Step 3: Gluttony

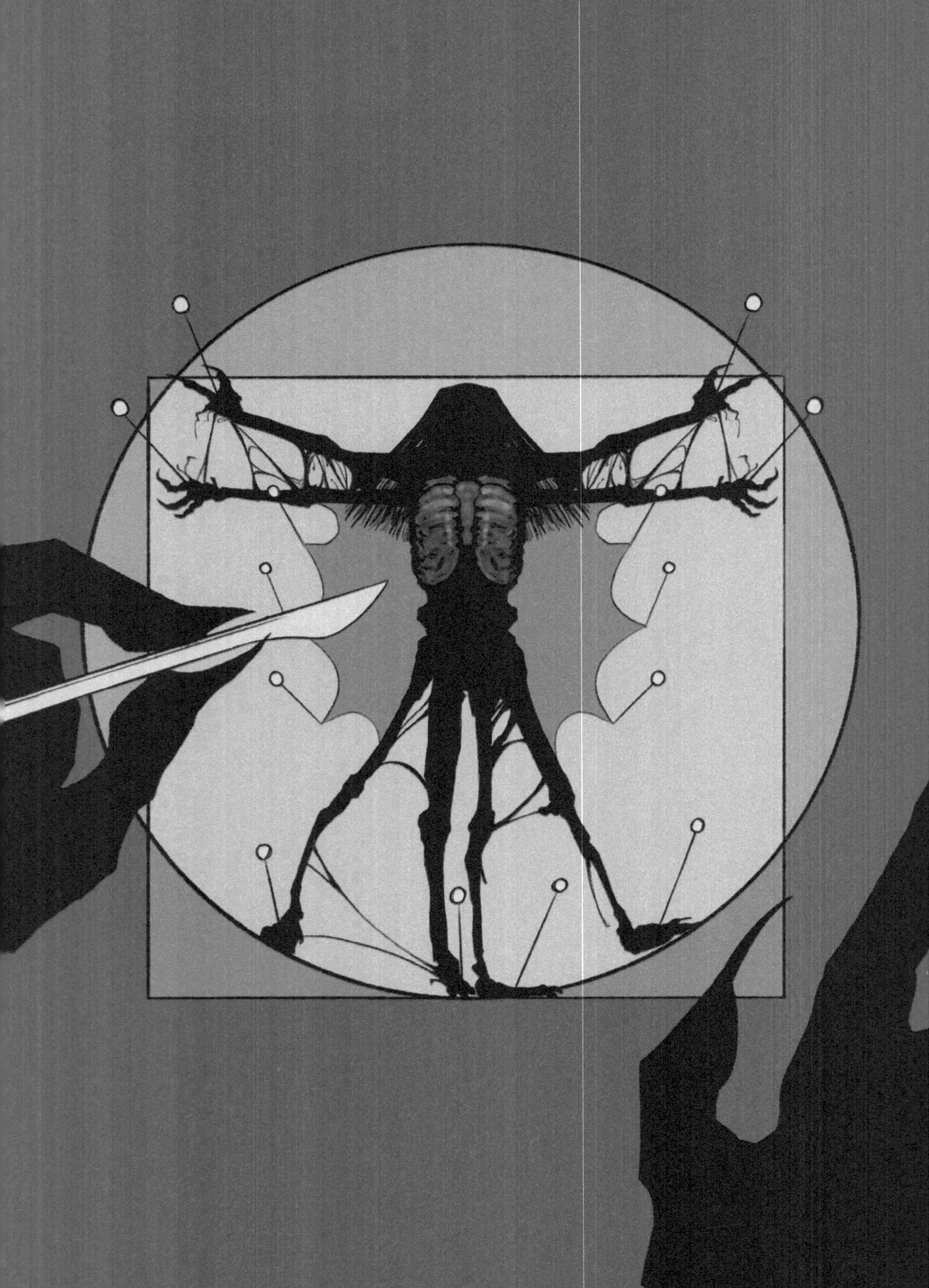

A GAMER'S GU1DE 2 BEATING TH3 TUTORIAL

Step 3: Gluttony

Palt

Podium

Podium

Step 3: Gluttony

FLOOR 16

THE HARSH CATARACT

I

Animus Vote

I'm not in the lobby. The status box lied to me.

I'm . . . I don't know where. To be completely honest, I know where I am, but I don't want to say it. If I admit that I'm in the play area of my old kindergarten, I'll have to admit that I can even remember what that place looked like. Now I've gone and said it, though, so, yeah. That's where I am.

My gaze slowly moves over the place. Soft, rounded plastic furniture. Soft playmat beneath my feet. Soft toys. Soft everything. Everything is soft and there's nothing sharp to stab my own throat with. Nothing to bash my head against that might scrub away everything that lingers inside my brain like the stench of rotten meat inside a refrigerator. As soft and padded as a pillow room.

Ah, well, I still have my claws, and most of my bones, so at least there's *that*.

Shaping my hand into a straight dagger, I press the needle-sharp tips of my claws against my throat. Bottom's up, and *adios!* Here we go—

<THE RESULTS OF THE VOTE ARE BEING TALLIED. PLEASE WAIT.>

My hand stalls. Vote?

Oh, yeah, now that I think about it, wasn't there some sort of vote mentioned in the floor clear message? Yeah, I wasn't too focused on it. I was more focused on the fact that—that . . .

My jaw clenches.

Vote. As if I care about that. You know what you can do about your vote? You can stick it right up your divine—

<THE RESULTS HAVE BEEN COMPILED.
100 OF 100 AVAILABLE GODS HAVE ANSWERED.>

Hey, not a bad answering rate! You want to know the *one* itsy bitsy teeny weeny problem?

I punt a tiny plush dog across the room.

I DON'T CARE!

Oh, but I guess since I'm one of your little all-terms-and-conditions-apply box-ticker guinea pigs, that means I'm obviously totally cool with anything and everything you do. Of course. I love this system. Hey, quick question, did you deliberately put me in a padded room so I couldn't go beddy bye-bye on myself? Did you *know* this was going to happen? Hey, answer me, damn it!

Did I do the right thing or not?!

<THE RESULTS OF THE VOTE ARE AS FOLLOWS:
<THE GOD OF COWARDICE IS IN FAVOR.>
<THE GOD OF HARVEST IS IN FAVOR.>
<THE GODDESS OF CHILDREN IS IN FAVOR.>
<THE GOD OF KNOWLEDGE IS IN FAVOR.>
<THE GODDESS OF LAW IS IN FAVOR.>
<THE GODDESS OF DRAGONS IS IN FAVOR.>
<THE GODDESS OF HONOR IS IN FAVOR.>
<THE GODDESS OF FORGIVENESS IS IN FAVOR.>
<THE GOD OF ADVENTURE IS IN FAVOR.>
<THE GODDESS OF COMPASSION IS IN FAVOR.>

<. . .>

<THE GODDESS OF WANT IS IN OPPOSITION.>
<THE GOD OF CRUELTY IS IN OPPOSITION.>
<THE GOD OF PAIN IS IN OPPOSITION.>
<THE GODDESS OF COMPROMISE IS IN OPPOSITION.>
<THE GOD OF GOBLINS IS IN OPPOSITION.>
<THE GOD OF COMBAT IS IN OPPOSITION.>
<THE GODDESS OF SOLITUDE IS IN OPPOSITION.>
<THE GOD OF WAR IS IN OPPOSITION.>
<THE GOD OF WILD IS IN OPPOSITION.>
<THE GOD OF WILL IS IN OPPOSITION.>

<. . .>

<50 TO 50 IN FAVOR OF REMOVING HELL CHALLENGER LO FENNRICK FROM THE TUTORIAL.>

Hang on just a second. Remove me from the—?

<THE RESULTS ARE A TIE. A TIE-BREAKER IS NEEDED.>
<THE GOD OF LOVE IS HEREBY CORDIALLY INVITED TO PARTAKE IN THE VOTE REGARDING HELL CHALLENGER LO FENNRICK.>

The God of Love? As in the God of Earth? Why should he have any part in this?

This doesn't make any sense. None of this makes any sense. What is even—

<THE GOD OF LOVE ACCEPTS THE INVITATION.>
<THE GOD OF LOVE CONTEMPLATES THE BEST COURSE OF ACTION.>

I'm just . . . what? No, seriously. If they hadn't shouted straight to my face that this was about whether I should *"stay in the tutorial,"* I would have assumed that this vote was about whether I did the right thing. To which the obvious answer is . . .

Is . . .

An image of a determined face and a sword pointed at me flashes through my head. I bury my face in my hands.

I don't know. I wish I knew. I don't know anything. Did I ever know?

It is clear to me that I was in the wrong. About Simel. About our time together. About what he thought of me, and about what he wanted. I was wrong. It's that simple. I never acted maliciously, but that doesn't mean I didn't hurt him. And I did hurt him. *Badly.* Ever since the start, that's all I've been doing. I didn't think I was hurting him, but that doesn't make it any better.

He didn't want me to kill the emperor. He didn't want me to kill *anyone,* as a matter of fact.

My only goal was to do what was right for him. In that sense, by doing the exact opposite of what he wanted . . .

I did the wrong thing.

<THE GOD OF LOVE HAS CAST HIS VOTE.>
<THE RESULTS OF THE VOTE HAVE BEEN RE-TALLIED.>
<THE RESULTS ARE NOW AS FOLLOWS.>
<50 TO 51 IN FAVOR OF REMOVING HELL CHALLENGER LO FENNRICK FROM THE TUTORIAL.>
<THE GODS HAVE HEREBY DECIDED THAT HELL CHALLENGER LO FENNRICK WILL NOT BE REMOVED FROM THE TUTORIAL.>

I stare at the screen. It doesn't go away, even after I stare at it for what feels like several hours.

They're keeping me in the tutorial. What would have happened if I'd been kicked out? Would I have been sent back home to Earth? Or would I have been stuck in Purgatory? Or, better yet, would I have simply dropped dead on the spot?

There's no answer. I'm a fool to expect one.

I can't even figure out if this was a good thing or not based on which god voted for what. The gods that like me and the gods that hate me all voted separately. Did the God of Love vote to keep me in here so that I wouldn't come back to wreak havoc on Earth and beat every high score there was using my superior gamer skills? Or was it out of some sickly-sweet bout of genuine compassion? I don't know. I don't know anything. How stupid can I be? Can't I learn a single damn thing?

I suck. I wish someone would shrink me and string me to a squirrel feeder so I could get what's coming to me. I'm sure the God of Cruelty would love that. Come on, people, let's make it happen!

Ahh, no answer. Of course, of course.

Reaching out, I grab a little plastic toddler stool and prepare to bash it against my skull, only for it to vanish from my hand, along with the rest of the room. Leaving nothing but an endless WHITE expanse. Ah. Ah. Ah. Bad. *Bad.*

A single splotch of color lights up my vision.

<THANK YOU FOR YOUR PATIENCE. YOU HAVE NOW BEEN RETURNED TO THE LOBBY.>
<PLEASE CONTINUE FIGHTING FOR THE SAKE OF BOTH WORLDS.>

That's where you're wrong, buster. I can't fight for your divine hineys if I'm *dead!*

<To repay your debt, your inventory has been sold for 3,119 points.>
<Current debt: 105,075 points.>

Aaaaaand there it is. Right. Okay, yeah. I was starting to wonder if they'd forgotten about my crippling life debt. It doesn't matter anymore, though. See, I have found a very simple solution to this whole mess.

Standing up, I stalk over to one of the nearby pillars. I grab it firmly, and then I do a somewhat professional impression of a woodpecker, minus the beak.

BASH BASH BASH BASH BASH BASH BASH BASH BASH BASH BASH BASH BASH BASH BASH BASH BASH BASH BASH BASH BASH BASH BASH BASH BASH BASH BASH BASH BASH BASH BASH BASH BASH BASH BASH BASH BASH BASH BASH BASH BASH BASH BASH BASH BASH BASH BASH BASH BASH BASH BASH BASH BASH BASH BASH BASH BASH BASH BASH BASH BASH BASH BASH BASH BASH BASH BASH BASH BASH BASH BASH BASH BASH BASH BASH BASH.

I remove my skull from the pillar. My head heals. I look down. The pillar is RED. My body is RED. My torn skirt is RED.

I tear off what remains from that floor.

Lying down, I crawl up into a little ball, with my face inches from the bloodied pillar. All I see is RED and the pink from my inside. I can't die in the lobby. I can't die in here. I need to go to the floor to die. Then I can be executed. Killed. Die. Like Simel wanted. He may not be my friend, but I'll be his, if it's the last thing I am. That's it. I just need to fulfill his plan. That's all.

Something hot and heavy wells up to my eyes and I feel my shoulders tremble.

I'm horrible. I'm the worst. I can't do anything right. I'm just a horrible person through-and-through. And every time I try to fight that, all I do is prove their words right, over and over again. Everything that's happened to me is my own fault. And I need to own up to it. Sure, Simel will never get to watch me be killed, to know for sure that I'm really gone, but . . . that's okay. Eventually, he'll know. Eventually, he'll understand that I really did do the right thing in the end.

Eventually . . .

<You have received a message.>

Through the blurred world, I read the words. I press the pop-up with a certain numbness, almost hoping for it to be one of those hate messages so I can tell them the good news.

<SuperMoleman[F67]: Hey Kitty! Congratulations on beating the fifteenth floor! I knew you could do it. Did you do the "right thing" in the end? And how did it go with Simel? You don't have to tell me, I'm just curious. And how did the gods react? I'm honestly so excited to hear about it! I feel like I ought to mention that I've heard some interesting rumors about a supposed tutorial-wide tournament. Spanning all difficulties and servers and floors, it would no doubt be the biggest event to happen in the tutorial so far! Personally speaking, I can't wait to test my magic against the other challengers. So far, I haven't heard of anyone else making it even close to how far you've gotten in the Hell Difficulty, but that doesn't mean we can't hold up hope, right? Anyhow, I look forward to hearing about how floor 15 went!>

I stare at the message. Rubbing my eyes, I read it over once more. It's still the same. I feel something hot rise to my cheeks again and I sit up fully, still facing the pillar. I start typing up a message.

<PrissyKittyPrincess[F15]: Moleman, am I ur friend?>

After a few seconds, a message dings in.

<SuperMoleman[F67]: Of course you are! Why, did something happen? I'm not sure if this helps but you are absolutely my friend. We've had some ups and downs but I would never call you anything but my friend, save for maybe a brother, haha. And, just so you know, I certainly hope that you see me as your friend too. Otherwise, this could get awkward pretty quickly, haha. Still, if something happened, you can tell me, okay? I'd be an awful friend not to hear you out, wouldn't I?>

The world blurs before my eyes and I let my face fall to the floor. My breaths are ragged and stagger up my throat only barely. I put my head in my hands and wait until my lungs are capable of breathing properly again. Through the gaps in my fingers, I stare up at the message and write a reply, mustering all the strength I have left to keep my finger from trembling too much to use.

<PrissyKittyPrincess[F15]: Ok thx i apreciate it cuz u mattr a lot 2 me thx bro ur 2 importnt 2 lose>
<SuperMoleman[F67]: You matter a lot to me, too! I'm not sure what you went through, but if it's too much to take over messages we can talk about it once the tournament happens, okay? Assuming it wasn't a hoax and I haven't been duped, that is. But I'll still be here if you want to talk. Otherwise, good luck with the next floor!>

I wipe the tears from my face.

<PrissyKittyPrincess[F15]: thx u2 bro>

I close the messages. And for the next twenty-four hours or so, I don't do anything. I don't train. I don't paint. I don't meditate. I don't think. I do nothing.

<Floor 16 has opened. Do you want to enter?>
<Yes/No>

I press the Yes button.
I enter the floor.

<Salrahna (Lv.17) Defeated.>
<Salrahna (Lv.22) Defeated.>
<Salrahna (Lv.23) Defeated.>

<. . .>

<Shade (Lv.64) [BOSS] Defeated.>
<Shade (Lv.71) [BOSS] Defeated.>
<Shade (Lv.76) [BOSS] Defeated.>

I beat the floor.

<You have cleared the sixteenth floor.>
<You have received 1,000 points for clearing the floor. You have received an additional 1,000 points for being the first to clear the floor.>
<For clearing the stage completely, you will receive an additional reward.>
<To repay your debt, the additional reward has been traded for 5,000 points.>
<4 Gods have shown a positive response to you. You have obtained 4,000 points.>
<43 Gods have shown a negative response to you. 43,000 points have been deducted.>
<To repay your debt, the floor clear reward has been traded for 1,000 points.>

I return to the lobby.

FLOOR 17

THE MURKY DEPTHS

Into the Abyss

<To repay your debt, your inventory has been sold for 0 points.>
<Current debt: 137,075 points.>

I paint the lobby. I stare at the RED. I wonder where it all went wrong.

I didn't die.

I lived.

I killed so that I could live again.

I miss Simel.

Gritting my teeth, I shake my head. I let my eyes fall to the floor. There's a spot between my toes that's still WHITE. It bores inside my skull like a drill, leaving a trail of horrible WHITE in its wake. It's only a tiny spot, but it's all I can see, burrowing deep inside me, filling me up, replacing my blood and flesh and bones with nothing but empty WHITE.

I want to meet Simel again. I don't know what I would say. Would I even say anything? I don't know. Maybe, maybe not.

I should ask Moleman about it once we meet again. He'll know what to do, like he always does. How does he do it? How can he keep being right, keep doing the right thing, effortlessly?

Why can't I be like that?

While the hole in my head yawns open and engulfs me like a massive beast, a little glowing box shines through the darkness.

<Floor 17 has opened. Do you want to enter?>
<Yes/No>

My hand reaches out and mechanically presses the Yes button and then the floor beneath me shifts from the single ever-present WHITE to a gritty, textured dark gray. I stare at it numbly. My feet shift a little. Rock. Cold, slightly wet rock. I hear a drop of water fall somewhere, the echoes of it plinking to the floor cascading through wherever I am without stop.

<Welcome.>

My neck pulls my eyes away from the rocky floor toward whatever's ahead of me, but I can't see it because my eyes get stuck on the status box explaining the floor.

<Tutorial stage, Hell Difficulty Seventeenth Floor: The Murky Depths>
<[Clear Condition] Bring enough purses to the Beast of Fraud to gain access to the abyss.>

After a second or so, the semitranslucent status box fades away to reveal the creature behind it. I meet its eyes.

<Beast of Fraud (Lv.89)>

I glance at my own status.

<Top—Status—Community>
<PrissyKittyPrincess
Human Level 74
Agility: 211
Strength: 138
Stamina: 242
Magic Power: 82>

It's doable.

I step closer to it. It mostly looks like a wolf, though it's about the size of a brown bear. Gray fur. Long, fishlike tail. It's got a crown clasped tightly around its neck almost like a collar, with chains connecting it to a not-comfortable-looking saddle on its back. It looks down at me with eyes that gleam of intelligence. When I scowl at it, it doesn't scowl back.

<You are more reckless than I had expected.>

My eye twitches. I twist my hand into a fist.

"And why . . ." I croak, "is that?"

<This floor was not designed to be beaten with me dead.>

"Oh? Is that so?" I suppress the urge to laugh in its canine face. "Do you think that's stopped me before?"

<No.>

It shoots a single, meaningless glance behind it.

<Though, I suspect, this time may be different.>

I arch my neck to follow its gaze. "Is that the abyss? That murky little puddle?"

It doesn't answer me. Typical.

Keeping one eye on the beast, I trace a wide circle around it to bring me to the puddle itself. The room as a whole is simply a single dome-shaped cavern. There are no exits or entrances. The only source of light is the clichéd glowing crystals embedded here and there in the seamless stone wall. Nothing else. Just me, this wolf, and a puddle on the floor. The beast doesn't move an inch or react to my movement in any other way. It seems content to sit there, with its back to the puddle, like a dog guarding an empty house.

I look down into the puddle. It's as black as tar. Experimentally, I lean down, bringing my face close to the surface. I can't see a single thing down there. Not one. It's just darkness, my own reflection, and a pair of gleaming eyes.

Wait a second—

Before I have time to react, a bloated head flies out of the water, a pair of soggy jaws closing around my neck, soon dragging me down into the ice-cold water, giving me no time to so much as realize what's happening. I can't see anything, but I can feel the jaws biting down around my neck, another pair of jaws soon clamping down on my arms, and then my legs. The water is infinitely dark, but the status screen still shines through.

<Drowned Dog (Lv.68)>
<Drowned Dog (Lv.70)>
<Drowned Dog (Lv.64)>
<Drowned Dog (Lv.66)>

Whichever way I turn my head, another status message pops up, not to mention the additional pair of jaws grabbing onto me, dead-set on dragging me
down farther, and farther, the waters around me as cold as dead flesh. My mind
shifts into gear without any need for thought and I plunge my one free hand into
the neck mere inches from my head, tearing out a soft, mushy throat as I do. But
the jaws crunching into my neck only clamp down harder, gnawing, making my
spine creak and my throat crackle. Soggy. Necrotic flesh. *Dead* flesh.

Zombies.

I grab hold of the jaw itself and tear it out, the tendons that would otherwise hold such a thing in place easily snapping off, the jaw easily loosening.
Going by where I can feel the other jaws, I begin carefully crushing skulls
and tearing off jaws, succeeding in escaping, but not in killing a single one
of them.

With enough of the hounds removed, I begin doggy-paddling toward what I
assume is the surface. My lungs are burning. How long have I been underwater?
My limbs burn coldly. I swim only reacting by pure instinct to kick away the
dogs snapping their jaws at me, the sounds echoing endlessly in the deafening
water.

My head spins. I can't tell which way is up or down.

Darkness. All around me. Jaws snapping shut, snap snap snap. Bones cracking, crack crack crack. Head spinning, lungs aching. Cold embrace of the abyss.
Can't see, can't feel.

I see the abyss. The abyss sees me.

And then I see no more.

My eyes flare open and I fly to my feet, briefly disoriented before keeling over to
regurgitate two lungs' worth of disgusting dark water.

Haah, haah, haah, I'm . . . alive . . . ?

<The next time you try that, you won't be quite so lucky.>

I turn to the Beast of Fraud with a glare.

"Why?"

If hounds could roll their eyes, that's what the beast would have done here.

<Are you asking me, or are you asking the tutorial?>

I open my mouth to answer but quickly close it again.

Slowly, I walk over to it where it sits. Then I sit down, facing it. Arms crossed,
I frown up at it. "I'm asking *you*."

<I see. Equally rude and clever, just as they said.>

I'm just about to say something sharp at it when it continues.

<Indeed, it would be a shame to lose such a valuable warrior so early.>

"I'm going to kill you," I say without the tiniest shift in inflection. "Your level isn't that high. Once I've ground a bit with these dogs, I'm going to defeat you."
It looks at me for a moment.

<If you are nonetheless to kill the dogs, you may as well finish the quest by bringing me their purses.>

I quirk an eyebrow at it.

<That way, I may at least fulfill my duty to bring you into the abyss before you defeat me.>

"And that's okay with you?" My eyes briefly dart down to look at its tight golden collar, then back up at its calm, icy-blue eyes. "You're totally okay with me using you, and then killing you? Do you even know what death means? And don't tell me there's a doggie heaven for good boys like you who go into their graves because your master told you to."

<Of course not. It isn't needed. There is no joy higher than to live and die for those you love.>

My back bristles and I briefly uncross my arms to run a hand through my hair. "Hang on a minute. One second. Are you trying to say that you love me, or that you love the gods? Because that was a really weird way of phrasing it either way."

<I love my creator, the God of Harvest.>

Its eyes sharpen.

<To you, I am ambivalent.>

"But you'll still die for me?"

<I'll gladly die for the sake of the world I was born for. However, that still assumes you are capable of defeating me.>

I leap to my feet. "H—hey! Of course I'll be able to defeat you, you big furry oaf! If I wanted to, I could tie a knot out of your limbs and go fishing with your wormy tongue!"

Somehow, in return, the beast actually smirks. Can dogs do that? Apparently.

<For now, why not focus on defeating the actual enemies of this floor?>

"The actual . . . ?"

And, as if on cue, a paw stretches out from inside the puddle, thin skin and loose fur stretched over a bony canine body. The rest of the creature soon pulls itself out, panting with every movement it makes like a malbred pug. The fur is wet and dark, saggy in some places where there is more bone than flesh, stretched thin where the dog's meat and organs have grown bloated. The neck is choked shut by a thin piece of rope, upon which dangles a soggy, wet purse. Like an actual money purse. The kind a little old lady would keep her coins and little notes in—that kind of purse.

<Drowned Dog (Lv.64)>

It turns to me, a spool of foamy saliva webbing down the side of its necrotic jaws. Empty eyes. Pupil-less. It doesn't really see me in the typical sense, the way the Beast of Fraud looks at me, or I at it. It's more like an animatronic creature, rigid as it steps toward me, fleshless limbs dragging a bloated body.

I point a finger at it. "That thing? I have to defeat a bunch of those?"

It doesn't answer me, probably because it knows that what I said wasn't really a question. Very well. If it wants to leave me to my fate, so be it.

I've dealt with zombies before. This will be no different.

I hunch down into position and the second it lunges at me, I in turn fly at it, rolling into a ball midair to briefly confuse it. But it isn't confused. Or, rather, it shows no confusion whatsoever. Like a dog flying after a ball that was never thrown, it keeps going, even though it doesn't actually know where I am. It leaps into the air, jaws wide, luck alone guiding it to bite into an arm I chose to sacrifice.

We both clatter to the floor. I scrape up my back a little and I can hear one or two of the dog's brittle bones breaking, but it doesn't care and neither do I. Jumping to my feet, I abuse every inch of my enhanced balance skill to keep on my feet, something that proves itself more than difficult once the dog pulls me into a tug-o'-war over my own arm. One made all the more difficult since the floor is about as slippery as any political slope.

I lose my footing within seconds, the dog mindlessly leaping atop me, jaws grinding the bones of my forearm to dust as its paws stab into my chest.

It's as heavy as you'd expect a drowned corpse to be, and it uses that to its advantage.

At this moment, the only thing between its frothing jaws and my head is my one arm.

Experimentally, I reach down and use my free hand to pop its bloated belly like a balloon. And it does indeed pop, releasing a stench more noxious than any can of surströmming alongside a homogeneous slurry of organs, each completely indiscernible from the other.

<You have learned: Enhanced Scent Lv.9>

Aaaaaaaand it just got worse. Ah, wonderful. Anyhow, I've had enough of this farce, so I reach up and tear out the jaw again, which is just as effective as it was underwater. Just as before, the dog isn't very interested in giving up and sticking its tail between its legs, so it keeps going, now trying to scratch at me with its paws. An ardent attempt to be sure, but I don't care.

I would have been more interested in how it keeps going even with its paws broken, but I've played this game before, and my stats are already perfected. Cut off the head, dismember the body, stick most of it into the inventory, wonder about how a cut-off head can still pant if it's disconnected from the mushified lungs in its main body . . .

Notice the purse. It's still connected to the bit of string, but the purse remains unopened. Out of sheer curiosity, I pick it up. It's far from heavy, though the being-fully-soaked aspect is weighing it down a little. Not as much as the small clinking things inside it, though.

Only now that I open the purse does the dog show any hint of emotion, whining in fear. Hm.

I peek inside the purse. I can feel my brows furrow as I remove the two coins from inside. They aren't from Earth, but they also aren't any kind that I can recall from Purgatory, though they're heavy enough to be made of some kind of valuable material. The two coins have the same design, that being a goblin on one side and a dragon on the other—which looks *really cool* if you ask me—but they aren't fully equal in shape, showing that they're handmade. I almost want to pop one in my mouth to see if I gain anything, but I don't think I'd get anything other than a stomachache and a judgmental look from the Beast of Fraud.

Remembering that I'm not alone in here, I peek over at the beast. It's looking at me. It doesn't even look away at my noticing it's looking at me. That's rude. I'm pretty sure that's rude.

"Don't you have anything better to do than watch me?" I spit at it.

<Such as?>

"I don't know. Chase invisible squirrels. Growl at empty corners. You know, typical dog stuff?"

<I have as much in common with dogs as you do with apes.>

Is it my imagination, or is the beast *smirking*?

<A surprising lot, that is.>

"Hey, stop making fun of me!" I say, giving it the stinkiest eye I can manage, unfortunately not beating the putrid stench caused by my defeating the dog. "I didn't ask for your *quips*."

<Would you rather I remain silent?>

I pause. Frowning, I turn to look at the still-whimpering drowned dog's head. Not really thinking, I mutter, "I don't know. *Do I?*"

Again, no response from the beast. Is it . . . no, is *he* making fun of me by trying to make my dreams come true? Hah! Does he seriously think I have some sort of *need* to talk? To *him*? To *anyone*? Idiotic. Dumb. Stupid. I can go months without talking, no problem! Just because there's silence where there could be conversation doesn't mean anything. Same silence as before. Doesn't mean anything whatsoever.

I grind my teeth.

"So, um . . ." I pick up the dog's head. "No comment on my tactics?"

<Is that what you call what you just did?>

"Fighting style. Strategy. Whatever." Growling, I turn to look at him again. "No thoughts about it whatsoever? With the ripping and tearing and disembowelment?" I hope I don't sound as desperate for conversation as I feel. "Most people don't like looking at it, you know."

<As a fellow beast, it would be hypocritical to look down upon your form of killing. It's mere survival. Those who fight with swords and arrows could never understand it.>

"Exactly!" I blurt out. "And then they still go and judge you because *you* didn't live up to the expectations they set on *themselves*! Like, sorry you've got high standards or whatever, but, like, that's just not me, right? I've got my own style, and—*fun fact*—if I did it like you did, I'd be dead! Easy as that, so, like—"

My jaw snaps shut. The beast looks at me oddly.

My teeth grind together and the sliver of a smile I'd mustered quickly slips off. "Never mind. You're just a tutorial construct. You can't possibly understand it."

For a few seconds, he just stares at me. Deliberating. *Thinking.*

<Bring me the two coins in your hand.>

I look down at the coins, rubbing them together for a moment to hear them scrape before standing up and wandering over to the beast. Holding out the two coins, I'm honestly not surprised when he leans forward and eats them out of my hand like a horse eating sugar cubes. He quickly swallows them, and the moment the coins leave his throat, I hear a sigh from behind me, only just having time to turn around before the status message pops up.

<1/50 purses collected.>
<Drowned Dog (Lv.64) Defeated.>

"Huh."
The beast licks his lips.

**<A simple purpose, as you see. My three brothers seldom speak. Most challengers do not need to be spoken to, and so they do not hear our voices.
I speak to you for the simple purpose that you need to be spoken to. No creator told me thusly. I chose this myself, as I chose to save your life. However, whether you listen is not my choice to make.>**

I look at the beast. My voice is even as I say, "I'm still going to kill you. You're useful to me now because you can help kill the dogs and you can bring me down into the abyss, but after that . . ." I almost smile. "Doesn't that bother you at all? That you're looking at your future killer? Shouldn't you be angry?"

His wolf's head doesn't even twitch. He's as still as a statue, but not out of fear, or any emotion like that.

<No matter how many times you ask, my answer will not change.>

His eyes narrow.

<Nor will I kill you.>

"What—" My voice gets caught in my throat. *What do you mean by that?* I want to ask, as if I don't know. As if playing dumb will get me anywhere. As if shouting accusations will somehow shift my anger away from myself. My fists clench and unclench, knuckles turning WHITE. But, in the end, all that leaves my throat is a little sigh. "Fine. Okay. You don't care . . . sure. What now?"

He tilts his head. You know. Like a *dog*.

"If you tell me that all I have left to do now is to defeat fifty—sorry, *forty-nine* dogs, feed you the coins and then go into the abyss, I'm killing you right here and now."

<I didn't take you for one to deny the truth when spoken plainly.>

"Yeah, well, we all have our moments to shine, don't we?" I huff.

A shadow of a smile flickers across his wolfish lips.

I roll my eyes since he won't do it himself. "Fine. Kill dogs. Easy peasy lemon squeezy. At least I won't have to eat like ninety percent of them to kill them properly . . ."

The beast watches with curiosity as I waltz over to the killed dog, grabbing its purse from the ground. So if I understand this correctly, the beast doesn't actually want the purse—he just wants the coins inside. Gotcha. Oh, I understand it now! Once he's eaten a hundred coins, he'll finally be heavy enough to sink rather than float! Ah, maybe I should suggest a lead-based diet? Oh, then again, this is a world where they've yet to invent bullets. Bummer. Guess coins of unknown value will have to do.

Removing the string from the purse, I grab one of the drowned dog's fangs and tie it to it, and if we then tie the other end to a dog femur, we've got ourselves a makeshift fishing rod! Amazing, wow, fantastic, best thing I've ever made, et cetera.

Taking a seat next to the puddle, I throw the hook inside and wait.

And I wait.

And I wait.

And . . .

I turn to the beast. He's still sitting with his back to the puddle, but he's got his head turned to watch me. "What?"

<Most challengers would use this time to rest before the next drowned dog emerges.>

"Rest?"

Curiously enough, the voice echoing through my head takes a turn for the amused.

<The first few drowned dogs appear with several minutes of rest in between, usually alone. Then, as time moves on, more and more will appear in greater amounts with a higher frequency. A natural increase in difficulty that you seem to have rejected wholly.>

Turning away from the beast, I pull up my line. Nothing. I throw it back in. "Yeah, well, maybe I don't have any need to spend minutes or hours or days waiting for my wounds to heal."

<There's more to rest than merely the physical.>

I smirk cunningly. "Well, funny thing to mention, because I also don't need to sleep, or eat, or drink, or . . . you know. Anything like that. I'm perfectly fine without it, so I don't."

<There's more reason to eat, drink, and sleep than the physical need for it. When did you last truly rest?>

Truly rest? Like, *actually* rest? Well, sleeping . . . I slept . . . I think I slept a couple of months back, probably. But that wasn't very comfortable, and I didn't exactly wake up too refreshed. Does it count when I passed out from drinking? No, I wasn't exactly resting . . . Then, drinking honeyed water with Moleman? That was pretty relaxing, but it wasn't exactly *rest* in that sense, so . . . Before the tutorial? But even then . . .

The beast watches me silently.

I bare my teeth at it and glower. "And? What's wrong with that? If you're trying to pity me, all I can say is that I don't want it. I don't want anything from the likes of you." A pause. "Except a little bit of help here and there, I suppose . . ."

<I will not pity the path you chose for yourself. I merely ask that you consider whether the trail you are on truly leads to where you want to go.>

"Of course it—" I bite my own tongue. A memory of a smiling face flashes through my mind and I shake my head. "It doesn't matter. None of that matters. I just have to survive, and keep going, and then the rest will solve itself."

He looks at me. When I find the strength to look back at him, all I see in his pale eyes is my own reflection, looking back at me. I see my reflection flinch.

<You don't have to fight on. You could stay here.>

I scoff. "Yeah, right. I've had that bone dangled in front of me before, and my answer is still the same."

For once, the beast makes a sound that isn't just telepathically shot into my brain. It actually gives a little dog-sigh.

<I had expected such an answer. Still, it is a shame that you refuse to rest yet. I can see why the creators have such faith in you.>

"Faith?" I say in sheer disbelief. "In *me*? Hah! You've got your doggy-wires crossed. The minute they have faith in me is the minute the world ends."

The beast watches me for a second before speaking again.

<It seems you've got something on the line.>

"Yeah, of course I know what I'm talking about! Psh, the gods? Faith? In *me*? Might as well suggest the world is carried on the back of a slug . . ."

<I meant it literally.>

"Huh?" My eyes flash down to the murky puddle. A pair of blank eyes look back up at me, the line clutched between the creature's loose teeth. "Oh!"

Heaving it into the air, I quickly dispatch it through a combination of beheading, dismembering, and robbery, stealing the coins from its purse without making the mistake of popping its bloated belly. And while the removed head is still snapping its jaws and yipping, I feed the coins to the beast, killing it properly.

<2/50 purses collected.>
<Drowned Dog (Lv.67) Defeated.>

With that done, I sit back down, throwing my line into the water. But I still can't calm down, and shooting seething glances at the beast is infuriatingly unhelpful. "So?" I say measuredly. "Why do you think the gods would have any sort of faith in me whatsoever?"

It meets my gaze patiently.

<You phrase it as though it were a matter of opinion.>

"Are you trying to say it isn't?"

And now I learn something fun. Namely, apparently, wolves can chuckle. That doesn't seem physically possible, but it's also huge and has the tail of a fish, so what do I know?

I grumble and toss a nearby stone into the puddle. "If you don't want to answer me, you can just say that."

For almost a full minute, we sit in silence. I fish, and it watches me, clearly in deep thought. Assuming beasts can have thoughts to begin with. I'm just about to assume that we won't be talking anymore on this floor when he suddenly shifts, standing up and turning around so that when he then sits, he faces me fully. Somehow, having two wolf eyes stare into me rather than one makes my heart waver a little.

<You are a survivor. In that way, we are the same.>

"Survivor . . ." I mumble. *For now*, I restrain myself from adding. I turn back to the fishing rod, the line making the otherwise motionless surface bob with little waves. "How can you be a survivor if you were made by the gods to be in the tutorial? That doesn't make any sense."

It blinks at me.

<Although you aren't quite correct, you aren't incorrect either.>

Before I can ask him to elaborate, he does it for me. Neat.

<I was not born in this place. I was simply brought here by the God of Harvest to help save the world. Our worlds. In return, He gave me a soul, split it into four, and left each of us to guide the challengers to beating this floor on each difficulty.>

I can feel my brows furrow, but before I have time to question him further, something tugs on my line and I pull it out, only to find the dog-tooth hook missing. Grumbling, I pull a new tooth out of my inventory. The beast absently continues.

<You've yet to ask it, however, I feel it pertinent to mention that at this moment, none of my three brothers have been killed, or even so much as threatened with death.>

I wipe at my nose. Sniff. "Are you trying to complain?"

Another wolfish smirk. He's got to stop doing that. It's really upsetting to look at.

<You are abnormal within the tutorial. That makes you special. And although that may scare some of the creators, to others it gives you all the charm of a hidden trump card.>

Now that I think back on it, even that herald seemed pretty surprised by my actions. But being unpredictable is only good in some situations. Certainty is valuable in and of itself, and apparently, I'm in sore lack of it. Okay, so, to summarize, he just insulted me.

Hey!

Ignoring my poorly hidden ire, the beast continues. How beastly.

<Personally, I can see both sides of the argument.>

"Is this about my planning to kill you again?" I say, smirking.

The beast smiles back at me.

<I'm a little torn on it, I admit. I don't mind dying to help you continue your quest; however, it saddens me that my death may become a bother for my creator. The temporary soul shard He granted me would be lost and would have to be remade.>

His smile turns sad.

<That is, assuming He doesn't consider it needless to provide another guide for this difficulty. I would not hope for it, but I can imagine that few of the creators believe that another challenger of the Hell Difficulty will reach this floor.>

I'm pretty sure that, going by the way he's looking at me, he wants a response of some sort. But I haven't got any to give. I just bite my tongue and continue fishing.

Not my problem. Whatever happens after this floor is up to the gods, not me. Not me.

Days pass comfortably. Like, unsettlingly comfortably. Just as the Beast of Fraud said—weird name, I agree—the dogs started willingly dragging themselves out of the water, more and more, with greater frequency over time.

And you know something interesting I learned?

The Beast of Fraud sleeps! *I'm serious!*

I asked him about it, and he straight-up told me that he simply enjoyed sleeping. Like, he didn't *need* to sleep, he just did it anyway. Like a lunatic. He didn't drink water or eat, but he told me with all the stonefacedness of a stoic philosopher that sometimes, before I showed up, the God of Harvest would appear *in person* to give him a big yummy bone to gnaw on while he waited for me to show up. *What.*

If anything or anybody else had told me this—that a *literal god* regularly appeared to grant treats and head pats—I would not have believed them. I would probably also have opened up their skull for a full cranial autopsy to ensure that they actually had a brain in there, though that's optional.

As a side note, I can say with fairly good accuracy that the beast does not lie. He says truths in a roundabout manner sometimes, but he doesn't lie. Never.

It's another one of those things he seems to have been born and raised without, alongside survival instincts and any and all rationality. Then again, maybe I'm expecting too much from a literal hound. Wolf. Beast. Whatever you want to call him.

Of course, as is typical, the drowned dogs don't stop their pursuit at nighttime. I say nighttime, but that's only because that's the time of day when the beast sleeps. Since we're in a cave, it doesn't actually mean anything. Either way, I politely interrogated the beast over how I was logically supposed to rest if I got attacked at nighttime, and he told me with actual nonsarcastic politeness that almost all other challengers, no matter the difficulty, are part of a party at this point. As in, they take shifts.

When I asked him why there were so few solo players, he told me frankly that most of them didn't make it this far, even on easy difficulty. Which is . . . Well, I should have known, but it was still a bit of a blow.

I mean, if someone else beat the first floor of the Hell Difficulty . . . I doubt they'd do it with an entourage. They'd be a solo player by default.

And, I admit, at this point, I did blow up a little at the Beast of Fraud. It wasn't very mature of me, but I did. Like, you're telling me that the highest difficulty can only be done solo? That people basically have no choice but to go solo, in a tutorial designed to be defeated in groups? How is that in any way fair?

And, as usual, he'd looked at me like he shouldn't need to spell out what I already knew. But, for once, he actually said the words, rather than forcing me to accept them myself.

<Whoever told you that the tutorial was meant to be fair?>

Which is, you know . . . Yeah. The tutorial isn't fair, this is the highest difficulty, yadda yadda yadda, but . . . still! Shouldn't there at least be a chance? *Someone* has to be able to do even the higher difficulties solo, right?

Sly as a fox, the beast only grinned at me.

I'm not sure I enjoy how highly he seems to think of me.

Either way, the days passed, I collected purses and coins, and in the end, I finally got the last two coins to fatten the beast fully.

<50/50 purses collected.>
<Drowned Dog (Lv.62) Defeated.>
<[Level Up]>
<You have reached Level 79.>
<Agility has increased by 2.
Strength has increased by 3.
Stamina has increased by 2.
Magic Power has increased by 1.
Cold Protection has increased by 1.
Frostbite Protection has increased by 1.>

As the beast licks his lips after a final metallic meal, I glance at the time.

<Top—Status—Community>
<20:01:54 Day 531>
<The eighteenth attempt will begin in 9:03:58:06>
<The Tutournament will start in 9:03:58:06>

I wonder what kind of dork would name the tutorial tournament the *Tutournament*. I mean, sure, they clearly saw a chance, and I suppose it's admirable that they had the gall to actually take it, but still . . . They really couldn't call it the tutorial tournament? Seriously? Well, anyhow—

<Tutorial stage, Hell Difficulty Seventeenth Floor: Boss Stage>
<[Clear Condition] Descend into the Abyss.>

Oh, that's vague. Either way, it's simple enough, so we might as well get on with it. No need to dilly-dally and all that. "All right, beast, time to get—"
The beast clears his throat, standing up fully.

<I accept your bribe of fifty purses. For this sum and no less, this amount and no more, I shall allow you a ride upon my back. With all of my power, I will bring you—>

"Why are you talking like that?" I deadpan.
The beast gives a little huff of annoyance.

<My brothers get to do this speech almost on the daily. Will you not grant me the joy of reciting these lines if only once, so that my debt to my creator may be repaid, at least in part?>

I tap my foot. After a second or so, I relent. I mean, who am I to keep a man-wolf-beast thing from his dramaturgical dreams? Sighing, I wave for him to continue.

The stoic wolf beams as best as such a creature may, and continues his speech. I listen with half an ear. I'm not actually too interested, but it would be rude to tune out fully, so, yeah.

After a while, his speech comes to a close.

<Now, leap onto mine back, and I shall bring both of us into the depths of this dark abyss. Come, challenger, and face the . . . the . . .>

I stare at him.
A single bead of sweat rolls down his nose.

<Excuse me.>

As I stare in mild disbelief, the beast pulls a tiny bit of parchment out of a pouch on his saddle, almost impaling his chin on the spires of his collar-crown as he does. Unfurling it on the ground, he carefully reads the words, a moment or so later rerolling it and stuffing it back into the saddle.

<Come, challenger, and face the darkness!>

Wow. I almost feel like giving him a small ovation purely out of pity. Luckily, I'm able to keep it in. Instead, I give him a thumbs-up. "Lead the way, pal."

I'm not entirely sure what I expected, but for some reason, I'm surprised when he turns his side to me, kneeling down a little for me to hop on. I still mount him, but that's purely out of instinct.

<Now hold on tightly as I descend. Keep your head close to my body, and you may breathe while beneath the water. And, as I've said before, I cannot assist in defeating the drowned dogs that may attack us in the darkness. That is your duty.>

"Yeah. Of course."

This feels . . . weirdly grand. I'm actually on a quest now. I didn't really think about it before, but . . . I'm going on a small adventure. I'm playing the game the way it's meant to be played.

I'm not sure how to feel about that.

But before we jump into the abyss, I need to get one more word in. "Remember to take your time diving down, okay? We need to defeat *all* the dogs. Otherwise there's no point in killing you."

The beast smiles.

<Of course. Now, take a deep breath, and hold on tight!>

And with those words, it leaps into the abyss.

The darkness swallows us and I instinctively pinch my nose shut, but I realize quickly that there's no need for that. By some divine providence, there's like a thin bubble surrounding the nearest parts of the beast, providing us with ample air. That would be one of two large differences when compared to my first visit to this abyss. The second being that this time, we brought one of the glowing crystals along with us. In other words, I can see the drowned dogs as they approach us, all in a swarm. I can't tell how many there are, but I don't need to know.

All I need to do is kill them.

Which is pretty simple, on account of how I've been killing these things for days now. It's easy. As long as you can get the purses away from them and feed the coins to the Beast of Fraud, they die. So that's what I do.

<Drowned Dog (Lv.62) Defeated.>
<Drowned Dog (Lv.68) Defeated.>
<Drowned Dog (Lv.72) Defeated.>
<Drowned Dog (Lv.70) Defeated.>
<. . .>
<[Level Up]>
<You have reached Level 80.>
<Agility has increased by 2.
Strength has increased by 1.
Stamina has increased by 3.
Magic Power has increased by 1.
Necrosis Protection has increased by 1.
Oxygen Deficiency Protection has increased by 1.>
<Drowned Dog (Lv.62) Defeated.>
<Drowned Dog (Lv.62) Defeated.>
<. . .>

In the darkness and its sparse light, it's impossible to tell the passage of time. I don't have time to check it, and I don't need to, either. We're done when the dogs are dead. Simple as that. And, eventually, they do die. Within time, there are no longer any dogs left to approach us, at which point the Beast of Fraud confidently increases his swimming speed.

Normally speaking, this would've been a good moment to relax. No enemies, no lack of air, no need to do much of anything other than clutch the saddle. And yet I didn't relax. Not that I felt afraid. It was more the opposite. I was . . . excited. It's that simple.

I mean, I was riding an aquatic wolf-beast through darkness at hyperspeeds, the two of us rushing through the water as though it was air! I understand cowboys now, and I also understand the Russian desire to ride bears. What would my moose-riding ancestors have to say about this? I don't know.

What I do know is that when the ride ended and we emerged into a tunnel which led to an air-filled room containing only a single brightly glowing crystal, all I felt was a mild sadness at the ride ending. Nothing else.

I step off his back and look down at the crystal. "That's it, right? I touch that and I beat the floor?" No response to my rhetorical question, as usual. "Seems simple enough. And, just to be clear, there are no caveats to this, are there? There won't be any snake to pop out and spook me or a pirate gh—ghost to do the same? Because, as I've said before, that would be mean and scary and I would hold it against you forever, so I would rather you didn't—"

Turning around, I find an answer to his lack of response.

Head bowed, eyes downcast, he waits. Neck bared.

I chance a chuckle. "Heh, um, what are you . . . ?"

His eyes briefly glance up at me. I see myself in their icy clearness. Rhetorical question. I know the answer, and he knows it. My hands start to tremble a little. "Aren't you going to . . . fight it? I mean, um, you're still, like, nine whole levels above me. In other words, if we fight, you might win! Then, you can go on living. Wouldn't that be nice, huh?"

No answer. I glance away from him to look down at the crystal. "Like, don't get me wrong, I just . . . Someone else will come along, right? Your precious harvest dude is planning on keeping this operation running for at least a little while longer, so someone else is sure to come along, and you can talk to them all you want. Maybe they'll even stick around? Heh, uh, assuming they don't decide to take a permanent vacation on floor four instead, but, you know . . . Up to them, right?"

What am I doing? Am I seriously trying to talk myself out of killing a willing opponent? Level 89. That has to give me at least one level-up. One more vital step toward not dying on the next floor, or the one after it.

So why am I hesitating?

I bring up my hand. Claws. My whole body is soaked down to the bone. A little bit of wolf's blood won't make a difference. I've killed for less.

Carefully, I press the sharp claws of my fingers closer to the beast's bared neck. Fur. Fluffy, thanks to the bubble. Soft. During the few days we've known each other, he's never refused a pet. He even let me scratch his belly, as weird as it sounds.

His eyes remain steadfast, even as his death inches closer.

And as my fingers brush closer, closer, I feel a sudden weight leave my shoulders.

Ah.

He doesn't have to die.

I look down at him. His eyes face the floor. A strange, ice-cold clearness spreads across my soul. I reach for his neck again, but instead of plunging my fingers into his throat, I brush them against his crown collar. Confusion flashes through his icy eyes and I kneel down in front of him.

"It's too tight," I mumble as my fingers loosen it just a little. His eyes meet mine and I smile. "Wouldn't want you to choke yourself before you get the chance to guide the next Hell Difficulty challenger, right?"

His mouth opens a little, then closes as I stand up, turning away from him, toward the crystal.

I reach it in four even strides, and as my hand hovers above it, light flitting between my fingers, I hear a voice bark through my head.

<I swear to you that I will guide them as well as I can! And when you meet them in what comes after, I'll tell them to say hello from me!>

I look back and smile at his bowing head. "I'll take your word on it, friend."

And then my hand falls on the crystal, and the floor ends, the last thing I see being the proud, confident head of my third-ever friend.

<You have cleared the seventeenth floor.>
<You have received 1,000 points for clearing the floor. You have received an additional 1,000 points for being the first to clear the floor.>
<16 Gods have shown a positive response to you. You have obtained 16,000 points.>
<34 Gods have shown a negative response to you. 34,000 points have been deducted.>
<To repay your debt, the floor clear reward has been traded for 1,000 points.>

I wonder, briefly, before I go, if one of those happy gods was the God of Harvest.

And then, just as briefly, I wonder whether he knew I'd spare his little doggie.

Then I wonder, finally—what kind of man would be willing to sacrifice his own pet for the sake of someone he doesn't even like?

FLOOR 18

THE DEEP MINE

III

It Ain't Over Till the Canary Sings

I appear in the lobby carrying a strange weight in my chest, alongside an even stranger emptiness. A kind of heavy weightlessness, as paradoxical as it sounds.

Sixteen positive responses.

But I didn't completely clear the stage.

Should I pull out my hair or pray to sixteen gods simultaneously?

<To repay your debt, your inventory has been sold for 42 points.>
<Current debt: 152,033 points.>

Or I could curse a hundred gods all at once. That feels more plausible considering my own skills, I think. Hmm, I wonder if a ritual using blood and organs might work better than simple thoughts and curses? Only one way to find out!

I don't know how offensive pentagrams would be to these non-earthly gods, so it's probably more offensive to draw the Christian cross, which is what I'm doing. In my own blood. Because what else is there to use? Let's see here, big cross, and a cool pattern surrounding it . . . maybe stick a few goblin skins here and there, I'm sure they'll dislike *that* . . .

And then, for maximum offense, I put myself—their greatest opponent and hater—right in the middle. And now, we wait for this dark ritual to gain power.

Ommmm. Ommmmm . . .

Hm. It doesn't seem to be working. Do I need to say a Hare Krishna? Ah, but I don't know how it goes . . . I knew it once, but then I forgot it, because why would I ever need to use the Hare Krishna in my day-to-day life, Mr. Davidsson?

Yeah, that's what I thought, teacher-I-haven't-seen-since-Swedish-middle-school-equivalent! Oh, if only he could see me now . . .

Anyhow. My ritual is a bust, so I cover up my mistake with a bit more blood, also returning the goblin skills to their pokeballs, that is, my tum-tum.

And from there on, you know the drill. Before I've even had time to properly test the true limits of my little toe in blood-stew-making, the next floor opens.

<**Floor 18 has opened. Do you want to enter?**>
<**Yes/No**>

Poke. *Yes.*

<**Tutorial stage, Hell Difficulty Eighteenth Floor: The Deep Mine**>
<**[Clear Condition] Save the unfortunate miners from their cruel oppressors.**>

The world shifts and what strikes me is a sudden and overwhelming sense of boredom. Is it too much to ask to *not* have two cave floors right next to each other? I mean, come on. First we have a circular cave, and now this? Well, at least I can see an orange fire torch in the distant tunnel, so I won't have to tear my eyes out to avoid the murderous blue lights of those magic crystals.

Anyone who says they prefer blue light to orange light is a liar whose brain has not been subjected to evolutionary psychology. In other words, they are monkeys and ought to be treated as such.

I'm no monkey, though. I am a proud ape, so I head toward the wonderful orange light.

And in the light of that torch, I meet a goblin. An orange goblin who takes one look at me before running off in such a hurry that he actually drops his pickaxe. Acting purely on gamer instinct, I pick up the axe of pick and put it into my inventory. Just in case. I doubt it'll sell for basically anything, but it's still nice to have.

Then I head into the same tunnel the goblin went down.

So, to make a long story short, this floor has a lot of goblins. It's a big mine, and it's full of goblins. Unfortunately, I couldn't smell any nearby natural gas deposits, so I couldn't take care of the whole thing in one fell swoop like that. Rather, I had to do it one by one, which took much longer.

But eight days *should* have been enough. I've handled a much greater amount of these things in a much shorter amount of time, so this shouldn't have been any issue. Might have been hubris on my part, but once I got it in my head that I could surely clear the whole floor in eight days, I went at it. The first days were kind of relaxed—I didn't want to cause an uproar or whatever—but then time got tight, so I dropped that whole plan. Take out the larger base camps, defeat the smaller mobs as quickly as possible, spend as little time as possible on the much more high-leveled whip-carrying red goblins, wonder about the level discrepancies, consider whether the normal goblins are actually meant to be defeated or if they're optional *like the beast was*, disregard thoughts since they simply stall me, and on it went.

But it all worked out in the end, because now I've got the final boss goblin at my feet, and I've got plenty of time to loot all the goblins I left to fester before. As I found out only a day or so ago, you don't actually need to join the Tutournament straightaway. You're allowed to take your time and join on your own initiative! Neat, huh? So that's what I'm doing.

The final boss goblin is breathing heavily in the corner and I'm walking around the large dining area I poisoned a few days back, and everything is okay. Every few steps, I bend down to butcher and loot another one of the little bodies strewn about. One little goblin hide, two little goblin hides, three little goblin hides . . .

"I . . . curse . . . you . . . demon . . . !"

I look back at the big boss goblin, mostly in surprise. Wow, it can still talk with only one lung? Impressive! Though, of course, I barely need lungs to talk, so it still has a long way to go. Not that there's much left for it to—

<The Tutournament will now begin.>
<Those who did not join early will be forcefully summoned in 0:05>

I blink at the screen in front of me. Huh.
Hey, wait a minute.

<Those who did not join early will be forcefully summoned in 0:04>

H—hang on! That's *seconds*?!
My face flashes toward the half-dead boss. I—I can still make it!

<Those who did not join early will be forcefully summoned in 0:03>

Throwing away the hide in my hands, I hurl myself across the room toward the final enemy.

<Those who did not join early will be forcefully summoned in 0:02>

Come on, just a little more, I can almost—!

<Those who did not join early will be forcefully summoned in 0:01>

I thrust my clawed foot at the goblin's exposed neck only to hit nothing as the world disappears around me.

Noooooooo—!

<Those who did not join early will be forcefully summoned in 0:00>
<Welcome to the Tutournament!>

IV

Tutournament

It's dark. It isn't cold, but the water and the humidity makes it feel colder than it really is. I'm . . . underground again? But not in a cave. There's dirt below me, and also above me. I can't hear much of anything beyond this, but I can see a pale stream of light fluttering in through a nearby hole leading up. Yeah, this is a hole. I can barely crawl, much less actually sit up. No, wait, if I allow my natural gamer hunch to solidify into a gamer crunch, I can sit upright.

For some reason, this is kind of . . . comfortable? I mean, with the non-warmth and non-cold of the dirt. And with the silence. Dirt is pretty soft, huh . . . Oh, shoot, I forgot to remove my goblin disguise! Better change into something more standard if I'm to meet humans . . .

Not that I got the opportunity earlier. You know. What with being *forcefully abducted against my will*, that is. Something we in the crime business colloquially call *kidnapping*. Yeah. That's what you did to me, *gods*. I know you're listening in! Don't think I can't hear your mouthbreathing against my neck, sodomites!

Grrr. And I was *this* close to beating the floor, too . . . !

Hmph. No use crying over spilled blood, I suppose. Though I do kind of want to stay in this hole for a little longer . . .

Just . . . to relax . . . a little . . .

<**Welcome to the Tutorial Tournament!**>

My eyes snap open. I—who—what—!? Oh. It's just the status thingy. What, *now* it's a *tutorial tournament*? No consistency. Typical.

<**Your current rank (group): N/A**
Your current rank (solo): N/A

[Sign up at the colosseum to receive your allotted time]>

Ranks? Colosseum? Well, well, well, now we're talkin' tournament arc!

I kind of wanted to snooze a little longer, but I'm not too interested in being a snoozer-loser, so although it pains me, I reluctantly drag myself out of my hole and into the light like a bear emerging from hibernation. Yaaaawn, okay, so, where is this colosseu—

I stare straight ahead. I blink once, and then another time for good measure. Experimentally, I turn my head to view what's behind me. Same answer.

I am surrounded by nothing but barren, arid wasteland.

I'm surprised I can't spot any dried-up ox skulls, or even one or two tumbleweeds, though I expect this world has neither. But still. It's just . . . emptiness. Ah, save for this one, lone sign right next to the hole I spawned inside. Pulling myself to my feet, I give it a good once-over. Now, let's see here . . .

<[Hole] Property of Hell Challenger Lo Fennrick>

Hole?

I glance down at the hole. Yep, that's a hole. It's . . . *my* hole. My own hole. No one else's. *Mine.*

I, uh. I don't think I've ever owned my own piece of property? Sure, if I'd played my cards right as a child and whatnot I might have stood to inherit the family home, but this is . . . This is something else. A hole. *My* hole.

The hole.

Biting a hole in my finger, I add *The* in front of *Hole*, to designate that this is not merely *a hole that happens to be owned by some dude*, but rather that this is *The Hole*, a much grander and more specific hole, owned by a much grander and more specific dude. Yes, this is correct. This is how it shall be. Good.

My hole. Hehehe.

That aside, I still can't see any colosseum. Which is, you know . . . not in my best interest. If I turn my face skyward, I find it dark, save for the five morbillion stars. If I turn my face to the clock, I find my answer.

<Top—Status—Community>
<3:58:54 Day 541>
<The nineteenth attempt will begin in 29:20:01:06>
<Tutournament Day 2 of 5>

Ah. It's the middle of the night. Yeah, that explains the dark sky. It does not, however, explain the lack of a colosseum. Am I to suppose that the ground eats it at night? No. I am not so *cleverless.* There is an answer to this, and I will find it.

And I have all I need right here. Sniff sniff sniff sniff. Object localized. Sniffer analysis engaged. Calculating distance based on sniff potency. Wind removed from calculations. Pants: shidded. Sniff inhibitors disengaged. Calculating . . .

I turn toward the hypothetical south. There it is. I can't see it, but I can smell it. Approximately seventy-five kilometers away.

Why the heck is my hole, *the hole*—aka the centerpiece of all future nightlife activity—seventy-five damn kilometers from the colosseum? Who is sabotaging my pimp potential?!

With such an accusation burning in the back of my throat, I get down on all fours and begin running toward the colosseum. The wind is on my back.

If you told me a year and a half ago that I'd become the type of person who could run seventy-five kilometers in the span of five hours without taking a single break other than to instinctively kill and butcher a two-legged goat within the span of only one minute, I would have asked you if you could spare some loose change. But you wouldn't have been wrong. Just the opposite, as a matter of fact.

And I didn't break a bone even once! Ahh, the sweet rewards of mindless grinding . . .

By the time I can actually see what I'm heading for, the sun is coming up a little and I have reached a Zen state. I am transcendent. However, transcendence doesn't actually grant wisdom, so it's only when I pull up to the twenty-meter-tall walls that I realize that what I was heading for wasn't a colosseum but rather the walls of a city surrounding said colosseum. It's a good wall, too. Very sturdy. Difficult to break down even with all the pent-up teenage angst I've saved for such an occasion.

Since I'm a rational person, I take a walk around the walls, looking for the entrance.

Spoiler alert, there is none. No way in, no way out. But I know this is the place, because I can smell people in there, and food, and items, and just the slightest twinge of bloodshed. I really hope they haven't started killing each other without me.

Okay, so since there's no entrance and I'm not beefy enough to Hulk-smash my way through, I'll simply have to let my recessive squirrel-genes do the talking and get climbing. Luckily the stones protrude pretty well, and there are a fair number of cracks and crevices to stick my grubby little fingers into, so the climbing goes well.

<You have learned: Climb Lv. 10>
<You have learned: Scale Lv. 1>

And with only a little bit of blood, sweat, tears, and a few fingers here and there as tuppence, I have reached the top of the wall. What lies before me is a perfectly circular city, each quarter almost exactly mirrored in the others, at least in terms of roads. In the very center stands what I can only assume is the colosseum, which is a grandiose but squat structure, carved out of WHITE stone with no shortage of indulgent swivelly details. If this thing had been built on Earth, I am assured it would have had gargoyles on it, as well as a few mobile phone advertisements. Instead, it just has stone statues of . . . people, I think? It's hard to tell, what with it being several kilometers away from the wall I'm sitting on. Even then, I can actually hear the excited cheering all the way from over here, which is a little insane.

The area closest to the colosseum is divided into four quarters, with three large buildings seemingly representing all quarters save for one. I call them buildings, but they really remind me more of, like, cathedrals or something. They're differently sized, but no less ornate than one another. Interestingly enough, each cathedral is surrounded by a luscious bit of greenery, the biggest by blooming trees, the second-biggest by regular green-leafed trees, and the third and last—also the least—surrounded by orange, crisp-looking trees. The fourth quarter, the hypothetical north, is filled up with what looks to be a bazaar. It does have trees—the desolate, leafless kind—but no cathedral. Interesting.

The bazaar in the fourth quarter actually spreads more, reaching a marketplace that joins with a larger, more standard area, with shops and libraries and what I think is a courthouse, alongside other official buildings. The last area, closest to the wall, appears to be more of a standard living area, with houses of varying size and quality.

Most interesting of all, milling about between these buildings and shops and tents and trees, like little ants marching about, are not goblins, but humans. *Humans.*

More humans than I think I've seen in over one and a half years. Thousands of them. It's honestly awe-inspiring, and as I sit perched up here like an owl trying to take in the sheer size of it all, a new smell slips into my nose, replacing the cold stone-scent of the colosseum.

I grin to myself. So Moleman's already here, huh?

Looking down, I see that the drop is only twenty meters. Yup, sounds good to me. Here we go!

With a skip, and a jump, and a—

Cra—ack!

Ah, whoopsie-daisy, looks like my leg didn't much like that fall. Still, I'm on the ground now, so there's no need to—

"Are you alright?"

"Hey, Lustrie, come heal this guy!"

Someone crouches down next to me and takes my hand.

"Keep calm, okay? Deep breaths. We'll have a healer here in just a minute, so there's no need to—"

All very swell and nice, but I'm in a bit of a hurry, so I pull my hand away from theirs, stand up, force my leg into place, and get moving.

"H—hey, wait a minute! Walking will only make it—"

Getting down on all fours, I begin sprinting. Ugh. I don't know why, but that felt gross. Oh, well. Despite how big this place is, it isn't actually jam-packed or anything. More like . . . custard-packed. Or something. Whatever that means. In other words, I can run without needlessly crashing into someone. That way, I can avoid a repeat of that thing that just happened. Ughh . . .

By the time I reach the colosseum and the cathedrals, my leg has healed and I can see him. He's in the opening of one of the colosseum's four vomitoriums, being harassed by . . . some group of humans. I feel like I might recognize one or two of them, but to me, they might as well all be strangers.

As I sprint toward them, my mind fills with possibilities. Do I leap at them? They have pretty good armor, but under that, they're still only flesh and blood. But what if they aren't harassing him, only talking? Yeah, sure, but what if they're robbing him and my hesitation gets him killed? Since the consequence is worse, I'll just assume the worst-case scenario.

Wait for me, Moleman, I'm coming to save you!

I leap at them. Wide eyes meet me but before my claws can meet their arteries, a clublike staff meets with my face and I go tumbling.

Ah, a worthy opponent! Allow me to lick the blood from my nose in a sinister manne—

Moleman?

As his brows furrow, Moleman's grip on the staff loosens slightly. "Kitty?"

In this moment, I have several thoughts running concurrently through my skull, one of these being *Why did Moleman hit me with a stick?* An answer soon echoes in turn: *Maybe to help increase my concussion protection?* But then another thought hits back, *But he doesn't like seeing me hurt,* so another thought returns with the screwball *He clearly didn't recognize me at first, so maybe—*

And by the time I reach *that* thought, the world around me has already started moving again and the people harassing him take defensive positions in front of him. Each one stands in a specific place, so it's clear to me that they have a lot of experience working together.

So it's a skirmish they want, eh? Well, in that case, they shall have it!

I crouch down further, like a cockroach, ready to strike once any one of them shows the slightest gap in their defenses.

"Stay behind me, Mole, this thing is clearly out to kill!" one of them, some archer dude, shouts out before hiding half his face behind his hand. "Kuh . . . I can feel its killing intent . . . it's so strong . . . and sharp . . . like a knife against my throat . . . !"

Uh. Okay?

Completely ignoring him, one of the others—a female warrior I somewhat recognize the hair of—steps forward, halberd drawn and ready. "Who are you?" she says in a familiarly accusatory voice. "Why did you attack us? Don't you know PvP is prohibited outside the colosseum?"

Ah, trying to draw me into word games, is she? Unnecessary. I can already smell their fear, roiling off them in waves. So, to unnerve them further, I begin slowly circling, trying to find a gap in their defenses. Won't be hard. Nervousness does that to people, even hardened warriors. If something that should speak doesn't, that's frightening. Useful. So I circle. Watching closely. Until . . .

"Wait!"

My whole body freezes up. The moment when Moleman now jumps out from within their barrier would be the best time for me to act but I can't move. Heh, j—just one word and I'm the one trembling, huh?

"Mole, don't get closer to that—"

Not heeding their words, Moleman strides up to me, grabs me by the shoulders, and pulls me to my feet. I feel dizzy. He won't let me look at anything save for his eyes. A—ah, uh, hello, Moleman. Um . . . let me guess, you didn't need saving from a poor little level 83 like me, huh? Yeah, I should've guessed, I just—

"Kitty? Are you okay?"

Ah. I forgot to speak aloud. Uh, I, um . . . My eye slowly falls down to the cobblestone floor. High quality. Yup. Good stuff. "I am . . . fine. Thank you. And how, uh, are you?"

His face scrunches up a little, and then he fully commits to this whole thing by violently shaking me by the shoulders to the point where I might as well assume he was trying to jimmy loose coins out of me. Not that any fall out; I haven't got any pockets. And with each powerful shake, he bites out, "Are"—a shake—"you"—one more shake, eyes burning—"*okay?!*"

The shaking stops. But I'm still shaking. Trembling. "I—I'm," I stammer, but then my throat gets all choked and nothing wants to come out anymore, it just goes all blurry and my arms and my legs are like soggy noodles and won't move good anymore. My chest heaves, all on its own, and I gulp down big breaths that I can't control, stammering breaths, I almost choke on them, warm tears and warm snot going down my face and *I must look like such a mess* but I . . . "I—I lost him, Moleman," I say, my voice in a constant, fearful vibrato. "I messed up, oh, God, I messed up so badly I want to die, I just . . ."

But I don't know what I just, because the story ends there, with Moleman putting his arms below my armpits, both hands on my back, and pushing my limp, bony little body into his arms. I can't fight it. I don't want to. But I don't deserve it. "Why—" I sob into his back, into his soft, warm back, "why are you still . . . ?"

"Of course I'm still here," he mumbles back. "I'd be an awful friend if I wasn't."

Only now can I properly hug him back. Tawny arms clutching at him like he might float away. But he won't. He's right here, and he'll never leave. Because he's my friend. And I'm his.

It takes a minute or so for me to calm down, at which point Moleman sends away his party members and moves to sit me down on a little bench outside the colosseum, in the spring park. Even then, I still can't really collect myself. I mean, I'm not wailing louder than the audience cheers anymore, but I don't . . . I can't.

A light blue handkerchief is nudged into my vision. I give Moleman a thankful nod before wiping my face with it, leaving it in a pitiful state.

What do I do with it now? Do I keep this soggy thing? I don't mind, but . . .

Before I have time to have a proper mental breakdown over it, Moleman gently takes it out of my hand, uses a little spell to clean it, and puts it back into his inventory, safe. At least until the next time. I sniffle. He sits next to me. There aren't many people here. There were a bunch of people inside and outside the vomitoriums, and especially in the bazaars, but right here, in the little park of blooming trees and flowers surrounding the largest cathedral, there's barely anyone around. The quiet is as comforting as a warm meal.

"I'll assume," Moleman says beside me, smiling gently, "that floor fifteen didn't go exactly as you wanted?"

I chuckle. "Not exactly, no . . ." He turns to me, eyes eager, but not pushy. I don't have to tell him. A while back, I would probably have kept it to myself. Most people don't talk about their big mistakes, even to their closest friends. But on the other hand . . . There's no reason to keep it to myself either, is there? I smile at him. "It's a bit of a long story."

He smiles back at me. "All the more reason to hear it."

So I tell him. I say my little jokes here and there, and he laughs along with me sometimes, not purely out of pity. I even tell him about the brand on my chest. It's easy to see. I'm only wearing a small hide around my hips right now, so it's very visible.

"Does it still hurt?"

I shrug. "It aches a little, but for the most part? Not really. Hurt a whole lot more when I got it, that's for sure." He laughs along with me, if only to be polite. I don't mind. "Compared to everything else that happened, this is the last thing on my mind."

Where he sits, Moleman gently leans forward, folding his arms across his knees. "So you pleaded guilty to killing the king of Acheron, and then you killed the Sun Emperor . . ."

A million justifications and accusations and excuses bubble up to the top of my mind, but in the end, all that's released when I open the lid is a tiny, honest "Yeah."

He pinches the bridge of his nose for a moment. Then he sits up straight and angles his chest and face toward me, his face set in a mask of determination. "You've been honest with me, and I appreciate that. So in turn, I'll be honest with you. Even if you might not like what I have to say."

I almost chuckle, but the atmosphere is wrong. *He's serious.* "Well, um . . ." I smile bravely. "All the more reason to hear it, right?" To that, he mirrors my smile, just a little.

He takes a deep breath. "This tournament . . . This is the first time all four servers have met. *Completely.* The leaderships of all four servers are here. There's our dictatorship—although Bach calls it a republic; Africa's representative democracy; Asia's democratic confederacy; America's non-appointed triarchy . . . Yesterday, all of these leaderships came together in a grand meeting. It's a shame you weren't there; your translation abilities would've been a great help. Nonetheless . . ."

He pauses, eyes hardening as he looks down at his lap and then back up at me. "You were mentioned." My mouth flounders open but he speaks before I have time to puzzle together a coherent string of words. "A fair bit, actually. You weren't the first thing or anything—we had a lot of things to discuss—but you did eventually come up."

My eyes fall to the ground, to the cobblestones beneath my bare feet. Absently, I push a little rock into a gap between two cobblestones. "So, um," I say after a pause, "what did you talk about?"

"A lot," he says, his voice shifting subtly, like he's suddenly giving a report instead of simply talking. "First, Bach ascertained how much the other server leaderships knew. It didn't take long for them to admit that they had—with the exception of the Africa Server—formed intelligence groups specifically to investigate the reason behind the residents of Purgatory's ire toward humans. Not that they needed to do much research."

"So . . ." I butt in. "They know?"

"Everything," Moleman sighs. "They know everything."

For a few seconds, I don't say anything, and neither does he. Only once the shock has worn off do I ask, in a voice tinier than a mosquito's buzz, "And you told them . . . ?"

"I told them nothing they didn't know already," Moleman says frankly. I release a breath. "They wanted to have you executed the second you showed up." I stop breathing again.

"Th—they did?"

He nods. "The Americans were very adamant. Said if we let you live, the goblins would resent us forever for letting a king-killer run free." Which is, in my opinion, not entirely incorrect. Actually, scratch that, I'm pretty sure that's completely correct. "Bach was on their side, but Flagship, the current president of the Africa Server, refused. Tried to pull a veto on the whole deal, which Bach obviously shot down. Almost threatened to personally join the tutorial tournament, against the agreement made earlier for server rulers to refrain from participating."

I blink. "Wait, you're not going to fight in the tutournament?"

His brows furrow. "What did you just call . . . ?" A shake of the head. "Never mind. See, that's the thing. Since our server is technically a dictatorship, our only ruler is Bach. The rest of us are free to play as we please."

"Oh, good," I say. Then I smirk. "I was starting to fear we might not get to have our long-awaited rematch after all."

He smiles back at me. "If you get that far in the *tutorial tournament*, I'll be sure to face you with everything I've got." We grin at each other for a few seconds before he continues. "Anyhow, Asia stood on the fence for a little while before deciding to support Africa and me. Though, in the end, we didn't exactly get through that you wouldn't be executed. Instead . . ."

"Instead?"

"Instead, we'll hold a trial. A proper one, with a judge and jury and lawyers. That's the least we can do, right? The Americans weren't too happy to hear it, but Flagship talked them into it, and with three to one, Bach had no choice but to capitulate."

"I'm going on trial?" I ask incredulously. "*Again?*"

Not responding to my words, Moleman continues, "However, with your reputation being as it is, the leaders weren't certain that you could be . . . *captured* . . . without any unintended casualties. So they . . ."

I look at him. He doesn't look at me. But I know what he's saying. "They asked you to get me, didn't they?"

"Not forcefully," Moleman quickly adds, "nothing like that. They simply asked me to try to get you to come peacefully, instead of making this into a huge deal." He turns to me, eyes drilling into mine. Earnest. "So I'm asking you. Will you allow yourself to be put on trial? *Again?*"

I blink at him and look down at my feet. My jaw works itself. Mouth opening, then closing again, lips slowly, almost reluctantly forming a little smile as I turn my eyes from the cobblestones up to him.

"Well," I say. "If it's for a friend, then . . ." I chuckle. "*Why not?*"

We smile at each other. Isn't life awfully simple sometimes?

"But, before that," he says, as though a thought hit him only now, "have you signed up for the tournament yet?"

"The tutournament?" I parrot. "No. I only got here just now, and then I saw you being harassed . . . um, *talking* with your *friends*, and after that . . ." I give a self-deprecating chuckle. "You know the rest."

He nods at me thoughtfully. "In that case," he says, standing up, "we'd better get you signed up before the preliminaries reach floor eighteen. Would be a shame if you missed the group tournament, I'd say."

Following suit, I stand up as well. A thought suddenly hits me, making me pause midrise. "Wait. Don't you need to be in a group to fight in a *group* tournament?"

He snaps his fingers. "You do. However . . ." He grins. "I think I can help you with that."

Not explaining himself in the least, he pulls me back to the vomitorium, not pausing at all to look at the single random saddled sprint-drake tethered outside, dragging me all the way inside the colosseum, into a pretty large hall. There are people doing the usual hustling and bustling. Some enter a hall that seems to lead to the various bleachers, while others head into some kind of back room. The room as a whole is quite large, the walls and the receptionist area hogging most of the human interest.

Moleman guides me to the receptionist area, or, rather, to the line heading to it. There are about two dozen people ahead of us.

"So, uh," I say, grabbing his attention. "Why did you—"

Interrupting me fully, he grabs my shoulders and pulls me up, bringing me from his chest level to his eye level. I blink at him and he smiles sheepishly. "Slouch all you want, but you can at least try to walk upright, okay?"

I look down at the floor, at my now-straightened knees. "Oh, uh, yeah. Of course." It seems I have acquired an unfortunate habit of not merely slouching but actually falling into an instinctual crouch, no matter where or when or why. Extreme cases can even have me assume Gollum-position without a single thought. A few people who were glancing at me from across the room look away now that I'm standing normally. Hm. Nevertheless, I turn back to Moleman, a hint of suspicion shining through my voice as I say, "If you already knew everything that happened . . . everything I *did* on floor fifteen, why did you ask me to explain?" *And why did you listen?*

I almost expect him to maybe shrug and explain it dismissively with something like *Oh, haha, I could tell you needed to talk it out,* but I don't get that. His expression turns somber. And after only a moment's pause he says, as plainly as the weather, "I had to know whether you regretted it."

For several seconds, I simply stare at him, lips sealed tightly. The line moves a step and we move along with it. I avert my eyes from his face and look down at the floor, at my blueish, reddened feet and his well-made, well-worn boots. In a whisper, I ask, "Did I pass the test . . . ?"

"Yes," he says, and a warm hand falls on my shoulder and my eyes snap up to him, to find him smiling broadly. "With flying colors." He chuckles. "If you hadn't, I would probably have had to *trick you* into coming down to the courthouse." My heart plummets and he must have been able to see it on my face, because he quickly adds, "Though I didn't have a doubt in my mind that you'd pass. That's just what Bach told me to do in the infinitely small chance you didn't. Heck, she actually wanted to keep a circle of guards around you at all times to ensure that you could be captured in case you tried to escape. But I talked her out of that, alongside all her other insane contingency plans."

I look around at the other people in the room. "So we aren't being followed?"

"Nope."

"If I suddenly went out of control and began biting everyone like a printer chewing through paper, a bunch of guards wouldn't suddenly appear to chop off my head and hammer a stake into my heart?"

"Funny way of putting it, but no, that wouldn't happen."

I can feel my brows furrow. "So, what you're saying is . . ." The thought is too unreal to think, so I have to say it. "You *trust* me?"

Smile not wavering for a moment, he nods. "I trust you, and the leadership trusts me enough for that to transfer." As we move further up the line, he actually giggles at the mere thought. "I mean, can you imagine if the leadership tried to treat you like some sort of beast that had to be put down? Put you in a cage, wind you up with chains . . . Like a medieval animal court?" He sighs. "No, we're more civilized than that." A frown suddenly slips its way onto his face. "Apparently, not civilized enough to fully condemn the death penalty, but all governments have their cracks, I suppose."

I almost want to respond with something, but by the time my brain has shifted into the right gear to formulate coherent thoughts, we've abruptly reached the end of the line. Namely, the reception desk.

A conventionally attractive *human* woman glances at me for a fraction of a second before looking over at Moleman, beaming the moment her eyes fall on him. "Oh, SuperMoleman! It's so lovely to see you again. Is there anything I can help you with?"

Her voice is pleasant, but it isn't memorable in the least. It's not bad to listen to, but I can't imagine it saying any word she hasn't already spoken. Her face is the same. Pleasant, but strangely ordinary. Only flawless insofar as there's nothing unpleasant about it. It's not a face you'd see on billboards, it's not something you'd call any extreme like *beautiful* or even *pretty*. Nobody could possibly envy or be disgusted by it.

The only feature of note is that somehow, despite the lack of wrinkles or pimples or any other human flaw, she looks kind.

Moleman smiles back at her. "It's nice to see you too, Patty. How are things going here? Nobody's harassed you or anything?"

"Oh, of course not! What a silly joke," she says in that pleasant, accentless inflection. "Now, let's not hold up the line for the others too much. How may I help you?"

"Well, actually, it's not me who needs help, but actually my friend, Kitty. PrissyKittyPrincess."

She doesn't even look at me. "A—ah. Yes . . . PrissyKittyPrincess. Of course. And he wants to sign up for both tournaments?" To avoid looking at her pleasantly nervous face, I glance down at an embroidered patch on the front of her vest. *Hi! I'm Compassion 28: Patty. How may I help you?* The weave shimmers oddly in my sight, and I've got a hunch that anybody else reading it would also read the exact same thing I did. Magic.

Moleman looks at her, and then at me. "I don't know, how about you ask him?"

"Huh?" she says. Her blandly kind smile twitches. "Oh, yes. Of course. You are perfectly correct, SuperMoleman. Forgive my rudeness."

"I'm sure Kitty will be forgiving if you say so to him," Moleman counters.

Ah, she froze. Is she even breathing anymore? No, now that I think about it, was she breathing to begin with? Right as I'm starting to consider the possible non-nature of the woman in front of us, she turns toward me. Oh, but only her body does. Her head remains fixed in place, like she's a chicken or something.

"Forgive me, PrissyKittyPrincess. To repeat my question, are you interested in signing up to both tournaments or just the solo?" And all this said while very clearly looking at Moleman, *not* me. Speaking of Moleman, he looks like he wants to say something about the status of her head, but he never told her to actually look at me, so . . . good enough.

"Um, yeah," I respond. "Also, don't you mean the *tutournament?*"

Her customer service *I-want-to-die* smile twitches. "No, that is simply how the God of Pain refers to the tutorial tournament. The Goddess of Compassion is not affiliated with His terms." I gawk at her. Wait, seriously? That stupid word is just what Pain calls it, and *no one* else? Did He alter my status screens to add it?!

Ignoring my grand internal conflict, Patty continues. "On the matter of the *tutorial tournament*, you are most welcome to join the solo tournament. However, as SuperMoleman is on floor sixty-six and you are on floor eighteen, it will be impossible to form a team with him. For a team, you need a minimum of two members and a maximum of seven to join the group tournament. Since you do not have any group to join, I'm afraid that—"

"He'll be joining floor eighteen's Team Wu-Li." Moleman just totally cut her off. Whoa, is that a vein popping on her forehead? I've never seen that in real life! Man, this is *exactly* like my animes.

Her eyes narrow. "Excuse me?" After a second, she regains enough composure to talk properly. "I'm sorry, but without a representative of Team Wu-Li, PrissyKittyPrincess will unfortunately not be able to—"

Interrupting her *again*, Moleman slams a parchment down on the reception-ist desk like it's key evidence in a murder case. "I've already received their permission. This written agreement should suffice."

In keeping with the courtroom analogy, Patty looks down at the parchment like it just sealed her fate on the scaffold. Hands moving like that of an animatronic, she picks up the parchment, which I now see does indeed contain a few signatures. Her eyes scan it for any inaccuracies. In the meantime, I throw a cautious look at Moleman.

Moleman . . .

How much did you plan in advance . . . ?

"Everything appears to be in order," Patty says with the same gravity as someone reporting on the death of a beloved family pet. She only lacks the mournful shake of the head, the wiping at the eyes, or any other shows of humanity. "The floor eighteen all-skirmish will be at a quarter past thirteen. It is recommended to be in the preparation hall—right through that door—at least a quarter of an hour before the allotted time. Your party wins if any of you are the last standing, at which point you move on to the quarterfinals, then the semifinals, and ultimately the spiraling finals."

"So if I understand this correctly," I say measuredly, only half wanting to see her get her panties in a twist again, "as long as at least *one* member of the party is left standing in the all-skirmish, that's the party that wins?"

The frustrated hesitation on her face is a wonderful sight to see. "Yes. That would technically work. However, as this is a measure of your teamwork and ability to cooperate, it would paint your aptitude in a bad light and would therefore not be a recommended strategy."

"Besides," Moleman suddenly says, "isn't it better to use it as a moment to make some friends?"

I make a face at him and turn back to Patty. "So, what's the grand prize at the end?" I flash a toothy smile at her. "If it's points, I'll maul ya."

Ah, unfortunately, she shows no reaction. "I am certain that your *companion* will be more than willing to inform you." I didn't know you could say *companion* like it's a four-letter word, but by golly did she do it. "Now, if you'll stop clogging up the line, I have other challengers to attend to."

Before I have time to argue and ask for her manager, Moleman grabs me by the arm. "Bye, Patty! I'll see you on floor seventy, yeah?"

She shoots him a cold glare but a warm smile. "If your *companion* lets you go that far, then sure. I'll be happy to answer your questions again, SuperMoleman."

And then we're too far away for me to stick out my tongue at her, so what's the point anymore. "Hey, Moleman, where are we—" Oh. We're by the wall. Which is apparently covered in timetables, various lists of rules (official and non-official), graffiti left by anyone and everyone, billboards for anything and everything, and the big centerpiece of it all: a huge poster showing a tournament outlay that really looks more like a death spiral. I'm not entirely surprised to find that the all-skirmish is indeed just a battle royale, but the rest of the outlay unnerves me. It's separated into floors, and the two first battles after the all-skirmish are totally normal, but then it literally becomes like a death spiral of some sort, with the winner of the first-vs.-second against third-vs.-fourth floor facing off against the winner of the fifth-vs.-sixth and seventh-vs.-eighth battles, and then either continuing up against higher and higher floors or being beaten and letting the new finalist move further. It looks absolutely insane.

"What the heck . . ." I mumble, which Moleman's super hearing apparently catches.

"It's not as complicated as it looks," he says, like a secret genius or something. "I asked the Goddess of Compassion about it, and it's because of the simple fact that you can't exactly do a normal semi-hemi-demifinals thing here. People get stronger pretty naturally as the floors go on, so if it had had a more standard tournament shape, the strongest player in the upper half of the floors would have had to spend the finals stomping the strongest player of the lower half of the floors. It wouldn't have been fair, so now they're doing this instead, where it's more like moving through a gauntlet. It has the same structure for the solo matches in two days."

I cross my arms. Yeah, no, I can't really understand it. All I know is that I've gotta defeat them all, and then I'll get to reap the sweet, sweet rewards of my bloodshed: more bloodshed.

Taking a step closer, pushing past one of the other dozens milling about in the room, Moleman points a finger at one of the timetables. "The time right now is . . . eleven-something, so we can already see who the winning groups are for floors one through thirteen. Once all the skirmishes have finished, the group-on-group battles will begin."

"You still haven't told me what the reward is for beating all of this," I say, almost dismissively.

He jumps a little, almost as if he forgot he was talking with me at all. "Did I? Sorry, I wasn't . . . Well, it's not exactly complicated." I perk an eyebrow at him. He simply shrugs. "It's a wish."

"Another damn wish?"

"Well, yes, but . . ." His smile turns enigmatic. "It's a wish from the *master of the tutorial.*"

I frown to myself. A wish again, huh . . .

Honestly, I'm not too interested. However, the concept of crushing those who dare oppose me en masse and in person is very attractive to me, far more than any monkey's paw fingersnap. Considering that my current level is probably barely half of whatever Moleman has, winning isn't on my mind in the least. It feels like a lifetime ago, but back during my pro gamer days, I mainly played for the PvP. Plot, actual gameplay, game design . . . All of that was secondary to being able to construct a powerful avatar to use as a battering ram against the collective player base. No boss, no matter how artificially buffed it is, can possibly compare to the sweet joy of beating someone with nothing but pure skills.

As I watch Moleman checking through the list of winning teams, I feel a competitive grin materialize on my lips. I take a step toward him. "Hey, Moleman, how about when I beat you fair and square, you have to treat me to dinner?"

Not looking away from the time tables, Moleman gives a chuckle. "Don't you think I'll treat you anyway?"

"Well, yeah, but I mean, like, a *big* dinner, a real nice one." I close my eyes for a second to imagine it properly. "Four courses, caviar, fantasy-world-lobster-equivalent . . . non-French champagne, gold leaf asparagus, beef Wellington but with whole minced truffles instead of meat, enriched mineral water taken straight from Mars . . . you know. The whole nine yards, and then a few inches more, just because."

He throws a sly, playful glance at me. "I think you might be overestimating the kind of points I rake in."

I hum loudly to show my lack of interest in his obvious excuses. "How about we have it once we both beat the tutorial, then?"

"I'll have to ask my parents, but I'm sure they won't mind."

I grin, for many reasons, not just because I conned myself into a six-star dinner. "Great! Glad we've agreed on tha—"

"*John!*" someone somewhere shouts, and I'm tackled to the floor, a pair of slim arms clutched around my torso. I reflexively slice at their neck but my claws bounce off because of the pink chain mail beneath their shirt, a few sparks leaping into the air and dissipating, leaving me to stare at their face. *Her* face. She blinks back at me. "Aw, shucks. You're not John, are you?"

Wild RED hair peeking out from beneath a flat-topped cowboy hat. Freckles. Smiling, even though I just tried to kill her because she literally tackled me to the floor. But between the thick, curling locks of ginger, a pair of crystal-clear blue eyes shine. Submerged diamonds. Playful. *Dangerous.*

Pushing her off me, I leap back, reflexively snapping into a ball to gain distance and distraction before falling into a crouch, fingers flexed and ready. My eyes quickly start moving about her shape, looking for an opening, instead finding what can only be described as the epitome of cowboy gear. Cowgirl? Ignoring the hat I want to ridicule but can't because it really *does* look kind of sick, she's wearing a leather vest, leather riding trousers, leather boots . . . good leather. It would take more than a few hits to get through that, not to mention that she's apparently wearing a chain-mail shirt beneath the white blouse I just ripped at the throat. To be honest, I don't know if it's a shirt or a blouse. Is it a blouse because it's a woman wearing it, or is it a shirt because everything else is so typically masculine? I don't know.

But the thing that grabs my attention the most isn't any of that, but rather something I hadn't even thought about before. I didn't notice it at all, but unlike almost every other challenger in the room, she wears a lot of satchels and pouches and things. Everything she owns is on full display, close at hand. Is she showing off, or does she not trust the inventory?

Either way, thanks to this, I can tell what kind of fighter she is. Namely: an archer. She wears her bow right on her back, together with her quiver of arrows. Not to mention the dagger and short sword hanging at her hip.

She looks fully decked out to go to war, but her face undermines that impression.

Big, innocent smile; eyes you can see right through all the way into her blindingly honest soul. "Man, I messed up, huh?" I don't answer that one, because I don't think it was aimed at me. I'm still thinking, though. See, she smells weird. There's all the leather, sure, but then there's something else, below that. Like eggs and ash. I can't really explain it, but it isn't a wholly bad smell or anything. Just . . . weird. Out of place. "Are you okay? You didn't get hurt, did you?"

I need to assess whether she's an enemy. But the more I look at her, the less I think she is. With the dagger and short sword and the bow, if she'd wanted to kill me, she would've stabbed me in the back earlier. She certainly could sneak up on me unseen, so slipping a knife between two of my ribs would've been easier than pushing me into a brawl.

For a few seconds more, I watch her where she stands, smiling sheepishly but widely. I can't tell how or why, but she doesn't smile like you do when you feign compassion, or when you pretend to be happy. Frankly, her smile is ugly. It's lopsided and oddly crooked but she still smiles it, doing so for no one but herself.

Somehow, she feels measured. Whatever it is she's doing, whatever it is she is, it isn't random or thoughtless. Even as we face each other in a silent deadlock, I can tell that she's ready. Her stance is relaxed, but my instincts tell me that if I attacked her, she'd have an arrow lodged in my chest before I so much as crossed half of the distance between us.

I don't think of her as an enemy, but simply because of the way she holds herself, I cannot let my guard down.

No, more than that, as strange as it feels to admit . . . I don't *want* to let my guard down. She's at ease now, but if I provoked her a little, I could get the match of my life. I don't know her level. That means it doesn't matter. I don't need to know my chances. I just want to—

"Whoa, whoa, whoa!" Moleman says, quickly stepping between us, his back to me, facing the girl. "I'm sorry, but could you explain yourself? If you have nothing to say for yourself, I won't hesitate to contact the Server Alliance."

Where I sit hunched on the ground, I can perfectly see the blank expression on her face. And not in a *who's-this-mob-character* kind of way, but more pure non-understanding. Like she's watching a dog trying to explain itself through barks and growls alone. "Well?"

She shoots a glance at me. I can instantly tell exactly what she's thinking, but I don't care about that. Instead, sighing, I straighten out and tap Moleman on the shoulder. He's hesitant to turn to me, but once I tap him a few more times, he finally relents, his quizzical eyes as perusable as hers. I simply ask him, "You can't understand what she's saying?"

His brows furl a crease along his forehead. "Well, I . . ." He turns around again to look at her. "To be honest, I have no idea. I think she's speaking English, but the accent is so thick I can't make out a single word . . ."

"Personally," the girl says, butting in, somehow answering both of us at once, "it's more that everyone else talks very strangely. Except for you! You talk my own language, so to speak." And then, as a cherry on top, she gives an innocent little smile. "But in your case, I guess it's more that everyone understands you in their own language, right?" Her smile falls a little and all of a sudden, before I have time to digest what she's actually saying, she gives a curt bow. "I'm sorry for tackling you; I overheard you talking and since I could actually understand you, I thought you were from my town. Will you explain to your friend that this was all just a misunderstanding?"

I cross my arms. "Can you not understand what anyone in here says?"

"None," she admits.

"You never learned a second or third language in school?"

"I didn't have time for school, I was too busy training my sharpshooting," she says, as if that's actually a real excuse for anything. Still, an accent so thick it's basically its own language . . . I'd be more skeptical if I wasn't from Skåne. While I think the whole thing over, she takes a step forward, removing the hat from her head and placing it on her chest as she does. And although he can't understand a word she says, her intention shines so clearly in her eyes that Moleman simply steps aside, letting her approach me.

She holds out a hand to me. "It's a pleasure making your acquaintance, mister."

I look down at the hand, up at her face, down at the hat in her other hand, and then finally at the hand itself. Despite the tremble in my hand, I grip hers. "Likewise," I mumble.

But all she does is smile.

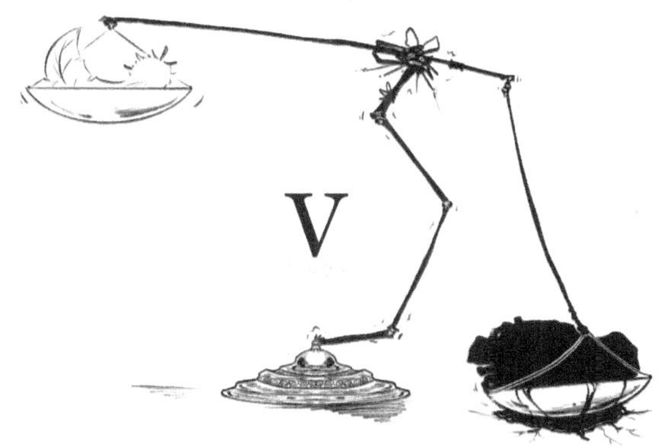

On Trial (Reprise)

"My username's BeatriceTheAngel, but I'd prefer it if you called me Rice. All the other parts are so needlessly grand, and Rice is pretty similar to my real name, anyway," she says as she shakes my hand.

"Kitty," I say, shaking hers. "PrissyKittyPrincess."

"And your friend?" She shoots a glance at the confused but not unhappy Moleman.

"SuperMoleman," I say. "Moleman or Mole works."

Moleman nods. "I'm fine with either." His attempt to join the conversation is unfortunately lost as Rice stares blankly at him, curious but non-understanding. The second he sees the look in her eye, he turns to me with a pleading face.

"He's saying that either one works," I translate.

"Oh! I see!" she says, grabbing Moleman's hand and shaking it for both of them. "Pleasure meeting you, Man!"

I can't tell if she's making a joke or what, but after about half a second of deliberation, I decide to neither correct her nor to inform Moleman of what his name has become.

What follows this greeting is a conversation that is simultaneously attended by two and three parties. By the end, I'm shoved into the role of translator as Moleman effortlessly befriends Rice. I couldn't even really tell what was happening. They would say things and I'd repeat them and they would go back and forth like that, with me squeezed in the middle. He was genuinely curious about her, and she was genuinely curious about him.

"You won't be participating in the group tournament? Why not?" As Moleman speaks, I repeat it for Rice to hear.

After nodding at me encouragingly, she shrugs at Moleman. "I fight alone," she says neutrally. Once I've translated it, Moleman and I both perk an eyebrow at her. Body language doesn't need to be translated, and she quickly explains her position. That is, being one of only a hundred or so Hard Difficulty challengers of the American Server, also being the only one to have reached floor forty-five. But even while she was in the same lobby as the others, the inability to communicate was simply too much. Even in Purgatory, she still can't find it in her to try to form a party.

"I see . . ." Moleman says, giving her a pitying look that I really don't like seeing. "But—"

"But you'll be joining the solo tutournament?" I ask, maybe a bit too eagerly. Moleman gives me a look of concern, but I'm too focused on Rice to care about it.

After a few moments of deliberation, she gives a toothy grin. "Of course!" Her eyes, still as clear as before, gleam mischievously—dangerously. "Wouldn't want to miss an interesting fight, now would I?"

Moleman glances at me with what I think might be worry in his eyes. Sometimes I really do underestimate how observant he is, because just a single look at my face told him everything he needed to know. "I see," I mumble to myself before giving her a grin in turn. "It'd be a shame to fight you with a bunch of meat bags clogging up the arena, anyway."

Rice seems to like what I'm saying, though Moleman appears to be of a different opinion. "As long as you don't overdo it, I suppose . . ."

As Rice watches him talk, her catlike grin takes on a mischievous curl and she turns her eyes back to me. "He doesn't like you fighting, does he?"

Giving a quick glance at Moleman to make sure he didn't understand her somehow, I briefly answer. "It doesn't matter."

And then there's that glint in her eye. Some little refraction leaping off the crystal-clear calm waters of her eyes, gleaming like the light stroking a knife. "I see. Interesting fella, you are." She puts her hat back on her head, face shadowed for but a second, one that feels much longer than it really is. Her eyes shine just beneath the hat's brim. "You better keep him close. When the time comes, I'll gladly fight you on your terms." She turns her back to us and starts walking away, only pausing to glance over her shoulder, through a gap between her bow and quiver. "I'll see you, Prince."

I don't even have time to say goodbye before she easily slips back into the crowd, mingling into them just as a roar of cheer roils over them, everyone falling over each other to congratulate and shake the hands of a team exiting the door leading from the scene. They smile and shake hands and pat backs, but I'm trying to look for Rice.

In the end, my search leaves my eyes to fall back on Moleman, who turns to me with a conflicted expression. "That last word she said," he says measuredly, "was *Prince*, right?"

I pause a second before answering. "No," I say. My nose can still make out the lingering scent of sulfur and ash. "She said, *Bye*."

We share a look, and then the world starts turning again.

Since my preliminary skirmish was still several hours away, Moleman decided for both of us that we might as well go to the courthouse early. "Is that really your decision to make?" I asked him, but all he did was shrug, so I guess it was. No idea how the trial itself is supposed to work. Honestly, the only reason I didn't feel more worried about the whole thing while walking there was that Moleman was at my side, and he seemed fully calm. We walked side by side as he led me away from the colosseum (interestingly enough, the sprint-drake previously tethered outside the colosseum was now gone) and toward the outer parts of the city.

While we were passing through the marketplace area, he actually threw curious glances here and there, downright promising me that we would get something to eat once the trial had concluded. The fact that he boldly assumed that the server leaderships wouldn't just execute me on the spot was weirdly comforting.

"So this is it?" I ask in reference to the unusually grand-looking building in front of us. Polished white marble, a statue of the same goddess I saw at my last execution, and a big sign above the front entrance that reads *House of Law* in bold, brassy letters. Looking at it, I can tell that it—much like Fatty's patch—can be read by anyone for what it is.

Moleman nods, his face and posture abruptly serious. "Yeah," he says sharply. "This is it."

As we stare in shared silence, my instincts whisper to me, and I glance stealthily to the side of the building. There, in the shadow of a marble wall, I catch the eye of a man who, upon making eye contact with me, speedily slips fully into the shadow. However, though I can't see him, his scent is not so easily hidden. Nor is the scent of his comrades. Fear, I've found, is a smell most distinct, even when mingling with the smells of iron, oil, and sweat. There are about thirty-two of them.

"Well?" Moleman asks. "Shall we enter?" There's a lilt to his voice that isn't usually there—worry? Not for himself, or for me. I let my eyes linger on him for just a moment, my mind grappling a few seconds with the fact that *he knows*.

But the seconds pass as they always do and I let myself sigh. Turning to Moleman, I smile. "Sure," I say. "Let's go."

We enter. I remember now that I hate stairs. The physical pain is minute and it's not like I haven't experienced worse bodily sensations, but the memory of the stairs at my old Swedish-high-school-equivalent is painful enough in its own right. The inside of the courthouse *appears* empty, but I can smell them. There's a stink in this place, produced by the frantic scuttle and shuffle of dozens of people. Not fear, no, but something adjacent. Worry? Yes, worry. Lots and *lots* of worry, all concentrated here and there in little blobs of stress amalgamate. It's honestly an interesting smell, and I'm a bit unwilling to relinquish it once we arrive at a small, inconspicuous door at the top of a long staircase.

Moleman opens the door, but instead of shutting out the odor of stress, it actually intensifies it, a wall of solid worry barreling out from within to hit me face-first.

<You have learned: Enhanced Scent Lv.10>
<You have learned: Greater Scent Lv.1>

And with that skill evolution, the scent almost becomes dizzying. Nevertheless, Moleman seems less than perturbed, entering casually. I follow him, remembering as I do that the smell is hardly new to him. He's exuding it in equal parts as them, after all.

There are a total of seventeen people already inside the room. But the room itself is . . . how do I say this . . .

Not exactly a courtroom?

I mean, there are all the necessary actors for a classic courtroom scene, but the room itself is just a room. No raised pedestal for the judge, no humongous gallery for the witnesses and audience, no dramatic tables to slam fists and evidence onto; and no stand for the jury, either. No, out of every type of room I can recall seeing, this one appears to me far more like a conference room. The room is fairly high, but I don't think it's designed to hold more than maybe thirty people or so.

There's a window facing a small courtyard, which provides most of the light. Much like every other room and house I've seen in the tutorial, there are no electronic or gas-lit lamps. Since it's daytime, there's no need for light of that sort, but . . . still. All seventeen people sit gathered around a fairly large oval-shaped table, the majority of them facing toward the opposite side of the door we entered through.

Moleman nods to them in greeting, and the man sitting at the Dracula-seat, farthest away from our side, nods back. Then Moleman guides me to sit at the seat on the very other side of the table, facing the Dracula-seat.

As this is happening, I notice with some amount of interest and suspicion that—once again—there isn't a single guard in sight.

I know they exist. Out in the streets, I saw a pair passing by, proudly wearing a patch showing the server they were from. They didn't look at me but I sure looked at them, because they were very interesting to see. But in here, where a known criminal is being put on trial, there isn't a single guard to be seen. I'm not in a cage. They didn't even put a pair of cuffs on me, or ask me to empty my inventory, or take a nail cutter to my claws.

I watch Moleman take a seat next to me, bringing the total number of attendees up to nineteen. Had this taken place in a normal-sized courtroom, like the ones in the movies or the one I was judged at most recently, nineteen people would have seemed like a tiny number, barely enough to fill the jurors' box.

But in this small room, around a single table, with all of them looking at me? Yeah, no, I feel claustrophobic.

I don't have time to think up ways to bodily vent the itch in my claws before the trial begins, all on its own.

"Thank you all for coming," the guy in the seat opposite to mine says warmly. Only a few heads turn to him, the rest still facing me. Among them, I only recognize one, though seeing Bach—former rebel leader and current Simon Says of the Europe Server—does actually surprise me a little. But she's looking at the guy speaking, so I do too. "I am John Logghammer of the America Server, Normal Difficulty, and I will be acting as judge for these proceedings."

Judge, eh? His first name is awfully droll, so I'll just call him Logghammer.

"The leaders of the Server Alliance have graciously decided to act as the jury to represent each server in the judgment." Presenting them, Logghammer gives the twelve of them a little wave. They don't say anything, but I can tell they're tense. More so than me. "For our prosecutor and defense attorney, we have VenedictAllegro and SuperMoleman respectively, both of the Europe Server."

My jaw drops a little and I turn to look at Moleman. He smiles at me, in a *sorry-for-tricking-you* kind of way.

Moleman will be defending me?

While I'm still reeling, Logghammer continues, each word he says being meticulously noted down by one of the many people in attendance. "To preface this simple trial, we are not following the laws of any specific country, or of any specific server. Each server has their own rules and corresponding penalties, some of which overlap, others that don't. Since the Server Alliance has yet to fully detail a collective lawbook for the use of all challengers, this trial will act as part of the foundation upon which any future trials may stand. At the moment, it is pertinent to assume that any act the majority of the challengers and the population of Purgatory deem as criminal will be considered and therefore punished as such. The punishments will be decided with time, but for now, we may assume that any penalty, big or small, is on the table." He looks over at the person closest to my left, sitting opposite Moleman. "Venedict, will you begin by presenting the prosecution's case?"

Nodding, the prosecution stands up, adjusting the collar of his shirt as he does. "Thank you, John." Going by how short his hair is, I can assume he hasn't been here for more than a few attempts. Doesn't look like much of a fighter, but he's got a good glint in his eye. "During the past three weeks, I became a slough."

I blink at him. Well, *that's* an opening statement, I suppose.

He clears his throat. "Being in the Europe Server, there was no lack of people who had an opinion on PrissyKittyPrincess—whom I will henceforth refer to merely as *Kitty*—be they good or bad. Mainly bad. A few older members spoke of his brush with death upon the execution block. Others, who had their efforts rewarded with only scorn in Purgatory, spoke angrily of the man who had single-handedly ruined the reputation of all humans.

"But when it comes to proof, crimes, and evidence, one needs only to look at the brand permanently seared onto his chest." A few eyes dart down to look at my bare chest. Ah, that's embarrassing. Couldn't you have a little more grace and tact about this? Not hearing my silent pleas, he continues. "I consulted a few well-known mages among humans, ones who had spent time in Purgatory. This brand, now widely known as the *Brand of Penance*, is already in use in several places across the central continent. Mainly on humans. From what I've heard, some die from the pain alone, others from the spiritual pain, choosing to die rather than keeping it. In the end, though, the pain of the brand is caused by the weight of the sins carried by the brandee. Nevertheless, the brand can only scar those guilty of the sin it was forged for."

He turns to me. There is no great flourish, no pointing of fingers, and no throwing of papers. Just his soft voice, saying, "I don't have to wonder the weights of the sins needed for that brand. Murder of a king, yes, but . . . The rest is just as heavy, if not more so."

Is this the moment when I'm supposed to stand up and shout, *Objection, Your Honor, it was self defense and also totally not me, I was nowhere near the scene of the crime!* or something? Because, well, I'm not doing that. I feel calm. He's right. The brand hurt like a dagger to the heart and my hands bear the blood of more than a mere king. It's almost eerie how calm I feel.

A number of eyes turn to me and I shrug. "Yup," I say. "Gu—" A thought rushes into my skull and my eyes flash toward Moleman. But he doesn't look angry. He doesn't even look as though he disapproves of anything about this. Isn't he supposed to be my defense attorney? Well . . . this is still *my* trial, so . . . "Yeah. Guilty. I did that."

Sue me, I almost say, but stop because that's exactly what they're doing.

"You plead guilty to the murder of the king of Acheron?" Logghammer asks, not sounding surprised in the least.

I toss a look at Moleman. "Yeah. You know I did it, and you know I pleaded guilty to it last time, too. Mass murder, arson, cannibalism . . . I did it." I hope the glare I give Venedict is as icy cold as it feels. I mean, why waste time laying forth an argument for what we all know I did? To show my irritation, I cross both my arms and legs. "You even know I killed Emperor what's-his-name and a bunch of his guards. None of it was in the clear requirement, so it isn't in accordance with the rules and laws whatsoever." I almost feel like sneering, but Moleman's calm, unfazed expression keeps me from it. "So?" I say instead. "What's the verdict, Your Dishonor?"

Logghammer waves a little. "No need for that *Your Honor* stuff, I'm technically nothing but a former attorney. John is fine."

"Okay, *Your John*," I snark.

He chuckles with mirth. My attempt to rightfully upset a few people has failed and I have instead lightened the mood for some old short-hair newbie. I must repent by jumping off a cliff. "To reach a verdict, the jury and judge would have to be in agreement, which we are."

As I knew they would be.

"However, although we know much about the events in and before the Split Horizon murder, there are some details we would like fully explained and described." His eyes sharpen slightly. "Would you mind writing a full confession of all crimes you can recall committing during your time in the tutorial? It's fine if you can't remember all of them, but a simple, summarizing account of your criminal history would suffice very well. After all, we can only judge you properly if we know exactly what you did."

I stare at him. He smiles at me. I glance at Moleman. He seems just as nonchalant about this as he has been by literally everything else that's happened so far. Leaning forward, I fold my fingers across the table. "Sure. Why not?"

To summarize, they gave me a stack of parchment papers, three quills of disgustingly high quality, two inkwells, an inkblot that I have no idea how to use, a list containing the full rulebooks of each server, and then also a small room to do my bloody business in. Oh, and they also gave me Moleman. He came along. You know. As moral support, I think.

Once the door is closed behind us, as soon as we both sit down, I say, "Thanks for telling them I don't like guards. And being chained up."

He smiles at me, the picture of well-meaning honesty. "Glad to hear it, Kitty. They were hesitant, but I explained that even if you did something, I could easily have you apprehended within minutes."

Oh, really? "Are you sure about that?"

He smirks. "Save it for the tournament." A grin. "Assuming you make it that far."

Alright, that does it. I chuckle at him and let the sourness leave my mind. And then work, work, work. It wasn't exactly easy remembering it all, but having Moleman at hand to refresh my memory and inform me about the nuances in the rules was very helpful. Where the lines went and all that. In the end, I found with some pause that the pieces of parchment that had felt so numerous before were exactly the right amount to write down each individual incident. I had to be detailed. Premeditating, assaulting, killing, dismembering, eating, and wearing their skin were all separate crimes, designated as one incident.

Moleman actually helped a lot. With my ever-dwindling focus, I doubt I'd have gotten even a single page done if he hadn't encouraged me to keep going.

Midway through page twenty-one, I put the dot on the sentence *Afterward, I butchered her body (defiling of dead body; AmS [2:12], AS [1:32], AfS [2:11], ES [3:1], [P]), consumed parts including thighs and neck (cannibalism; AfS [2:12], [P]), placed remaining parts in inventory (unsafe keeping of food items/handling of criminal evidence; AS [1:12], AfS [7:2] / AfS [2:11]), and set loose a sprint-drake (stealing of live animal; AmS [4:3], [P]) to make it seem as though she had eloped in the night (framing; AfS [5:2], ES [6:5])* and turn to Moleman. He's carefully inspecting a piece of paper I recognize as page eighteen, which I'm pretty sure details my killing of the prince. Ah, the prince of the empire, that is.

My throat feels a little dry, but I still speak. "Hey, Moleman?"

"Mm?" he hums in response, keeping his gaze on the paper, eyes narrowing a little.

I watch him reread a passage before speaking again.

"What's your plan with all this?"

"My plan?" Moleman repeats innocently.

I won't let myself be fooled. "You knew I was going to confess from the start. Like I did last time. Why?"

"Why, what?"

"Why didn't you stop me?"

Only now does he glance up at me. His eyes remain narrow, and I find on his face an expression I see all too often on goblins whenever they catch me with my hand in someone's guts. Somehow, it feels like they see me more clearly than most humans do. Nose wrinkled, he speaks openly. "Over a year ago, we both agreed that you would follow the rules. You haven't. Therefore, it is only right that you be punished by the law."

Hard words. Cold as stone. But I expected them, so they don't hurt so much. "Would you . . ." I hesitate saying it, but only for a moment. "Would you have preferred it if I had been executed on floor fifteen?"

"No." Not a single pause. No conflict. Eyes back on the paper, he writes something in the margins that I can't read. "You need to be judged *fairly*," he says. "Not by a biased judge and jury who use such medieval punishments as branding and the death penalty. That would be revenge at best, far from real justice."

Strangely enough, those words do actually put me at ease. If Moleman hadn't cared at all, or if he had decided to gloss over it, I'm not sure if I'd like him as much anymore. It wouldn't be righteous of him. *This is.* Being able to point out the wrongdoings of those you love is an invaluable trait to find in a friend, and I appreciate him for it. So I feel calm. I continue writing, knowing that Moleman is still Moleman, and I'm still me. "What do you think they'll do to me?"

For once, Moleman frowns. "I don't know," he admits. "I genuinely don't know. But I refuse to let them choose the option of barbarism."

"How virtuous," I say, and though it may sound like sarcasm, I'm fully serious.

"Thank you," Moleman says, equally honest.

We smile at each other.

After an hour or so, the full list is complete, and Moleman's eyes look just a twinge deceased. But when I ask him whether he is okay, he tells me he is fine, so I'm sure that's the case. Also, I was expecting a pretty instant sentencing and verdict and punishment, but not so.

"It will take us some time to review the list. We'll resume the trial tomorrow," Logghammer says, and everyone accepts it. Not a hint in anyone's mind that I will try to escape. Not that I will, of course, but what if I really am as crazy as people think I am?

Nonetheless, just like that, the first day of my third-ever trial ended.

As we exited the courthouse, Moleman turned to me and asked, "Want to go grab some lunch?"

There's no refusing that one.

One-Man Skirmish

Lunch was good. Need I say more? We stumbled around for almost a full hour, moving around the entire circumference of the market district. We saw pubs, grand restaurants, small shops for armor and weapons and even magical items, alongside the whole of the marketplace itself. It was in all honesty pretty cool. There were so many players selling so many things, others advertising their party and trying to gather more members to tackle Purgatory.

I was fine with any kind of food, but Moleman disagreed. He clearly wanted to bring me someplace nice, with good, standard cuisine. A task we soon found to be a fair bit more difficult than otherwise expected.

In the end, we started to run out of time, so even though Moleman was still hesitant, we settled for a bit of street food. Moleman said it tasted like dog food and I agreed. It was delicious.

But now, with the food and trial done and over with, there was only one thing left to do. The colosseum stood before us, overflowing with wild roaring and cheering. It was a little daunting, but I felt excited nonetheless. We entered, and Moleman brought me to the door leading into the challengers' preparing room. He couldn't accompany me inside since he wasn't taking part in the skirmish, so I bid him au revoir and received his promise that he'd be watching me from the bleachers. Worrying, or kind? Both.

I enter. There have to be at least two hundred people in here, all gathered in small crowds around tables and on uncomfortable-looking sofas. But that's just the common area. Closer to the walls are several different shrines to various gods, whetstones and water and oil, cauldrons and mortars and accompanying ladles and such, alongside various other things I'm sure are to be used to prepare for the battle. Not a lot of people are using these various preparatory items, but the ones that do seem almost masterful at it. Armor is polished to a sheen, weapons are given intense care, sticks of incense and other small such offerings are left at the various shrines, and potions are brewed.

There's also a wall of dummies and punching bags and such things, all of which have clearly been put to use. Poor things.

Of all the people in the room, I have the longest hair. It goes down to just above my shoulders, whereas the standard hair length in this room is very short, only barely longer than a buzz cut for most, with the longest having a pretty standard haircut. They can't have been in the tutorial for more than a few months.

The difference between us is clear, and the second I step inside, they notice it. A few groups closest to the door turn and look at me like I just stepped into the women's bathroom, whereas a few others look at me like I'm not even human.

"Excuse me, sir—" a voice I recognize says, her words cut short once our eyes meet. I recognize her as Patty, but the patch on her chest introduces her as *Cathy*. But she looks exactly the same. It's just that her hair is blond instead of brown, and the smile she gives me is wryly uncomfortable. And now she's looking away. In a single breath, she mumble-raps, "OhsorrysirIddn'tknowitwasyo upardonme," and then she hastily steps away, flat-cap heels clacking frantically as she goes.

Yeah, that's right! Better not mess with me, lady! Still, that's kind of weird. Identical twins? No, this is something else. I just can't really figure out what.

"Wow," someone says, whistling. I turn to see a young face, even younger than me. He smiles excitedly. "Even though Mole told me this might be the case, I can't believe the Goddess of Compassion actually *hates* someone." He holds out a hand toward me. "ReefCounter, or Reef for short. Hard Difficulty, and the party leader of Wu-Li."

Ah. This is the guy, then?

Flanking him are four other party members. From what I can tell, they've got two magicians, a spearman, an archer, and a heavily armored tank. Good balance, and they seem to be well-coordinated. I wonder how Moleman knows them? Even more, I wonder how they know Moleman.

Reef, the spearman and leader, waggles his hand a little, but after a few more seconds he understands that I have no intention of taking it, so he pulls it back.

"Well, erm, I guess there's no need for introductions on your end, Kitty. Mole told us that you might be reluctant to outright join the party, so if you want, you can just consider us your backup. Fight as much as you want, and then once the skirmish ends, we'll be standing next to you and move together to the semifinals. So it's more like we're forming an alliance instead of you joining our party. Does that sound alright to you, Kitty?"

Yup, sounds perfect. I'll be sure to keep that in mind.

With the conversation finished, I spin on my heel and start walking away, toward . . . anywhere, really.

"H—hey, wait!"

I peek over my shoulder.

"Before the skirmish starts, you have to have a shard installed at the reception desk, otherwise you can't join!"

Ah. Okay, thanks. I do a thumbs-up for him and head toward the reception desk. There's a line, but that's fine. I can wait at least semi-patiently. The looks people give me are somewhat disconcerting, though. After almost six months on floor fifteen, it feels weird to no longer be the tallest person in the room. If my posture hadn't resembled that of a shrimp, I might not have been the shortest, but as it is, all gazes turned my way are looking down at me. I don't really like it. Makes me antsy.

I keep myself from bodily reacting by recalling that in a few minutes, I'll get to tear all of these snoopers apart with my bare hands. It's a good thought, and it makes me smile—and drool a little. Ah, conditioning works way too fast . . .

Before I know it, I'm at the front of the line, and Cathy still won't look me in the eye. "You want, um, a shard, I take it?"

I nod at her.

"Of course. Not a problem. Please, remove your . . ." Her gaze briefly crosses my chest to realize that, yeah, I'm not wearing anything. She clears her throat into her fist. "Er-herm, please grip the handles."

Handles? Oh, these. I hadn't noticed them before, but there are a pair of handles stuck to the receptionist desk. Although I'm wary of divine tricks, I take hold of them and watch as Cathy conjures a BLACK and RED shard from thin air. It looks like obsidian dipped in blood, and as she holds it up, I feel something within me resonate. It feels . . . oddly familiar.

My thoughts are interrupted as she leans forward and pushes the shard inside my chest. It slips through skin and bone and flesh easily, all the way into my heart, which experiences a sensation closest compared to cardiac arrest.

—*Guhh . . . !*

<SHARD OF DIVINITY HAS MERGED WITH YOUR INCOMPLETE SOUL TO FORM A TEMPORARY SOUL.>

Ahh, so that's what it was, eh . . . ? It hurts like hell, but knowing that it's nothing I haven't experienced before makes it manageable. I clench my teeth hard enough to feel a few creak dangerously, and after a few seconds, the throbbing pain in my chest fades into nothing but a mild heartache.

While I'm clutching at my chest like a stock image of a heart attack, Cathy apathetically tells me to get out of line, and I do just that.

Outside a large door, I hear the rupturing cheers of the crowd going wild. A message appears before my eyes.

<The floor 17 All-Skirmish has ended.>
<The floor 18 All-Skirmish will begin in 4:59>

Five minutes left. Five minutes to spend somehow, hopefully without having to talk to anyone and therefore start the skirmish early. To avoid other people, I stalk over to a corner and sit down, hugging my knees to my chest. It's kind of funny to watch everyone in the room suddenly confused, but my fun is ended by Cathy's icy-cold glare. Either way, I remain in the fetal position, waiting for the time to pass.

And, eventually . . .

<The floor 18 All-Skirmish will begin in 0:00>
<The floor 18 All-Skirmish will begin shortly. Please make your way toward the arena.>

Everyone got the same message, and as I had hoped, they all begin moving toward the same place. I follow, hidden between plates of armor and quivers and sheaths.

We step out into the glaring sunlight, and I have to briefly shield my eyes to make out the arena we're entering. The scene itself is a large, round platform, surrounded by a moat containing disturbingly delicious-looking water. I'd expect there to be like sharks or whatever in the moat to eat the dumb losers who fall out-of-bounds, but no. The water looks supernaturally clear, and as we're walking above it across a small wooden bridge, I hear someone mention in awed, hushed tones, "Th—that's first-class divine water . . . !"

Since I don't know what that is, I keep walking out into the middle of the arena. While the slowpokes catch up to the rest of us, I turn my gaze toward the bleachers. They're hardly full, but there are still quite a few members in the audience. I don't need my eyes to find Moleman, though. His scent is unmistakable, and he's . . . right there! Sitting next to a group of people, watching curiously. I wave at him. He waves back at me. Wonderful. Motivation: gained.

As the final few challengers cross the bridge, it's drawn up, leaving us stranded on the arena. Just as I'm beginning to wonder when I'll get to shed some blood, a voice speaks. An upsettingly familiar one, too.

"And with that, my beloved audience, the fighters of floor eighteen have arrived! For those not in the know, I, Hell Administrator God of Pain, will be your commentator!" My head turns with a creak toward the sky, where the sound is coming from. Up there, sitting on a cloud of stars, is none other than Pain. He gives a sly grin that I know is for me, and me alone. **"Is everyone down there ready?"**

The collected fighters turn their heads to look at each other, clenching weapons in their hands and preparing spells at the tips of their fingers. We're packed too tightly on too small a stage to make proper space between everyone, but people still try, trying their damnedest to not turn their backs on anyone but their party members.

"**Glad to hear it!**" the God of Pain booms. "**In that case . . . Ready, set . . . "Go!"**

Swords slash, spears stab, arrows fly, magics magic, and I take it all. One spear goes into my stomach, an arrow stabs through my shoulder, a sword slashes my forearm, and a bit of magic bounces off me harmlessly. To the people around me, it must have seemed like I willingly took it, which I did. However, I made sure to move just enough to ensure that no weapon hit any critical areas.

Like this, I will be more disturbing to look at.

My apathetic reaction to it all is enough for the person who stabbed me with a spear to freeze in place, the realization that he stabbed a human crashing down onto his conscience like a cinder block on a mouse. "A—ah . . . !"

Not giving him time to mourn himself, my flared claws shoot out to gouge a slash across his neck and upper chest. He grabs at his neck, eyes wide in surprise, trying to talk but unable to. Killing him straightaway would be a waste, though, so I pick him up, hold him above my head, and thrust my hand into his belly, tearing out a spool of glistening intestines. I toss his dying body back to the floor, ignore an arrow striking me in the back, slice off the ends of the intestine, and throw it into the air like a handful of confetti, splashing the nearby fighters with blood and intestine and various other bodily fluids.

The horrified screams erupting around me tells me that my *spook them stiff* strategy has worked. Now, I just have to get to work.

Tearing out the arrows is more trouble than it's worth, so I ignore them, even as more thump into my back. I don't think much. I don't have to. My fingers slice, my teeth bite, and people die. It's effortless. A few people see the purposeful mess I've made and let out screams like schoolchildren finding a dead squirrel, which only adds to the psychological damage of the whole thing. Yes, all things considered, this method is the best for fighting large groups of people. If people are scared, they will be more reluctant to fight the thing that scared them, and if they do, they will fight in a state of terror, making more mistakes than otherwise. In the best of cases, this can actually make people run, crushing others underfoot. Effective.

"**RunAndKick and YourNameHere are locked in a battle! Who will win: the sword, or the spear? And on the other side of the arena, my lovely friend PrissyKittyPrincess is living up to his namesake, playing with people like a cat toys with mice!**" the God of Pain comments.

I don't actually care about what He's saying, but I still pay half an ear to it while I tear the head, spine, and attached nervous system out of a woman I feel like I might have seen before. Hm. Looking at the bit of exposed, RED flesh, I decide that if I'm going to do the *spook them stiff* strategy, I might as well commit fully. I take a bite of the flesh, tearing out her still-twitching cheek and chewing it fully. Hm. Compared to the flesh of goblins, it's . . . more. More meat, more fat, more skin. I like eating the skin together with the rest of the meat, since the salty sweat is basically the only seasoning I can get.

Yeah, not too bad! It isn't gobling meat or anything, but I wouldn't say no to it if the chance arose.

I make eye contact with someone. Oh, hey, that's Reef, isn't it? I wave to him, but he doesn't wave back. I take another bite of the head in my hand. He goes totally pale. As in ashen. He's got less color than a BLACK-and-WHITE silent film, but that's all dispelled in an instant as his face goes RED with rage and he flies across the arena, spear raised. "Ho—how could you—!?" I easily dodge the strike with a simple sidestep. "She—she's our *teammate*! Our *healer*! Why would you—"

Stepping around him easily, I stab my hand clear through his chest, tearing out a twitching and trembling heart.

"Well, well, well! Looks like the Wu-Li party is about to be defeated from the inside out. Who would have thought that their own teammate would do a full wipe?"

Reef staggers, one hand at his chest, the other waving his spear like it's a magic wand. "I . . . I can still fight . . . ! Damn it, just because Mole told me to, I accepted, but I didn't . . ." He falls to his knees. I take a bite out of his heart like it's an apple. His face wrinkles up in despair. "He . . . tricked me . . . !"

I pause midbite. Okay, now he went too far. Stepping forward, I kick him in the chest, forcing him fully on his back, and I stand on top of his chest, foot grinding into the hole that used to hold his heart, feeling the flesh twitch beneath my sole. "Now, listen here," I say. Even though battle is raging all around us, no one will approach us, and in the silence between us, I know he can hear my voice, as soft as it is. "Moleman didn't trick you. What would he even gain from that?" Bending my knees, I crouch down atop him, my eyes locking onto his. They're dim. Dying. He can barely even look at me, so I grab his face and angle it toward me. "I didn't fool you, either. I'm keeping my promise. This battle will be won by your team." The final flickers of life begin to fade from his eyes. "*Just not by you.*"

And like that, he dies. But the instant he does, or maybe the millisecond before he truly dies, he disappears, turning to ash. I'm holding ash in my hands. What the—

"Remember, folks, those killed won't actually die! With the help of the divine shard, they will be able to survive death and return, unscathed in all but mind!"

Aww, that's a shame. But it does also raise a few questions. To answer these, I continue my little massacre. People begin fleeing me, some even jumping out of bounds into the pool of super-powered healing potion to alleviate the pain, even at the cost of losing. Weird. But I still get my answers.

Only the part connected to the heart turns to ash; the rest stays fleshy and yummy. The heart itself can be removed, but once the brain dies, the heart turns to ash. Not yummy.

The upsetting thing about the whole ash thing is that by the end of the skirmish, I was almost completely covered in it, ash sticking to blood like feathers to tar. It felt horrible, but it did scare people enough to surrender rather than die. Of course, people who surrendered were just extra easy to kill, so . . . yeah.

In the end, I stand alone, pulling my sole remaining hand from the chest of the final challenger, in an arena covered with dissected and half-eaten body parts and puddles of blood filled with ash. *Spook them stiff:* very effective.

"And it seems we have a winner! Everyone give a hand for PrissyKittyPrincess of Team Wu-Li!" Silence. But only for a few seconds. Then the booing begins. In every single corner of the colosseum comes the sound of booing, every single person in attendance finding my display worthy of jeer. No, not *every* single person. Up there in the bleachers, there's one person who doesn't boo. He isn't cheering either, but at the very least, he isn't booing.

Moleman sits alone, watching me.

In the wall of booing, I meet his eyes, and he meets mine. I almost raise my hand to wave at him when he shakes his head. My hand stalls halfway up. Ah. I . . . see. It falls to my side again, throwing a few drops of blood to the floor.

"Congratulations to the winner! Now, if all remaining contestants . . . Oh, sorry, there's only one! Kitty, will you please leave the stage to make space for the next skirmish?"

Numbly, I head toward the drawbridge. As I walk, I pull arrows out of my back and swords out of my abdomen and spears out of my chest, tossing the lot into the ever-blue waters below. On the other side of the bridge stands Cathy, who looks neither angry nor disappointed. I suppose you can't exactly be disappointed if you never expected anything.

I'm just about to stalk past her when she steps in front of me, plunges her hand into my chest, and plucks the shard of divinity straight out of my heart, which actually hurts more than it did going in. I don't show it. I clutch my hands, give her a glare, and continue. I leave through a hallway and into the vomitorium receptionist area. People turn to look at me, and then they look away. They aren't in the bleachers anymore, so they can't boo me from the safety of their seats. I'm right in front of them, and even if their levels are higher than mine, that doesn't matter to me.

Scowling, I move past them, and the crowd opens up before me.

I leave the vomitorium. I can tell that the breeze is soft and nice, but I can't actually feel it. Silently, I walk across the spring square, bringing myself back to the bench I shared with Moleman earlier. Sitting on it alone feels weird. It's empty. I should talk, but I don't want to talk to the air. That's even worse. I don't want that.

My back hunches, my neck slouches, and I let my eyes fall to look at my dirty feet.

A handkerchief appears in my vision. I look up to find Moleman, nudging it toward me. I take it. He sits down next to me. I wipe my hands with the plain handkerchief, staining it with BLACK and RED.

We sit in silence. I look at the blooming trees, petals of pink and yellow and blue dancing down to gather in little cuddle-puddles on the ground, leaned up against the stones and buildings like multicolored snow. "Did you . . ." I change my mind. "I didn't—" No, that isn't right either. My gaze falls to the handkerchief, snuggled closely between my fingers. At one point, my claws accidentally tore a little hole. I run my fingers over the hole, unwittingly making it a little bigger, snapping a few more seams. Closing my eyes, I take a deep breath and turn to Moleman. "I'm sorry."

Moleman reaches over and plucks the handkerchief from my hands, cleaning it with a single brief spell. Then he opens a little satchel on his belt and pulls out thread and a needle. I watch closely as he bites off a length of thread, threads it through the needle's eye, pulls it double, makes a double knot, and begins sewing the hole shut. It only took a few minutes, but it felt like seconds. It wasn't effortless or fast and it didn't turn out pretty. He pricked himself on the needle, got the thread all wound up, and made several tiny mistakes. But in the end, the handkerchief was fixed. It was obvious it had once been hurt, and that scar would never go away. But it didn't need to.

He holds out the patched-up handkerchief to me. "I think you'd better keep it," he says mildly. Not answering, I accept it, putting it safe and secure in my inventory. Standing up, he holds out his hand to me. I take it, and he pulls me up as well. He looks me up and down. "Say, what kind of house did you get? Does it have a shower?"

House?

Correctly assuming my ignorance, he gives a brief explanation. "Everyone spawned inside their house, where they would be able to stay and rest over the coming days. Did you . . . not get one?"

Does he mean . . . ? "I got, um . . . a hole."

"A hole?"

"A hole in the ground."

"Ah! I see. A hole in the ground." He nods as if that's normal. "I'll assume you don't own a shower, then?"

"I don't," I answer with a mix of confusion and bitterness. I can't believe I don't own a shower.

He scratches his neck. "In that case, would you care to use mine?" After a second or so he adds, "The one in my house."

My jaw falls open. "Y—yes," I say. "Of course I do."

We go.

The shower wasn't exactly a shower, but it *was* warm water that fell onto me, so I had no reason to complain. I took my first proper shower in . . . two years, technically speaking? Then again, I wasn't much of a shower-goer even before that, so it could have been longer.

It was nice. I had soap to use that smelled herbal and a little weird. I even got to dry off with a towel, and when I exited, Moleman had left me a change of clothes. Nothing extravagant, just a pair of dark pants and a light cotton shirt, but it felt like an Armani suit with gold buttons. Moleman didn't mind me keeping them, but I swore on my life that I would return them before the next battle tomorrow. Otherwise, I'd no doubt ruin them beyond repair.

He made dinner for us both to eat. I had almost expected us to go out to find a restaurant, but with our shared experience of trying to find lunch fresh in our minds, we agreed to eat something simpler.

Meatballs. Meatballs with potatoes and brown sauce. No lingonberry sauce, but we survived. I didn't entirely catch on to what meat was used, but I was reasonably certain it was neither beef nor pork. Still good, though that might just have been thanks to Moleman's methods.

I wasn't sure if this counted as a fulfillment of our promise to get dinner, but according to Moleman, that only counted when his mother made the food. Not him. Well, if he said so.

Nevertheless, after a good dinner, we decided to head out on the town to celebrate my win with a drink or two.

There was no shortage of pubs to choose from in the city, some smaller, some larger, some fancy, others less so. Drinks were bought with points. Depending on the place, so were the reservations. At first, Moleman had wanted to go to a nicer place, but I had succeeded in convincing him to instead enter a smaller, more typical pub.

Funnily enough, when we went inside, I had sort of expected that Wild West trope to happen, with the music abruptly stopping and for everyone to turn to me, silent and staring. But no. People didn't even glance my way, too occupied with drinks and food and company to stare at . . . a guy who looks completely normal. I've got a shirt, I've got pants, and my hair isn't as greasy as a knot of rats. I refused socks and shoes, but other than that, for once, I actually look . . . *normal.*

The only people who pay attention to our arrival is a small group I don't recognize who notice Moleman—*not me*—and wave at him. Moleman waves back at them, and then we go over to the counter.

We sit down, and I notice with a smidge of interest that the bartender isn't one of several dozen copies of the Goddess of Compassion but is, in fact, a dude. Just a man. A man with an intense, powerful look in his eye that leaves me almost wanting to kowtow. Instead, I sit down at the counter, Moleman taking the seat next to me. "Two beers," Moleman says. "Anything light you've got on tap."

The bartender nods and pours us a glass each. I take a sip and remember only once the brew touches the back of my throat that I don't like the taste of beer.

Moleman chuckles at the face I make. "It's alright, nobody actually likes the taste. We all just pretend we do." He lifts up his glass toward me. "Anyway, congratulations on winning the all-skirmish!"

I clink my glass against his. "Thanks," I say. In accordance with the laws that govern toasting, I take a swig, forcing it down even though it tastes like monkey butt. I kind of want to slam the beer mug onto the counter like they do in the pictures, but I don't want to break it, so I set it down normally. "So," I say to Moleman, "when's your skirmish?"

He swallows down a mouthful of beer, brows furrowing as he turns to me. "Didn't I tell you? My party is alone on floor sixty-six, so we'll pass straight from the preliminaries into the semifinals."

"You're alone? Does that mean all the other cool parties are above you?"

He shakes his head. "No, we're actually the only party to have reached this far. It won't be long until we're dethroned, though, since I'll be staying in Purgatory for a while on foreign relations business. At least until Bach arrives to take over, that is."

Oh. Oh? Wait.

—*Oh?!*

"Y—you're the best player in the entire damn *tutorial?!*"

He laughs at me. "Well, *best* might be a bit of an overstatement. We simply happen to be the group that's cleared the most quests. If anything, we're the *luckiest*," he says modestly. Grrr, Moleman and his dumb humbleness . . . ! I'd be more upset if he hadn't been completely genuine. "No," he continues absently, "if we're only talking *best*, I'd put my money on you over me any day."

I do a comedy spit take of my beer, successfully covering the front of the bartender's apron. "Oh, shoot, sorry—"

Before I can register it properly, the stain is gone, and the bartender turns a heavy eye to Moleman. "I wouldn't be so certain." His voice is as weighty as his gaze.

"And why's that, Will?" Moleman asks.

The bartender's eyes narrow. Piercing. "I don't need to explain what you already know."

The impromptu staring match that follows only lasts a few seconds, but it feels like minutes. I can't tell who won, but afterward, Moleman turns to me and shrugs. I, confused, shrug back on instinct.

And then someone stumbles up next to me, drunkenly slamming his hand onto the counter for support while a friend of his, less obviously drunk but equally noxious to the nose, holds on to his shoulders to keep him from toppling over. The clearly drunker of the two eyes me up and down. "What the hell . . ." he mumbles groggily, and pulls a rolled-up piece of parchment from inside his coat. It's stained with beer and several other kinds of alcohol, the stickiness granting it a sound like unrolling tape when he opens it up. He looks at me, back at the parchment, and then down at my chest. He reaches out and I let him fumble my shirt open, with him tearing it open just enough to see the brand on my chest.

"*You motherfuck—*" he roars, and a clenched fist flies my way, knuckles aimed for my eye. I let him connect, but move my face enough to make it hit my cheek instead of my eye. The punch is powerful and sends me crashing to the floor, head banging against the wood like a gavel and the stool I was sitting on clattering down right next to me, only barely missing my head. The same can't be said for the drunk himself, who either leaps or stumbles atop me, one hand powerfully gripping my collar to hold my head up and the other, clenched, going at my face, getting in one, two, three solid hits before his friend grabs him, trying futilely to pull him off.

"Tyre, come on, stop, it's not going to bring him back—"

"Shaddap!" the drunk slurs, his upper body swaying back and forth even while sitting. "This—this *asshole* got Dave killed! This fucking douche—all because he had to go and—and burn some fucking city, kill some fucking kids, *eat babies*—all because of him . . . !" Spittle and stuff that smells like bile flies out of his wide open maw. "This—this fucking guy—!"

Angry roars give way to equally uncontrolled sobbing, and all of a sudden my face is covered in not just spit but also tears. A fist is thrown at me but the impact is soft and he breaks down into a mess of heaving sobs and hiccuping gasps atop me. "It's his fault, all his fault . . . !"

I look at him, and I look up at his friend, now also sobbing, one hand on his friend's back, and then I look up at Moleman. He's half slid off the chair, fingers almost formed into a point, halfway to acting, but stopped before it got there. He meets my eyes. There's a brief indiscernible emotion in there, soon replaced by confusion and worry, the latter not for me.

The grip on my collar is loosened. Still, I remain where I lie. Only once the friend picks up the drunk atop me—pulling him high enough to drape him onto the counter—do I stand up as well, dusting off the front and back of my borrowed clothes. Leaning down, I pick up the stool and retake my seat at the counter. I grab my beer and take a sip. Eugh, still gross.

The drunk has now started pulling himself together, just a little. "Oh, God, Dave, I can't—we can't . . ." Sorrows are soon replaced by rage and he turns a flaming eye my way. "Bastard . . . bastard . . . ! I hope they kill you, I hope the goblins get you, and kill you like they did Dave . . . !"

I don't respond. He makes a guttural, growling sound and then something wet hits my face. I touch my finger to it, the liquid viscous enough to form strings of slime. *He spat in my face.*

"Come on, Tyre, let's go, come on," the friend urges, doing so with great difficulty, all the while the drunk swears loudly at me. But in the end, they do leave me alone. Suddenly, the bar feels much quieter, much colder. I pull my handkerchief from my inventory and wipe off the spit. Next to me, Moleman slides back onto his seat.

I take another sip of my beer. I can feel his gaze on me.

"Why didn't you do anything?" Moleman says with a frown.

Another sip, and a little look his way. Foul taste, but it fills the time. "It wouldn't look good for my trial if I killed someone while it was still proceeding."

Words measured, voice low, Moleman says, "One more or less wouldn't make any difference."

"It would make a difference to you," I say. "In how you see me."

"Yeah," he agrees quietly. "It would. I just . . ." He shakes his head, and I can tell he doesn't know what to say either. "A guy *attacked you.* A year ago—no, even two years ago, you would've . . ." I know, and he knows. "But now, you don't even seem to care. At all. You've . . . *changed.*"

"For better or worse?"

He gives a hesitant smile: a sad one. "I don't know yet." Turning away from me, he takes a sip of his beer. "But I do know," he says mellowly, "that you're still my friend."

I smile, lift my glass, and clink it against his.

Right now, that's all I need.

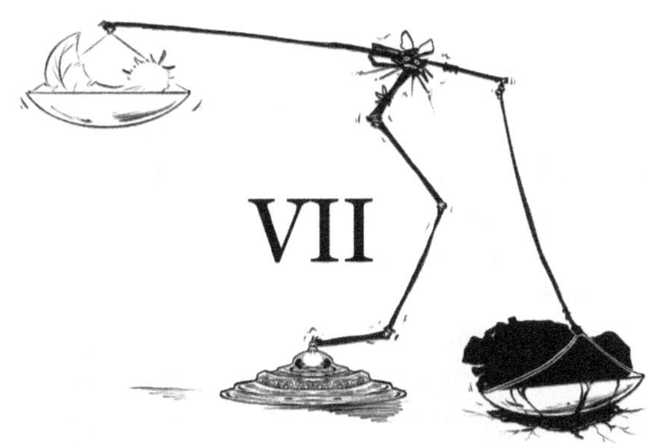

VII

On Trial (Cont.)

When we arrive for the trial the next day, there's a crowd outside.

Where did they come from? Why are they here? I don't know. What I *do* know is that a lot of people are shouting very loudly that I ought to be hanged. Moleman mutters something under his breath about word of mouth moving quickly in the tutorial, which does appear to be the case.

When they spot me, the shouting intensifies. Signs and boards are raised angrily and—hey, wait a moment. Isn't that my picture?

I snatch a sign out of someone's hand and guards quickly swarm me, though not to do a police brutality for my theft but rather to make distance between me and the people. *Protective.* This distance gives me more than enough time to take a good, long look at the sign. I tear off the picture and . . . Yeah, that's me. *Wanted by the Acheron Kingdom, Dead or Alive: Tallthing.* There's a seal in the bottom right of a phoenix rising from the ashes of a city, but I don't really care about that. I recognize this picture.

This is the picture Simel painted of me. It's . . .

It's *really* good! I mean, sure, I look kind of like a hairless rat and my expression is weirdly intense, but it is very much in my likeness. He's so talented! It also shows the brand on my chest, even though it wasn't on me at the time of painting. Ah, I'm so proud of him.

I stick it in my inventory for later use. Humming happily, we enter the courthouse, ignoring the shouts from the crowd outside.

How did we get here, you ask? Well, um . . . Moleman wouldn't let me sleep in my hole seventy-five kilometers from the city, so on his recommendation, I spent the . . . I slept . . . you know. At his place. On the couch. The most comfortable couch I've ever slept on. Not that I slept. I just pretended I did so

Moleman wouldn't worry. Then we had breakfast in the morning and headed straight here.

The crowd is effectively shut out by closing the front door behind us. Since only those taking part in the proceedings are allowed inside the courthouse, the guards quickly dislodge from us, leaving us to our business. We walk up the stairs, and I feel very calm. Maybe I should feel worried, considering everything. There is a fairly good chance that whatever happens in the trial today determines whether I'll live to see tomorrow, but I'm still relaxed. Maybe I'm just in denial about the whole thing.

If I die, Moleman will be sad, and maybe Rice since we won't be able to have our fight. But overall, a lot more people will be happy. They'll be able to use my execution as a bargaining chip with the goblins, to be able to say, *Hey, look, this guy is not one of ours, so let's be friends, okay?* and then they can work together with the goblins. Easy peasy. They'll make an alliance, I'll be dead, and a lot more people will be able to survive going forward since they won't pay for my crimes, directly or indirectly.

Somewhere, sometime, I read that people who have been falsely convicted can't sleep well in prison. They toss and turn and shout about their innocence, trying to convince anyone who'll listen that they didn't do it. But guilty people sleep like babies.

I'm glad I never tried to fool Moleman about any of this. I couldn't bear trying to keep something like this a secret from him.

Before we enter the courtroom, Moleman pats me on the back and gives me a look, silently asking if I'm okay. I nod back at him. We enter.

The air inside is cold even though it should be choked with breathing. Same people as yesterday, in the same places, wearing almost the exact same things. All of them look substantially more exhausted than they did yesterday. I'm still wearing the clothes Moleman gave me. Bach isn't the only one surprised by my being dressed, but nobody mentions it.

Logghammer looks me up and down before turning to the secretary, giving her a curt nod, then turning back to look at us. "Welcome back, everyone." A few nods pass between people, a formal but silent greeting. People nod at Moleman, but not at me. Unsurprising. My eyes fall to the stack of papers pinched between Logghammer's fingers, which I recognize by the tears and sweat stains as being those that Moleman and I labored over yesterday.

Logghammer soon begins speaking gravely. "I and my fellow jurors have spent much of the evening and some of the night going through the full written confession of PrissyKittyPrincess, making note of which incidents are criminal and which are not." A look of deep, spiritual fatigue briefly passes his face before being masked by professional apathy. "Due to the extensiveness of the crimes listed, a complete record may be found in the appendix, figure two. However, most notably, the murder of the king of Acheron will not be counted due to it being part of the floor clear requirement. Antithetically, the murder of the Sun Emperor, although it did count toward clearing the stage, will not be counted as *necessary* and thus remain first-degree homicide.

"Similarly to the king of Acheron, the killing of shades will not be considered criminal in nature. However, I feel it pertinent to note that killing *all* shades on floor seven was needless and is—in lack of adequate character witnesses—a good example of the kind of person the defendant is." He glances my way, and I can tell somehow that the way he looks at me has shifted somewhat. A twinge of fear. "The judge and jury are in agreement that the defendant is guilty on all charges."

The single certainty of the day.

"However . . ." The room holds its collective breath. "The question, then, comes to what a proper penalty would be."

Moleman stands up, his chair giving a jarring squeak. "John, if I may—?"

Logghammer seems briefly stunned by the turn, the same reaction as mine, but a warm nod tells Moleman to continue.

"I believe," Moleman says, "that the best possible penalty would be house arrest."

"House arrest, you say?" Logghammer asks. Curious, without a twinge of sarcasm. "Please elaborate."

It takes a second or two for Moleman to gather his thoughts before he speaks, gravely enunciating, "Prison is not possible unless he were to beat the tutorial or someone else in the Europe Server were to reach the eighteenth floor of the Hell Difficulty, which is nigh impossible. Physical punishments would be medieval and ineffective. Banning Kitty from participating in activities, the forums, and likewise is trivial compared to the crime committed. He owns nothing to be taken as a fine." Moleman takes a deep breath. "No other penalty would be anywhere near as effective as house arrest."

"Would you care to explain what you mean by *house arrest?*"

"House arrest, in the context of the tutorial, would involve the punished offender remaining in the floor lobby for a specified number of attempts until he is allowed to leave by moving on to the next floor. This way, the offender will be incapable of causing harm to others or other such future damages."

"That is, unless he chooses to leave of his own accord," the prosecutor Venedict says, butting in. His eyes fall on me sharply. "Or until the time runs out, and he leaves to terrorize the population of Purgatory once more."

Moleman's jaw snaps shut and he turns to Logghammer, who simply shrugs. "Since this is an open debate, there's no need to speak in turn."

Grinding his teeth, Moleman continues his argument. "It is the most humane option."

"Were you at the eighteenth floor all-skirmish yesterday?" Venedict asks. "No, actually, don't answer that. I know you were there. I saw you." His sharp eyes home in on me. "That's why I know you saw the offender maim, kill, dismember, and *eat* his own teammates—not to speak of the other unlucky contestants." What a total non sequitur. Where is he even going with this? And, better yet, why isn't Moleman speaking out against him? Ignoring my pleas, Venedict carefully folds his fingers across the table. "Since you won't say it, I'll ask you straight out: why should we show any humanity toward someone who clearly lacks it?"

"Because," Moleman quickly answers, "he's *still human*. Although he may not, at times, act like it, should we as humans choose to no longer treat him as a human, it would make *us* inhuman in turn."

Venedict rolls his eyes. "Instead of arguing about whether we should put the monster in a self-inflicted *house arrest* in the hopes that it won't leave at the literal press of a button out of the goodness of its shriveled husk of a heart, why don't we just have the actual argument we're all really thinking about?" He leans in, his eyes taking on a half-desperate, half-determined luster. "*Should we have it put down like the animal it is or not?*"

Moleman's mouth opens but he's interrupted by Logghammer, who speaks up instead, saying, "Venedict, will you please refer to the offender by his name and proper pronoun?"

"You clearly weren't at the floor eighteen skirmish, I see," Venedict mutters. "But sure. I'll rephrase my question: *Death penalty, or no penalty?* How's that?"

"It's reproachable," Moleman chides.

"It's the truth," Venedict rebuts. "Physical punishment, house arrest, stoning, imprisonment, verbal warning, fining . . . *nothing* save for the death penalty will actually do anything in this case."

"It's inhuman!"

"No less than letting that *thing* go free!"

"Please refrain from shouting!" Logghammer shouts. For reference, it's been less than half an hour and the court has already deteriorated into . . . *this*. I'm more impressed than surprised. I mean, I had sort of expected this to happen at some point, but hearing Moleman argue this fiercely in such brief sentences really does make me realize he has a lot of missed potential as a rap artist. If only he'd cuss, I'm sure he could get a platinum album in no time.

While he and Venedict are still going at it, the jury starts getting involved, discussing the whole thing with each other in louder and quicker tones. Many looks are thrown my way, some disgusted, some appalled, some disturbed, some fearful, all with some degree of hate.

"*Silence!*"

There's a *bang* and I turn to see a gavel materialized in Logghammer's hand.

His gaze moves over the collected group, eyes burning. "It is clear to me that this debate—no, *argument*—cannot continue in a civilized manner. As much as I despise adjournments, this discussion will have to be postponed to let all gathered members formulate their own thoughts in a proper fashion." Looks are shared, and in the end, people can only nod regretfully. "Good. Spend the day, evening, and night contemplating what you all believe the proper course of action to be. That includes *you*." He points at me and I twitch a little, expecting magic but getting nothing but a scalding look. "As for the rest of you . . ." His gaze slowly glides from one person to another. "You may assume that the death penalty is on the table; *however*, it is not a verdict to be made lightly. Once we execute one murderer, that option will never disappear. Try to find other options if possible.

"That is all for today. Court adjourned."

It feels strange. Life continues. Somehow, I didn't expect to survive until lunch. Or, at least, that if I were to receive lunch, it would be in the form of my final supper. Instead, I'm looking into a bowl of clear broth, a piece of bread in my hand, and my own face staring up at me. I don't recognize it too well. The surface of the broth has left it deformed in both shape and color, so the eyes that stare up at me aren't liver-failure yellow, but instead RED.

Sinking my spoon into the bowl, I take a sip. It's good. Going by Moleman's words, it was pretty cheap, too.

Looking up and across the table, I find him staring down at some kind of porridge, with a square of butter in the middle. He hasn't touched it yet. I wonder if there's something wrong with it. But I can't smell any mold or worms in it, so it should be okay. It's already been a couple minutes since we got our food, so he might still be waiting for it to cool off a little. I watch him for a few more minutes, but he still isn't touching it. I'm actually starting to get worried, so after waiting for another minute or so, I ask, "Hey, Moleman, are you—"

"I'm fine." He doesn't look up from the now-cold porridge. As a matter of fact, to intensify his porridge-watching abilities, he puts his head in his hands, eyes shadowed so I can't see his face anymore. But I *can* hear him mumble, "I'm not the one who might get *executed* tomorrow . . ."

"No," I admit, idly stirring my lukewarm broth. "But . . . I'm also not the one bearing the weight of a friend's life on my shoulders."

He peeks up at me through a crack between his fingers. I've never seen him look so exhausted. "And that's supposed to be worse?"

"It is," I say. "If it were me, and I had to try to argue *you* out of getting killed . . . I'd be so nervous, I wouldn't even be able to eat!" That got a chuckle out of him, at least, though it was a slightly bitter one. "But when you're nervous like that," I continue, "what you need the most isn't to grind your teeth and pace in circles. It's a bit of food."

I slide my bowl over to his side. It's still a little warm. Better than his cold, dry-looking porridge.

His gaze falls down into it for a second, looking up at himself, seeing himself—maybe seeing how tired he is. He almost looks as though he's about to refuse, but then he smiles mellowly, shakes his head, and lifts his eyes to me. "Thanks."

We finish lunch.

The time for the semifinals of the group tournament is at hand. "And you remember what I told you?" Moleman warns.

"Yeah, yeah," I say dismissively, but the look in his eye gives me pause. "No killing my teammates."

"And?"

"And . . ." I huff at the air. "*No* eating people."

He smiles wryly. "Yeah, something like that." He looks me up and down. Reaching out, he fixes the collar of my shirt. I'm just about to start objecting about this whole thing when he preemptively shuts me up, saying, "The jury and judge will no doubt be in the audience today. We were lucky they were too busy to attend the preliminaries, but now you'll have to make a good impression. Look like a person, act like a person. Follow the rules we agreed on. And maybe, just maybe, if they see your human side, they might show a little mercy on the whole having-you-killed thing."

I frown down at the clothes. They aren't uncomfortable or anything, but . . . "There isn't a chance in hell that these won't get bloodied beyond belief. You know that, right?"

"In that case, the chances are about the same as me *not* being around to clean them afterward."

Cheeky. I smile at him. He mirrors my expression and we share a fist bump as I enter the preparation room. Both opposing teams and all their members are already here, apparently. Surprisingly enough, they're already on good enough terms to stand huddled in a single big group, both parties mixed as though they were all on the same side. And . . . *wow* is the look they give me harsh. Just one of them has enough poison in their gaze to kill a fully grown elephant, and combined with the eleven others . . . Yeah, it's not exactly welcoming.

Even though all of my instincts are screaming at me to run away from this skin-crawlingly awkward atmosphere, I remain steadfast. Moleman's words echo through my brain and I try to keep in mind that he's seldom wrong. If an earnest apology goes a long way, then a long way I shall go.

I confidently stride up to the gathered party members.

Technically speaking, they didn't exactly *open up to accommodate me*, rather, I think they *collectively retreated in mild fear and disgust*, coincidentally creating enough space for me to join the gathering. Now that I'm among them, I can tell that Reef is actually here. Our eyes meet and—oh, I'm having a few flashbacks here. I mean, this is *exactly* how most goblins reacted upon meeting me a second or third time. Even the trembling jaw and wide eyes are exactly the same!

I almost want to point it out as a sort of fun ice-breaker, but I know that it wouldn't be the right moment. Instead, I give a measured bow, lower my head, and say with full honesty, "I'm sorry."

Since I'm not looking at them anymore, I can't entirely tell what their reaction is. Trying not to think about it, I resume my apology. "Yesterday, I acted like . . . I was . . . The things I did were . . ." I shake my head. Okay, okay, I *have* to get my head in the game. Moleman and I went through this! I just have to remember what we talked about . . . "I'm sorry. There are no excuses. I was caught up in the moment, and I was acting like a beast, all because I thought that it was the best way to beat the floo—erm, the *preliminaries*. But I was wrong. It wasn't the best way, and I completely ignored how it would make you guys feel. I'm really sorry." Now, I lift my head. "So . . ."

They're gone.

In front of my eyes, a single message hovers.

<The floor 17 vs. floor 18 semifinals group battle Team VielSpass vs. Team Wu-Li will begin shortly. Please make your way toward the arena.>

I blink at it. In the corner of my eye, I can see the light of the outside arena shining in through the open door.

I exit the preparatory room.

As I exit, Cathy inserts the shard in my chest again. It doesn't hurt too much. Crossing the drawbridge, I find myself in the arena. On one side is the opposing team, seven in total, bundled tightly, and on the other is Team Wu-Li, all five members standing closely together. Oh, and me, off to the side, looking at them both. An unwanted third party.

And the crowd? Yeah, uh, the arena is packed. It wasn't empty yesterday, but now it is absolutely jam-packed. And, let me tell you, it doesn't take many seconds after my entrance for the audience to start chanting, in unison:

"*SKIN—THE—CAT!*"

"*SKIN—THE—CAT!*"

"*SKIN—THE—CAT!*"

Which is, all things considered, not especially nice. Even worse, one of the fighters on the other team actually gives a thumbs-up, which only makes the audience cheer even louder, booming, exploding through the arena. Pouring over me like boiling oil.

"What an audience!" the God of Pain comments. **"It seems to Me that almost every single participant in the tutournament has decided to come and watch a certain cat get his comeuppance, including our very special**

Server Alliance Leaderships! Isn't that right?" Cheering. Clapping. Laughter, even though I'm certain not a single thing He said was actually any funny. **"Keep yourselves restrained, lovely audience! No need to try to join the fray. Remember: even the tamest of housecats still has claws and fangs!"** Why do people keep laughing at this guy? Don't they know they're only encouraging Him?

"And now, without any further ado, we shall watch the match of a lifetime—will Kitty persevere or be dragged down by the weight of his own sins? Let us see! Are all you brave fighters ready?" In response, the audience cheers, bloodthirsty. Nobody on my own team or the opposing team says or does anything. **"Great, love to hear it! In that case: ready . . . set . . . *Go!*"**

A spear is plunged into my back. I whirl around, claws shooting out to gouge the flesh out of someone's throat, only to freeze midair as my eyes meet those of Reef. I blink at him. "Huh?" Wild cheering explodes across the bleachers.

While I stare at his determined face, a sword finds its way across my stomach, neatly slicing open the skin and flesh to reveal the coiled intestines inside. Much like a prank snake let out of its innocuous can, my intestines all leap out, which is quite a gruesome sight to see. The audience squeals with glee. I don't recognize the woman who slashed me, she isn't on my team, so I plunge my claws into her neck. A bolt of some sort of lightning hits me, but it doesn't do anything, so with my hand still in her neck, I turn to the aggressor. One of the girls on my team. Ah.

A sword falls and severs my hand at the wrist. Booms of adulation. With the death of the one who sliced my stomach, her body turns to ash, leaving my bisected hand lying in a pile of soot. I turn to the swordsman, but I recognize him, so I can do nothing as he stabs his sword deep into my chest, one lung down, one to go.

"SKIN—THE—CAT!"

"SKIN—THE—CAT!"

"SKIN—THE—CAT!"

I open my mouth and blood I didn't know was in there spurts out, down my face, onto my chest. I look down. Blood stains the light shirt Moleman gave me RED. Blood from my throat. Blood from my chest. Blood from my stomach. It's sliced up. Too much. As I watch, another sword slices the shirt, another spear stabs it, another arrow plunges into it, tearing it up so much there's no salvaging it anymore. It's gone. It's dead. It's in pieces and you can't sew it together anymore.

So what's the point in even wearing it?

I stand, listlessly, watching the blood leaving my body, the only sounds I can hear being the booming roars of the audience echoing through my brain like the thunderclap following lightning. *More, more, more,* they demand. Blood isn't enough, guts isn't enough, flesh isn't enough. They want my life.

So I'll give it to them.

The torn strips of shirt fall off my body.

I move. They only realize it once one of their own falls to the floor, turned to ash before their back could touch stone. They start shouting but I can't hear it. In my head, there's nothing but endless cheering, a thousand voices all as one, shouting for me, for me to fall, for me to show them what they want to see. And I show it.

One hand is enough. No, it's *more* than enough.

Hands meet flesh, teeth meet blood, and both are turned to ash. I dance among the piles, even as the floor is littered with more of my own blood than theirs. Cheering, cheering, cheering, cheering. *Hooray! Hooray! Hooray!* Three cheers for Kitty!

See me! This is who I am! This is what you wanted! Aren't I beautiful?

Among piles of dead ash, below, with his back to the floor, lies Reef, spear desperately clutched in his hand, saying something, saying anything, but I can't hear it, and I don't need to, his sort, his type, is prey, and I am their predator, above them by divine decree, so I put my foot on his chest, same as yesterday, another enemy to be crushed, to be defeated, foot raised, claws ready, lips salty with the taste of blood, and—

"Wait!"

The cheering stops. There are no boos either. It is silence, save for one voice, one person, one gaze that sees me for what I am, below that, below it all, and I feel it.

Slowly, I turn, and I see Moleman, up in the bleachers. Looking at me *like that.*

Huh?

Something stabs my heart. Something went through my back and through my heart and through my chest and I see it. It's a spear. I touch it, pricking my finger on the tip. A little bead of blood forms on the tip of my finger. It hurts. It . . . *hurts. It hurts!*

The cheering becomes deafening again, roaring, booming, atom bombs going off, the sound barrier being broken, planets crashing and the universe being born and then dying, over and over again, explosions of sound, and it hurts it hurts it hurts *it hurts*—

My heart ends,

and I turn to ash.

I wake up. I'm in . . . a hospital of some sort.

Not dead. Alive.

But I died.

And before that . . .

Cheering explodes across my skull and I press my hands against my head, hoping to silence it, if only a little. Wait. *Hands?* Yeah, now that I look at it, I've got hands. Everything else is healed, too. Except my clothes. Actually, if I look under the thin WHITE blanket I'm covered with, exactly nothing of that sort has regenerated. I'm in the nude.

Approaching footsteps in the hall outside makes me quickly cover myself again. A shadow approaches the doorway to my lone room. *M—Moleman?*

Ah, no, it's just Cathy. Or Patty. No, wait, if I'm reading the patch correctly, this one is named *Mary.* The only difference between her and the others is that her hair is a light RED, and she's wearing a doctor's outfit.

She enters the room without speaking a word, barely sparing me a single glance. In the silence between us, I crane my neck to look down the hallway, checking for . . .

"If you're looking for SuperMoleman," Mary says, "he's currently fighting in the floor sixty-six vs. floor sixty-four group tournament match." She doesn't say it, but I can tell by her tone that she's thinking, *And even if he wasn't, why would he be here?*

I can't help but agree.

I sit up in bed, sliding my feet off the side, letting them touch the cold floor below. Standing up, I pull a leopard hide from my inventory, tying it around my waist. It feels more natural than the soft fabrics. More . . . *me.*

Mary speaks as I stand up. "Your body is fully healed, re-created from the template submitted before battle. It isn't strictly necessary, but I will inform you, as I tell the other fighters, that although your soul and body have healed, the mental effects of the battle may remain, and that there is help to be had if you feel any ill effects moving forward."

Ignoring her words, I step out of the room.

There's a person in the hallway. The swordswoman from the fight, from before. Our eyes meet and I can see the slot game of *fight-flight-freeze* roll in her head, eventually falling on *fight.* She charges at me, fist raised. I'm not in the mood. She's full of openings. The second she's in range, I'll stretch out my hand, and she'll decapitate herself on it. It'll be so simple. It won't even be funny.

Less than one meter from me, fist still raised, before I even have time to raise a finger, she suddenly freezes. Her chest falls up and down, eyes widening to show her WHITEs, and her forehead starts gleaming with sweat. She must have seen it in my eyes. Because now, I can see her life flashing before her eyes. "Ah—ah . . . !"

Turning around, she runs away in such a frantic scramble that she slips and falls to the floor trying to turn a corner, crawling the final bit out of my view on all fours.

That was . . . something.

Since the exit is the other way according to my nose, I turn away from where she went, ignoring the sound of her hyperventilating down the hall.

A few minutes later, and I'm at the colosseum again. The cheering is still there, loud and booming, resonating with the grating sounds inside my head. But it isn't bloodthirsty. It isn't like the cheering of those watching the execution of a hated criminal. It's just a sports game, and they're excited to see the outcome.

I enter. There aren't as many people, but it's still a good crowd. I remain standing, watching the fight down below ending. I was too late to see it at its peak, but I do see the results and aftermath.

There's no ash in the arena.

Five of the nine total fighters stand upright in the moat, happily cheering on the remaining four, standing side by side with no care for the fact that they're supposed to be enemies. The four still in the arena are shaking hands, laughing and smiling, all to the backdrop of the audience cheering.

"What a match!" the God of Pain comments. **"It was a close one, but it seems that Team Jormungand has decided to surrender the victory to Team Mole and the Mice! Give a big hand to the proud fighters and the final winners of the semifinals!"**

Standing ovation as the final members of the losing team wave to Moleman and his group, willingly leaving the arena and jumping into the out-of-bounds pool of healing elixir, the few small scratches and burns they've incurred easily mending themselves. Then Moleman and his remaining allies walk over to the edge of the arena, pull the losing party and losing members out of the moat, and bask in the clapping and cheering together, as one.

Next to me, I feel someone looking at me, and I turn to see a person I've never met, never learned the name of, never done anything to, looking at me *like that*. How else would they look at me? I don't know. Their hands freeze midclap, making it look like they're about to pray.

Turning around, I leave the colosseum. I walk down the stairs, and then I begin to hurry, and then sprint, and now I'm running, running, trying to get the cheering and clapping out of my head, trying to replace it with the howling of the wind, trying and failing oh so miserably. People who see me freeze up or run or try futilely to stand their ground before capitulating, throwing themselves out of my way in terror. Afraid, angry, disgusted eyes are all that I see. Darkness all around me. Hatred, hatred, hatred, eyes like Simel's, bearing down on me, righteous, justified—they know what I did and they hate me for it, and they're right.

It's dizzying and my head reels and spins in circles, orbiting itself like a pair of stars going supernova together, imploding to form darkness, sheer darkness, all-consuming darkness, one that feeds and feeds and never stops even when the universe is eaten, only stopping once its gluttony eats itself, only then will I finally receive the sweet release of—

I crash into someone—some*thing*—and fly to the ground, eyes moving erratically, teeth clacking together like a wind-up toy, claws ready, always ready, but—I look up. There's a sprint-drake in front of me, clad in a leather saddle. And above that . . .

My eyes meet those of Rice. She smiles down at me, her eyes bright. "*Howdy!*"

Haah, haah, haah, haah. My feet hurt. They're bleeding, from running barefoot on gravel and rocks, but I pull myself to my bloody feet, staggering, swaying, before finally being able to stand upright. She doesn't seem to mind it. She doesn't mind anything. Not what I'm wearing, not the way I look, not the way others are looking at me.

She leaps off her steed with an acrobat's grace, her spurred boots touching the ground with a melodic jingle. "What a match!" she says. "I could tell by the look of you that you weren't exactly any normal fighter, but—*wow!* In the preliminaries, with the way you spooked them silly, and then herded them all to their deaths? Expertly! Were you a herding dog in your past life or something? Ah, though, with how you sliced through them all, I'd probably put my bet on a bobcat instead!"

I breathe heavily. My eyes dart about her form, unwillingly looking for places I could fit my claws into, places I could bite off arteries, ways I could kill her. Openings.

She has few.

"It was a shame your teammates turned on you—very weird, considering you won them the match. But don't be sad, Prince! In the solo tournament, you won't be dragged down by those kinds of weights. You'll be free to fight in whatever way you want!" Her eyes gleam dangerously. "For people like us, there's no alternative to winning other than *death*, right?"

Something clenches in my chest and I start running again, barreling past her, ignoring her confused cries, running, running, running down the street again, clambering up the walls of the city like a headless cockroach, across the top of it, plummeting down to the arid wasteland outside, ignoring my broken legs to keep running. I don't know where I'm running until it's dark and I reach my little hole in the ground and I crawl inside, dragging my broken and aching and heaving body inside the coldest, dampest part. There, I curl up, pulling my legs to my chest, hoping that maybe, just like a dying star, I'll collapse in on myself, and no one will ever see me again.

Darkness around me, darkness abundant, inside me and outside me.

Sleep comes to me like an old, beloved enemy, and I let her take me.

I drift endlessly, my curled-up body knocking against other planetoids, comets drifting around my head, space dust in the shape of rings hula-hooping across my midsection, stars dancing in the distance, all going round and round and round together in a big galaxy dance, dancing around the maypole together, all holding hands. Cosmic laughter and photons forming into smiles and squinting, happy eyes. Galaxies of light bound together in eternal embrace, all the stars and planets interconnected, together, never separated even in brightest death.

But I'm not with them. I'm far away, in the cold and the darkness.

Alone.

"No, no, he isn't in here," someone in my dream says. "If Granny can't smell him, he isn't there."

"Thank you for getting me this far, Rice. I'll take it from here."

"No—*no*. Not. Here. Granny's nose . . ." Huff of annoyance. "Okay. Yes, no problem. I'll return in an hour or so. One hour. Yes?"

"Yes, one moment. One moment."

"Good, good . . ." The sound of padding, animal footsteps leaves, alongside the sound of jingling spurs and heavy leather. Alone remain the gentle steps of someone outside my hole.

Someone approaches in my dream, leaning down, briefly blocking the entrance to my hole. Then they carefully slide down, no doubt dirtying all of their fancy expensive equipment in the process. The hole is low, so they have to crawl forward, hands groping about the dirty ground blindly. Eventually, they touch my foot in the dream. "Hey, there you are."

My eye rolls to look at Moleman. He sits down next to where I lie, still crawled up. I don't move.

"What did Rice say out there?" Moleman asks. "I couldn't understand her at all, but . . . It was something about one. Something like that."

"One," I mumble. "One hour."

"One hour, huh? Yeah, that's a good amount of time. Plenty enough to talk." While he's talking, he keeps one hand on my leg, as though he's afraid I'll vanish into thin air. "Rice brought me here on her sprint-drake. You told me which way this place was so I kind of knew, but it was easy to follow your footprints. I mean, you must have left five buckets' worth of blood out there!" A little laugh. I don't share it. "Yeah."

We're both in the darkness now. I can't really see him, but I can feel his hand, warm, on top of my leg.

He takes a deep breath and I catch a glimpse of his eye, looking toward the entrance to the hole, to the stars shining outside. I don't know what the time is. When did it get so late?

"I'm sorry I wasn't there when you woke up." I don't answer him. "I knew you needed me, and I wasn't there."

It's okay. The sun had fallen a lot when I woke up. It must have been hours. And your party needed you. It's fine. You're here now, aren't you?

His hand squeezes my leg. "The next time you feel horrible," he says, "so horrible you just want to crawl up inside a hole and never come out again, I'll be there." He turns to me. Even in the darkness, I can see his eyes shining like a galaxy's worth of stars. "No matter what."

But I'm fine.

It's okay.

You didn't—

I just . . .

My shoulders begin to tremble and I feel heat rise to my cheeks. Burning hot tears well up and out of my eyes and my chest hurts horribly, terribly, worse than ever. I sit up and find his arms already spread wide. I fall into them. My thoughts are all jumbled together, like unwound yarn put together erratically, nothing making any sense, emotions and reasoning all knotted together limb over limb. "I'm sorry" are the only comprehensible words that escape my heaving throat without being turned into sobs.

"It's alright, you're okay" are the only words I can hear properly. Warm hands pressing against my back.

Hiccuping breaths, too overwhelmed to even consider trying to make it stop. Speaking without thinking. "*I don't want to die, I don't want to die, I don't want to die,*" pleading, trembling, said so quickly the words merge together into one singular expression of everything I didn't want to say.

"It's okay," he says, "you'll be okay. I won't let them."

I'm a coward. I always have been. Why can't I just accept my fate? I'm pathetic.

While I'm still slobbering and sniffling, Moleman takes me by the hand, telling me to hold on, to come along for just a second. And I let him lead me out of the hole, crawling after him, up into the open air, my neck craning to look up at the stars, the endless blanket of stars, a field of shining flowers in the sky, a million billion suns, beautiful and ever present, there before me, there after me. There always. Beauty everlasting.

He sits me down on the ground, on top of a little blanket he brought. We watch the stars.

I decide, beneath the light of the endless stars, beside the only friend I've ever truly had, that no matter what happens tomorrow, it will be alright. I'll let it happen. This night is beautiful, and I don't mind if it's the last one I'll ever have.

I just hope Moleman won't take it too badly.

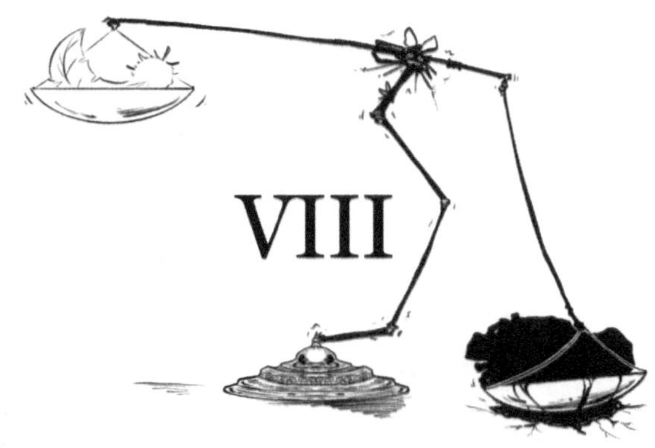

VIII

Death Penalty or No Penalty

Courthouse, exterior. Crowd is even bigger than yesterday. More signs, more shouting, more things thrown at me, more guards trying to suppress the rioting with less fake enthusiasm.

The only major difference would be in the addition of an anti-riot, consisting of a whole two people. When Moleman and I pass them by, Virgil tries to wave my way, but I ignore her. If the other people in the tutorial knew we were actually friends, I can't imagine how they'd treat her. So, although it pains me, I turn the cold shoulder. She seems hurt, but it's necessary.

A few people actually try to push their way inside as we enter, but a wall of guards keeps them at bay. I'm unhappy to find that there are now a number of guards inside the courthouse as well, likely to counter the increased interest in the trial. Normally speaking, at least in Swedish courts of law, civilians have a constitutional right to partake in trials since the law is meant to be an extension of the civilians' rights and such. However, this is not that kind of case, and we aren't exactly following Swedish law, so . . . yeah. I wonder how the outside governments might react to this whole situation? I mean, if they decide to execute me, it could very well be considered murder, maybe even vigilantism, assuming Sweden has laws against that.

Nevertheless, my thoughts are interrupted as we take a wrong turn, head down a number of stairs, and go through several confusing, winding hallways to finally enter a room that seems more like a bunker than a courtroom. Security reasons, I suppose. Same as why there are guards now on standby outside. Not a single one in here, though.

The judge, the jury, and other various members look kind of undead? The jury all seem positively constipated, and the judge is even worse off. Pale, red-eyed, hunched . . . He looks *really* bad, which is made a twinge worse by the fact that he also looks at me *like that*.

The only one who doesn't look like he belongs in hospice is the prosecutor, Venedict, who only looks arguably more tired than yesterday. Sleepless. Same as Moleman. Unlike Moleman, though, Venedict has a look on his face that radiates *I told you so.*

"Welcome back, everyone," Logghammer says, voice heavy. "I hope you've all gotten some rest and relaxation." Sarcasm, in the first two sentences spoken? Bad sign. "Let's not dilly-dally. Since the prosecution is in favor of the death penalty, I'll ask Venedict to begin with his argument. Please."

"Thank you, John," Venedict says, standing up. I don't know whether the cue cards in his hands are worrying or not. Moleman seems to think it's the former. I really am lucky to not have to partake in this myself. "I was very happy to see you all in the colosseum yesterday, where we were all witness to the barbarism of the offender, alongside what the general public's clear desires were. Was there a single person in the audience yesterday who did not partake in the chant, who was not filled with unfathomable glee and relief when said cat was skinned? That is, aside from our dearest defense." Venedict shoots a jeering little glare not at me but at *Moleman.*

I can feel myself bristle.

"This jury, these separate leaderships coming together, were all formed to speak for the people of the servers—to introduce justice and law where there were confused and frightened people. You are the will and want of the people." He turns grandly to the jury, pointing one big finger at the ceiling, where you can yet hear the murmurs and stomping of angry people. "Even down here, can we not hear the people clamoring? Through meters of earth and stone, we can still hear the will and want of the people." *The will and want to see my head roll.* He gives a coaxing smile. "Isn't it your duty to follow it?"

Moleman stands up. Logghammer nods at him, and with that, Moleman begins to speak. "Although the government is formed to speak and act for the people, the people are not always in the right morally. When many people shout, the logic is often lost. Your duty is not to obey those who shout the loudest, but rather to bow down and listen to the small voice of reason." Mcleman penetrates the jury with his sharp gaze. Bach squirms a little in her seat. "You must uphold civility even against the barbarism of the people."

"Even against the barbarism of the criminal?" Venedict retorts.

Moleman nods deeply. "Yes. Civility must stand strong. The way to defeat barbarism is not to kill it but to reason with it."

Venedict takes one look at me and goes, "Some barbarism can't be reasoned with." While he smiles about his clever turn of phrase, I try my hand at telekinetically twisting his head off. Unfortunately, it doesn't work. Bummer. "Some people simply can't get better. They kill and then they kill again. Maybe they give a show of repentance and humility, but in the end, they always do it again. These unforgivable people can only be dealt with in one singular way."

"Nobody is unforgivable," Moleman bites out. "Anybody can get better. You can't assume that everyone who ever commits a crime will be a repeat offender. If that was really the case, all prison sentences would be for life."

"We both know that the offender is an exception to the rule."

"Yes, but if we make *one* exception, it opens the door to make future ones as well. At what point is a criminal *unforgivable*? When do we as a society decide to give up on those who need our help the most? When they kill ten people? Five? *One?*"

"When," Venedict enunciates clearly, "they willingly burn a city to cinders." He thumbs his lower lip. "Or how about *when they kill, dismember, and eat children*? Is that specific enough?"

Moleman's face crumples up and he turns to Logghammer. "Could we take a small breather, please?"

Logghammer nods. "Of course."

The break lasts three minutes and it is spent in horrible, uncomfortable silence. A guard, or maybe a bailiff of some sort, came in and left water for us. Moleman didn't touch it. I wish I could tell him something to turn this all around, but I can't think of a single idea. I've never thought much about the death penalty myself, and when I hear Venedict speak, I can't help but think that it isn't horrible. It's basically just life in prison with fewer steps and expenses.

Before I've realized it, the break ends and Moleman speaks first, saying, "There must be no exceptions. If there's no first, there won't have to be a last, either. Death, killing . . ." He gropes for words for a moment. "It is the greatest tragedy of life. If we decide that there's a certain group of people who cannot change, who cannot get better, who may not be forgiven through anything other than death, then we place ourselves above the order of death and life. The power to order the death of a person should never . . ." He abruptly shakes his head. "No, sorry, let me start over."

"By all means," Venedict says casually. "Take all the time you need, Mole."

Moleman bites down on his lip, chewing, brows heavy with thought. "I, um . . ." He chuckles self-deprecatingly. "I'm the opposition, I don't . . ." Another shake of the head. He takes another moment before speaking again. "If we begin designating certain people as *unforgivable*, then—"

"Slippery slope fallacy," Venedict says sharply.

"I—" Moleman gulps. "S—sorry. Yeah, I . . ." He tugs at his collar. When did he get so sweaty? "Heh, I haven't been in a debate since high school, so . . ." Cold crowd. The way they look at him . . . it's changed. They see him standing next to me, and they don't just see *him* anymore—they see him *together* with *me*. An ally of the monster. "Simply put," he says, taking a long time to find the right words to follow, "the death penalty is simply morally unjust, and ineffective at what it is. Simply, it lacks the deterring effect often associated with such barbaric punishments, alongside being inherently immoral, since killing is always wrong. To live is a perpetual, self-making good, and to end that is therefore evil." Moleman gives Venedict a long look, clearly hoping desperately for him to give a response of some sort.

Going only by Venedict's casual, half-leaned posture, I can tell that he knows how this game is played. Instead of making his own argument, he convinced his opposition to try to flounder for arguments, making a fool out of himself while making Venedict seem to be in a much better position than he really is. If Moleman had been of sounder mind, I'm sure he would have noticed it and returned fire much earlier. But now it's a stalemate.

One that Venedict would probably have continued in perpetuity, had Logghammer not said, "Well, Venedict?"

"Hm?" Venedict says. "Oh! Yes, of course. If it is inherently evil to kill, then does that mean you find war fully unjust?"

"My opinion on the necessity of war is unrelated to the discussion."

Although Venedict seems to want to argue it, he can't find the words and instead says, "Some evil is necessary for the betterment of society."

"An argument that could be used to excuse any number of genocides."

Venedict pauses briefly. "Yes, but a valid argument nonetheless. The ends justify the means."

"And what ends are you looking to achieve by executing the offender?"

"The prevention of an untold number of future deaths."

Now Moleman hesitates. "We can never know for certain whether a criminal will—"

"I'm not talking about a nondescript everyman criminal. I'm talking about the *offender*."

Moleman bites his tongue. He glances at me for just a second, pleading, hoping to hear me say *I will never reap another life again!* or *I've turned over a new leaf—I'm a new man, Your Honor, and I'll never eat a baby moving forward!* or some other such lie. But I don't say anything. My eyes are stuck looking at the judge, looking at the jury, who are all looking at Moleman as though he's as much of a madman as I am. As though we're both lunatics in this together, and *maybe, just maybe, he also deserves what's coming to him.*

Sin by association. An ancient, long-disproved notion that wrongdoing tarnishes like crude oil to silk.

It is as old as it is human.

They look at me and they look at Moleman and they see one. *I can't stand it.*

Opening my mouth, I finally speak up for myself, and say, to Moleman's horror, "I'd do it again."

Silence. Everyone looking at me like I just told a locker room full of classmates that I've been having homosexual thoughts lately. Moleman worst of all.

He stares at me for almost a full minute before the reality of what I just admitted sets in and his head flies to face the judge and jury, mouth moving rapid-fire, saying, "He isn't—he doesn't know what he's saying, once he leaves the tournament, he'll be of a different mind, and when he beats the tutorial, he'll be perfectly ready and willing to help Earth defeat the threat of the—"

"And," I say, my single word choking all noise again, "I don't regret what I did one bit."

Moleman's jaw trembles. "He—he doesn't—"

"It kind of sucked that people didn't like what I was doing, and that I lost my friend over it, but the actual things I did? I don't regret it in the least. It was totally worth it, and if I went back in time to before all of this happened, I'd still do all of it over again." I turn to Moleman. One final nail in the coffin. It'll hurt, but I have to do it. I can explain it all afterward, so for now, I just have to make this convincing, at any cost.

"Including killing you."

Moleman looks at me. I look up at him. My words echo through the bunker briefly before fading away. And in those little moments, where I can still hear the calm, icy-cold words I just said, I can see a little something form in Moleman's eye. A look of realization. An understanding of who I am when I'm not his friend. I see him, and he sees me, for once.

He turns to the judge and jury. The silence in the room chokes everything save for his words. "If anything else," he says, quietly, "letting him live will surely grant him more pain than the absolution of death ever will." He takes a trembling breath. "And maybe, one day, he'll come to regret your mercy."

Logghammer looks up at Moleman and smiles softly, eyes bright.

"Thank you, we'll be sure to keep it in mind."

"But you understand why I had to do it, right?"

"Of course," Moleman says, head in his hands, back hunched.

"I didn't mean it," I lie. "I was just making things up to—you know. Seem horrible. More than I really am, that is. But I didn't mean it. If I went back in time, I'd clearly do the right thing, not *this*. I mean, can you imagine? Going back in time and *not* changing anything? That would be totally—"

"Hey, Kitty?" Moleman says.

"Yeah?"

He peeks up from between his fingers, eyes dark. "Could you please be quiet for a moment?"

"Oh," I say. "Y—yeah. Of course. No problem. I'll be . . ." A pause. He doesn't move from where he sits. "Quiet."

He puts his face back in his hands, elbows resting on his knees. I quietly, very quietly, take a seat next to him. I don't know why, but I'm surprised that they've got such comfortable couches in a *courthouse* of all places. Maybe I should tell Moleman? Something like *Hey, why do you think they have couches in a courthouse? For all the non-existent criminals to sit on? Haha!* maybe? Yeah, that might be good!

I turn to Moleman, mouth open, only to feel it instantly snap shut as I notice his back trembling.

M—Moleman . . . ?

I touch a hand to his back only for him to jerk away, breathing heavily, eyes RED and dark, and his head snapping to face mine, his features holding so many different emotions and thoughts and frustrations that they all become weighted down into a single all-powerful frown. My hand retreats.

In his eyes, I see a mirrored version of my own face, my terrible, horrible, infinitely pained face. His eyelids tremble wide and all of a sudden he doesn't look *like that* anymore, he's just Moleman again, *my friend*, and the regret overwhelms everything else. "I—I'm sorry, I—" He grits his teeth. I pull my hand to my chest. He looks back down at the floor. "I just . . . have to think . . . for a little while."

The unsaid word rings out and I realize that's my cue. "Oh—yeah. Yeah. Sorry, I'm . . . Yeah." I stand up again. Back turned to him, I wonder if there's anything I can do to fix this. Some magic word I could say to make everything right again, to make Moleman smile, to put the planet back into orbit. Oh, and maybe solve world hunger, too. Aw, heck, while I'm at it, why not create world peace?

I walk away. I didn't even say goodbye. Then again, neither did he.

I leave the courthouse through the back door, emerging into an empty alleyway. The final words of the court proceedings echo through the back of my head, accompanied by a chorus of cheers.

The final sentencing will occur tomorrow, alongside any possible penalties.

One more day. Is this what it feels like to be on death row? Endless tomorrows that all feel as final as the last? It's enough to make a man give *himself* the death penalty. As I stand here in this shaded, somewhat cool alley, a thought occurs to me. If I just showed up in the middle of a crowd, could I realistically be executed by lynching? Sure, it wouldn't be pretty, but I can be fairly certain that a good number are far, far stronger than I am, in stats and equipment and everything else. If I just get killed by one of those, I don't have to bother with any of this anymore. No paperwork for the leadership, the goblins will be happy, and Moleman—

Moleman . . .

Actually, never mind. I'll stick to back alleys and rooftops. I sort of wish there was some way of procuring a skin to wear without upsetting Moleman or the general human moral consensus. As is, I suppose I'll simply have to try to be a bit careful about being in public and all that.

Making sure to avoid crowds and to abuse the fetal position and my other stealth skills, I make my way to the colosseum.

<You have learned: Hidden Lv.10>
<You have learned: Unnoticed Lv.1>

It isn't as loud as it usually is, which is nice. Since things are the way they are, I have no choice but to go in through the front door. I'm almost surprised that nobody bodily attacked me on the spot, which is very likely to be a result of the new skill. Nevertheless, I make my way over to the wall, which shows the results of the group tournament.

Let's see here, the winner of the whole group tournament was . . . *ChemistsStink*? First up, weird name. Secondly, I really thought that Moleman's group would be number one! Instead, they're actually in second place, and that's only because they were the final obstacle in the spiral-of-death gauntlet. That's . . .

"You really are still up to your old tricks, aren't you?"

First instinct: stab. Second thought that follows: *But Moleman wouldn't like that.* Resulting action: do a midjump pirouette to face the voice; affix with glare.

Hm? This woman . . . haven't I seen her before?

"But less talkative," Ursula comments. "I don't know which I prefer: chatty but harmless, or . . . *this.*" I'm not sure what she's talking about. I'm the same as I was when we last met and she tried to have me arrested. I've changed a little, sure, but I'm still *me.* Putting a thumb to her chin, she rubs it in circles. "Let's see, going by what you were looking at and what's been happening lately . . ." Her eyes fall on the group tournament results. "You're wondering why our team didn't cream those Yankee bastards, aren't you?"

I don't nod or show any other sign that she's completely correct, but she still takes my silence as affirmative, which it is.

"The answer is simple. Mole didn't show up for the semifinals or the finals. We could handle the semifinals on our own, but the finalists were able to beat us since we were already tired." As she speaks, I listen in stunned silence. Moleman left his team to lose? Why? "Going by the look on your face, I can't believe that that actually surprises you, considering that you were the one he prioritized over winning the tournament."

I stare at her. I . . . what?

She crosses her arms and looks back at the wall, to the list of when the solo all-skirmishes are going to take place. "Well, would you look at that? Nobody wants to play with you anymore."

I follow her gaze, my eyes falling on the list of skirmishes. The eighteenth floor isn't there. I quickly turn to look at the tournament results so far. They're only at the thirteenth-floor skirmish, but the eighteenth-floor results are already tallied.

I won by default. Nobody else signed up, or they all withdrew before the match even began.

"Poor, poor Kitty-cat. How will you sharpen your claws now?" Ursula tuts at me condescendingly. I draw back, away from her. She steps toward me, closing the distance again. "Will you even be able to survive going a whole day without killing anyone? Is that even possible?"

I reconsider the choice of not trying to kill her on the spot.

She blows a strand of hair out of her face. "You're an animal. I could tell it the moment we met first. In that sense, you haven't changed a bit." Something sad shines in her eyes. "But there used to be something else in there, too. I can't see it anymore. What happened to that little glint, Kitty?"

I turn away from her and run away.

A few hours later, I return to watch the floor forty-five all-skirmish, getting a good seat and view by climbing up the side of the building, leaving a few fingers chiseled between the stones in a trail. The match is . . . interesting. I think, all in all, only a few people were actually turned to ash. The rest either surrendered and lost or were injured and willingly went out of bounds. There were a lot fewer people than there were at my skirmish. I count less than a hundred, I think. With more space, people were able to fight in a much different way compared to the chaos of my match. Most people were defeated by being forced out of bounds.

Nobody booed for anyone.

And I saw Rice. I saw her be a flurry of arrows and clever tricks. Not much in the long range. People would rush at her to try to close the gap as quickly as possible only for her to engage them in close quarters as willingly as long distance. But the real highlight was her archery. Skilled, quick, and most damning of all: accurate. If she put her eye on someone, they would undoubtedly get an arrow to the shoulder or knee or elbow. Never anywhere truly dangerous. Just enough to incapacitate them long enough to surrender.

And surrender they did. As people became exhausted from the fighting, she remained active, ready, always moving, always acting. It was mesmerizing. Not like a dance of death or anything like that. It was more like watching a peerless musician, moving in incomprehensible but deeply purposeful ways to create music that touched the soul. It was simply that. Beautiful, like a flower caught in a dust devil. And the audience roared for her. She would shoot someone clean through the shoulder and receive the praise of thousands.

Effortlessly beloved.

In the end, when all was said and done, could I really say I was surprised when she emerged victorious? And then she stood there, looking around at the cheering as though it was a mysterious new noise coming from an old television.

"And there we have the winner of the floor forty-five solo all-skirmish, our lovely BeatriceTheAngel, of the Hard Difficulty!" the God of Pain announces happily. **"Let's all give a big hand to her and the other valiant fighters!"**

A hand is more or less an understatement. The whole arena is in a joyous uproar, making noise for a girl who doesn't even seem to realize that they're clapping for *her*. Instead, she's going around the stage, pulling people to their feet, shaking hands and smiling broadly at anyone and everyone who put up an interesting fight. And they love it. The atmosphere is incomparable to anything I have ever produced.

Even back in my pro gamer days, although people were clearly awed by my skill and tenacity, they still refrained from cheering. So I'd cheer for myself. I'd pat myself on the back by gloating at the losers. *Better luck next time* was used as a sarcastic insult, because we both knew there'd be no next time.

But these people, with her . . .

Clapping, and they bow together. Even the losers are still happy. That shouldn't even be possible, but she makes it possible.

And as the fighters wave and pat each other on the back, I feel a pair of eyes train in on me where I sit on the wall above everyone else. A pair of crystal-blue eyes that light up when I turn to her. She waves at me. Tentatively, I wave back at her. Her smile grows broader, and when everyone else leaves the arena, she hesitates to go, shooting me a quick, happy look before doing so.

I watch her back fade into the darkness of the colosseum, a sense of nauseous bitterness forming in the pit of my stomach.

Before meeting Moleman—no, *LetsFraternizeTogether*—I hadn't felt much of anything. Another foolish enemy to be defeated, to prove my overwhelming might against. Only once he'd already beaten me did it sink in that he was on a different level. But now, with Rice, it's completely different.

For some reason, I've got a feeling that she's one of few opponents I can't defeat.

A few hours later, Moleman and his party take the stage for their skirmish. Since they're alone on floor sixty-six, it's only them. They could've just decided on a winner beforehand, but no. Apparently, they've got too much respect for each other, so they decide to waste everyone's time by having a genuine battle.

Maybe it's hubris on my part, but watching Moleman pull out all stops and become a whirlwind of magic was startling. It felt like watching a beloved family pet suddenly rush a home intruder, except with magic instead of claws and teeth.

Maybe if I was a total battle maniac, I could have spent these minutes watching him by trying to dissect his fighting style. By the time I have this thought, though, it's already over. Using his wind-lifty-up magic and a barrage of other nameless spells, Moleman has either pushed the rest of his party members off the stage or otherwise incapacitated them. The whole thing couldn't have taken more than ten minutes.

And by the end of it, people are cheering and Moleman is shaking hands and the God of Pain is talking and I just . . . I can't do this anymore. I feel sick.

Not waiting for the ceremonies to end and the cheering to fade, I turn away from the arena, toward the city. I'm just about to start climbing down when I spot something I hadn't noticed before. It really feels like I should have seen it earlier, considering just how obvious it is.

Stuck in the middle of the northern park, the one square filled with a bazaar and people instead of trees and a cathedral, stands a chapel.

It's small and dull-looking, the walls made of aged, BLACKened sandstone. Squeezed between the food stalls and the mats and shouting salespeople, it feels oddly malplaced. Like someone put the wrong texture on a single square of the map. Even weirder, the more I look at it, the stronger I feel that it isn't the chapel that's malplaced, but rather everything else. A million little insults to the sacred ground upon which the chapel stands.

Guided by nothing but my own heart, I climb down the side of the colosseum. My feet lead me to the chapel. In person, it looks even smaller than from up above. The man in the stall next to it stops shouting about sprint-drake gear and foldable bicycles the moment his eyes fall on me. He knows.

I put my hand on the door handle, pushing it down. The heavy wooden door slowly creaks open, a sliver of pure darkness gaping wide before me. I slip inside.

The door closes with a thud behind me. After a second or two, my eyes get used to the darkness.

The only light to be seen is a tawny stream, as thin as a spider's thread, shining in through a small window in the roof. But it's enough to see by. Calling it a *chapel* was really more for the outside appearance, because the inside looks way more like a jail cell of some sort, if a bit larger than most that I've been in. There's a single bed, a chair and table, and then . . . an altar, I guess? I don't know what else to call the carved stone slab leaned against the farthermost wall. The thick base of it is inscribed with five different sigils, and there's a silk cloth draped over the top, so it looks very religious. Or, it *would*, if it had held any sort of religious paraphernalia on it. Instead, there's just a single vase with five flowers in it. A red rose, a yellow lily, a butter flower, a . . . marigold, I think? And then another pink-white one I don't recogni—

"That's a dog rose!"

Jerked out of my thoughts, I leap four feet into the air, bang my head against a wooden pillar, and crash down onto the floor like a swatted fly. Who—what—where—

My eyes fall on the God of Pain. He smiles at me. He's a lot smaller than the last time I saw Him, but He's still the same annoying moon-man. Wasn't He supposed to be at the colosseum? What the heck is He doing here?

"I was wondering whether you'd found your way in here yet, and I'm happy to find you have!" He says, smiling. Always smiling. Grrr. Moon-face frozen in that ever-smile, He wanders over to the altar and plucks the so-called dog rose from the vase. **"This is the one I picked, you know. The God of Love sent Us a whole list of all His flowers, and I'm quite happy with My choice."**

"Why are You here?" I bark at Him.

His smile turns obnoxiously elusive. **"Don't you know? This is My temporary abode for the tutournament."** Before I have time to reel from that insane statement, He puts the dog rose back in the vase and grabs the butter flower. **"You didn't ask, but this is actually called a kings cup flower."**

"Sh—shut up, I knew that!" I lie at Him, for absolutely no reason. Before the word shifts back to Him, I quickly add, "And, besides, why are You lying to me? No god would be masochistic enough to live in this dinky little cell. Are You trying to get on my good side by pretending to be mortal or something?"

He's got the same expression as before, but something in His eyes looks a fraction quizzical. **"Didn't I tell you I'm the God of Pain? Tut tut, Kitty. Now's no time to play games."** Enigmatic smile, now. Can't He stick to one? My brain can't handle deciphering the tiny quirks of a single smile for more than a minute straight.

Returning the flower to the vase, He waltzes over to the bed and pats the part next to Him. A silent request. One I *really* don't want to follow. He quirks an eyebrow at me. The awkward silence is worse than the possibility of Him touching me, so even though I mostly just want to run away, I step up to the bed and sit down next to Him. Thankfully, He doesn't put His arm around my shoulders or anything parental like that.

"If you'd like," He says, **"you are most welcome to stay the night here."**

My head flashes to face Him. "What do you mean? Didn't You just say that this was *Your* place?"

"Don't you worry about that—I'll crash at Will's place. He hates Me, but He just can't say no to My infectious smile!" To punctuate His dumb joke, He sticks His fingers in the edges of His lips to form a bloodcurdling grin. Since my reaction is one of mute horror, He quickly releases it, returning His expression to the ordinary. **"So, what do you say, Kitty?"**

"About what?"

He shrugs. **"You'll have a bit of silence, some alone time, away from the crowds . . ."** A gleam in His eye tells me He already knows exactly everything there is to know. As though He's reading my heart directly. **"With a day as tumultuous as this, a bit of time to think might be just what you need, no?"**

My hands curl into fists atop my lap. "I . . . I don't . . ."

"If not for you, then for your friend. Does that make it easier?"

No. It really doesn't. If anything, trying to factor Moleman into this whole thing just makes it harder. I clench my teeth and bite out, "I don't . . . want to bother him. He told me he wanted a bit of time alone, so . . ."

"How about we put it to the test, then?"

"What? Test what?"

What the heck is this guy on about now?

Aaaaand now His smile has gone all mischievous. He seriously can't pick one, can He?

"I'll send a little system alert to SuperMoleman about where you're at, and then we'll see if he shows up. How's that?" He asks, like a psychopath.

"Why—why would You do that? *Can* You even do that?"

"I'm a system administrator!" He says. **"I can do *anything*."** A chill runs down my spine. When I'm around this guy, I keep forgetting He's a god. An actual divine being. It's hard to remember considering the way He acts. **"So?"** He says. **"Do you think he'll show up or not?"**

Saying so, He leans in closer. I scootch away. "I—well, I think I'd rather he . . ."

"It's not about what you *want*, Kitty." His face twists in dark glee. **"It's about how well you know Moleman."** He carefully strokes his pointed chin. **"So? What'll it be?"**

I gulp. "I . . ." I shake my head and affix the God of Pain with my gaze. "He'll be here."

"I see. In that case, I'll bet he won't come. If I win, you'll spend the night, and if you win, I'll help you out a little when the time comes! How's that?"

"Uh . . . sure?" That's ominous.

He turns away from me. **"Now, while we wait, would you care to teach Me one of your Earth games? Love mentioned something called *tic-tac-toe* last time I spoke to Him. Would you care to explain?"**

"Alright." So I teach Him. Tic-tac-toe is easy enough, so to up the ante, I teach Him tramp chess, ergo the variant where you can move your pieces around once you've used three. We do this for a while. I'm ashamed to admit that once He understood the simple rules, He beat me. Every time. Didn't matter where I put my piece, once He got a taste for it, He knew just what to do. Didn't help that He quickly integrated a little punishment game where if He won, He got to poke me. In return, if I won, I was allowed to insult Him to His face. In hindsight, I'm not so sure if it was worth it.

To continue passing the time, I taught Him checkers, which I can only barely play myself. Why did I keep playing even though I got zapped every game? No idea! Better than facing the silence, I suppose.

If I taught Him to play, I also didn't have to look at the time.

How long has it been since Moleman got the message? Is he still coming, or does he need more time to think? I'm sure he's got a lot to think about. I don't mind if he doesn't come. It's up to him, really. I'm used to being alone, so this is nothing.

Nothing at all.

<Top—Status—Community>
<22:30:02 Day 543>
<The nineteenth attempt will begin in 27:01:29:58>
<Tutournament Day 4 of 5>

I'm starting to think he might not be coming.

"So? How about it? One more game, right? We'll play one more game, won't we?" the God of Pain says, practically begging.

I look at Him, and then toward the closed door. "He isn't coming, is he?"

Pain tilts His head at me like a dog. **"Hm? What's that?"**

Anger bubbles up in the pit of my stomach. "You've just been distracting me to make the pain worse. Isn't that right, *Pain*? The longer I waddle around with false hope, the more it'll hurt once it breaks. So You've been distracting me. Even made it into a fun little game." I stand up, fists trembling. "So stop it. I don't care anymore. He's not coming, and I'm not staying here. I'll go live in an alley or something. That's nothing new to me, unlike this damn—"

Knock knock knock.

I freeze in place. My head slowly turns to face the door.

Knock knock knock knock.

I turn to Pain, breath held, only to find His face as serene and placid as a moonlit lake.

Turning away from Him, I move toward the door, big, confident strides hiding my fear. I pause briefly for a second in front of the door, my trembling hand hovering over the door handle. I grit my teeth and push it down, heaving the door open.

It's raining. I hadn't noticed that before, but now that the door is open, I can hear it plainly. Smattering down, loudly, harshly. Glints of light in the night darkness. And there in the rain stands Moleman, panting like he just ran a marathon, clothes and cloak and pants and hair all soaking wet, raindrops streaming down his face to mask the scent of sweat. If I hadn't been paralyzed by the look of deep, deep relief on his face I might have noticed the fact that he's half leaning on a bicycle, of all things.

My jaw works itself. "M—Moleman, you—"

Throwing himself at me, the bicycle clattering to the ground, he clutches me in his arms, the cold rainwater and his feverish skin painting a very strange picture. He quickly unlatches from me, keeping his hands firmly on my shoulders. "Are you okay, Kitty?"

"Yeah, of course, what are you—"

"Would you like to step inside, Moleman?" an undeniably divine-sounding voice rumbles from behind me. His smile makes Moleman twitch. Or maybe it's the simple fact that there's a god standing in front of him. **"You'll be no good in the tutournament finals if you catch a cold now."**

"Oh, uh . . . Y—yes, of course," Moleman answers hesitantly.

We enter, leaving the bike tethered outside.

There's a fireplace in the chapel now, lighting up the room. Not to mention the couch facing the bed. The God of Pain seems positively giddy with the developments, but I feel nothing. Considering the fact that I won our "bet," shouldn't He be the unhappy one? I don't get it.

Moleman gives me a meek look. "Sorry I was late. I was halfway to your hole when I got the message, and by that point I thought I might as well check it out to make sure that you weren't—that you hadn't . . ." He shakes his head. "Really, I'm sorry."

"No—no, there's nothing to apologize for." I look at the fire to avoid having to watch his expression shift. "You're here now, aren't you?"

He follows my gaze into the fire. A long pause passes between us. He's the one who breaks it, saying, "Listen, about the trial . . ."

"Let's not talk about it," I quickly say. We share a look. "It's been a long day, and tomorrow will probably be no different, so . . ." I muster a smile of some sort. I'm not sure if he's falling for it. "We'll take it when we get there, okay?"

He slowly nods. "Yeah, alright."

Silence. Horrible, painful, awkward silence. If only to break it, I ask, "So, what's with the bike?"

He blinks at me. "Oh, that's . . . One of the people in the Africa Server was able to make a Purgatory-compatible design. He's been selling foldable, inventory-sized bikes and building plans in the bazaar, so I got one. They're really useful, but since they're made of wood, they aren't very long-lasting."

"Okay," I respond. And then silence again. Itching silence. "Um . . . It's kind of late, isn't it?"

"Yeah, it is," Moleman says. "We should probably head back home. Regain some energy for tomorrow and all that."

"So . . ." I look down at my folded fingers and then back up at him. "You're okay with me sleeping at your place again?"

His brows furrow. "Why wouldn't I be?"

"Well, I . . ." I . . . *What?* We didn't exactly split on good terms, so I thought . . . But it's not like he's cruel enough to ask me to sleep in the hole just for that. That's why he literally spent hours biking all the way to the hole and back. To make sure I didn't have to sleep in the mud and the rain. I look down at my feet, and at the shadows dancing in the fire's living light. I smile. "No, nothing." I look back up at him. "Let's go home, yeah?"

He smiles back at me. "Sounds good."

On the way out, Pain stops me briefly to pat me on the back (horrifying) and give me a cheeky wink. Whatever that means.

IX

Spiral of Death

"Kitty, hey, Kitty, wake up . . ." Someone's gently shaking my shoulders, but I'm pretty content just lying here, meditating, not really thinking about much of anything . . . "Kitty, come on, wake up!" There's a gentle slap against my cheek, but that's okay. I'm fine right where I am . . . "I didn't want to do this, but . . ." There's a pause. Snore, honk, mimimi . . .

"Wake up, Kitty, time for school!"

I fly to my feet. "Whu—where?! I'm awake, I swear. I just have to—" I pause. Standing up, I find that I'm not at home, in my bed, late again. Instead . . .

I turn to Moleman with barely hidden ire. "What's up?"

He puts away the pots and pans he was slamming and gives me a cheeky smile. "Thought it'd be a shame for you to miss your quarterfinals match because you overslept. Don't you agree?"

"Well, yeah, but . . ." I cross my arms defensively. "I wasn't sleeping, okay? I was just . . . *resting my eyes a bit*, that's all."

"Sure, sure," Moleman replies as he starts setting the table. The smell of fried eggs makes me drool. And is that bacon? Oh, boy. As per our usual routine, I help set the table, giving us both cutlery and a plate and cup. Normally I don't really use this kind of stuff, but Moleman told me that if I wasn't going to eat with proper manners, I wouldn't get to eat at all, so now this is how we do it. After a few minutes, breakfast is served, and we both take a seat.

Bacon, eggs, potato pancakes, and a tragic lack of lingonberry jam. Still delicious, though. Moleman is a surprisingly good cook. Actually, no, he feels like the exact kind of guy who'd be a great cook, but he's even better than that. I eat greedily. Man, this is good. Crispy eggs, flaky bacon, tender potato pancakes . . .

I glance up at Moleman. Luckily, he's also eating. I was a little scared he might still be sulking about the whole me-being-executed thing, but he seems to have cheered up a bit. Enough to eat, at the very least.

I swallow down a mouthful of egg whites. "Hey, Moleman." Looking up, he meets my gaze, sipping on his water. "You're okay, right?"

He gulps the water down before responding. "Yeah, sure I am." He perks an eyebrow. "And you?"

"Of course I am!" I answer quickly. "I was just, you know . . . thinking." My words aren't making sense anymore, so I pause by cutting a piece of bacon into slices. "I mean, today, if things don't go the way you want . . ." I poke at my egg yolk to stall. "Will you be alright? I mean, without me?" Dumb question; I'm sure he'll be alright. If he was the one getting executed and me being left behind, I would probably handle that as well as a child losing his brother would. But Moleman has tons of other friends. He'll be fine. I'm not even sure why I asked.

He falls silent. After a while, he mumbles, "You tell me."

But I don't tell him, because I've learned from experience that that expression is rhetorical and not meant to be taken literally. Still, I kind of want him to talk. It's not like this is mainly my issue. I won't have to worry about this when I'm dead, while he's the one left to grumble about how he could have handled it. What he could have done, what he should have said . . .

Unfortunately enough, I don't think this is the kind of thing I can force out of him. Maybe breakfast isn't the best place to have this conversation, I suppose.

I turn back to my plate, with all the items neatly separated, and continue eating.

A while later, once the food is eaten and the dishes done, we head to the colosseum. I don't know who designed the timetable for the solo matches, but the first quarterfinals match between the skirmish winner of the first floor and the skirmish winner of the second floor took place at six in the morning. I can't imagine there were many spectators.

The same can't be said for the match I'm about to have. Oh, yeah, apparently, my quarterfinals against the seventeenth floor is at twenty minutes past seven. In the morning. Who decided on these times? Might it have been Pain? Ahh, who knows.

Then again, I think I remember something about the group tournament going on way too late into the evening, so this might be in response to that. Maybe.

Either way, since the trial stuff has a long way to go, I'll do my quarterfinals first and then we'll see if I'm alive to do the semifinals.

I say goodbye to Moleman outside the preparation room, he wishes me luck and recommends me to not fight too creatively, I give a roundabout answer to avoid lying to him, and then I enter. Surprisingly enough, there are more people inside the preparation room than I'd expect. Not a single one of them will look me in the eye. When I approach the receptionist desk for the shard, the queue that was there before dissipates, letting me go up to Cathy without having to wait at all. She gives me the shard, I pretend it doesn't hurt, and then the pop-up appears.

<The Floor 15 vs. Floor 16 quarterfinals has now ended.>
<The Floor 17 vs. Floor 18 quarterfinals will begin shortly.>
<Please head toward the arena, Hell Challenger Lo Fennrick. If you are not present at the arena within 4:59, the match will be forfeit.>

Right, right, I got it.

As I head toward the entrance to the arena, I watch the parting crowd around me, trying to parse who my first victim is to be. And from the crowd steps . . . Hm? Don't I recognize her? . . . Well, either way, she certainly recognizes me, considering the look on her face. Maybe there's even some old blood at play here, because for how terrified she looks, she's still decided to face me. Brave, but foolish.

We head out onto the drawbridge, and then into the harsh, glaring sunlight of the arena outside. The arena isn't quite as crowded as it had been at my latest matches, but it's still a pretty good amount.

"And let's welcome our next two challengers with a big hand! Here we have GlowingGlyphs of the seventeenth floor, coming in from the Hard Difficulty at an impressive level of thirty-nine, finally facing off to take revenge on our dearest PrissyKittyPrincess of the Hell Difficulty, at a stunning level of eighty-three!" At Pain's intrusive and frankly uncalled-for exclamation, the crowd is split, some cheering, others murmuring among each other, maybe about my level, maybe about something else. Pain doesn't care, as He excitedly continues His introduction: **"Will GlowingGlyphs avenge her fallen teammates and finally defeat Kitty once and for all, or will yet another challenger fall victim to Kitty's horrid claws? Let's find out! Is everyone ready down there?"**

He looks down at us. I nod up at Him. I have to show *some* appreciation for yesterday. Glyph, on the opposite side of the arena, also nods at Him, though only after a little pause.

"Wonderful! With that said . . . Ready . . . Set . . . *Go!*"

I don't move. I don't need to. Heck, I don't even crouch down or anything. I'm standing, casually, watching as she with trembling hands tries to unsheathe her sword. Oh, yeah, now that I'm looking at her, isn't she the one I saw in the hospital the day before yesterday? I recognize the scent of her fear. It's very distinct.

While I'm thinking, she actually drops her sheath, the whole sword clattering to the floor. With the arena being so silent, the sound feels much louder.

She almost reaches down to grab it, only to stop once she sees my eyes. Ah, she's petrified. And no magic needed, either. What, does she think I'll kill her while she's trying to pick up her sheath? I mean, I *could*, but where's the fun in that?

I wave my hand at her. "Go on," I say, loud enough for her to hear. "Pick it up."

Wow, now she's *really* sweating. I wonder if there's a telepathy skill or something. At this moment, I'm very curious to hear what kind of thoughts she's having. Considering the way she's looking at me, I wouldn't be surprised if she thought I was playing 5-D chess in my head. The unfortunate fact of the matter is that I don't need any clever strategies to defeat her.

"Come on, Glyph, don't let him psych you out!"

"Yeah, Glyph, just kill him! You can do it!"

"Don't fall for his mind games, Glyph!"

I turn toward the voices and the group instantly falls silent. Hm. These people . . . aren't they the rest of her party? That makes sense, I guess.

Unfortunately, it seems Glyph has decided to take their advice. She bends down, keeping her eyes on me, fumbles for the sheath, grabs it, and stands up straight again, clipping it to her belt before I have time to wonder why she didn't just keep the unsheathed sword in her inventory. Maybe there's something in the rules I don't know about because I didn't read them?

Nah.

Spurred on by the cheering of her friends, Glyph takes her sword in both hands, points it toward me, and . . .

Freezes again.

It seems to me that no matter how much she tries to transform her fear into a fighting drive, she can't help but get stuck on the far more primal *freeze* instinct. I guess I've got no choice but to help her.

I start walking toward her. The audience holds its collective breath as I stroll up to her, hands on my hips.

I'm not even taller than her or anything, but because of the way she cowers from me, she certainly feels smaller. The tip of her sword trembles mere inches from me, but with how stiff she is, she won't be able to use it. Am I really going to have to do everything here?

I grab the blade. Good sharpness. Even just holding it like this has already sliced up a gash in my palm, making my blood trickle down the edge, all the way down the hilt to soak into her gloves. She won't move. Her eyes remain glued on me, waiting for me to do something. So that's just what I'll do.

Holding the sword in place, I step closer, forcing the tip to stab into my stomach. Her entire body gives a jolt, but that's hardly enough. Another step and the sword slides in a bit further, the muscles of my abdomen twitching and spasming around the intrusive metal. One more and I can feel the tip pressing against the skin of my back, so with another step, I stab it onto me fully. Now we're face-to-face. Close enough to kiss. I release my grip on the sword.

"Well?" I ask her. "What now?"

She looks at me, mouth opening briefly, and then . . .

Her hands lose their grip on the hilt and she falls to her knees, mouth opening and closing rhythmically, eyes staring straight ahead, no longer at me, staring at anything and everything and all that's in between. "Ah, ah . . ." And now, just to complete her impressive display: tears. "P—please . . ."

I look down at her. It would be easy to kill her. Maybe even dissect her while she's alive as a threat to future enemies. On the other hand . . .

My eyes move up to the bleachers, up to where Moleman sits. Next to Rice. Surprising, but a nice sight nonetheless.

Sighing, I turn back to Glyph. I let my eyes sharpen threateningly. "Do you surrender?"

Her head jerks up and down, nodding frantically.

I sigh and look up, toward Pain. "Hey, Pain, she gave up. That counts, right?"

He blinks down at me from atop His cloud of fireflies. **"Huh? Oh, yes, of course!"** Sitting up properly, He clears His throat and starts actually doing His job. **"It seems GlowingGlyph has unfortunately decided to surrender! What a shame. Nonetheless, let's give a big hand to Kitty for winning without laying a single hand on his opponent. What an achievement!"**

Silence. I expected as much, but . . .

Someone claps.

Huh?

No, not just one. *Two.* Up there, Moleman and Rice both clap. I think I can even hear Rice yelling something. And then, on the other side, there are two others clapping as well—Virgil and Almos. And with these four clapping, a few others join in. Not everyone, but a few. Some.

But even more than that, nobody's booing.

"So when's the next one? I'm in great shape, I could take anyone on right now!"

Moleman rolls his eyes, but he's smiling. *Proudly.* "You took a *sword* to the *stomach.* How the heck are you in great shape?"

I pout at him. "Don't underestimate my auto-healing skills, Moleman. With my skills, I can lose an arm or two and be fine within the hour! Or the next couple of hours, at least."

He chuckles at me. "In that case, you might as well drop an arm or two." I perk an eyebrow at him. In reply, he simply points at the tournament schedule. Let's see, floor eighteen vs. floor twenty semifinals . . . My jaw falls open. "Yep, it's in four hours."

"F—four hours? Why?! How?"

"Well," Moleman says, "there's a lot of quarterfinals to be done before then. Mine included." He winks at me. To mock him, I do a one-at-a-time frog blink. It makes him laugh. But the laugh is short-lived as a shadow falls over his face. "Though, before that . . ."

"Brunch?" I suggest. It makes him chuckle, successfully lightening the mood, if only a little.

"I don't think they have that at the courthouse."

"Not even as a final supper?"

He pauses in his step. "We don't know that yet."

I don't correct him. But the mood has shifted. Nevertheless, we head toward the courthouse. My steps feel light. Making Moleman a little proud was a good final act, I think. It may not have been as effective as some other strategies, but if I'm not alive four hours from now, then it doesn't matter.

We approach the courthouse. It's early, and it's not like the leaderships are up and about when the trial takes place, so not a lot of people are gathered. We approach the entrance without issue, open it, and . . .

"Huh? You need more time?" Moleman asks the person in the doorway. The secretary, I think.

She nods in reply and affixes her glasses. "Yes, the deliberation is still ongoing. It likely won't finish before the solo tournament concludes."

"I see, that's too bad . . ." Moleman says. "In that case, I guess we'll just have to keep fighting in the tournament to pass the time. Right, Kitty?"

I give him an *are-you-kidding-me* look. Should I be surprised or relieved that he still has this much sway over the leaderships? Either way, he's waiting for a response, so after a few seconds, I reply, "Yeah. *Right*."

"Great!" Moleman says. "In that case, we'll be back later, and, for now . . ." He smiles sheepishly. "Brunch?"

I want to point out that he really didn't need to pretend about this whole thing, but the suggestion to get food is overpowering. I can do nothing but agree as we go grab brunch.

On the way to the bazaar, I have time to think it through. He doesn't need to know I know. Considering his current position in the leadership, with the way they treated him yesterday . . . He must have pulled every string he had to make this happen. Maybe even snapping a few of them. All to let me participate in the tournament.

There's no need to spend the final hours we have together talking about useless things. So while we buy some drake skewers, I decide to talk about other stuff instead. Future fights. *Our* future fight. Tease him about what'll happen once I beat him. Make silly jokes about random things that don't matter. We went and watched Rice's match, and it was as impressive as expected.

When the time came, I happily watched his quarterfinals. It was exciting, and although he unsurprisingly won in the end, the fight itself was still really cool. I think he might have used different spells than he did last time, but when I asked about it, he wouldn't answer.

And just like that, the hours passed peacefully.

<Top—Status—Community>
<11:03:32 Day 544>
<The nineteenth attempt will begin in 26:12:56:28>
<Tutournament Day 5 of 5>

It's time.

We enter the vomitorium.

Before I headed straight to the preparation room, I decided to check the schedule, just to know the name of the guy I was up against. However, what I found was far worse.

"He—he *surrendered*?!" I exclaim.

Next to me, Moleman shrugs. "Can't say I'm surprised." I give him a hopefully only mildly incredulous look. "Sure, you didn't kill her or anything—*which I'm very proud of*—but it was still a fairly intimidating display. Not to mention that your level was—let's see . . . yeah, almost twice as high as his. Surrendering beforehand was a wise choice."

I wave my hands in the air to try to make the words go. "Well, yeah, maybe, but . . . *Still!*"

Moleman easily capitulates. "Still a shame, yeah."

Frowning, I check at what time I'll finally get to fight. Let's see here, floor eighteen in the finals . . . "Thirteen-thirty? That's in over two hours! I can't wait that long! What kind of—"

"Hey, no need to be upset about it, alright?" Moleman says, trying his best to calm me down. "You'll get to fight eventually."

"But I want to fight *now* . . ." I grumble, which is admittedly a little childish. I just . . . I was really looking forward to it, okay? Nevertheless, two hours isn't too bad. Less than last time. It gives us plenty of time to . . . "Hey, Moleman." He tilts his head at me. "I'll stop sulking if you treat me to lunch."

"I treated you to brunch less than an hour ago!" he complains, but going by the smile, I know I've won already. "Is there nothing but food that makes you happy?"

I rub my chin. "I'm not sure it's advisable for me to answer that from a legal standpoint."

"I'm your lawyer. I've got a vow of silence—you can tell me *anything*."

"That's a misconception and you know it!"

We chuckle and head to lunch. A while later, we watch Rice's semifinals match, and then Moleman's. And then, finally, it's time for me to have my match.

I'm in the arena. On the other side stands my opponent, a middle-aged man with a scythe. He looks pretty tough. A few seconds ago, I was pretty excited to fight him. But that's all changed. Now, the arena simply echoes with the sound of what he just said.

"Yeah, uh, I'd like to surrender."

So now I'm staring at him, and he's looking down at the floor.

"How impressive! That's the quickest surrender we've seen inside the arena so far! Might Kitty have some special skill that lets him sap the will to fight with a mere glare?" Pain narrates. **"Nevertheless, with the floor sixteen winner having surrendered, that means Kitty moves on to—"**

"W—wait just a minute," I say. "We didn't—I didn't even—"

Not waiting for me to explain why we should fight even if just a little, the scythe guy turns around and jumps into the moat.

"Ouch, what a retreat! Seems like Kitty got the cold shoulder. Either way, this means Kitty will now continue in the *Spiral of Death*! As is customary, our current finalist will be offered a ten-minute break to recover from any injuries incurred in the last battle. So, what do you say, Kitty? Do you want to take a little nap before continuing?"

"No, I don't need a nap, damn it! I want to *fight*!" I shout up at Him, shaking my fist. This is probably the closest I've ever gotten to cursing God.

"Great, that's what we love to hear! In that case, I would like to welcome our next challenger to the scene. Everyone give a big welcome to TinCan-Goodness of the twenty-fourth floor Hard Difficulty, weighing in at a stunning level of fifty-six!"

He arrives. A piercing light in the darkness, descending like an angel to rescue the poor and downtrodden. A dove's blessing to a lonesome funeral.

Big, burly, buff. A man roughly the size of a barge, or maybe even bigger. Hard to tell. And then with the gapless armor and the mace in one hand, shield in the other . . . He looks like a dragon slayer or something. The only thing offsetting the perfect knight visage is that the armor is a light shade of pink, but that's forgivable.

A real fight.

I'm too excited to even pay attention as Pain goes through the regular spiel of asking if we're ready, and then the countdown, and . . . *go!*

I fly across the arena, heart beating out of my chest, legs aflight with guidance from both mind and instinct, ready to run or to leap away or to curl up if the need presents itself. Claws at the ready, mouth half-open, I attack, every muscle in my tawny body clenched and ready to let skin taste blood.

Except, once I get close, something is wrong. There's an odd smell that shouldn't be here, and a sound I haven't heard before, like hail on a tin roof or nails against nails.

My eyes focus on a chink in his armor at the level of his chest, a spot where my claws will fit perfectly to preface the amazing fight to come, but as I come nearer and as my hands shoot out to gouge him open, I find myself freezing in place, needle-sharp nails mere millimeters from his wide-open chest.

The sound is him trembling.

Huh? Wait a moment, that isn't—

The mace falls out of his hand, the shield soon following suit. Through the slit in his helmet, I can see a pair of terrified eyes staring down at me.

"I—I give up—" he says between tiny panting breaths.

I blink at him in equal parts astonishment and indignation. "No, wait," I say. "What are you—"

He falls to his knees. This massive, hulking warrior of a man falls to his knees before me, his armor clinking and his weight kicking up dust around him. Even on his knees, he remains massive, now at the height of my chest. His trembling hands move into the air, palms up, like he's submitting to arrest. "Please, please don't kill me," he whimpers.

"I'm not—" Okay, I might have, but . . . "Why the heck are you surrendering? I didn't even lay a finger on you!"

"Please, please," he says, sniveling like an idiot, going so far as to tear up. No, not just tear up, he's full-on crying. What the heck is even going on anymore? Is someone pulling a prank on me? Am I on reality TV? Where are the cameras? I'm not laughing, damn it!

"Ooh, what a shame! It seems yet another one of Kitty's playmates has decided to bail on him. Isn't that tragic? Well, since the twenty-fourth-floor challenger has surrendered, we'll have no choice but to move on," Pain narrates insufferably. **"Will someone please remove TinCanGoodness from the arena? Oh, thank you, Compassion!"**

Turning away from Pain, I watch in stunned offense as a pair of Goddess of Compassion clones literally drag the poor guy off the stage.

H—hey, that was my challenger! *Give him back, damn it—!*

"With that done, let's all welcome our next challenger to the stage! Give a big hand to AccordingToAccordion of the twenty-eighth floor, who despite his diminutive size weighs in at a level of seventy and is still somehow taller than Kitty!"

That one went over well. Lots of people cheered for that one, yessir. Not me, though. I'm too busy trying to look non-intimidating. See, so far, people have surrendered because I looked spooky scary, right? And, of course, part of my strategy so far has been to be a bit spooky scary to psych people out. But I don't need that kind of strategy if I'm fighting a chump. For chumps, I just want to beat 'em up. Easy as that.

Is it so much to ask for to be allowed a chance to actually fight in this damned tournament?

However, thankfully, this guy I'm up against might be able to pose a threat against me. Maybe. See, he looks pretty stinking cool. Guy's got the whole outfit. I'm not the type to have favorites when it comes to colors, but BLACK and yellow is such a classic combination. And with the robe and the satchels and the hat? Oh, yeah. That's a good outfit. I can't tell if he's a thunder or bee wizard, though. Only one way to find out!

"Ready, set . . . go!"

I gesture at my chest. *Come at me, bro.*

Damn, I love how serious he looks. He's not completely ice-cool, but he's far less overtly afraid than my previous opponents. Like this, I might actually get to have a good fight, and if I'm even luckier, I could get a new resistance! Mmm, bee resistance . . .

"You're quite cocky, aren't you?"

I perk an eyebrow at him. "I like to think I've got a good grasp of my own abilities and limitations." I lick my lips. "That's why I'll ask you again. *Come at me.*"

That finally gets him moving. Pulling a long, ivory stick-looking thing from his belt, he points it at me with his left hand, his fingers seemingly slipping into five specific grooves. Interesting. Dark cracks along the staff suddenly begin being filled with a webbing of light, the smell of thunder and rain spreading across the arena. Spider legs of electricity dance at the staff's tip, pointed right at me.

Huh. So no bee magic, then——

CRA—ACK!

Lightning flashes across the arena, striking me square in the chest, the sheer light of it briefly blinding the entire audience, and in the aftermath of that immense shock . . .

N?

I look down at my chest. There isn't even a mark. I touch my chest, finding it slightly hot to the touch, but otherwise completely fine. Uhh . . .

On the other side of the stage, my opponent stares at me, and then at his staff, and then at me again. "Huh?" He doesn't say this loud enough for it to be directed at me, but thanks to my senses, I can still hear him say, "The heck? Did I miss . . . ? Did the God of Speed revoke my blessing or something?"

"Is everything okay over there?" I shout across the arena.

"Sh—shut it! Just keep quiet for a moment, okay? I need to . . ." Pulling a little amulet out of a satchel, he begins praying. That's what I think he's doing, at least. In the end, the little amulet begins to shine brightly, making him sigh in relief. He turns back to me with a flourish, raising his staff again. "Prepare yourself. This time, I won't fail!"

I shrug at him. Oh, yeah, sure, cool, I'll just keep standing here and letting you shoot me with lightning. That's totally normal and not at all weird to do in a death battle. But, yeah, just let me prepare and I'll—

CRA—ACK!

Another stroke of lightning arcs across the arena, very clearly hitting me in the chest, doing absolutely nothing. No, not *nothing*.

<You have learned: Paralysis Protection Lv.6>
<You have learned: Electrocution Protection Lv.2>

Heyyy, been a while since I saw those two! Maybe I should thank him for raising them?

Nah, going by the way he's hitting the staff like an old remote, I doubt he's in the mood for compliments. Still, this is no way to conduct a proper match. "Hey, dude, if it isn't too much of a bother, how about you just surrender and we can—"

Zap!

And now he's using his right hand to shoot lightning at me. To absolutely no effect, mind you. I'm not even feeling slightly tingly, so although I'd love to drag this out to get some higher resistances, I doubt his dollar store lightning will actually grant me anything beyond what I've already gotten.

Ignoring his pathetic displays of magic, I approach him, zaps and bolts of lightning bouncing off me like water off a duck's back. With every step I take, he grows increasingly desperate, panting and trembling as he exerts every effort to keep shooting ineffective, useless spells at me.

By the time I'm standing in front of him, he's no longer able to fire off a single spell, the sound of his hare's heart echoing rapidly through the air, his breathing heavy and labored and his arms trembling. Is magic really such a physical endeavor? Apparently it is. Unfortunately, there's still a spark of fighting spirit in his eye, so to extinguish it fully, I grab both of his wrists, squeezing them hard enough to make him drop the staff and fall to his knees, though not enough to actually break them. I mean, I *could*, but it's not like he actually hurt me any, so . . .

I look down at him. "Well?" I ask. "Do you surrender *now?*"

He breathes heavily. I squeeze his wrists a little harder, feeling his bones creak threateningly. "I—I give, I give! I surrender, so, please . . ." His head falls to face the floor. "Don't . . . don't hurt me . . . !"

I wasn't going to! Well, not *grievously*, but . . .

"Another opponent surrenders within mere minutes! Kitty is on a *roll!*" Pain unhelpfully narrates from above. He grins down at me, and at the confused audience. **"For those who might not understand what you just witnessed, I can gladly tattle on the fact that dearest Kitty's divinity protection is currently at level four, meaning that no low-tier lightning magic will have any hopes of getting through. With that said, the same can't be said for ordinary weapons! So while this sad excuse of a magician drags himself out of the arena, let's welcome our next challenger, the lovely PinPrickPrecision of Hard Difficulty floor twenty-nine, with her shocking level of seventy-one!"**

Only seventy-one? Wasn't the guy I just creamed at level seventy or something? No, considering that she's only on floor twenty-nine while this guy was on floor twenty-eight, wouldn't that mean that she fought challengers from the beginning of the thirtieth floors? And she *won?*

That's . . . quite promising. But I shouldn't get my hopes up. I mean, my level is still higher than hers, so there's still a chance that she'll be a chump like the rest.

Somehow, I can't help but feel a little more excited when she comes on stage. Leather armor, chain mail, and once our eyes meet properly, she puts on a helmet, one with long ends to hide her neck. Like this, her entire body is protected, without any visible gaps. However, since she's only wearing chain mail in certain places, and since the rest is mainly protected by leather rather than actual metal, my claws can still get through.

As I'm beginning to wonder if she's supposed to be an archer or something else, she pulls a long, thin blade from her side, taking a pose that I'm pretty sure is mainly used by fencers.

No way. Am I seriously about to face off against an actual *fighter?* Someone who knows what they're doing? Someone who can match me, and more?

I feel myself tremble with excitement.

No, no, I need to control myself. Just because she's showing a little promise doesn't mean that—

"Go!"

She flies across the arena, her rapier flashing as it goes directly for my eye, an instinctual side step being the only thing to save me from a one-hit KO.

She's fast! is about all I have time to think before she draws back her blade, readying to stab again—stab what? My chest? My stomach? My neck? My face? With the helmet hiding her eyes, I can't get a grip on where she's aiming, so instead of waiting for the answer to stab me, I forge an answer for myself, refusing to back down and instead approaching her, arms raised to defend my skull while the other goes for her rapier. If I can just get it out of her hand, then—

She side-steps and swipes at my feet. I dodge it, but in the brief moment of distraction, she stabs her sword at me again, aiming for my neck. My hand moves quicker, letting her instead stab my wrist. I almost grin. See, a funny thing about how the wrist works is that the two bones comprising the wrist and arm actually cross each other when you turn your wrist. In other words, now that her blade is stuck between those two bones . . .

It's a rather simple trick to twist that wrist a hundred and eighty degrees, crossing the bones and capturing her sword.

The grip of her rapier leaps out of her hand with the force of my turning hand, its weight causing the blade itself to slip out of my arm, clattering to the floor. I stomp on it. "Well?" I ask. "What no—"

A knife I didn't notice before flashes out at my neck, but thanks to my impressive instincts, I'm able to catch it in my wrist. I look at her. She looks at me. I can't see her face through the helmet, but I can still practically taste the sheer indignation.

You know, it feels kind of cruel to do this, but . . .

Yoink!

The knife flies through the air and I grab it at the same time that she does, leading to a single breathless moment when it's just me and her, our fingers interlocked across the hilt of the knife . . . And then she uses the knife to stab me in the chest. Very rude. Since she clearly can't be trusted with weapons, I jimmy the knife out of her hand and toss it into the moat. There: disarmed.

I grin at her like a cat. "So? What now?"

No answer. Well, I'm still holding her hand, so I might as well force it out of her.

With a simple movement, I remove her helmet, before just as easily grabbing her by the neck. She's kind of heavy, but not much more than a goblin, so I'm still able to lift her up with one hand without making it too obvious that this is a strain on my musculature. "Come on," I say to her choking, gasping face. "Just a little word and you can leave without getting hurt at all. Wouldn't that be nice?"

Her eyes burn something fierce. It's seldom I see eyes as determined as these, so even as her face turns RED I can tell it won't be enough.

Without waiting for her to pass out, I toss her in the moat.

"Another bloodless victory! Has Kitty turned over a new leaf, or is he saving his claws for the big finale? Let's find out! Everyone, please welcome the Hard Difficulty floor thirty-six—Wait, hang on . . ." Pain abruptly pauses, turning away from the audience. While He's nodding and listening intently to what looks to be a firefly whispering into His ear, the audience mumbles among each other. Confusion and uncertainty seems to be the biggest reaction, not that I care. What I care about is the fact that Moleman and Rice are still cheering for me. That's all that matters.

After about half a minute, Pain turns back to us. **"Yeah, uh, it seems the next challenger has decided to throw in the towel! Unfortunate, huh? In that case, I suppose we'll move right onto the next challenger, assuming Kitty doesn't** want to take a break?" I glare up at Him. He smiles down at me. **"Thought not. In that case, let's all welcome the skilled GlintInShadow of the fortieth floor Normal Difficulty, with his stunning level of ninety-six, a whopping thirteen above that of Kitty!"** There's a pause. **"Uh, you *are* willing to fight, aren't you?"**

A ninja shows up in the arena in a puff of smoke. "Yeah," he says once the audience has calmed down a little. "I'm willing to show this beast how a *true* battle goes."

"Is that so? Wonderful! In that case, let's get right into it. Ready . . . set . . . *Go!*"

The ninja throws something at me. Ah, there's a needle in my forehead.

"That," the ninja says, "is one of the strongest poisons in all of Purgatory. It is so potent that it remains nameless, though the account of its lone surviving eater has dubbed it *Yellow Fluffylady*, in reference to its deceptively beautiful outside. Within moments, you will lose feeling in your tongue and face, and your brain will start to shut down. You are already—"

I pluck the needle from my forehead and stick it in my mouth.

Mm! I *thought* I recognized lady number two! It sure has been a while since we last met, huh?

<You have learned: Poison Protection Lv.10>
<You have learned: Poison Immunity Lv.1>

Whoa, that's new! Immunity? Is that what the next step is called? Whoa.

"What the hell did you just—"

Ignoring the ninja's insipid ramblings, I pull up my skills menu. Let's see here . . . Ah, there it is!

<[Poison Immunity (Lv.1)] Evolved version of [Poison Protection]. Grants strong immunity toward poisons and venoms. Body becomes slightly poisonous to counteract poisons as needed.>

Wait, what? Seriously? That last bit is a new clause, and I'm not sure how to feel about it. *As needed* suggests that I'm not always poisonous, but the system's skill explanations have always left a lot to be desired, so it's not like I can take it at face value. No, I'll need to test this out. And I happen to know the perfect guinea pig.

"Hey, stop ignoring me! Damn it, I'll show you . . . !"

Throwing down another smoke bomb, he uses a skill or something to approach closer, which was probably not a very good idea, because as soon as he's next to me, I simply snatch the knives out of his hands, throw them in the moat, and swipe his feet from under him, taking a page out of my former opponent's book. With him on the floor, I kneel down across his chest, shove my hand inside the stab wound I got earlier, grab a handful of tissue, and shove said handful of tissue into his loudly cursing mouth. His eyes go wide and he seems like he's about to spit or puke out what I just put in his mouth, and I can't really have that, so I lean down and force his mouth closed.

He tries to fight it, screams muffled between my fingers, and after a few seconds he passes out.

But he didn't technically *die*, and I have no idea if he got properly poisoned, so . . .

I'm just about to slice open my wrist and stick it in his slacked-open mouth when Pain calls it quits.

"Putting his enemy out of commission nonlethally, Kitty has once again won the match! It almost seems like Kitty wanted to go further, but since his enemy has indeed passed out from fear, there's no need for it. What a bold strategy, to make someone surrender simply by forcing them into becoming a cannibal! Devious as always, Kitty."

No, wait, I didn't find out if he got poisoned or not! Don't you dare—

While I'm still trying to feed him blood, two copies of the Goddess of Compassion saunter in and grab him, dragging him away with ease and leaving me to tumble off as if someone pulled the rug out from under me. How dare they steal my guinea pig? Give him back, damn it!

Ignoring me and my righteous anger, Pain continues talking. **"Now, unfortunately, it seems the next challenger has also decided to surrender. Apparently, the prospect of being forcefully fed someone's blood has a deterring effect. Who would've thought it? With that said, our next challenger is one who needs no introduction, but will get one anyway.**

"Ladies, gentlemen, and sewer creatures, I present the beloved desert flower of the America Server, the pioneer of the Hard Difficulty, former sharpshooter Olympian and current archeress, with her shocking level of one hundred five, entering on stage left: *BeatriceTheAngel!*"

The audience roars.

I turn to watch her approach.

She grins at me.

Rice

Her spurs jingle with each step, her face shadowed by the brim of her hat, yet still clearly grinning. Casual. Her posture is full of holes and openings, so many places I could attack from, but at the mental image of myself sinking my claws into her stomach, the vision of her planting an arrow straight to my forehead forcefully materializes in my brain.

But maybe if I rolled across the stage and leapt at her back, then—arrow to the skull.

What if I pretended to shake her hand and then—arrow to the skull.

If I were to attack, then—arrow to the skull.

Her eyes gleam at me, diamonds underwater. I feel a chill across my back.

She's going to kill me.

She's going to play with me, tear me apart with her bare hands, splatter my blood across the arena and pick her teeth with my bones. Death. End of the road. I see it in her eyes. Calm, clear, unafraid. Calculating the best, easiest, *most interesting* way to kill me. It's so clear. Her posture, her face, her eyes, everything radiates that one simple fact of life: *She's going to kill me.*

My breathing suddenly feels very heavy. Like her spurred boots are already pressing down across my chest, cracking ribs, stomping my lungs into nothing-ness, grinding my heart to mush. I'm scared.

I'm . . . *scared?* Me, *afraid?* Th—that's stupid! Why would I ever be afraid of *Rice*, of all people?

Her level is only a hundred and five. Twenty-five above mine or so. That's nothing. I've defeated enemies with a way higher level gap than that, probably.

But they were only animals and monsters. Not like this. Not calculated, clever, cool. *She is.*

I put my hand to my chest, trying to calm down my breathing, only to find my heart beating quickly against my fingers, sweat slipping between my pronounced ribs and the grooves of the brand. I'm not scared. I can't be scared. It's not possible. Not me.

I am *not* a coward, damn it!

But as I look up at her again, my heart, previously so quick and alive, stops beating fully. I stare, eyes wide, as she calmly draws her bow.

Wait. Has the match already begun? I—I didn't hear Pain say anything, so why is she—

But when I look up, I find Pain silent, already having said everything that needed saying. The audience is likewise silent, anticipating what's to come. Waiting, watching for my righteous demise. Execution.

My eyes flash back to face Rice. She's moving. Slowly, deliberately, she pulls an arrow from the quiver on her back. No hurry. No rush. She raises her bow, loads in the arrow, pulls it back, and points it at me. At my skull. Bull's-eye.

She takes her time. She knows I won't move. I'm as frozen in place as a cow about to be stunned. She has made me livestock, more aware than ever of the fate that awaits me, while still too docile to change it. Prey before predator. No, she isn't even that. She's playing for sport. I'm just a target.

I'm nothing.

Her hand twitches, one eye closed, and as calmly as ever, her fingers loosen their grip on the arrow and bowstring. It's like watching a master craftsman at play. Absolutely entrancing. Unlike any bowman I've seen before. And the loosened arrow begins its maiden voyage, its body swaying back and forth midair, its flight altered by the wind, but in that perfect way where the wind is not only calculated for but indeed depended on, as the arrow saunters pridefully through the air, head glinting with a cocky flourish, right at me, right at my skull, right at that little bridge between my brows, right at that one spot where I'll be killed, quickly and painlessly. *Bull's-eye.*

Ah. I'm dead, aren't I?

"*KITTY!*" someone shouts, far away, but so familiar, so close, and as the word penetrates my skull, I realize how stupid I am, how much of a damn idiot I've been—to think that this place would be my grave!

My feet are uprooted, my heart begins to beat again, and I move, instinct and rationale cooperating to make my head move, neck jerking to the right and jaw jutting out.

The arrow, flying true, is caught by my cheek instead of my skull, passing through my mouth and jaw harmlessly, only chipping a single tooth and slicing my tongue before it passes through the other cheek, leaving me and my head only slightly damaged as it flies to the boundary around the arena, harmlessly bouncing off the barrier around us. Behind the barrier, I spot Moleman in the front row, sighing in relief. I smile at him before turning back to Rice.

"Thanks," I say, rubbing the holes her arrow made in my cheeks. "I'd been considering a cheek piercing, or whatever they're called."

She smiles at me. All of that pressure is gone, replaced with a playfully innocent face and eyes that glitter with excitement. "Are you ready now, Prince?"

I spit a mouthful of blood and a chipped tooth onto the ground. "Yeah, I'm ready."

She looks up to face Pain. "Mr. Bread, would you please do a restart of the match? We weren't quite ready."

Pain smiles down at her, more obviously amused than His moon-face should be able to show. **"Oh, please, Mr. Bread was My father. But since it's a request from our dearest angel, I can't refuse. Are both sides ready?"**

She turns to me. I look up at Pain and nod resolutely.

Her smile widens a smidge. "We are."

"Great, love to hear it! With that done and over with . . . Ready, set . . . Go!"

She looks at me, a silent question shining through her crystal-clear eyes.

Want to play?

I smile at her, crouch down, and ready my claws, letting my stance speak for me.

I certainly do.

She grins, and so it begins.

Without waiting for her to start, I flash across the arena, briefly jumping into a ball to get her off guard, but when I arrive at her side, all I find is a smiling face peeking out from just beyond her drawn bow. I grin back at her, jerking my body to the right just in time to catch her arrow with my shoulder instead of my face. When I look back at the path I took to get to her, I find a trail of blood drops left from the holes in my cheeks. I see how it is.

Leaping back, I evade another arrow flying at my face with an acrobat's grace, doing a somersault for the sheer style and landing a pace or two away. As soon as my feet touch the ground, an arrow stabs into one of them, nailing it to the floor. I quirk an eyebrow at her and she pokes her tongue out teasingly.

Well, it's not my first time dancing with arrows, so I simply step off the arrow. Leaning down, I remove it from the ground to put it into my inventory, away from her.

<Alert: In accordance with the Tutournament Rules, access to the inventory has been restricted during arena combat.>

Ah, is that so? Luckily enough, I happen to know another place I can put this arrow where she won't be able to get it.

I toss the arrow into the moat.

Two down, approximately two dozen more to go. I was a bit worried that she might pull arrows from her inventory, but if she can't use it, then this becomes a lot simpler. It also means that the weapons on her person are all she has. Her bow, a quiver of two dozen or so arrows, a short sword, and a dagger. There might be something hidden under her vest or in her boots or under her hat, but I doubt it. She's not the type to keep things hidden. We're very alike in that sense.

An arrow whizzes through the air, seemingly going for my chest but instead impaling my right shoulder—again.

Apart from our fighting style, at least. Heh, I can't believe she won't even give me a break to think.

I'd better take this a bit more seriously, then.

Hunching down, I kick off the ground, running on all fours toward her, only for her to sidestep me with routine ease, not even needing a RED flag to distract me with. Blood is starting to drip generously from my various wounds, soon joined by yet another as she plants an arrow to my shin. Her strategy is as deceptively simple as my own.

I just have to get close, and then I'll win.

She just needs to disable my limbs, and then she'll win.

That's the thing here. She isn't actually trying to *kill* me. There's no fun in her outright killing me, and I'll pay her the same courtesy. This is much more fun.

It's like a high-stakes game of tag. As ridiculous as it sounds, it soon boils down to both of us just running around the stage, her shooting arrows at me, me trying to catch her and failing, splattering blood everywhere I go . . .

Within only a few minutes, the entire stage is covered in blood, my arms and legs and back are riddled with arrows, and her quiver is starting to look awfully empty.

My efforts are finally starting to pay off.

She's breathing heavily and smiling, holding her bow in one hand with her other hand resting on the hilt of her short sword. I'm also breathing heavily, though I'm not really in any place to use my right arm. I should have recognized what she was doing earlier, focusing all her efforts on my right shoulder specifically. By this point, it's almost more useful to pull it off if only to get it out of the way.

However, after close to twenty minutes of bleeding like a stuck pig, I've finally achieved what I was going for.

On the other side of the arena, Rice takes a long look around her, at the completely RED floor. Then she looks over at me. "You're pretty clever, Prince. But are you sure it'll work?"

I cackle to myself. "Oh, yeah. It'll work." If it doesn't, I'll look like a massive doofus and she'll probably laugh, which isn't too bad, now that I'm thinking about it. Either way, it's time for some Metroid action.

I practically throw myself into a ball, rolling speedily across the arena, the slippery blood beneath me acting as grease to make me go even faster. It's beyond difficult to ascertain her facial expression since the world as a whole is zooming by so fast, but I can assume that she's astonished. I mean, who wouldn't be?

Rolling in a wide arc around the circumference of the arena, I head toward her, ready to spring up and at her like a leaping hedgehog.

"You know, Prince . . ." she says, her voice ringing clearly even over the splashing of blood, "I can still see the trail of fresh blood."

Ah.

I can't see it, but I can hear the sound of her bowstring being drawn, and then the whistle of the arrow piercing the sky, and it's only by instinct that I leap up and out of the way, letting the arrow bounce out of bounds as I touch down on the floor again. Only to then realize that its slipperiness combined with my momentum has allowed me to expertly imitate a ballerina on ice, sliding and slipping and—isn't that the edge of the arena right there?

Hey, whoa, wait just a minute, I don't mind being embarrassed a little, but I can't lose like this! D—damn it, why can't my claws find grip on this damn arena—?!

My feet leave the sanctity of the arena. And for just a moment, I hang in midair. A million thoughts going through my head. None of them expressed in words. None, save for one.

Crap.

But right as my toes are about to be dipped into the moat and my last few shreds of honor forfeit, I feel something slip over my head, around my arms and chest, then suddenly tightening with all the force of a constricting boa. Suddenly no longer falling, I bump my back against the wall of the moat, where I hang loosely for a moment. I look down to find a rope snaking around me. No, not a rope, a *lasso.*

Did she—

My thoughts go no further as the rope constricts even tighter, my body being pulled up from the moat and back onto the arena. Rice looks beyond happy. These are levels of smugness no non-feline should be able to pull off.

While I'm still on the floor, she strolls up to me, spurs jingling, walking a wide arc around me to wind the rope across my chest and arms properly. Then she takes her due distance again. I'm impressed that she still manages to show a bit of caution. If I was in her place, I would've gone all-in on the foolhardy cockiness by now.

With a bit of effort, I'm able to stagger to my feet. Unfortunately, I'm not in much of a position to escape these ropes. Or to do pretty much anything, as a matter of fact. *She's caught me.*

"Well?" she says from across the arena, bow in hand. "Do you surrender?"

I give a smirk to match hers. "You should know the answer to that one, Rice."

She nods solemnly. "What a shame. I had hoped we might end this without bloodshed, though you've done plenty of that so far." Pulling the final arrow from her quiver, she loads it into her bow, pointing it right at my heart. "If you stay still, this won't hurt one bit, not that you mind." Closing one eye, she smiles. "We'll take the handshake after you wake up. See you in a few hours, Prince!"

A chill passes over my back again. Like the cold fingers of the dead, poking me, reminding me, telling me that soon I'll join them. It's only for an hour or two. When I wake up, it'll have felt like an instant, same as how all the time that passed before I was born didn't feel like anything. But in that absence when I'm dead before I'm alive, there's an infinity, one that I don't feel. One that I never want to feel again.

Ah, ah . . .

I don't want to die.

Sweat mixes with blood across my back. Behind her, sitting in the audience, I spot Moleman. I haven't had my rematch yet. I need to have my rematch with him. I can't die here. And we promised that he'd get me dinner. I need to live so I can do all of that. I can't die here. I just—

The bowstring is drawn, and the arrow flies.

On instinct, on nothing but instinct, I duck.

Thump.

Ah? There's something in my . . .

<You have learned: Brain Damage Protection Lv.3>

I turn to the left, I turn to the right, but the thing on my forehead remains in sight.

What

is

this?

Across the place, she's talking. Something about how I'm still alive. Something else about how I should stay still. Something more about how if I just stay still, it'll be over soon.

Over? Why? We're still going, aren't we?

I can still move. But I'm a bit restrained. Snakes around me, tight, holding me down. Not good.

But she's coming closer now, with a knife, which is good, a knife will be good to get out, to free me. I turn my head back and forth, watching the thing on my forehead sway. I'm like a narwhal. Should I push it through or pull it out? Push, pull, push, pull.

I fall down and roll myself into a ball and bite the ropes, gnaw gnaw gnaw gnaw, the ropes fall off. There we go. When I stand up again, she's closer, eyes like a wolf, knife in hand. The thing on my forehead looks twofold and she stands between the semi-tangible things, ready. It's a fight?

I take a step toward her but things are wrong. There's something warm and wet running down from my forehead and I lick at it. My legs are bad, there are arrows in my knee. But my right arm is the worst. It's almost gone. Just a dead weight. I don't need it anymore, so while she's approaching, I stab my left hand into my shoulder, flesh twitching around my fingers, claws gouging and slicing off muscle and tendons. I can feel my own collarbone, its sharp, broken-off edges cutting me a little. Squishy.

I saw my arm off and remove it. I hold it in my hand by the wrist, like a bludgeon. Wasn't there a comic book hero with this power? Arms falling off? Arm garde?

I experimentally swing it at her, succeeding in knocking the knife out of her hand. It goes sliding off and into the moat. Ahaha! So this was the answer all along? Arm? Clever!

Arm! Arm! Arm!

Aha? Now she brings out her sword? Very well!

Have at thee, harlot! Like this, I'm just like that one I fought before, though I can't seem to recall her face. I strike out, stepping closer, and she steps back, away. There's an odd look on her face but her face looks foggy and I can't really see it at all but her eyes are there.

I strike at her with my arm and she tries to not fight back much but her sword keeps getting stuck in the flesh, keeps chipping at the bone, and the blood splurts like confetti or maybe like candy from a pinata. I wonder if pinatas are real? I was never really invited to parties and nobody showed up for the few I had so I never saw one, is there really candy in them? I don't know!

Her face twists. Blood on her face. I see the blood. RED splattered against mist.

And she takes a bit of distance, and she raises her sword, pointing it at my chest, to stab me there and end the game early.

But I don't want that, so I hold up my arm, my upper arm, the one in my non-attached arm, and her sword goes in between the wrist bones. I grin at her because I got her and even though she doesn't understand what I'm doing, why I've got the sawed-off part of the arm in my mouth and the hand in my living hand, she understands it when I twist my hand, twist the wrist, and,

Yoink!

Gotcha, gotcha, gotcha!

The sword goes flying and then it skids across the floor and there it goes off the moat, gone, her last weapon exhausted, *gone*! Ahhh, what a shame she has no claws with which to slice and no fangs with which to bite!

For the love of all that is fair and just, I toss my arm away, letting it join her sword in the moat. See, now we're on the same level, nothing between us anymore!

One arm grabbing her shoulder, I tackle her to the ground, down into the slippery bloody mess below. Neck. Neck. Neck. Bite. Claws: rip. Jaws: tear. The nail of my one thumb scratches a deep line across her face. Now she's bleeding, too. More RED so her face isn't covered up by all the mist. Her hat is somewhere else, her hair bright and exposed, wiry and everywhere.

Bite, bite, bite, bite.

I press my face against hers to bite to rip to tear out her throat *to win* but I find myself stopped by the thing in my forehead, the butt of it pressing into *her* forehead. Ah? Ah? Ah? Weird. Push, then. Push push push. Drops of blood go down the thing on my forehead, connecting to her forehead. Streaking across her misted face. A little more and I win, a little more and I can *bite*.

I hear words. Her mouth is visible through the mist. They say,

"Prince, I'm . . . sorry"—through gritted teeth—"to have to win like a coward . . . !"

I can feel it, I can feel the head of the arrow, poking into the back of my skull, just a little bit more, and . . .

She reaches inside her vest.

The smell of sulfur, and of ashes. The smell of . . . of asphalt being laid, of heavy machinery, of work and of . . .

An old memory deep in my mind is scratched. When I was a kid, no older than six, I had a little toy revolver, with a little holster with Lucky Luke on it, and with that revolver, I had these little cartridges you could put in, so that when you pulled the trigger of the revolver, there'd be a *bang!* and it would smell like eggs and ashes, like, like . . .

Gunpowder.

Inside her vest, clipped to her chest, is a holster. From it she pulls a revolver, a crude one, a homemade one, one that smells like cast iron and smoke, and she puts it to my chest, only a little above hers, its cold nose pressing against where my heart is, and she pulls back the hammer, puts her finger on the trigger, and—

BANG!

I turn to ashes.

But before I go, I see her face, her smiling face, covered in rose petals, and although I can't hear the words, I can read her lips, mouthing,

"Good night, sweet Prince."

XI

The Winner Shares It All

I wake up by way of instantly entering a sitting position, almost throwing my covers clear off, my face flashing back and forth, memories of arrows and guns and roses crashing and tumbling through my mind like elephants on skates. Who—what—where—

Someone grabs my shoulder. "Hey, Kitty, calm down!" I turn and find Moleman looking at me. "You're okay now. The fight's over, you're alright." His soothing voice successfully brings my heart rate down from dubstep tempo to something more manageable, like a fast waltz. While I'm trying to breathe more normally, he props up a pillow behind my back, gently pushing me onto it. I lean back. "You're back at the hospital. It's been"—he quickly checks his status screen—"almost two hours." He looks back at me, his brows scrunched up in worry. "How do you feel?"

How do I . . . feel? I turn my face down to my lap. Oh, would you look at that; my arm is back. And—my fingers brush against my forehead—I no longer have a thing in my skull. So, yeah, all things considered . . . I'm not dead.

I look back at Moleman.

Not yet.

I try to muster a smile. "I'm—" His hand is warm against my shoulder, his gaze soft and his expression mild. Ah, that's right. He's my friend, isn't he? No need to lie. The smile leaves my face. "Scared. I'm scared. That's all."

"Being afraid is only to be expected," he says. Then, with a chuckle, he adds, "Still, it's a bit ironic, isn't it?"

"What is?" I ask.

"I mean, the way you were frozen stiff there at the start . . . You looked *exactly* like all your opponents did in the earlier rounds," he explains. "If that isn't ironic, I don't know what is."

I blink at him. "Oh, yeah. It *is* ironic, isn't it?" I chuckle. Yeah, that's . . . I mean, it's *all* ironic, isn't it? Here I am fretting over being killed. *Me.* Isn't that so very ironic? My chuckle soon turns into full-on laughter; from the very deepest recesses of my hollow chest, I laugh. Loud and clear, and after a few seconds of stunned silence, Moleman starts laughing too, tentatively at first, before throwing all inhibitions to the wind and joining me in full-on belly laughter, soon slapping my back as the ridiculousness of us laughing to begin with becomes the catalyst for even higher levels of laughing, the sounds of our ruckus echoing down the halls.

I have no idea how long we spend laughing, slapping each other on the back over the absurdity of it all, occasionally devolving into wheezing chuckles only to look at each other and break into teary-eyed laughter again.

But as all good things do, this does eventually end, in this case by the unwanted intervention of a nurse. Mary, I think her name was.

While we were still laughing, she suddenly poked her head in through the doorframe, and once she recovered from the slight shock of our situation, she said, quite clearly, "Excuse me, SuperMoleman . . . BeatriceTheAngel has already been waiting for over half an hour. Although she has agreed to wait for as long as needed, and although you *are* the final challenger, we encourage you to take your place in the arena as soon as possible. If you do not join within five minutes, I'm afraid we will need to forfeit your—"

"I'll be there," Moleman says once he's recovered a bit. "Just give me a moment or two longer, yeah?"

She glances at me, but only briefly enough that our eyes don't actually meet. ". . . Very well. *Five* minutes."

Moleman nods at her, and she leaves. Then he turns to me, smiles for a few seconds, and asks, "Do you still have that handkerchief I gave you?"

"Huh?" I say. "Oh, yeah, of course." As if I would ever get rid of it. "Why do you ask?" He stares at me. I blink at him. "Oh! So that's . . ." I pull the handkerchief from my inventory and deposit it in his hand. "If you wanted it, you could just ask for it, no need to be all cryptic about i—"

While I'm still talking, he presses the handkerchief against my cheek, interrupting me.

What the heck is he—

When he pulls the handkerchief back, it's a little wet. Huh? I touch my cheek. Oh, yeah. It's wet. I can't recall when that happened. As I'm thinking, Moleman wipes my other cheek too, before using a spell to clean the handkerchief. He hands it back to me. "I want you to keep it, but more than that—*use* it. Okay?"

Use it for what? What could possibly happen in these last few hours that would require the use of a handkerchief?

Not counting crying hidden by laughing, that is.

But he nudges it at me, and even though I want to point out that there's no chance I'll be able to use it before I'm gone, I accept it, slipping it back into my inventory. Maybe if I'm lucky, I might drop it as loot after my execution, so it won't be gone forever. On the other hand, I've heard that you can live for several minutes after your head gets cut off, so if I'm able to, I might be able to spend my last few moments alive removing it from my inventory. That wouldn't be so bad, I suppose.

"Well then," Moleman says, abruptly standing up from where he'd been sitting. "How about we get going? I've got a match to fight, and you've got a front seat to occupy."

Huh? Right now? Already? But . . . Okay, it's a selfish thought and I know it, but it would be nice to stay here for a little bit longer. Can't I enjoy this a bit more? But I can't say that, so I simply smile, say, "Yeah," and stand up out of bed. Then I remember that I'm naked and before either of us has time or cause to comment on it, I pull a leopard skin from my inventory, wrapping it around my midsection with expert ease. Our eyes meet. "You didn't see anything."

"Absolutely nothing."

And then we head out.

Being a real gentleman, Moleman escorts me all the way to the seat he formerly occupied. And as I take a seat, I notice with some interest that the people around me, the people he sat next to before, are actually those teammates of his. I look at them in mild bewilderment, and they meet my gaze evenly. I would have expected them to stand up and walk away—that's how people usually act when I sit next to them—but they remain. They even nod at me. As though my presence isn't an intrusion. Like I'm supposed to be here.

I don't have time to question Moleman about it before he slips away to take his place in the limelight. And now I'm sitting here, squeezed between that archer from before and Ursula. Ah. So this is the true essence of torture? Crushed awkwardly between two people who clearly don't like you? Makes sense, I suppo—

"Nice fight!" someone who must be a hallucination says. Huh? What? Where—oh, it's the . . . archer? He's talking to me? Why? And why did he say that? But instead of realizing the absurdity of what he just said in relation to *everything*, he simply grins. "I've gotta respect a man who can subdue his foes without a scrap of violence. That's a true show of power! And your tactics there at the end with that cowgirl? Sure, you didn't win or anything, but you really pushed her to the edge!"

Uhhh . . . Why is he talking to me? I look at the arena to try to catch Moleman's gaze so I can send a telepathic message asking if he put him up to this. But Moleman's busy shaking Rice's hand, so it's up to me to solve this, hopefully without bloodshed. I turn to him stiffly. "I have no idea what you're talking abou—"

Before I can finish my loss of accountability, he grabs my hand out of the air, shakes it, and says, "I'm Rat! Short for RatAttack. Dumb name, I know, but we all have our issues, don't we?"

As soon as he lets go of my hand, I pull it back, resisting the urge to hiss at him. Since he already knows my name from Moleman or Pain, I refuse his unspoken cue to introduce myself. Instead, I turn back to the arena, watching with true interest as the exciting finale begins.

After shaking hands, they both take their places on the opposite sides of the arena, eyes locked and faces set in resolute excitement.

"Since everyone down there looks ready, I believe it's about time we let this final battle take its course," Pain says grandly. **"Now, ready, set . . . *Go!*"**

Neither side moves. Then, after a moment, Rice draws her bow with all the solemn care of a funeral archer. On the other side, Moleman inexplicably undoes the clasp holding his right arm behind his back. What the heck is he doing . . . ? However, the two people on either side of me, his comrades, don't react in the slightest. No, as a matter of fact, Rat is grinning even wider, and Ursula . . . She's got a small smile resting gently on her stiff face. As I look at her in mild confusion, she meets my gaze, which makes me want to run away a bit.

She chuckles at me. "Haven't you ever seen him fight properly?"

Well, uh, I've seen him in the earlier rounds, of course. But he never needed more than one arm, so I don't see what he might accomplish by involving his unusable one.

She ignores the words I didn't speak aloud and turns back to the arena, even going so far as to point at Moleman. "Watch this, then."

Following her finger, I look back at Moleman.

Even though the match started almost a minute ago, and although Rice is actively aiming at Moleman, she still lets him continue what he's doing. It's a bit amazing that she's gotten this far despite being so chivalrous.

Fully trusting that she won't just shoot him in the heart while he's prepping, Moleman turns the straps around, affixing his arm in a weird way to where it's formed into a fist just above his heart. Then, without even the slightest hint of hurry, he opens up one of his satchels and pulls out a blue crystal orb. No, it isn't *just* a crystal orb—inside it, suspended in animation, is a single bloomed flower of some sort.

No, not *of some sort*. I know *exactly* which lady that is.

Lady 1,777.

What the heck is she doing here? And stuck in an orb, too?

Before I have the time necessary to answer all of these questions, he carefully pries open the fist of his right arm, depositing the orb within the firm cage of fingers. I wouldn't have been able to see it from a more distant seat, but as close as I am now, I can tell that the fingers of his right hand actually slip perfectly into five intricately carved grooves in the orb. And then . . .

Not much. I was expecting some awesome effects to show up, like a pair of glowing wings or a halo of light, but there's nothing like that. On the other hand, the complete lack of visual indication that anything is happening *does* grant an effect in and of itself. Namely, bewilderment.

An effect Rice doesn't seem to notice.

In fact, now that Moleman has returned his attention to her, she understands that it's time to begin. Smiling a twitch wider, she perks an eyebrow at him. He nods back at her. No words needed.

She pulls the arrow back an inch, lets the bowstring tremble, and then . . .

Fhew!

The arrow flies true, whistling through the air with pinprick precision, aimed perfectly for Moleman's heart, ready to take him out in a single strike.

Or, at least, it would have, had it not abruptly swerved out of the way to slip right over his head. The audience goes silent. For a moment, Rice stares at the path it took from behind her bow. But then a grin splits her face and she pulls another arrow from her quiver, loads it up, and in less than a second it's up and flying, flashing through the air like a bolt of lightning, only for it to once again curve around Moleman. It doesn't look real. As a matter of fact, it looks fake. If you showed me a video of this, I would've declared shenanigans.

But Rice is persistent—or maybe she just likes the way it looks—so she fires again, and again, and again, sending more and more and more of her arrows into the moat just behind Moleman. In the end, she's exhausted at least half of her supply, and Moleman hasn't even moved a single step.

Moleman raises his hand, pointing it at her. "I hope you're happy with that, because now, it's *my* turn."

Despite her not understanding a word he said, his declaration does nothing but feed the fire of her excitement.

Realizing her arrows were useless, she pulls her sword from her sheath and dashes at him, ready to close the distance and end the fight quickly. Not that Moleman lets her.

He may only be able to equip five spell rings—or whatever they're called—at a time, but he switches them out often enough that I can't keep track of them even when I try. He's got a penchant for wind magic, but he'll often switch it up with water or various miscellaneous types, just to keep on his toes.

From the very first moment of their match, there was the sense that Rice was hopelessly outmatched. Not because of any skills or in terms of pure experience, or even intelligence, but rather because of the simple fact that he outleveled her by close to thirty levels. Combined with his superior gear and a moveset that naturally beat hers, it was only a matter of time before she had to admit defeat.

Still, they had fun with it.

And throughout it all, she never once pulled her revolver. I could tell Moleman was wary of it, but in the end, it was a non-issue.

After around a quarter of an hour, it ended, as simply and politely as it had begun. Not a drop of blood was shed, and neither of them was turned to ash. Honestly, I'm not sure how I would've handled it if one of them had hurt the other. Luckily, I didn't need to find out. Instead, what I got to see was Rice surrendering while being held in a small bubble of air above the moat, Pain announcing Moleman's victory, Moleman returning Rice to solid ground, and then Rice trying to shake his right hand before correcting her mistake and extending her left hand instead.

"What a thrilling end to an exciting tournament! With that, we have our winner, and our proud second-place contestant! Now, as is customary, let's welcome up the third-place runner-up to join them on the pedestal!" Pain announces. I clap alongside everyone else, even cheering as I stand up for the obligatory standing ovation. True to His words, a pedestal has indeed appeared out of nowhere in the middle of the arena. Rice and Moleman both take their places atop it, Moleman highest, Rice second highest. As I clap along with everyone else, I can't help but wonder who the third-place contestant is. I mean, it ought to be the guy Rice beat before fighting Moleman, right? At least, I think so, but I can't be sure—

Up on the pedestal, I can see Moleman and Rice turning to me. "Kitty, what are you waiting for?" Moleman calls out. "Don't keep the audience waiting!"

Huh?

Rice soon chimes in, "Hurry, hurry! Don't you want your medal?"

What are they talking about? I'm not—

"Is Kitty absent? Here, kitty kitty kitty . . ." Pain says, peering out across the crowd until His eyes fall on me. **"Aha, there you are! Trying to skip out on the ceremony, are you? My angels, carry him here!"**

With that beyond-grandiose statement, a part of His firefly cloud suddenly departs from Him, descending on me to crowd around my form, tiny insect arms grabbing hold of me and hoisting me into the air. W—wait a moment, what the heck is happening!? L—let go of me—!

My protests unfortunately go unheard as the fireflies excitedly pull me into the air, over the moat and all the way to the arena, depositing me right in front of the pedestal. I look up with wide, uncertain eyes at Moleman and Rice. They smile at me like I'm an idiot to think I shouldn't be here. Still, they can't stop me from protesting. "I—I think there's been some sort of mista—"

Nobody lets me finish speaking, not even Moleman, as he points at me and uses literal magic to fly me into the air, setting me down on the third-place spot, right at his side.

I—I'm . . . this is . . .

I look ahead of me. There's a wall of people, cheering. Thousands of people. Standing, clapping, shouting, cheering. This is . . .

A hand touches my shoulder. When I look up, I find Moleman, smiling at me.

And I have the feeling, the overwhelming feeling, that even if all of these people had been cheering for me and not for him or her, I wouldn't have cared. They don't matter. The support of thousands means nothing compared to the pride I now see in his eyes, in the eyes of my closest friend. In fact, compared to everything else, nothing seems to matter much at all anymore.

I made him proud. That's all the happiness I need.

"Congratulations, Kitty!" Pain says, but all of a sudden He isn't all the way up there, no, He's right in front me. Holding . . . a medal? A dark, dull-colored medal that shines a rusty RED when the light hits its edges. What is He . . . ?

Looking to the right, I find a pair of other people; one I recognize as the Goddess of Compassion, and the other being . . . Will? The bartender from the other night? Well, either way, they're hanging a pair of medals on Moleman's and Rice's necks, giving them words of congratulations. I look back at Pain. He smiles at me. Oh—I'm supposed to . . .

I bow down. He hangs the medal on my neck, pats me on the shoulder, and when I straighten back out, I notice Rice and Moleman looking at me. They grin at me, holding up their medals, and I somehow muster the strength to smile back, medal in hand.

The crowd in front of us claps.

All things considered, this isn't too bad for a final memory.

A few minutes later, after everything's done and over with, we leave. I shook Rice's hand, she told me that she would be looking forward to our rematch, and I didn't have the heart to tell her that might have to wait until we meet in hell. Assuming she doesn't go to heaven, that is. Oh, but wait, we could always have a go at it in Purgatory! Ah, the joys of compromise . . .

As we leave the vomitorium for the final time, squashed on all sides by the crowd of challengers, I put my hand to the medal around my neck. "I wonder what this thing is even made of," I note absently. "I mean, Rice's medal was like blue, and yours is pink, same as her chain mail. What kind of metal is pink? Or maybe it's like an alloy or something, it *is* a pretty nice shade . . ."

"The crowd's pretty thick," Moleman says.

"Huh?" I look around us. "Oh, yeah, it is." Furrowing my brows, I look back down at my medal. "Feels kinda soft. Maybe if I bite it . . ."

"In a crowd like this, it's no wonder you escaped."

I freeze in my step. Turning to him, I say, "What's that supposed to—"

But he's smiling, not looking at me, looking straight ahead. And he says, "Not to mention the fact that while I'm super tired from that fight in the finals, you're fresh and ready. Sure, I won the tournament in the end, but a surprise attack can get the best of anyone, right?"

I blink at him.

Oh.

Oh.

I look down at the cobblestones beneath my bare feet. "You . . . you really don't have to—"

"I did my best," Moleman says with a sigh, smirking at me while still keeping his eyes straight ahead, "but, in the end, no one can beat the unkillable Kitty. At least, I think so." A teasing glance. "I won't know for sure until I have a proper rematch with him."

I turn to him, unable to keep a disbelieving chuckle off my lips. "You really are too kind, Moleman. Don't you know I'm going to be the death of you?"

He stifles a laugh. "You already have been. Now isn't it about time you get goi—"

I clock him clean across the face, fist closed, my knuckles making perfect impact with his right temple, sending him flying off his feet and crashing to the floor. While he's still on his knees I take off on all fours, shooting a quick "*Sorry, dude, it had to look real!*" behind me as I fly into and through the crowd, weaving between and through legs like a fleeing rat. At almost the exact same moment, a bunch of guards lying in wait emerge from their hiding places, trying to get hold of me. I, however, am one with the wind and cannot be stopped. Utilizing all tactics I've become proficient at, I shake off all followers, only climbing the walls of the city once I know for certain I'm no longer under attack.

And then I take off toward my dearest little hole.

Once I get there, though, I find something interesting waiting for me. Namely, a bouquet of . . . of *dog roses*, I notice now that I'm holding them. Honestly, not my favorite type of flower, but there's an accompanying card I can't ignore. Even without recognizing the handwriting, it doesn't take a wild guess to realize who sent it.

<Hi Kitty! As per our agreement, I've done you a little favor. Enjoy the peace and quiet! //Your friend and benefactor.>

The heck does that mean?

Well, in a purely literal sense, the sign outside my hole is now missing. What does this mean? What does this actually do? I have no idea. Anyhow, assuming they don't have a blood compass or something, it's unlikely I'll be found all the way out here.

So, with my escape successful, I take a seat outside the hole, and let the time pass by.

"Hey Kitty!"

I jerk out of a state I hope was meditation. Who—huh? Oh! Standing up, I wave at Moleman as he approaches on his simple bike. "What took you so long, man? I thought I was going to fall asleep!"

Stopping a pace or two away, Moleman folds out the bike's leg to park it. "Sorry, it was a bit harder than I expected to shake people off. After the first hour or so, people wanted to party, not search for some common crook, so I had to pull the old *He may have betrayed me but he's still my friend, I need to make sure he's okay* schtick, which worked."

Walking up to him, I lean down to get a better look at his bike. More specifically, at a motor-looking thing attached to the back wheel, with a wire or something leading to the left front handlebar. "What's this thing?"

"Oh, that?" Moleman says. "Well, it's just a simple little thing . . ." But I can hear the pride in his voice, so I nod at him to continue. "Heh, yeah, I met up with the guy who designed the bike originally, you know, the guy from the Africa Server? He actually didn't speak English, but he did speak Afrikaans, and I speak German, which is pretty similar, so . . . Anyway, we talked a bit, and I told him about my idea for a magic-fueled motor. I've been trying to pitch it to the various kings and nobles I've met so far, but they fear the possibility of upsetting the gods. Not this guy, though. No, heh, he was totally on board!" Smiling broadly, Moleman pats his bike. "With this, you'll be able to keep biking for hours on end without issue! Neat, huh?"

I give him a teasing look. "Nerd." But the smile on my face betrays my true feelings of admiration. "Do you really want to industrialize Purgatory that badly?"

He hums a little. "A bit, yeah. If it can save lives, then . . . absolutely."

We smile at each other for a few more seconds. Then, standing back up, I ask him, "So did you bring the goods?"

"I certainly did," Moleman says, his face turning mischievous. "And did you . . . ?"

I nod at him. "Indeed. See, there's a hill right over here, and if you climb to the top . . ." He knows exactly what I mean, and that's why I don't need to say anything else. We head to the hill, climb it to the top, and spend a few minutes squinting at the hypothetical south. "We *should* be high enough to see the fireworks. Right?"

"Probably," Moleman concurs.

I shrug. "Eh, good enough."

With the spot chosen, Moleman removes a blanket from his inventory, having me grab one side while he takes the other, letting us spread it perfectly across the ground. And then plates, and cutlery, and cups, and a pitcher of water, and all that sort of stuff . . .

As I place the plates properly, I lightly ask, "So, what was the sentence?"

"Death," Moleman replies in the same tone. He puts a bundle of grapelike fruits on a plate. "I didn't ask about the method, but they would probably have gone with beheading for the sake of simplicity."

"Mm-hm," I hum. "Public?"

"Unlikely," he replies.

He looks at me. I look back at him.

We burst out laughing. It takes a couple of minutes for us to gather our wits again, at which point my stomach is hurting and Moleman's wiping his eyes. Without waiting for him to calm down fully, I slip my handkerchief out of my inventory and hand it to him. The sight of it makes him chuckle. Once he's wiped his tears, he hands it back to me.

It's dark now, close to midnight. We take our seats, facing the hypothetical south.

"The fireworks start at midnight, right?"

"That's what Will told me," Moleman says. After a second or two, he adds, "The *God* of Will, that is."

"Yeah, yeah, I understood that," I lie. My hand hovers over the various delicious foods he brought from the party he was supposed to be the recipient of. Let's see here . . . Ah, meat! Always a classic.

"Kitty, could you show me your medal for a second?" Moleman asks.

"Hm?" I respond, mouth full of meat. "Oh, yeah, shuwe," I say, threading the medal over my head and handing it to him.

"Thanks," Moleman responds, accepting it. After a second or so, he pulls his own medal from his neck, holding it out to me. "Mind holding this for me?"

Fighting the urge to tilt my head like a dog, I accept the medal. Then I watch as Moleman without saying a single word or even looking at it threads the medal over his head. Silently imitating him, I hang the pink first-place medal around my neck.

We look across the arid wasteland and watch as the first fireworks rise into the air and burst into flowers of light.

"Oh, yeah, I forgot to tell you," Moleman says, "I finally know why you can't learn magic."

My jaw falls a little. "Seriously?"

"Yeah," Moleman says. "I asked Pain about it. Most of the other admins are kind of standoffish about this sort of stuff, all *You need to have a wish to ask Me that* and stuff, but Pain was really cool about it."

"Okay, so . . ." I lean in closer. "What's the problem?"

"Well, um . . ." Dodging the question, Moleman lunges into an overview of magic. "See, when you learn magic at first, it's kind of like doing an audition. You understand the core elements and by doing that you open yourself up to the prospect of being sponsored by the gods. We're always sponsored with our skills and stuff, but magic is granted by one god in particular. When you audition to learn magic, you might get a couple or a bunch of gods who notice you, some who have noticed you since before, and they'll do a bit of an auction over the chance to sponsor you. The winner of this bidding gets to become your sole provider of divinity, and by acting in ways that they like, you can increase your sponsorship of divinity, becoming stronger. If you're wondering, I'm actually sponsored by the God of Knowledge. He views curiosity, active learning, and a humble attitude as important."

I stare at him. "Are you saying that—"

His lips turn into a thin white line. "See, it sounds pretty bad, but—"

"Not a *single* god wants to sponsor me? Not *one*?!"

He holds up his hands placatingly. "It's a bit more complicated than that, but, uh . . . *kind of.* To begin with, sponsorship is a pretty complex deal, but your situation is even more unusual than that, so there's a lot of factors to consider . . ."

"Not a *single* one . . ." I mumble listlessly.

Moleman looks at me, looks at the fireworks in the distance, and finally decides to simply pat me on the back. "There, there, Kitty. Maybe one day you'll get to shoot lightning bolts out of your fingertips."

"One day . . ." I murmur.

We watch the fireworks. The food is eaten, we share drinks. Moleman brought a bottle of some kind of high-percentage sweet liquor, which we drink together, clinking glasses and watching as the fireworks fade over the city. Soon the bottle is almost emptied, and the sky is dark, save for the endless stars and moons. Lying down, we share the blanket, watching the clouds blotting the glittering stars.

"That's the bowman," Moleman explains, pointing out a cluster of stars. I can't tell how it's supposed to look like a bowman, but I don't question it. "And that over there is Prince Lumit, and his wife Elysia. And then the royal dog, which is chasing the twin cats . . ."

The hours pass easily.

When the hour is late and the moons stand high, painting the world in monochrome, I ask, in a voice gentle enough to hide my own uncertainty, "Do you think you're making the right choice?"

He's silent for a moment. Then he points up, at a constellation I think he called the Brothers and says, "If you set port in Ret-inn and sail toward Oulm, you'll begin with the brothers. Halfway to Oulm, one brother kills the other brother, and he disappears down the horizon. And when you reach Oulm, the second brother disappears too, replaced by the Fire King, who brought righteous fury upon the second brother for his crime." His finger trails back over to the brothers. "But . . . when you start out at Oulm, it's a different story. The king has one son, a mischievous child who frequently gets into trouble. To make him better, he sends him away across the seas, where the son has a child. This child goes on to become a great warrior, eventually returning to take his father's place as the true heir to the throne."

I feel my brows furrow. "I don't get it."

He chuckles. "Neither do I."

"So you didn't really answer my question," I theorize aloud. "It's two completely different stories. I don't . . ."

"Don't worry about it," Moleman says calmly. "This isn't for you to worry about."

Right. My gaze soars high above, to the stars, and to the brothers. I can't tell whether they look happy or sad. Why did one kill the other? Couldn't they keep being friends? Did something happen? Was he redeemed through his death, or . . . ?

There's a *ding* as a bunch of status messages suddenly roll in.

<Thank you for participating in the Tutournament!>
<Your stats are as follows: Group rank: 54th place; Solo rank: 3rd place>
<The Tutournament has now ended. Unless chosen otherwise, you will soon be returned to your lobby.>
<Would you like to remain one additional day?>
<Yes/No>

The status screen appears as an intrusion on the quiet moment, but I can't find it in me to instantly press the Yes button. Instead, I look over at Moleman, quietly reading his stats. Group tournament: fourteenth place. Solo tournament: first place. And then, below that, there's an added message that I don't have.

<Congratulations! You are eligible for a Wish. Would you like to redeem this Wish now?>
<Yes/No>

Without any hesitation, he presses No, letting the status message fade away. Then he turns to me. He smiles gently. "You should probably get going. Soon enough the leaderships will notice I'm not actually looking for you anymore, and you don't want to be around for that."

"I guess so," I answer. "But . . ."

"What is it?"

I sit up, turning to look at him. "We'll meet again, right?"

Mirroring me, he sits up as well, face confused and voice almost incredulous as he says, "Well, *of course*. Why wouldn't we?"

I blink at him. The sheer, unquestioning certainty in the way he said it makes the other words buzzing through my brain suddenly feel awfully stupid. "You know. If I were to die, or if you . . ."

"I'm not going to *die*," Moleman says as though dying was some exotic disease. "And neither are you. We'll meet again, and we'll share a meal, and that can take however long it needs to." He suddenly smiles. "What, are you thinking of going and dying on me?"

"N—no! Of course not!"

"Good. In that case, there's nothing stopping you, is there?"

Ah. He caught me. "I guess not, huh?" He pats me on the back, making the pink medal still around my neck jingle. Reminded, I grab it, saying, "You'd better take this back; if I have it, it might get sold, so—"

"Keep it," Moleman says, pushing it back onto my neck. "And I'll keep yours. If you want it back, you'll have to live to do it. Got it?"

My eyes fall to the third-place medal slung around his neck. "Alright." I look back up, straight into his eyes. "It's a promise."

He grins, shakes my hand, and says, "Promise."

After that, I say my goodbyes, press the No button, and smile as I'm transported far away from that place, all the way back to a certain RED lobby.

Well, might as well get right back to it, no?

A few days later, thanks to my staunch efforts, I finally clear the eighteenth floor. Interestingly enough, no new goblins had spawned in, so I just had to kill the one guy I missed last time. Curious. Either way, there was one clear and obvious reason that made me hesitate to clear it fully—a reason hanging proudly around my neck.

Nevertheless, I had to clear it eventually. So I did.

<**You have cleared the eighteenth floor.**>
<**You have received 1,000 points for clearing the floor. You have received an additional 1,000 points for being the first to clear the floor.**>
<**For clearing the stage completely, you will receive an additional reward.**>
<**To repay your debt, the additional reward has been traded for 5,000 points.**>
<**18 Gods have shown a positive response to you. You have obtained 18,000 points.**>

<40 Gods have shown a negative response to you. 40,000 points have been deducted.>
<To repay your debt, the floor clear reward has been traded for 1,000 points.>

And just like that, the next floor began.

FLOOR 19

THE AVARICIOUS FLAMES

XII

Don't Need No Magic

I arrive in the lobby. WHITE, WHITE, WHITE. The standard, that is.

<To repay your debt, your inventory has been sold for 32 points.>
<Current debt: 166,001 points.>

Considering what it should have sold for, that feels like a strangely small amount.

Suddenly, this silence feels a bit overwhelming. I only spent like five days constantly surrounded by people, but . . . No, not *people*. Moleman. Five days in the presence of a friend, and now I'm alone again.

Alone . . .

Something jingles.

Hm?

I touch my hand to my neck. There's a band, and something metallic. When I look down, I find Moleman's medal, still hanging there.

What? But—but *how*? And why?

<The God of Cowardice solemnly affirms that some battles cannot be won alone.>

I can't believe my eyes. Am I seriously seeing this right? No way.

The God of Cowardice has balls?!

My eyes instantly flash to my inventory.

I—it's still there.

His handkerchief. I still have it.

I pull it from my inventory, if only to make sure that it's actually there, that I'm not being pranked or something. But, no. It's here. In my hands, snug between my REDdish fingers.

The realization that my bloodied fingers might be tarnishing it almost makes me fling it away, but I'm able to keep my wits in place and simply return it to my inventory. My breathing is quick. I can . . . keep it?

I pull the medal from my neck, holding it in front of me. The pink, almost pearlescent metal glints back at me. If I put it into my inventory, it won't disappear. It won't get sold off to some divine pawnshop and melted down for two points per gram. It's mine to keep.

I . . . I don't know what to say. Or even what to do.

In the shine of the medal, I can see my own face, looking down. Splattered with RED.

For now, I suppose, I might as well put it in my inventory. I can only assume that Cowardice's protection will stay true even when I beat the next floor. If not, I know exactly how to handle such liars.

<THE GOD OF COWARDICE HESITANTLY AGREES THAT HIS PROTECTION WILL REMAIN FOR THE FORESEEABLE FUTURE.>

Is that so? Good. It better. If I find out that this was only applicable under specific circumstances, I will make him regret it.

Now, I suppose there's no reason to delay the inevitable.

Before the horrid color once again burns itself into my retinas, I cover up the WHITE with the infinitely superior RED. And then, since I've got a fair number of hours left over, I train my resistances a bit. Since most of my resistances are now at either the resistance or protection level, it's gotten fairly hard to raise them. In the absence of fun status messages, I instead work on a few other skills.

It's kind of interesting that no matter what I do, neither my claws nor my teeth can so much as make a scratch on the floor or the pillars. I've been sharpening my claws on this one specific pillar for almost the full duration of this stay and it hasn't even stopped shining. Divine protection, I suppose. Maybe if I had some *magic*, I might have been able to do something about this.

Yes, now that I think about it, having a scrap or two of magic would *absolutely* make my position more enjoyable. Heck, even just the ability to make sparks would be enough to give my brain a full rehaul, transforming me from this beastly form into something much more suitable for this divine audience, like a squirrel or something.

I repeat, a bit of magic would make me *super nice* and remove *aaaaaaall* need for flesh and gore!

I pause. The sound of silence meets me.

Ah, screw it. Damn divine bastards couldn't make the right decision if it was the only choice they had left! I bet their mothers had to babyproof the chemicals cupboard so they couldn't make themselves a world-bettering cocktail.

Still . . . Not even Want or Cowardice could be bothered to give me a bit of thunderhoney? Considering that they want me as their apostle, shouldn't they have at least a little interest in sponsoring me?

<THE GODDESS OF WANT GLANCES AT THE GOD OF COWARDICE.>
<THE GOD OF COWARDICE TUGS AT HIS COLLAR EQUIVALENT.>

Hm? What is it, Goddess of Dumb and God of Dumber? Is there something you'd like to tell your favorite defier of hell's calling?

<THE GOD OF COWARDICE DECREES THAT HE WILL ONLY EXPLAIN THE SITUATION IF HELL CHALLENGER LO FENNRICK AGREES TO NOT BE TOO MAD.>

Seriously? You want me to promise not to be angry? What are you, some kind of child?

Silence echoes across the lobby.

No answer. Should've expected as much.

However, since we've already gotten this far, I might as well, right? Who knows when this information can become vital?

So, yeah, sure. I promise I won't be mad.

<THE GOD OF COWARDICE RELUCTANTLY EXPLAINS THAT THEY HELD A VOTE REGARDING THE SUBJECT, AND THAT THE GENERAL CONSENSUS DEEMED HELL CHAL-LENGER LO FENNRICK UNFIT TO WIELD MAGIC.>

I—

You—

What!? Unfit? Unfit how!? I am perfectly fit to wield the vast unknown powers of the elements! You're telling me that I can be trusted with claws and teeth but not the ability to make a feather levitate? What is this, some sort of layman's psych evaluation? Oh, so just because I'm a bit quicker to violence than most, that makes me evil and unsuitable for your frankly pathetic spells and invocations? Is that it? Simply because of my actions on floors one through eighteen, I can't be given magic?

Well, I'll tell you what—I don't want your stupid magic anyway! Making balls of air? Shooting lightning bolts? Bah! Humbug! I didn't need it for the past eighteen floors, and I certainly won't need it for the coming eighty-two floors, either! In fact, I bet having to juggle your idiotic demands and desires would only slow me down!

So you better write this down, because I'm not saying this again. I don't need your damn—

<Floor 19 has opened. Do you want to enter?>
<Yes/No>

My hand flies out on instinct to press the Yes button, only to realize my folly and jeer out of the way, almost pressing No by accident.

I—I can't leave now, I'm still giving these divine dishrags a piece of my mind! I only need one more minute to—

<If no answer is chosen, [No] will be chosen for you and the floor may be accessed next attempt.>

Damn it, damn it, damn it . . . !

Okay, fine!

I press the Yes button, instantly finding myself transported to a place that feels about as hot as the inside of a volcano. Combined with the enemies seemingly being little salamanders of some sort, I've got my work cut out for me.

Still grumbling about magic and how I *absolutely don't need it at all whatsoever*, I set out to beat the floor.

The whole thing took around two weeks, and by the end of it, I had thoroughly grown tired of the taste of charred lizard. Or, technically, *amphibian*. And now here I stand over the corpse of some big salamander queen or whatnot, trying to discern whether her flesh is tastier than that of her children. However, her body wasn't capable of withstanding my sudden French urges, so with a final silent skin-breath, she dies.

<Queen of Magma [BOSS] (Lv.97) Defeated.>
<[Level Up]>
<You have reached Level 85.>
<Agility has increased by 2.
Strength has increased by 3.
Stamina has increased by 2.
Magic Power has increased by 1.
Burn Protection has increased by 1.
Heat Protection has increased by 1.>
<You have cleared the nineteenth floor.>
<You have received 1,000 points for clearing the floor. You have received an additional 1,000 points for being the first to clear the floor.>
<For clearing the stage completely, you will receive an additional reward.>

<To repay your debt, the additional reward has been traded for 5,000 points.>

<7 Gods have shown a positive response to you. You have obtained 7,000 points.>

<50 Gods have shown a negative response to you. 50,000 points have been deducted.>

<To repay your debt, the floor clear reward has been traded for 1,000 points.>

FLOOR 20

THE SORCERER

Helper

And just like that, I'm back in the lobby.

Now, where was I? Oh, yeah. Since your magic is dumb and useless, I have no need for it, and will therefore be—

I . . . What? Wait, who are you? Goddess of *Children?*

Now listen here, lady, I'm not one to go and tell other people their business, but . . . You *do* know who you're talking to, right? Miss *goddess of tasty treats?*

Save . . . ? Lady, are you sure you didn't get the wrong number? I don't know if you've been watching the PKP Broadcasting Network recently, but I haven't exactly been *saving* people, if you know what I'm saying. It's closer to the opposite, all things considered.

And, also . . . now that I think back on it . . . Weren't you one of the people voting against me remaining in the tutorial? Sure, I still don't know if this was for better or worse. But considering that *you* were one of the gods and goddesses trying to get me removed, I think I've got my answer.

So I guess what I'm trying to say is, *Why the heck do you think I'd go along with your wants?* Answer that one and I might consider it. Oh, and unlike you, I'm in no hurry. No, I'm actually having a pretty grand time painting these pillars, enjoying the sound of a divine dingus actually treating me respectfully for once.

<The Goddess of Children bows Her head.>
<[Please help Me.]>

I perk an eyebrow at the messages.

You *do* know I can't see you, ri—

But I can. Sitting on the floor, head bowed, is an outline. A spot not covered in blood, that shifts and moves. A WHITE silhouette placed on the floor like a shadow, at an angle that makes it look as though it's actually a person.

Her ears are long and goblinlike, her body small but still motherly in shape.

I freeze looking at it.

<[I do not wish to send other challengers. They would not survive.]>

What makes you think I can?

The silhouette doesn't move. There's a long moment of silence.

<[One of My children has fallen. I cannot save him anymore. No one can.]>

The silhouette's face rises. Eyes like sunbeams.

<[None but you.]>

You're a fool to think I can save anybody. If you send me to wherever this guy is, I'll kill him. You know that, right? You have to. You've been watching me, like a filthy voyeur.

The air around us feels stiff. Like the lobby is holding its breath.

I'm just about to say something else when it breaks the silence.

<[Yes. I know.]>

You know, so . . .

Why?

It bows its head again, eyes of shining light hidden once more.

<[Only in death may he be saved from the influence of the God of Kings.]>

The God of Kings? Is that what this is about? Wow. Can't you handle him yourself? I really don't see how a measly human could possibly help in this situation.

For a few moments, it keeps its head bowed, almost contemplating. Then it raises one clenched hand up to me, the blood on the floor shifting to account for its new position. The fist shines oddly.

<[IF YOU HELP ME, I WILL GRANT YOU A PORTION OF MY POWER.]>

For real? Seriously?

Well, why didn't you say so? A portion of your power will be a wonderful addition to my collection! Why, with this literal bribe, there's no reason for me to refuse anymore!

Not!

You can't seriously think a vague promise of *power* is enough to convince me to run into danger for your sake, right? I mean, really. And what is your power anyway? You're the Goddess of *Children*, for crying out loud! Are you going to give me the power of supersonic screaming? Hiding under tables? Ankle-biting? Fun fact: I've already got all of those!

I stare down at the silhouette. It doesn't budge.

My eyes slide down to the clenched hand, to the light held within its grip.

I lick my lips.

Well, I mean . . . I glance away. You aren't going to, like . . . change your mind or anything, right? Such as, you tell me I can only get it after I beat the floor, and then when I do you're surprised because you thought I'd die, so you retcon the whole thing by adding a clause like *Oh, sorry, you could actually only redeem this portion of My power if you did a midair twirl and sang the Danish national anthem backward. Guess it's no power for you!* Because that would honestly be—

There's a chuckle. I look around frantically, because *I* certainly didn't chuckle, but there's no one there. Who the heck . . . ?

I look back down at the silhouette. Did it just . . . ?

But before I can determine whether that little chuckle I heard was actually from the Goddess of Children, she answers me.

<[NO, I WOULD NOT BREAK SUCH A PROMISE. SHOULD YOU AGREE TO SAVE MY CHILD, I WILL GRANT YOU A PORTION OF MY POWER. THIS I SWEAR BY THE GODDESS OF HONOR.]>

No backsies?

<[NONE WHATSOEVER.]>

Well, erm, I mean . . .

I'll enter the next floor eventually, and it's not like I wouldn't be putting my life on the line anyway . . . And if the God of Kings is involved, I *might* get to eat some more grape jelly . . . And to get a portion of divine power, even if it's a little useless, might not be too bad, so . . .

I look to the left.

I look to the right.

Nobody's watching.

I look back down at the hand stretched toward me. Hesitantly, I reach for it.

Fine! I accept. But not because I actually want to help—this is purely for monetary reasons, alright?

Is it just me, or is the silhouette smiling?

The hand stretched toward me unfurls, its shining palm soon pressed against mine as our hands shake together.

<You have obtained:>
<[Innocent Adoration (Lv.MAX)]
The Goddess of Children, who watches over the young and the innocent,
has granted some of Her powers to Her potential helper.>
<Under the effects of this skill, the user will always be known, trusted, and
beloved by all nearby children and innocents.>
<[SOVEREIGN SKILL]>

Wait, what? H—hang on, I've changed my mind, I don't want the skill anymore!

Take it ba—

The world shifts harshly and the ground beneath my feet sways, catching me just before I can tumble ass over kettle. As soon as I'm able to stand upright again, the smell of ash and cinders hits me like a truck, almost sweeping me back off my feet.

Squinting, I take a look around me. This place . . . has probably seen better days.

It seems to me that just a few days ago—no, *hours* ago—this place was a small village. Like, really small. I can count a maximum of a dozen used-to-be houses, now little more than charred and smoking foundations. Still, the placement of this village is weird. Take this with a grain of salt, but I'm pretty certain that we're on top of a mountain. The view is not shy, and with the sun going down over the horizon, it's a beautiful sight, only sullied a little by the fact that I'm standing in the remains of what was once a mountain village.

However, the devastation isn't actually the most interesting thing to be found. No, I would say that the several dozen kowtowing, goblin-shaped mounds of ash and embers takes that cake. Even stranger is the fact that they aren't just placed nilly-willy, no, they're all lined up on the large road I'm standing on, facing an empty throne farther down.

That's . . . a bit odd, I'd say.

<[As per the Goddess of Children's request,]>
<Tutorial stage, Hell Difficulty Twentieth Floor: The Sorcerer>
<[Clear Condition] Reach the misguided apprentice before it's too late.>

Quite the dramatic way of putting it. And I did agree to do this, so . . .

However, I feel that there's something that needs to be said in regard to that *reward* I got.

[Innocent Adoration]? What? What the heck is this supposed to do for me? Better yet, why in the world would you give *me* of all people a skill that makes children like me? Have you not been keeping track of what I've been doing!?

I suppose rational thinking is too much to ask from these supposedly divine beings.

Ignoring the child-summoner deluxe 5000 skill, what do we have here?

Sticking my nose in the air, I take a deep breath.

Grape.

I turn back toward the empty throne. Yeah, the smell is coming from down the road. From what I can tell, the road actually continues for a while, heading into and up the mountain. And up there, just a bit ahead, I can smell my target. Alongside what I think is a pretty fair amount of blood, and . . . three, four corpses, I think? Fresh ones. Very recent.

Alright then. No need to dilly-dally, I suppose. I'm not personally in much of a hurry, so I *could* just take it easy, but the clear requirement pretty clearly states that this is a time-limited situation. Combined with the fact that my skills improve more when I'm running, I quickly go down on all fours and set out, weaving between the kowtowing mounds of goblin-shaped ash and past the empty throne of gravel and dirt, down the road and up the mountain. After some time, the road transforms into steps, which I scale on all fours with an intense amount of nostalgia. I wonder why I ever stopped climbing stairs on all fours? This is obviously superior!

As I keep running, I eventually notice a strange ringing coming from the distance, like the pealing of church bells, dinging and donging constantly without pause. The closer I get to my goal, the louder it becomes.

Running without hurry but with interest, I soon reach the end of the road.

I'm not sure whether to describe the building half-attached to the mountain face as a wizard's tower or as a church. It looks very similar to both, in terms of both height and general shape. The whole thing is mainly made with what seems to be stone, the roof formed out of what appears to be ornately shaped and carved clay. It's an interesting building. Shame it's on fire.

Yes, for as lovingly intriguing this building is, it is currently being eaten by hungry purple flames. How can fire burn something as inorganic as rock and clay? No idea! Must be magic fire. The color certainly suggests as much.

And right there, by the flaming entrance to said standing pyre, are those dead bodies I'd been smelling, suspiciously uncharred. However, despite being spared from the flames, they are even more mauled than the kowtowing corpses down in the village. Their chests are ripped open, faces twisted in horror and despair, the whole nine yards. From what I can tell, there are two goblings, maybe ten years old, and an older goblin, middle-aged at the very youngest.

Kneeling over them like a grieving widow is the one I'm probably supposed to *save*.

It's small, hardly bigger than the little bodies in front of it. With it wearing oversized robes fit for an adult, it looks even smaller than it really is. It's just a kid.

However, the positioning of the little thing is . . . *weird*. See, I know it's kneeling, and its arms are grasping at the dead bodies, but its body isn't actually turned toward the dead bodies. No, in actuality, it appears more that the body itself is facing one way, with the head facing another.

Only once it notices me do I fully understand what I'm looking at.

It flinches, jerks back and forth, and then it stands up, wobbling, its feet hidden by the vast length of the ornate robes it's wearing. Unsure of its own movement, it staggers back and forth, turning itself around to make its back face me. And there, I finally see its face. In movies, you sometimes see characters getting their necks snapped and broken, leaving their heads owlishly facing the wrong way. That's what I'm looking at here. The neck is twisted and elongated, slung around and over the shoulders, leaving the head to dangle down the back like the tail end of a scarf. The child's face is upside down as it stares at me, one eye glazed over with purple, the other wide and trembling and crying, tears streaming down its forehead.

<Tutorial stage, Hell Difficulty Twentieth Floor: Boss Stage>
<[Clear Condition] Put the misguided apprentice out of his misery.>
<Lett Ne'harr Lv.4 [BOSS]>

This is it? Level four? Seriously?

On the other hand, the last herald I fought didn't have any level at all, so I can't judge it on level alone. More importantly, this one doesn't seem to have been completely flooded quite yet. It looks—dare I say it—half-baked at best. There's something about the way it staggers toward me that feels childish, not at all like how the last herald moved. Nothing is regal about this little guy.

"M—mister, please." A hoarse, childish voice tumbles out from its upside-down lips. Its arms stretch toward me, one normal while the other's skin is cracked, long veins of purple webbing across its palm and fingers. One step closer, and then another. Tentatively, I match its pace, walking backward as it comes closer. "Please, help Father and my brothers, they—they aren't moving anymore . . ."

Is this a trick of some sort? Is the God of Kings trying to pull a bit or something to catch me off-guard?

No, he's too proud for that. This is something else.

The apprentice wipes at his eyes, not that it helps much. Hiccuping, he pauses a pace or two away. I stop as well. "P—please . . ." he says, voice trembling as badly as his form. "I don't know what's happening anymore. The man with the crown said if I shook his hand, I could become just as good as Father at magic, but now Father isn't moving, and everything hurts, and—"

He points one cracked hand at me, and I burst into flames.

<Ablaze.>

Everything goes BLACK as the fire eats my eyes, every nerve in my body screaming out in pain before being snuffed out by the flames, replaced by a cold nothingness—just like how it felt last floor when I accidentally stepped in a patch of magma. This fire is eating me a bit quicker than the normal one, but I can still think and I've got pretty good muscle movement, so for a couple of moments I remain standing, trying to ascertain the actual strength of this flame. And after a few seconds . . .

<You have learned: Burn Protection Lv.9>

Neato!

With that, I drop to the floor and start rolling back and forth, only stopping once I can no longer feel myself actively losing what little mass I have. While standing up, I carefully remove the charred things inside my eyeholes, activating moving meditation to ensure that my eyes return quickly. My nasal cavities are still in good shape, so I can tell that the apprentice hasn't moved an inch since he set me on fire, but I'd still like to have eyes.

<You have learned: Moving Meditation Lv.10>
<You have learned: Feeding Healing Lv.MAX>

Hm? What's this?

While my eyes are still recovering, focusing a part of my attention on the non-movement of the apprentice, I pull up the explanation of whatever skill this is.

<[Feeding Healing (Lv.MAX)] Through the consumption of organic matter, the body may be healed to the same mass as what was consumed. Healing may be focused to any specific part or spread across the whole body.>

Huh. So if you're saying what I think you're saying . . .

I take a bite of my arm, burnt and charred skin going crunch-crunch-crunch between my molars, and with a chew and a swallow . . .

After only a few seconds, my vision is back. I only got enough to heal one eye, but this is still insanely overpowered. To be completely clear, with this skill, if I get a broken arm, I could literally heal it by eating it and regrowing the entire thing in a matter of minutes. Well, eating an entire arm might take a little longer, but still!

This is . . . *really* powerful.

With my eye healed, I look back at the apprentice. He's standing in the same place as before, clutching his arm to what's technically his back. More interestingly, though, despite the fact that I no longer have skin and just committed an act of auto-cannibalism, he doesn't look afraid in the least. He looks scared, sure, but when he looks at me, there's an impression of clarity in his eyes, no confusion whatsoever.

Is he stupid or something? Doesn't he know what I'm going to do to him?

I step closer to him, eye set on his face. Soon, I'm close enough to touch him, or to maul him, or to dissect and eat him alive. But he still has that look on his face. A weird, strange look that I think I've only really seen on Moleman.

It doesn't leave his face even when my claws grab hold of his head and pull him off the ground, his feet dangling and his neck making crunchy noises. Grabbing a proper hold of his head, I twist it around until it's the right way up. But he's still giving me that weird look. Not to mention that he hasn't moved even a little since I picked it up.

Squinting at him, I finally say, "You're awfully okay with what I'm doing to you."

He blinks at me, tears in one eye, purple goop in the other. But the look in his clear eye doesn't shift. "For some reason, it just . . . I can tell you're here to help, mister, so . . ." A smile. A knowing, trusting, loving smile. "Please. Help me."

I almost throw the thing away. It's weird. It's wrong. *Don't ask me for that. I can't save you—I can't save* anyone. *Please stop expecting things from me that I can't give you.*

But I can't bring myself to drop him. I can't even bring myself to behead him like I was going to.

Instead, I just grumble a couple of curses a child really shouldn't hear and lean in closer to his face, or, more specifically, to his eye. "Keep still," I growl at him. Painfully enough, he does exactly that, exerting a clear effort to keep himself from trembling. He thinks I can save him. He thinks I can fix this—this . . . *eye*. I'm looking at it. It's purple and smells like grape. It feels oddly familiar, almost magnetic, and not just because I've seen people with eyes like this before. The inside is kind of muddy, so I can see my own reflection. My face is just one big mass of RED and BLACK, all surrounding a single yellow eye.

I lean back out. Yeah, no, there's no way of fixing this. None that I can think of, at least. There's just no way. It's like the Goddess of Children said—all there is to be done is to put him out of his misery.

"Am I . . ." He looks up at me, trying so hard not to quiver. "Am I going to be okay . . . ?"

I look away from him. Down there, away from the burning church, is a ledge. A cliff. Still holding him, I walk toward the ledge. As I approach, I find that it overlooks a massive drop, easily several hundred meters high. From this height, he'll die instantly. No pain. Gone before he even has time to be afraid.

Turning my face back to the apprentice, I see him looking out over the ledge, across the nearby mountaintops and the carpet of trees, through the snaking rivers and all the way to where the sun is still setting, painting the clouds in yellow and pink. Normally, goblins like him wouldn't dare remove their eyes from me. They treat me like I'm a tiger of some sort, waiting for them to turn their heads so I can attack unseen. But this kid . . . I wonder if that thought crossed his mind for even a second? That I might be here to kill him, and not to save him?

Nobody can save him now. I don't know how long it'll take until he becomes a full herald, but . . .

If you look at it from a logical perspective, I'll get more purple goop from a fully formed herald than a half-transformed one, right? Yeah. So there's no hurry.

I sit down, dangling my feet over the ledge, keeping the apprentice on my lap. This way, the second he transforms fully, I can kill him, or drop him, or anything else like that.

For now, though, I guess we'll just watch the sunset a bit longer.

The apprentice trembles in my arms. "I'm scared, mister," he says quietly. I pat his back. "My eye feels cold, and—and my chest, too." He pauses for a moment. With my eyes on the sunset, I can't see his face. "Father is dead, isn't he? . . . And—and Luvid, and Gyem, too." His back shivers. "*I killed them.*" That last part comes out like a whisper, still holding all the emotion of a mourning cry. "They're dead because of me, because I trusted the crown man, because I wanted to show that I could do magic, too. All because of me, the village . . . !"

"Hey," I say, flicking the kid on the head. "Shut up, man. What the heck are you even talking about?"

He rubs his head. "S—sorry, mister. I just . . ."

"If you're going to be angry, be angry at the right person—ergo, the dumb idiot god who decided that a tiny kid like you would be best for making a herald out of. I mean, why not grab an actual adult? So dumb," I grumble.

For a few seconds, he just stares at me, eyes wide and glittering. Then he looks back at the twilight. "Thanks, mister. And thanks for being here, too. I'm scared, but . . ." It's faint, but I'm pretty sure I can hear the way his small mouth quirks into a smile. "Now that you're here, I feel calm. I can just tell that every-thing's going to be okay."

I almost tell him. I want to tell him, if only because not telling him makes my heart ache like I'm about to choke on words unsaid. But I can't. The aching in my heart has made my throat thick and stuffy and now nothing will come out. Trying to keep my eyes on the sunset and nothing else, I press him closer to my chest, his face squeezing against my bare breast.

Thump. Thump thump.

Something's weird.

Something feels very, very off.

I push him away a little, and it's gone. That oddly magnetic feeling is gone, replaced by his vaguely confused face. But his right eye, the purple one . . . It's no longer as foggy. That . . . that *has* to be a hallucination or something. It can't be that—

A sudden desperation claws hold of me and I press the apprentice against my chest again, squeezing him as close to my heart as I can without hurting him.

Thump thump, thump thump, thump thump.

I can feel my heart, beating rhythmically through both of us. Gently, as gen-tly as I can, I take hold of his right hand, the cracked one. With eyes as wide as saucers, I watch as the purple retreats from within the cracks, slowly leaving his hand fully. I put my hand on his back again, pressing him closer. My breathing is quick, chest rising and falling against him.

What is this? What is happening?

I hug him close to me. As close as I possibly can. Closer than I've ever hugged anyone.

Across the horizon, the sun finally breathes its last, falling below the horizon, leaving the light to scatter endlessly before fading away.

<SHARD OF DIVINITY CONSUMED.>

The instant I receive the message I grab him, pushing him away from my chest. His eye is normal. He's looking at me. He smiles at me. But his neck—

<[THANK YOU.]>

A hand reaches out from right next to me. I want to scramble away in fear—it would be the most normal reaction—but I can't. If I move hastily now, we'll both go tumbling off the cliff. Instead, I simply turn, only now seeing the person beside me. No, *goblin*.

If that's what she is.

She smiles at me, the edges of her eyes wrinkling in joy and mirth. She looks old. Adult. Motherly. But she's also crying. She's smiling in bottomless relief, but she's crying. I don't understand what I'm looking at. She doesn't smell like anything, but she looks perfectly ordinary. I've met countless goblin women who look like this.

Her aged hands reach out toward the apprentice.

<[MAY I HOLD HIM?]>

My gaze hops restlessly between the message and her face. Too stunned to do anything else, I hand the apprentice to her. She takes him in both arms, and I watch perplexed as even more arms appear, inexplicably normal-looking, and gently take hold of his head and neck. And with a little tinkering, and a tiny crack . . .

His eyes open again. His neck is okay. He's okay. There's nothing wrong with him anymore. He's alive, and he's fine, and . . .

And I saved him.

His eyes are wide and surprised, but with the way she's holding him and looking at him . . . Any fear instantly melts from his form. He knows that he's in the arms of someone who loves him, and so he has no need to be scared. Looking up at her, he says, "I—"

She shushes him, one finger to his lips.

<[YOU'RE ALRIGHT NOW, MY CHILD. REST IN MY ARMS.]>

He doesn't question it for a single second. With that simple command, his eyes flutter shut, and he slips into a deep but easy sleep.

She turns to me, smile unwavering, eyes like beams of sunlight.

My trembling eyes move between her and the boy. "Is—is he . . . ?"

<[THANKS TO YOU, HE IS SAVED. HE WILL BE OKAY, EVENTUALLY. BUT FOR NOW, HE
NEEDS TO REST.]>

Her smile widens a hair, and still holding him in her arms, she bows.

<[YOU HAVE DONE ME A FAVOR I CANNOT REPAY. FROM THE BOTTOM OF MY SOUL, I THANK YOU.]>

I, well, uh . . . Really, I only did what I promised, so . . .

Righting again, she speaks once more, her face set in a grave but gentle expression.

<[I DOUBT YOU WILL FORGIVE ME AS YOU HAVE EVERY RIGHT NOT TO, HOWEVER, I WILL STILL EXTEND MY APOLOGIES. FOR WHAT YOU HAVE DONE TODAY, HENCE-FORTH, I WILL SUPPORT YOU TO THE BEST OF MY ABILITIES.]>

That's really not necessary, I've been doing perfectly fine on my own, so there's truly no reason to—

She smiles again. What is it with gods and enigmatic smiling? Don't they have any better ways to use their faces?

<[I WISH YOU LUCK IN YOUR FUTURE ENDEAVORS, KITTY.]>
<[I WILL NOT FORGET MY DEBT TO YOU.]>

And just like that, she's gone, taking the apprentice with her.

What the heck just happened?

<You have cleared the twentieth floor.>
<You have received 1,000 points for clearing the floor. You have received an additional 1,000 points for being the first to clear the floor.>
<For clearing the stage completely, you will receive an additional reward.>
<To repay your debt, the additional reward has been traded for 5,000 points.>
<54 Gods have shown a positive response to you. You have obtained 54,000 points.>
<6 Gods have shown a negative response to you. 6,000 points have been deducted.>
<To repay your debt, the floor clear reward has been traded for 1,000 points.>

Wait a minute. Freeze frame. Zoom in, enhance . . .

Fifty-four?!

No—no. I must be imagining things. Heh, silly brain, stop making up your own ideas and things! Dumb, dumb. Okay, let's read this thing again . . .

Sold for debt, sold for debt, fifty-four gods have shown a positive response, sold for debt . . .

My gaze slides back up to the reaction part. I carefully rub my eyes.

Fifty-four.

That . . . is . . . uh . . .

<THE GODDESS OF CHILDREN HAS INVITED ALL AVAILABLE GODS TO A DELIBERA-
TION IN REGARD TO HELL CHALLENGER LO FENNRICK'S DEBT.>
<THE GODDESS OF HONOR HAS AGREED.>
<THE GOD OF DUELS HAS AGREED.>
<THE GODDESS OF COMPASSION HAS AGREED.>
<THE GOD OF ART HAS AGREED.>
<. . .>
<THE GOD OF PAIN HAS REFUSED.>

Hey, what the heck, man?

<THE GOD OF PAIN EXPLAINS HIMSELF THE FOLLOWING WAY:
[I'M BUSY, TEE-HEE!]>

Pardon me?

That's not an excuse, damn it!

<Congratulations! You have beaten the twentieth floor of the tutorial on Hell Difficulty. You are hereby invited to meet the Hell Difficulty Adminis-trator to make a request.>

Don't try to distract me with—

Oh, wait, busy as in *fulfilling my wish*?

. . . Okay, carry on, then.

<Please stand by.>

Considering the fact that I know You're right here, listening to me, there really shouldn't be any need for me to wait.

<Thank you for your patience. The Hell Difficulty Administrator will see you now.>

Patience? What patience? This is completely—

The world spins and I'm abruptly deposited in that familiar space except, no, it's quite different. It feels the same, oddly enough, but instead of being a big BLACK empty space, I'm standing in a doctor's office of some sort. Like, a fully modern hospital room, complete with papers I can't understand and various tools and—most importantly—a stretcher. One with the sandwich paper on top.

Purely by instinct, I take a seat on the bed, trying to get comfortable even though it's as stiff as wood. Hm. I wonder what the purpose of putting me in a hospital room is supposed to b—

The door to the room is slapped open and Pain literally sprints inside, His weirdly fitting doctor's coat flapping as He skids to a stop in front of me, putting the cold listening-piece of a stethoscope against my chest. What the heck is He—

Removing the piece from my chest, He affixes me with a suspicious gaze. **"You *are* Kitty, right? Say *meow meow* if you're being coerced or puppeteered by the God of Kings."**

I—I'm not—yeah, it's me! What the heck are You on about?

He squints even harder. **"I'm sorry, could you repeat that?"**

I said, it's—

My mind flashes back to what He said the last time I absorbed a shard of divinity. I look Him up and down, withholding a smirk. "Can you . . . *not* understand what I'm thinking?"

His mouth opens and then closes just as fast. **"I, erm . . ."**

My face splits into a grin. "You *can't!*"

"I can! It's just a little garbled, is all," He defends weakly.

"Oh, yeah? How many meows am I thinking?"

Woof.

He makes a funny expression. **"That was . . . *one*, I think?"**

My grin widens. "Trick question. I woofed."

"Oh, come on, don't be like that!" He says, throwing His arms in the air before crossing them and turning away from me. He huffs a little. **"Hmph. And here I was going to give you a free soul evaluation to make sure you weren't about to be forcefully made into a herald . . ."**

"Yeah, well, I didn't ask for it, so—" My jaw snaps together. Hang on. What the heck did He just say . . . ? "Uh, say, Pain . . ." I gulp. "That thing I did earlier . . . I'm sorry, okay?" He peeks over His shoulder at me. "I got carried away, so . . ."

"You mean it? You won't pull any tricks on me again?"

Sighing, I briefly consider the pros and cons of pulling tricks on a divine entity versus the possibility of being forcefully turned into a herald. In the end, there's only one unfortunate answer. Slumping down on top of the stretcher, I let a sigh of the soul leave my lips. "Yeah, I promise."

Content with my answer, He twirls back around, face once more lit in a pure grin. **"Wonderful! In that case, I'll get right on it."** And without warning, He stabs His hand into my chest.

Wh—whoa, hey! What the heck are You— .

"Let's see here," He says as He pulls my heart right out of my chest. Though, on second look, He isn't *actually* pulling out my heart, but rather what looks like a half-translucent copy of my heart, with two shards of purple crystal stabbed square into it, one of them surrounded by what looks like indigo mold. **"Yep, there it is. See these veins right here, the BLACK ones?"**

Following where he's pointing, I notice that there are indeed a couple of BLACK veins blossoming across my heart. "Uh, are those supposed to be there . . . ?"

"Oh, yes, absolutely! This is very good progress. Now, your level is a bit lacking, but with your resistances and skills, this is a very good form. Once you mature a bit more, I haven't got a doubt in My mind that you'll be mowing down the soldiers of the God of Kings with ease!" As His attention moves, He points a finger to one of the two purple shards instead. **"These two are a bit more worrying, though. You're the first case We've had of this, so I can't make any statements in complete certainty, but being one of the oldest gods in the God of Multitudes, I'm pretty certain that this isn't good.**

"See, the past two times when We've had a human like you fight and defeat a proper herald—not the little, non-sentient ones—they handed the shard of divinity to Us so that We could cleanse it properly and even put the divinity back into the system for other challengers to soak up. But you, heh . . ." His grin widens. **"You just went ahead and *ate it!*"**

I shift a little atop the sandwich paper of the stretcher, trying to ignore the feeling that I might get wrapped up at any time. "So, um, was that a bad thing, or . . . ?"

"No clue! When you did it, I couldn't believe My eyes! I was very impressed, no doubt. Especially since you didn't just die instantly from the sudden influx of divinity. I would personally place My bet on the fact that if your divinity tolerance had been even one level lower, you would've died right on the spot." He looks down at my heart, still in His hand, and I follow His gaze. **"However, as you can see here, it might still have had its effects. Not least in allowing you to draw the divinity from an incomplete herald. Not even We can do that!"**

"So it's good?"

The shrug He gives as a response certainly doesn't speak for certainty. **"As I said . . . We don't know! For now, We don't even know if you're stable. So far, the two types of divinity in here aren't exactly clashing, but that might not always be the case. There is a chance that should you ever use magic**

consciously, you might explode, or die some other horribly gruesome death.” Apparently, the look on my face is enough to make him muster a calming look. **“But We won’t allow that. You’re one of Our most promising challengers, in the purely physical aspect. What you did on this floor . . . Maybe that’ll get a few more Gods to see what I see in you? Who knows!**

“Either way, for now, I think you’ll be fine. This might not look too good, but for the time being, I’ll try to find some way of solving this—one that won’t result in you losing one or more limbs.” Smiling, He leans back out, letting go of my heart to make it slingshot back into my chest. I touch a hand to where it went in, finding the patch of skin slightly cold.

“Thanks,” I say.

He blinks down at me, briefly still. **“You’re sure you haven’t been replaced by a tallthing?”**

“Yeah, I’m sure!” I say, crossing my arms over my chest defensively. “Why do You keep asking about that? I’m the same as I’ve always been.”

He looks me up and down, face blank. **“I’m not so sure about that.”** Without waiting for me to have time to ask Him what the heck He means by that, He breaks out into a smile again, and asks, **“So, on to the wish! What is it your heart desires, my friend?”**

Well, I used to know what I was going to wish for, but now I’m a bit confused. I mean, from what He said . . . Part of the reason I can’t use magic is that they won’t let me, since it might make me explode or whatever. In that case . . . “Can you remove my magic stat?”

He blinks at me.

I make a few movements in the air. “I mean, like . . . You don’t *remove* it totally, per se, but rather relocate it into my other stats. And then when I level up in the future, I get the points in the stats that actually do something, instead of the stat that’s functionally useless for me.” I perk an eyebrow at Him. “Would that . . . be doable?”

Closing His eyes, He hums for a few seconds, rubbing His chin. Then His eyes flash back open, and He says, **“Maybe!”**

Oh, come on! Can’t I get at least *one* real answer today?

While I’m still mentally complaining about the whole deal, He slyly wiggles a finger at me. **“I didn’t say *no*, now did I?”** Hope rears in my chest for the second time in the past hour or so. W—wait, is it really possible? **“It would be a complicated process, but I believe that it might be possible. Your divinity tolerance is high enough to where it should be able to handle the leveling process and the God of Kings’s divinity, so . . .”** Mumbling to Himself, he says something like, **“Yeah, if you concentrate a portion around his semi-formed soul, and boost the potency of a few skills . . .”** Nodding to Himself, He finally reaches an answer. **“It’s doable! It won’t be instantaneous, but I think I can** squeeze it into a single day. You might feel a few of your bones shifting, but I wouldn't worry. To account for your loss of the divinity stat, I'll be making a skill that adequately contains the uses of the divinity stat without the ability to actually use the stored divinity."

"That's . . . *good*, right?"

"Yep! All in all, you get your wish, and by the next floor, you'll be able to put your heightened stats to good use," He says. Then, stretching his back, he happily says, **"Wow, that was an effective meeting! Glad I could help, and if you find yourself fighting more heralds, be they half or fully formed, don't feel scared to absorb the divinity! If things go south, I'll try to help—if I can!**

"Now, until the next time . . . Have a good one, Kitty!"

FLOOR 21

THE BLACK PITCH

Tar without the Feathers

I come to, already standing in the lobby. How long have I been here . . . ?

Not very long, apparently. Ignoring all of that—

<You have been given: Don't-Worry-About-It! Lv.MAX>

Is that . . . ?

<[Don't-Worry-About-It! Lv.MAX] Has the same defensive and Soul-forming effects as Magic Power(96). Currently loading . . . 3% Complete.>

The name's a bit on the nose, but other than that . . . This is pretty much what I asked for, I think? I mean, really, I was more or less expecting the whole thing to go a bit smoother, but this is still good, even if it wasn't at the snap of His fingers.

But with all that done, there's only one thing left to check out.

Strength: 168 (+1(32))
Stamina: 284 (+1(32))
Magic Power: N/A
Currently loading . . .
3% Complete.>

So by the end, I'll have an extra thirty-two points in each stat? Nice.

In that case, there's nothing left for me to do other than the standard. Floor needs a new coat of paint, I need to experiment with selective organ loss, and through it all, I have to not think about all of the weird things happening around me. Yes, this is how it should be. Simple and normal. It's almost calming, at this point, to have something I'm used to.

Is anyone listening? How's the deliberation going? A—about my debt, that is. I don't mind whichever way it turns out, I'm just, you know . . . curious *as to what Your answer is. That's all.*

<Automated response: Divine Deliberation regarding Hell Challenger Lo Fennrick's debt remains in progress. Please hold.>

Ah, right, yeah. I see. Yup, I get it. Totally normal, I don't mind at all, sounds perfectly good. I'm in no hurry to hear about what the status of my fifty-million-point debt is.

I glance slyly between the cut-off arm I'm munching on and the static status message.

But even after hours have passed, it still doesn't change. No updates; just a big hole where there could be an answer. That's fine, though, because there are a lot of things to be distracted by. For one, the feeding healing skill I got! It's good. Like, *really* good. If I bite off my finger, then I'll heal that finger in a snap. It isn't instantaneous, but it's fast enough to make the eating part worthwhile. More importantly, it can combine with my other healing skills seamlessly, allowing me to heal things fully without necessarily eating enough to actually heal it all in one go.

However, it's good to note that caloric mass is important. If I slice off my finger and bleed everywhere before eating the finger, that won't regenerate the lost blood. I'll still be alright thanks to my bleeding protection, but if the thing I'm eating isn't caloric enough for whatever reason, I'll need to eat more. Simple math.

My only grief right now aside from the obvious is that I want to test out the innocent adoration skill. But I can't. The reason for this is simple: there are no children here. Oh, unless I count myself.

Well, technically speaking, I'm not exactly a kid anymore. Yes, as of five days ago, I successfully became a nineteen-year-old almost-adult! I only noticed because Moleman sent me a happy birthday message, otherwise I would've been completely in the dark. It's a bit unfortunate that we couldn't celebrate properly, but it's fine.

He promised we'd share a cake next time we met, and that is enough for me.

Without much trouble aside from my obvious worry in regard to the debt situation, the time passed easily. With each hour, the stats progressed more, and after a short twenty hours, they had been converted fully, leaving me a new man, ready to take on the next floor with even greater strength than previously.

Soon enough, the time came.

<Floor 21 has opened. Do you want to enter?>
<Yes/No>

Without a shred of hesitation, I press Yes.

Only to find myself instantly dumped into liquid fire. Something burning and boiling and awkwardly sticky covers my entire body within the fraction of a second it takes me to spawn in, allowing me to experience what it must be like to get broiled on high heat, or perhaps cooked in a way-too-hot pot of soup. I try to paddle but the stuff I'm in isn't a pure liquid, nor is it thick like the mud was—no, this is far worse. It's *viscous*.

I thrash my arms and squeeze my eyes and mouth shut, but it worms its way into my nose and my ears, burning off my eyelids and lips to slip in that way, too, brushing against my teeth with such heat that it feels cold instead of hot.

<You have learned: Heat Protection Lv.9>
<You have learned: Burn Protection Lv.10>
<You have learned: Burn Immunity Lv.1>

This is . . . pretty bad, I think.

I can't even tell if I'm moving. It's like I'm trying to swim in slime, but every stroke I take just skims over the surface, leaving me in the exact same place as before.

But there's no way I'll drown in this burning sludge before I get the answer on the deliberation, right? Wouldn't that be too cruel? Not even the gods would be *that* evil. I think so, at least.

Just as I'm about to lose hope, I feel my right hand break through something, the cool air pricking my exposed, skinless muscle like needles. Revitalized, I swim harder, my other hand soon breaking through and my head and chest following suit moments later.

Pah—!

I try to take a deep breath, but with my face still covered in sludge, all I breathe in is a thick layer of mucus that had formed across my lipless mouth. I cough and gack but it hardly helps. Maybe I should rip out my throat and hope it re-forms in time? No, I'd probably die.

Instead, I stick my bony, skinless hand into my mouth and pull out the goop, only able to use three of my five fingers since two of the carpal tendons burned off. While gagging silently and kicking my legs, I toss the removed goop away, shoving two of my fingers in my mouth and biting them off to quickly regenerate one of my eyes. And what I see is . . .

<Tutorial stage, Hell Difficulty Twenty-first Floor: The Boiling Pitch>
<[Clear Condition] Reach a safe place.>

Around me, covering every direction no matter which way I look, is a sea of BLACK—of bubbling, boiling tar. I think it's tar, at least. I can't be certain, but the floor description gives me good reason to think. *Pitch black* is an expression for a reason, and here it is. The pitch.

Bubbling and boiling and churning and endless.

And as for the clear condition . . .

Safe place? So, like . . . *heaven*?

I have a sneaking suspicion that I might die on this floor. I mean, I've already lost my left foot, and my fingers are looking a bit too crispy for my liking. If things continue at this speed, I'll be dead within the hour. Hm. I had a good run, though, right? Hopefully my debt won't be dumped on Moleman or my family back on Earth. That'd be mean. Mean enough for me to return from the grave to haunt the gods for sure.

Still, I might as well try. So, hoping that my remaining digits will be enough, I begin doggy-paddling.

And after less than a minute's effort, my prayers are answered.

Something stirs in the tar. I don't like doing it, but since it might be critical, I bite off a finger to recover the hearing in one of my ears. The moment I do, the sound of screaming and hissing and shouting hits me, coming from behind me. What the heck is—

Before I have time to painfully turn myself around, something crashes into me. Or, rather, it bites a hold of my leg, mercifully dragging me high into the air and away from the burning tar. Less mercifully, this bite is powerful enough to shear through what little flesh still remains on my leg, sharp teeth scraping against bone, making my femur creak dangerously. As I'm hoisted up, I'm given a pretty good view of what exactly just made me its dinner. A sea serpent. It's covered in tar and completely eyeless, large as two semi-trucks with a head to match. But as its upper body enters the air, a number of thick, armorlike scales covering its neck pop out threateningly, like the hairs of a cat puffing up, scattering the tar it was previously covered in. Steam billows from the now-exposed flesh.

But for as interesting as this massive sea serpent is, my one eye instead falls on the large metal harpoon jimmied into its side, connected by a metal chain to a metal ship. Actually, I don't know if the boat is made of metal through-and-through. Might just be that the hull is covered in metal sheets. Either way, I have no idea what a boat could be doing out here, or what it might be doing hunting a sea serpent.

As I watch the boat, I wonder idly if the skull-on-black flag has the same meaning here as it does on Earth.

I don't have time to wonder for long, though, as the sea serpent buckles, pulling away from the boat, dragging it along as it tries to escape. With my newly made ears, I can hear well how the harpoon's chain whimpers and groans, the ship likewise trembling under the sea serpent's strength. It's only a matter of time before . . .

Ah, there it went. The chain broke off. But just as it did, another harpoon went flying, aimed right at . . . me?

The harpoon shoots at incredible speeds, skimming off the sea serpent's head like a stone skipping over the surface of a lake, gouging off a good chunk of flesh without succeeding in killing or harming it properly. The sea serpent roars in pain, releasing me from its toothy grip. Not without biting off my leg, of course. Still, a removed leg can easily be recovered by consuming a bit of conveniently placed sea serpent flesh. With my claws mostly burned off, I latch onto the sea serpent's jaw like a leech, biting as hard as I can even as it thrashes sternly.

<You have learned: Dagger Tooth Lv.10>
<You have learned: Dragon Fang Lv.1>

Hm? Hey, that's nice—

My jaws clamp off the bit of hard flesh I'm attached to in a single bite. I instantly plummet to the tar. My descent is thankfully stopped by a massive clawed flipper smashing into me, making my head reel and fill with static and nothingness. The last thing I notice is the iron hull of the ship approaching me at breakneck speeds before I crash into it.

<You have learned: Unconsciousness Protection Lv.8>
<You have learned: Coma Protection Lv.4>
<You have learned: Concussion Protection Lv.7>

And just like that, I'm gone.

FLOOR 22

THE IRON SHIP

The Evil Claw Pirates

I jolt awake, lungs burning from the fact that I'm miraculously alive. I do a quick inventory check—conscious: yep. Arms: still there. Legs: back. Ribs: in their places. All five senses: up and running.

I'm alive. I think. To ensure that I'm fully operational, I engage all five senses in turn. I can feel a blanket on top of me, and something coarse but bedlike below me. I can hear the creaking of a ship. I can taste the half-hardened tar sludge still coating the inside of my mouth. I can see nothing because my eyes are closed, but if I open them, I can see a grayish roof. And if I take a deep whiff . . .

I can smell that I'm not alone.

Jumping up, I instantly form myself into the typical spherical shape, becoming invisible at the same time as I retreat from whatever I was on top of, tumbling down onto the floor. I'm just about to retreat farther away, anywhere, when a sudden keeling of the ship makes me roll helplessly across the room to bash my face into a wall. I splatter and slide down onto the floor in a puddle.

Okay, that could've gone better. My neck feels a bit too creaky for comfort, but—

"Impressive ability. Can all humans do that?" a voice says smoothly.

My hair stands on edge and I leap back to my feet, turning around in the same movement to face whoever said that just now.

In the middle of the room, sitting on a stool next to the bed I was on top of moments ago, is an odd-looking goblin. His entire body is dark and covered in long-since-healed burns, aside from a few parts that are stained BLACK by . . . something. One of these unharmed parts is a triangular shape around his right eye, the left being nothing but a skin-covered burn. Oh, and he's got a metal hand. Which is awesome, but I'm not quick to verbalize such a compliment.

Instead, I remain where I stand, eyes trained on him. He doesn't have any weapons, but that doesn't mean he's docile. He could be a magician or something. Or he's a mimic, taking the shape of a goblin, waiting for me to let my guard down so he can bite my head off.

Smiling lightly—an expression his scar-covered face seems reluctant to make—he leans closer. "You're welcome."

"What?" I blurt out unwittingly.

His one eye widens and he barks a laugh. "Well, would you look at that? It talks! Not that I had expected anything else from a two-time crownkiller."

Crownkiller? I feel my fingers twitching. What is this? This isn't how it usually goes.

As if searching for some sort of explanation, my gaze moves about the room, registering everything I see as a clue of some sort. There's the bed and the stool next to it, the bed bolted to the floor. There's also a cupboard, a desk, a chair for said desk, and various writing supplies weighing it down. Both the floor and the furniture are made of wood, but seem to be covered in an oily varnish of some sort, giving them a vaguely green sheen. However, ignoring all of that, my eyes fall on a single detail, nailed up above the desk.

Wanted posters. At least a dozen or so. All, save for one, are for goblins. And that single one, with a bounty in a completely different currency, authenticated with the seal of three separate royal families, is for a person I happen to know very well.

Me.

The goblin in front of me calmly follows my gaze, looks over at the wall, and then looks back to me. He jerks a thumb at my poster. "That *is* you, right?"

I hesitate to answer. Maybe he wants to turn me in for the reward. Maybe he wants to kill me for it. And if he doesn't know that it's actually me, then maybe, we don't have to . . .

Before I have time to decide, he confirms it himself, nodding at my chest. "The brand gives it away." A cold sweat breaks out across my back. Ah. Is that it, then? I click my claws against each other, wondering in what order to do away with him, when he suddenly brings up both hands in quasi surrender. "Not that I'm going to turn you in, of course! Calm down, won't you?" He chuckles briefly. "You've got to be the jumpiest fellow I've ever seen. Not to mention the most *selfish*."

What's that? Why, you—

He looks back at the wall with the wanted posters, turning away from me as though he's certain I won't pounce. "Yes, if you were only a little bit less egoistic, you might have noticed the fact that it would be a bit problematic for *me* to turn you in." More confused than insulted, I look up at the wall. And right there, as obvious as a clown's nose, is a wanted poster for the goblin right in front of me.

Claw-Hand Malacoda, captain of the Evil Claw Pirates. Wanted dead or alive for seven thousand yills.

He's . . . a *pirate?*

Does that mean I'm on the iron ship that saved me earlier? They saved me *twice?*

Why?

"The name's as mentioned, but my friends call me Coda. You'll do the same, won't you?"

Considering how scrunched-up my face is, I'm surprised he looks so . . . *calm.* This is the kind of expression that would make most beasts freeze in place. But he's casual about it. Is he putting up a front, or is he actually *that* strong?

<Claw-Hand Malacoda Lv.22>

He's stronger than most goblins I've met, but not to the point where he's got anything to back any supposed arrogance. No, this is something else.

Crouched where I am, I slowly straighten out until I'm standing properly.

"And why should I call you that?"

"Impressive, a full sentence! Now, assuming you haven't got the memory of a whitefly, I believe you'll find my answer in the sentence you're replying to."

I cross my arms. I don't like tricksters, but for now, there's no reason to kill him straightaway. Might as well try to squeeze some information out of him. "I'm not your friend, though."

"*Ouch!*" he exclaims comically, clutching at his chest in mock pain. "And after we saved you and everything! First you're egoistic, and now you're cruel? Oh, this is simply too much!" Wiping imaginary tears from his one eye, he takes a deep, shaky breath. "Alright, alright. How about this, then?" He smirks. "My enemies call me Mal. Would you rather use that, *human?*"

I glance to the left and right. Ugh. What the heck is this guy? I try to distract myself by surveying the room, but it looks the same as it did before, so I'm forced to look back at him. I grit my teeth and bite out, "It's not like I'm your *enemy* either."

He blinks at me. "Is that so? Hmmm . . ." Rubbing his chin, he hums thoughtfully. "Well, I can't have you call me *A,* now can I?"

Something in me rears up at the opportunity to jab back at him. "Sure you can, *Goblin A.*"

"Goblin A? Oh, how painful! No, anything but that!" he groans melodramatically. Squirming where he sits, it takes him a few seconds to pull himself together, at which point he suddenly stands up, his leather coat flapping with the movement. "No! So it cannot be. I cannot be a mere Goblin A, and you . . ." He shakes his head, making it suddenly very obvious that his ears are actually prosthetics of some sort and not normal flesh. "You, my newly found friend, cannot be *human*. Instead, if you'll permit, I would love to hear your name."

My name? Doesn't it say on my wanted poster?

But when I look down into his eyes, I find no such jest. He's serious. He's introduced himself by the name he wants to be called, and he expects me to do the same. He expects me to be respectful.

I sigh. Then I look away from him. "Lo Fennrick," I say, after a few seconds. "But my friends . . . my friends, they call me . . ." Curious. Usually, I would feel so ashamed by this name that my ears would go RED. But now, it feels almost normal. Actually, it feels *right*. It's the truth, after all, so what's there to be ashamed of?

"Kitty." I stand with my back as straight as possible, my eyes meeting his gaze evenly. "My friends call me Kitty."

"If you'll permit me, may I call you that as well, friend?"

Damn it. I grind my teeth, but it doesn't help the fact that once I part my lips and let myself speak, what I say isn't *Why the hell would I call some random green bag of exp like you* friend? it's "Yeah. Sure, Coda."

He smiles at me, and although he's so much shorter than me, he feels as tall as any fully sized man. "That makes me happy to hear, Kitty!"

While I'm still reeling from whatever just happened, he strides past me, fearlessly showing me his vulnerable back, and puts his hand to a strange groove in the wall. He turns back to me again, grinning with obvious and alien excitement. "Well, would you like to meet the rest of the crew, friend?"

And he waits for me to answer. And against every instinct in my mind, I say, "Yeah. Okay."

His scarred face wrinkles up in joy and he presses his fingers into a specific groove, letting the door slide open. I duck to pass through it, and we're suddenly in a hallway. He walks with learned confidence and I stumble after him, a dog off the leash, more confused than anything else, watching his back as though it was a mountain.

He knew. And he still saved me. He gave me a bed, and . . .

I look down at my body. At what I'm wearing.

Clothes. Stiff, itchy, too-small clothes that restrict my movement and leave my chest mostly uncovered. But they're clothes. He would give a known criminal clothes and a bed to rest in, for . . . Why? What reason? He's a pirate, too. I know I'm hardly better than a pirate by this point, but just because I happen to be somewhat of a wanted criminal doesn't mean I can go ahead and trust any lawless scoundrel I meet willy-nilly. That's dumb. Dumb and stupid.

I shake my head as I walk. I can't trust him. I can't trust anybody, aside from a few people who are exceptions and should not be counted.

I absolutely cannot allow myself to be lulled into some sort of false sense of security. Any time now, a monster could jump out from behind a bend to attack and kill me, or to maul me, or tell me something mean, or . . .

"We're here!" Coda says cheerfully, sliding open another door, bringing us out of the darkness and into the light of the ship's deck.

A little less than a dozen gazes turn to us, and I suddenly feel myself freeze where I stand.

Ah. I forgot I kind of despise having people look at me like this.

This is . . . somewhat bad.

"Kitty's awake and fully healed!" Coda exclaims loudly to the gathered crew members. Now that I'm counting them, there are actually only twelve of them, including Coda. Can you really have an entire ship with only twelve people to operate it? Is that even possible? Either way, the average level is nineteen, which is pretty damn high. More importantly, their reaction to me is very mixed. A few are celebrating, others are neutral, and a few are looking at me as though I personally killed their puppy. Well, I say *a few*, but it's actually only one. It's just that his eyes hold all the venom of a full group. "In other words," Coda continues, "those who bet that he'd heal within a single day have won. That one person being myself. Cough it up, friends!"

Bet on *what now*?

While I'm standing here as lanky as I am confused, people reluctantly walk up to Coda, grumbling and mumbling as they hand him coins and pressed metal rods. Grinning to himself, Coda happily pulls out a pair of small satchels, depositing half in each. And then he holds out one of them to me. I blink at it. "What are you . . . ?"

"You're the one who healed, aren't you? It's only fair you get half," Coda says casually, as though this isn't one of the nicest things anyone has ever done for me. I almost reach out to grab it, only to snatch my own hand back.

"No—no, I can't. If I take that stuff, it'll disappear when I clear the floor. That's *your* money, so—"

"You're arrogant to the point of rejecting a gift given in kindness?" Coda shakes his head disapprovingly, and to pour salt in the wound, a few of the nearby pirates go so far as to mirror the movement. "We may not know each other too well, but I had thought better of you, Kitty.'

I clench my teeth. Th—this guy . . . !

"Fine!" I exclaim, snatching the little pouch from his hand. "But don't blame me when you never see this money again!"

He looks at me with an odd mixture of entertainment and confusion, though I have a feeling the latter is for show. "I didn't expect anything different. What kind of goblin would demand his gift returned?"

U—ugh . . . For some reason, this guy feels like the kind of person I can't win against no matter what I do. He reminds me of a certain other guy in that sense . . .

As I'm silently seething, he loops the band of the satchel around his finger, twirling it around and around with an infuriating smirk on his face. "And here I thought the stereotype that humans were mannerless beasts was an exaggeration."

Mannerless? Oh, I'll show you manners, alright—!

Not giving me time to test out my choke skill on him, he turns his back to me, facing the gathered crew members. "Is everyone on board with teaching our new friend Kitty some manners?" A few excited whoops ring out, feeding Coda's theatrics. "Great! Now, can someone tell me what a well-mannered goblin would say to someone who just gave them a selfless gift?" A few hands shoot up and he lets his eyes glide over them, eventually pointing out a single one. "Yes, Al?"

"You'd say *thank you*, Cap'n Coda!" the goblin named Al practically shouts.

But a few hands are still up, so Coda points to one of them and says, "Anything else you might say, Cal?"

Cal's hand falls down and he quickly shoots a sly look at Al before turning back to Coda. "If you don't like the person giving you a gift, you can refuse the gift and call them a mean name!" He looks back at Al and shows a toothy grin. "Such as *Alchino!*"

Al leaps to his feet, eyes burning, and grabs Cal by the scruff of his shirt. "The hell are you trying to say, gallbladder!?"

In return, Cal merely shrugs. "I don't see why you're getting so mad about it. Or is this about how I didn't want your old moldy rations? Gee, Al-*shit*-o, you shouldn't make the lesson all about yourself!"

I can practically see the moment when whatever was holding back Al snaps and his eyes go RED.

Coda must've seen it too, as he quickly approaches them. "Alright, that's enough, you two." One hand on Cal's chest and his claw hand against Al's shoulder, Coda lets the silence linger for just a moment before speaking again, his voice soft and sharp in equal measure. "You wouldn't want our new friend to think this is how friends treat each other, now would you?"

A flash of remorse passes over Al's face and he deflates, ears drooping down. "Yes, Cap'n Coda." Turning back to Cal, he gives the smaller goblin a stinker of a glare before lowering him back onto the deck.

Cal, in response, does as any younger sibling would and is just about to double down when a goblin next to him smacks him over the head and whisper-shouts, "Don't be an idiot, Cal."

As Cal grumbles something and Coda thanks Al, a couple of the other goblins snicker, a few throwing out jokes. However, once Coda takes his place at the head again, slapping his one hand against his thigh, the group falls quiet. "Great teaching, everyone! Now"—here he turns to me, eyes glittering—"would you like to show the class what you've learned?"

I look back at him, turn away to look at the gathered, expectant goblins, and then down at my toes. But I can't show myself as cowardly. Not here. So I turn back to him, affixing my gaze to his. The little coin purse jingles in my hands. "Thank you."

His grin is practically radiant. "You're welcome, Kitty!" He turns to the gathered goblins. "Isn't he, friends?"

"*HE IS!*" the crew exclaims as one. Almost, at least.

"And what do we tell new members of the Evil Claw Pirates?"

I blink. Huh? "Hang on a moment—"

All in unison, all ignoring my pleas: "*ONCE A CLAW, ALWAYS SCARRED!*"

"And with that," Coda says warmly, turning to me, "I welcome you to our little crew."

"But I'm not—" Gazes. So many gazes, all on me. Looking. Seeing. Expecting one answer and one alone. I clutch the little purse in my hand. "Thanks."

With the joining ceremony already done and over with, Coda took me around to greet everyone properly. Their full names were all as stupid and insane as Malacoda's, so I was beyond happy to hear that everyone had their own nicknames to make things easier. All but one, at least. Most of them introduced themselves politely enough, though a few were restrained and suspicious. None more so than Barbariccia, who not only refused to let me use his nickname but wouldn't even shake my hand. Then again, with a nickname as dumb as *Bar*, it's not like I wanted to use it anyway.

I wanted to tell Coda about how I wasn't interested in actually joining their crew, but it was impossible to get a word in while being strung along. I resolved myself to tell him later, hopefully in private.

Among those I met, Cal, Farello, and Nazzo were the most curious about me, asking me how I ended up in the jaws of a steam eel, to which my response elicited as much confusion as entertainment.

"What, you just . . . *appeared* here? Like, out of thin air?" Cal asks, his back against the railing.

"That shouldn't be possible. Goblins, not to mention tallthings, can't just appear out of nowhere. It's against the laws of reality," Farello explains analytically, the barrel he's sitting on creaking with every movement.

"Um, Farello, you probably shouldn't call him a tallthing, I've heard humans really don't like it . . ." Nazzo mumbles from his position on the floor.

"What, you're telling me that *tallthing* is as bad as calling a red *bloodskin*?"

"Honestly, it might be worse."

And here, as Farello geared up to explain why he wasn't anti-human, I felt the need to poke my head in. "What even is a tallthing?"

They turn to me. Farello seems a bit shocked that I'd even ask, shifting atop the barrel he's sitting on before explaining. "My mom used to tell me wolf stories, and this was just one of them. I think it was something like, if you leave the window open at night, then a tallthing will creep inside and eat you, and if it happens to find your skin cozy enough, then . . ." He pauses for dramatic effect, his thin lips twisting up. "It'll wear your skin and replace you!"

Really now? As I listen closely, he goes on to explain that tallthings are tall, bone-pale creatures with long, knotty manes of pure WHITE and sharp claws to skin you better.

Watching Cal and Nazzo shudder gleefully at the horrors of tallthings makes me feel weirdly melancholic.

At least, until a warm hand falls on my back and I look up from where I sit to find Coda smiling gently. "Shapeshifting by wearing someone's skin? What a useful ability!" Did he just wink at me? Yeah, he totally just winked at me.

Cal, Nazzo, and Farello share a look.

"Yeah, it *would* be pretty cool," Farello soon admits.

Cal and Nazzo nod approvingly, Cal soon adding his own thoughts. "Would be pretty cool to kidnap like some judge's kid, wear their skin, and live a life of luxury and easy choices. What do judges even do? Decide who's guilty or not? Anyone with a brain can do that!"

Nazzo leans back where he sits. "Sure, yeah, but wouldn't wearing a skin be kinda gross? It's bound to start going bad eventually."

Nodding, my arms crossed, I can do nothing but agree. "Yeah, after a few days, it starts to get pretty slimy, but then after a week or two it dries out enough to act more like a leather suit than actual skin. The *real* issue is when the joints start to dry up and moving begins to rip the suit. But if you just slit a few lines along the limbs, head, and midsection, then—"

Ah. They're looking at me oddly. It seems I may have said a bit too mu—

"And that actually works?" Farello asks, eyes shining. "Is it still usable after that?"

"Well, that's . . ." I glance away, down at the floor. "It depends on the size of the skin, but most skins usually last around a month or two. But it really differs depending on how much you use it, and for what." I can feel myself sweating a little. "Generally speaking, strenuous activity should be avoided, as well as broad movements . . ."

They're looking at me with such big, curious eyes. They want to hear more. They want me to explain. To hear what I have to say.

And I give it to them.

I tell them about my adventures with Simel, when I wore skins fairly often; about what happened when someone saw through it; about the trial and how it went. And through it all, they listened with perfect interest, only interrupting to ask me to elaborate on minor points.

It almost felt unreal, and it only ended because we were called to our stations.

I, of course, didn't have a station. Nevertheless, Farello dragged me together with him and Nazzo over to manning the sail. I helped them as well as I could, even though there was no reason for me to be there. Soon, the issue that had forced us to our stations was resolved. We returned to relaxation.

And I forgot all about telling Coda how I wasn't interested in joining the crew.

The rest of the day passed quietly. We had lunch, and I enjoyed some goblin cuisine for the first time in a while. I tried to tell Coda how I didn't need to eat, but he forced food onto me, so I really didn't have any choice. The eel stew was good, though, and when I tried to give compliments to the chef, Coda just said, "Thank you!" for some reason.

Then I was finally given a proper station. Tar duty. The other goblins pitied me for it, which I didn't understand even as I began my work: removing pieces of dried, hardened tar from the deck and railings. As I removed them, more appeared, usually quite small, sometimes fairly big and still-molten. I didn't mind it.

At dinner, they toasted me, and I toasted with them. I got really drunk, and at some of the younger members' coaxing, I wore a few of my skins, parading around to their amusement, doing theater while wearing different skins for different characters. They laughed and I laughed and I forgot to guard my back. But nobody stabbed it.

The evening concluded, night duties began, and although I insisted to Coda that I didn't need to sleep, he was adamant in preparing a hammock for me in the common sleeping room. I relented.

However, once night fell, I couldn't sleep. So I spent my first night on deck, helping those there with their duties. Barbariccia, ever the grouch, refused to let me help him keep a lookout in the drake's nest. His argument was that since I was a human, the second he turned his back, I was sure to leap at him and tear him to bits and pieces within minutes to then replace him by wearing his skin. I didn't have it in me to admit that it wouldn't even take a minute. Nevertheless, I continued my other duties.

Days passed in a similar fashion. Every day, I told myself I'd tell Coda I couldn't stay on the crew, and every day, I decided to postpone it one more day.

A week into my stay, I began to notice something. The crew didn't exactly have groups. It wasn't a matter of the twelve goblins being split into three or even two friend groups, but rather, they just . . . were all friends. It was hard to explain, but no matter how people were mixed and matched at the dinner and lunch table—which had gotten a little crowded with my addition—they always spoke as friends. Openly, friendly, happily.

And worst of all, the same happened with me.

Even if the group I was with consisted of Cir, Cocco and Nazzo, we still talked normally. Scar, Al, Cante, same kind of dynamic. Sure, different people had different friends and enemies—Nazzo and Cir were practically brothers, Scar and Dragon had a mutual, mature respect, Al and Cal couldn't be alone in the same room—but all in all, everyone liked each other enough to laugh and be friends. I even saw Barbariccia laugh once! He was in the captain's quarters with Coda late one night, sharing a glass of liquor. They seemed like very old friends then; deep down, I hoped that Coda's inviting me into the crew hadn't caused any rift in their friendship.

Without any other way to react, I had stalked on by, returning to my post in the drake's nest.

I found with some degree of horror that aside from Barbariccia, I could talk to all of the pirates. Farello liked to hear my thoughts on the wildlife in Purgatory, and how it differed from wildlife on Earth. Cante was childishly excited by the stories I told of my times on different floors in the tutorial, and how the tutorial itself worked. Cane constantly wanted to try sparring, though I far preferred forcing him to fight with his mind, engaging him in logical debates to the delight of all the younger members. I didn't get on too well with Scar, Dragon, and Cocco. They were the adult members who had been a part of an older crew before the Evil Claw Pirates were formed. From what Scar told me in between puffs of colorful smoke, he, Coda, Dragon, Cocco, and Barbariccia used to be fellow members in one of the first pirate crews to sail the black sea. Their captain had been the one who invented Ferriccia, the resin used to make wood resistant to extremely high heat, with the added bonus of ensuring that dried tar didn't stick to it. Unfortunately, because of an issue with the metal they chose to use for the hull, the ship broke and most of the crew died.

The surviving members formed a new crew, calling themselves the Evil Claws Pirates. Though once Coda was chosen as captain, he changed it to Evil Claw Pirates because it "sounded better."

Ridiculous reason, but they were cool with it, so who am I to judge?

Funnily enough, although the older members were a bit more reserved, they were oftentimes just as interested as the younger members by the hijinks I've been up to. During some of the nights, when members took turns sitting on a stool and telling stories to the rest, I was allowed to take my place and tell my own stories. Not a few gasps were uttered those evenings.

And just like that, a full month passed seamlessly.

"But I didn't *have* to run away all because of that; maybe if I'd just stayed, then . . ."

I shake my head at Nazzo. "It wasn't to be. I mean, wasn't she in love with someone else, too?"

"Yeah!" Nazzo cries bitterly, draping himself across the dining table. "Some ashy bloke down the road without so much as a roof to house his bumpy head! And all because of that . . ."

"Look, brother," Cir says, a frown hiding most of his deformed teeth, "what's important isn't *why* you chose to run away from home." Nazzo's ears twitch. "The important thing is that you feel happy where you are." He smiles. Nazzo reluctantly looks up at him. "Well? Are you?"

Nazzo turns away from him again, but only to hide a small, almost unnoticeable smile. "Yeah," he says, softly. "I am."

The admission brings a smile to my lips. "Yeah, I—"

<A CHANGE HAS BEEN MADE.>
<THE DIVINE DELIBERATION IN REGARDS TO HELL CHALLENGER LO FENNRICK'S DEBT HAS CONCLUDED.>

Wait, seriously? It took a month?! Why the heck—

"Hey, Kitty, are you okay?" Cir asks, snapping me out of it. "You look a bit . . ."

"Oh, yeah, yeah, I was just . . ." I gesture at the air. "I got a status message."

Nazzo lights up, quickly swallowing a mouthful of bread. "Whoa, for real?"

Dragon, who had quietly been listening until now, shows an expression of pleasant surprise. "Really, now?"

Leaning across the table, Nazzo tries to interact with the invisible screen that only I can see, pushing his hand through it and making the words briefly unintelligible. "Is it here? What does it say?"

I read it again. "Remember how I told you I'm indebted to the gods?"

Cir, who hadn't heard me explain this the other day, furrows his brows. "As we all are?"

"No, no, I mean—"

Nazzo quickly chimes in with a helpful explanation. "The gods don't like him!"

Stroking his chin, Cir thinks it over before smirking. "So the same as the rest of us?"

"No, it's a bit worse, because . . ."

While Nazzo tries to explain the concept of divine debt, a bunch of status messages blot my view.

<A TOTAL OF 88 GODS AND GODDESSES AGREED TO ATTEND THE FOLLOWING DELIBERATION.>

<THE GODDESS OF COMPROMISE HAS AGREED TO WITHDRAW FROM THE DIVINE DELIBERATION TO KEEP VOTES ODD.>
<THE RESULTS OF THE DIVINE DELIBERATION ARE AS FOLLOWS:>
<THE GODDESS OF CHILDREN HAS PRESENTED THE FOLLOWING SUGGESTION(S):
POINT 1. [CHALLENGER'S DEBT SHOULD BE CLEARED AND POINTS RESET TO 0.]
POINT 2. [CHALLENGER SHOULD HENCEFORTH BE EXEMPT TO THE POSSIBILITY OF BECOMING INDEBTED.]
POINT 3. [CHALLENGER SHOULD HENCEFORTH BE TREATED WITH THE SAME RESPECT AS OTHER CHALLENGERS IN REGARDS TO FOOD, HOUSING, ACCESS TO SHOP, AND PERSON.]
POINT 4. [CHALLENGER SHOULD RECEIVE 100,000 POINTS UPON CONCLUSION OF DIVINE DELIBERATION AS REIMBURSEMENT FOR PRIOR TREATMENT.]
POINT 5. [HELL DIFFICULTY CHATROOMS IN THE EUROPE SERVER SHOULD BE MADE ACCESSIBLE TO HELL DIFFICULTY CHALLENGERS IN LOBBY 1.]>

What is this? Isn't this a *lot*?
Why would she—

<FIRST ROUND OF DIVINE DELIBERATION CONCLUDED AS FOLLOWS:
POINT 1 WAS ACCEPTED 56 TO 31.
POINT 2 WAS REJECTED 42 TO 45.
POINT 3 WAS DISMISSED FOLLOWING INVESTIGATION.
POINT 4 WAS REJECTED 17 TO 70.
POINT 5 WAS REJECTED 39 TO 48.>

Well, that's . . . Um. Nice that my debt got cleared, but everything else was rejected, so I guess once I beat this floor, it's back to the sharks for me. Hooray!

<THE GODDESS OF WANT HAS PRESENTED THE FOLLOWING AMENDMENT: POINT 2A. CHALLENGER SHOULD HENCEFORTH BE EXEMPTED FROM DIVINE JUDGMENT.>
<THE GOD OF SPITE HAS PRESENTED THE FOLLOWING AMENDMENT: POINT 2B. CHALLENGER SHOULD HENCEFORTH BE EXCLUDED FROM THE GAINING OF POINTS.>
<THE GODDESS OF DRAGONS HAS PRESENTED THE FOLLOWING AMENDMENT: POINT 2C. CHALLENGER SHOULD HENCEFORTH BE REWARDED ITEMS OR SKILLS RATHER THAN POINTS DURING DIVINE JUDGMENT.>

Now hang on just a second. Why is a guy called the God of Spite allowed to have a say in this? And why isn't anybody stopping him?!

<Second round of Divine Deliberation concluded as follows:
Point 2A was accepted 52 to 35.
Point 2B was rejected 10 to 78.
Point 2C was withdrawn following discussion.>

I want to breathe a sigh of relief for point 2B being rejected, but at the same time I can't help but wonder if point 2A being accepted is a good thing or not . . .

<Following discussion, the following amendment was presented:
Point 2D Challenger will henceforth be rewarded items or skills for the clearing of floors instead of points.>

As I'm staring at the status message in front of me, I notice Farello lean close to Cir and whisper, "Hey, is Kitty . . . ?"

To which Cir responds, "Yeah, he's reading the air. No idea what it says, but it doesn't look good."

If I hadn't been as conflicted as I currently am, I might have told them that everything was okay. But I'm far from sure that that's the case, so instead I just read the messages as they drop in.

<Third round of Divine Deliberation concluded as follows: Point 2D was accepted 53 to 34.>

So, what this means is that I won't receive points anymore? Like, at all? Never ever? I don't—

<Main Deliberation has concluded. Additional suggestions are made as follows:>
<The God of Cowardice and the Goddess of Want request permission to handle a situation following the steps presented in point 6.>
<The God of Cruelty requests permission to merge the Floor 21 and 22 Clear Requirements and Floor 21 and 22 Boss Stages as per point 7A.>
<The God of Cruelty requests permission to alter the Floor 22 Clear Requirement in accordance with point 7B.>
<The God of Comedy requests permission to send Hell Challenger Lo Fennrick a gift as per point 8.>

Okay, uh-huh, yeah. Right.

Cowardice and Want are being purposefully vague, Cruelty is doing something worrying, and the God of Comedy . . . Who is this? I don't think I've ever even seen him named? The doubts I have toward him are only amplified by the fact that he appears to want to do something completely selfless for me. A gift? Well, I don't know about you, but the only gift I could ever imagine getting from a clown would be a pie in the face.

<THE ADDITIONAL SUGGESTION DELIBERATION CONCLUDED AS FOLLOWS:
POINT 6 WAS ACCEPTED 72 TO 15.
POINT 7A WAS ACCEPTED 59 TO 28.
POINT 7B WAS ACCEPTED 49 TO 38.
POINT 8 WAS ACCEPTED 44 TO 43.>

I'm not sure if that makes me happy or not. I guess I won't know until the time comes, whenever that is. All I can hope is that the close to fifty-fifty split in regard to the God of Comedy's *"gift"* was because it was so awesome that forty-three gods didn't believe me capable of handling it.

<THE DIVINE DELIBERATION HAS CONCLUDED.
THANK YOU FOR YOUR ATTENTION. THE RESULTS WILL SOON BE EXECUTED.>

I let myself breathe a sign. Okay, yeah, alright. It's over.

A hand is placed on my shoulder and I look to find Scar giving me a calm, mature smile. "Everything alright, Kitty?"

I smile back at him and nod. "Yeah, I'm fine. A bit of information overload, is all. Didn't really mean all that much, though, so now I can go back to my lu—"

<A CHANGE HAS BEEN MADE.>

<THE GOD OF CRUELTY GRINS EXPECTANTLY.>

<Tutorial stage, Hell Difficulty Twenty-second Floor: The Iron Ship>
<[Floor Clear Condition] Defeat the Evil Claw Pirates.>

XVI

I Guess I'll Stay a While

My eyes slowly move over the message.

I'm on the twenty-second floor now, huh? That explains what the God of Cruelty was on about. *This.*

A warm hand rubs my shoulder and I look to see Scar, still looking at me, his fatherly worry shining through an appropriately scarred face. "Are you sure you're alright?"

Across the table, through mouthfuls of gruel, Nazzo pipes up, "Yeah, what did the thing say? Does it say something funny?"

I look away from Nazzo and back to the status message. It's still floating there, demanding a reaction from me. Maybe it wants me to be indignant, throw a tantrum, cry and scream like a child, or even flip the table. I'm sure that's what Cruelty wants me to do, at least.

With a wave of my hand, the status screen disappears. "It was nothing," I say. "Just another hate message."

"The ones other humans send you?" Cir asks curiously. I nod at him, taking a bite of food. He hums to himself, absently breaking apart a cracker. "Amazing power, that. Sending messages across the world without the need for flapping fiend or post carrier . . . If every stupid king had that ability, there'd be a damn lot less wars going on, I'm sure of it."

Under my breath, I mutter, "I wouldn't be so certain."

As Cir resumes his musings about the use of instant messaging across continents, I pull up my status screen, quickly flipping over to the shop menu. And right up there in the corner, where it usually says something like *negative X million points*, there's nothing but a single line. *N/A.*

I don't know why I feel surprised that the whole deliberation actually made any changes.

So from now on, I can't gain any points. But I also can't lose any.

Does this mean that my inventory won't be emptied every floor? I can actually put things in there without them disappearing?

My fingers brush against the fabric of my pants pocket, feeling a small satchel of coins jingle.

Maybe this isn't too bad. One of the topics brought up in the deliberation also said that instead of receiving points, I'd get items and *skills*. The latter being the important thing to me. Considering that I've spent close to two years without needing to use points, not being able to use them isn't much of a loss. And not having to hear the gods booing me every floor isn't too bad either.

And all of this because a single goddess decided to repay a little favor. What has the world come to?

"Alright, work beckons! Let's get to it, friends!" Coda calls, as he does every day. Moving by routine instinct, I begin gathering the plates. This week, I'm on dish duty. With the way things are looking though, I'm bound to do dish duty for a good bit longer. After all, I'm the only one who can do the dishes without needing gloves.

With all the steel plates and metal cutlery and cups in hand, I head to the kitchen. I put the plates to the side while I open up the dish locker, not even wincing as a puff of four-hundred-degree smoke escapes the insulated metal box. Seems like the pots and pans are done charring, so I grab them, ignore the way my palms sizzle, carry them over to the dish pit, and refill their spot in the dish locker with the plates, cups, and cutlery. With that done, I begin the only slightly grueling work of scrubbing the pots and pans with crystal moss to remove the charred and burnt pieces of leftover food. A simple wipe-down with a dishrag ensures that they are ready to be used again for dinner. It usually takes an hour or so for the dish locker to burn everything off, so while that's going on, I head back to deck to continue tar duty.

As I intermittently scrape and sweep the deck, I absently listen to Cir and Nazzo discussing the best ways to crack open crabs. I keep sweeping, trying to hear what fantasy aspect makes their crabs different from Earth crabs. Nazzo complains about how he once got pinched by a crab while trying to go skinny-dipping, dropping his towel in the process and being made a fool of by the rest of the village youths. So they still have pincers. And since it didn't pinch off his entire toe, it's fair to assume it's normal crab size.

"How was I supposed to see it? It looked like all the other rocks!"

Rock shape, pincers, small, edible, requires opening to eat . . .

Crabs are the same here as on Earth, then. What a quaint realization. Then again, considering everything, this place has more in common with Earth than it doesn't. Both have a breathable atmosphere, enough dirt to go around, and people who will have a heated argument about whether you're supposed to eat the goop inside the crab's head or not. Ah, the wonders of life.

"What do you think, Kitty?"

I look up from where I stand, scratching my head a little before answering. "Well, the only time I've ever eaten crabs, I ate the entire thing with shell and all . . ." But I wasn't exactly in a good state of mind back then, so if they gave me a crab now, I might eat it with more manners.

Nazzo nods a bit while Cir shakes his head and grumbles about how it doesn't count.

The smaller goblin, on the other hand, is far more positive toward my primal feeding habits. "Yup, yup. Exactly! More flavor, and with the shell . . . More nutrients! My sister used to say that eating eggshells made your bones stronger, and I agree. After all, I haven't broken a bone yet!"

"She only said that to see if you'd actually do it, which you *did*. And then she didn't have the heart to tell you it wasn't true."

Arms crossed, Nazzo shows no sign of backing down. "But I haven't broken a bone yet. Unlike a certain someone." Considering the insufferable smirk on Nazzo's face, it's amazing that Cir can restrain himself from personally changing that fact.

I return to sweeping, and later that evening, I visit Coda in his room to talk.

The room is dark, mostly lit by a crystal lamp, though the moons outside are almost brighter. The floor rocks gently beneath my bare feet, as it always does. I haven't had to chew on a tripseed for almost half a month, and by now, the gentle bobbing of the ship—the *Frisky Lady*, or *Frisk* for short—feels more soothing than nauseating. While standing in the doorway, I let the rocking calm my anxious heart, my attention focused on Coda where he sits at his desk.

After a second or two, he looks up from his papers, smiling as he notices me in the darkness. "And there you are, Kitty. Silent as your namesake, and just as much of a shadow when you want to be." He stands up, walks a few steps across the room, and grabs a stool for me to sit on, bringing it over to his desk so we can sit facing each other. "Come, take a seat. I believe you said we have business to discuss?"

"Yes," I choke out. "*Business.*"

I sit down. He sits down. We stare at each other. I really want him to say something first but this meeting was called by me, so it's my responsibility to—

"Whoa!"

Startled, I jump a little. "Wh—what is it?"

He blinks at me, amusement shining in his eyes. "For a moment there, you perfectly melded with the darkness. I couldn't even tell you were there! Can all humans do that?"

"No, not really."

"I see. A shame. I would have loved to form a human hit squad to use such abilities for the betterment of the Evil Claw Pirates. With a few more yills in our purses, we could buy a new figure piece no problem!"

"I don't think a new figure piece should be our number one priority," I say warily, remembering how last night a stray bit of tar burned an unwaxed part of the sail again.

He frowns before turning away, like a reluctant toddler. "I suppose . . ." Then, with a shake of the head, he looks back at me, smile reinstated. "So! What business did you have to discuss?"

"Oh, yeah, right, it's . . ." I gulp and look down at my lap. Clothes. Pants, actually. Not the most comfortable or anything, but Coda personally altered them to be long enough for me to wear. Same as the shirt I'm wearing. I swallow down a lump again and look up at him, steeling what little spirits I have left. "It's about my membership in the Evil Claw Pirates."

He tilts his head. "What of it?"

"I'd like to join properly." I inhale sharply. "To be a real member."

His brows furrow, a pause hanging between us for several long seconds. "But you already are?"

"No, I mean, like . . ." I make a few movements in the air. "Properly. I want to actually be one of you. Not just a tag-along, until-later kind of deal." He tries to say something, so I quickly continue my piece. "Yeah, sure, you made a show of my joining the Evil Claw Pirates, but that was just for the other members, to justify my brief stay with you, so they wouldn't treat me badly. You didn't *actually* make me a real member. But . . ." A deep breath, to give myself the strength to continue speaking. My eyes are on my lap, on my balled fists. "I want to change that. I don't want to leave you guys. Not yet. Maybe . . . Maybe *never*."

When I look back up, I flinch back at the face he's making. I'm not sure when I last saw a face so worried as his. Brows pinched together, lips twisted into a slight frown, his attention fully on me. And in a small, almost grieving voice, he asks, "How long have you been feeling this way?"

"What way?"

And now it's his turn to steel himself. "That you haven't been one of us."

I blink at him. Something in my chest drops. Ah. I said something wrong. My face falls to my lap again. "I—I didn't . . ." I shake my head. That isn't right. "Never, I guess . . ."

The deep, heartfelt sigh of relief that leaves his lips rends my heart worse than a knife to the chest. "Good, that's good. I had been worried that I may have pulled you along too quickly, but when you fell into the rhythm, I could tell you enjoyed it, so I thought . . ." He shakes his head, and before I can understand what's happening, he suddenly lowers it, giving a small bow where he sits. "I'm sorry. I should have been more open with you. I simply assumed that you were happy to go along with it, and . . ."

"No, no, you don't have to apologize, it's fine, really—"

A sharp glare slits through the air and I freeze where I sit. "Please," he says. "Let me take responsibility for my actions." There is no room for argument. No possibility of disrespecting him further by refusing his apology. No way for me to disobey my captain. His eyes are clear and he raises his head, a light smile on his lips. "I'm glad to hear you'd be willing to stay, even if you didn't feel that you had full agency in your joining. Would you like us to hold a proper party to commemorate your joining us fully?"

"Ah, uh, no, that won't be needed. I just, well . . ." I can't help but smile. Honesty is a wonderful thing, isn't it? "I'm glad to hear that you're okay with me joining. I was afraid that you'd be against me being a real member, since I'm, you know . . ." A human? A murderer? A cannibal? A crownkiller? I chuckle bitterly. "*Me.*"

All he gives me is a soft smile as he reaches out and puts a hand on my shoulder. Warm. As warm as his gaze. "That's the best part about you."

And weirdly enough, if only because he's the one saying it, because my *captain* says so, I can't find it in myself to disagree.

That night, for the first time in maybe forever, I felt as though I truly belonged.

Days turn into weeks. I have it good.

For one, I get to experience my first real pillaging. It was exciting. Suddenly everyone was so serious, being fully aware that any of us could die. People seemed to know their roles, but few felt truly comfortable in them. A general rule was to leave as many people alive as possible since they were valuable hostages, though anyone with rebellious intent or actual combat power had to be dispatched swiftly. I didn't mind it in the least. A few of the younger members were hesitant to actually hurt people, but with my lack of such inhibitions, it turned out a raging success. Once we traded the hostages and grain for a few thousand yills, we went on our way, stopping at a port town to celebrate. They cheered for my first successful pillaging and I got really, really drunk. The rest of the evening was a blur, but I'm told I was very silly all night.

Of course, during these months with the pirates, I kept in contact with Moleman. He wasn't too happy with my new profession, but he was happy to hear that I felt content in being with them.

However, one thing he warned me about was that I might not want to join the upcoming Server Symposium. This was a fair thing to say, considering that I was wanted by the server leadership and would likely be executed upon capture. I agreed to stay in the Hell Lobby, until a particular change made the whole ordeal a fair bit easier.

<As per popular demand, the Administrators have decided to allow challengers the choice to abstain from the Server Symposium. Happy New Earth Year!>

<The Server Symposium has begun. Would you like to abstain?>
<Yes/No>
<If no answer is chosen, you will be automatically summoned in 4:59>

Although I wanted to join if only to meet up with Moleman a little, I decided to follow his suggestion and abstain fully. Instead, I spent New Year's Eve with the Evil Claw Pirates. When I explained that it was New Year's Eve, they didn't understand. Apparently, they have New Year's Eve on a completely different day. After an extensive discussion, connecting their date system with my own, I found out that the day they have their New Year's Eve on is June twenty-eighth. The night before my birthday. Sometimes you have to appreciate the little coincidences life throws your way.

Nevertheless, I forced them to celebrate the New Year—*human style*. In other words, we got very drunk, counted down the last ten seconds, and sat up until four in the morning playing cards and telling stories. A lot of grouchy goblins roamed the ship the next day, that's for sure.

Time passes smoothly. We pillage another ship, have a run-in with the steam eel I fought earlier, feel like Captain Ahab for all but an hour, spend our time in relaxation, tell stories, chat and argue and discuss and laugh . . . Sometimes we visit a small town at the edge of the tar sea, where we stock up on supplies and spend our pocket money in pubs and stores. Some of the older members sneak away to spend their pocket money on the girls you can find on dark street corners, but that's their business.

<Top—Status—Community>
<10:37:01 Day 824>
<The twenty-eighth attempt will begin in 25:13:12:59>

It has now been a little over nine months since I joined the Evil Claw Pirates. Today is a fine day, and going by the smell I'm picking up, it's about to get even better. "It's moving really quickly," I tell Coda. "But if we just move a little bit farther to port, we'll be able to cut it off pretty neatly."

"What features does it have?" he asks, already turning the wheel.

"Small," I say, taking a few deep breaths. "Good-quality wood. Weird metal, and the sail is . . . leather, I think? Smells like drake hide, but weird. Unsure. There seem to be twenty-seven members operating it. *Very* fancy clothes on some of them." I say that last part with a wink and a smirk. "All in all . . . Small, expensive—good target."

"I haven't had any reason to doubt your nose yet."

"And you never will."

But even though I try to appear confident, I feel just a little unsure. There's something off about the ship. Not the first time today, I wipe at my nose, sniffling a little to ensure it's actually clear, and that I'm as levelheaded as I hope to be.

Coda watches me from the side. "Is it still like that?"

"Yeah," I say unhappily. "Still smells weirdly familiar."

"And it might not just be that you've smelled the same material somewhere?"

"No, I don't think so. But I really don't know."

"Not yet, at least," Coda says calmly. "With the speed they're keeping, you're bound to know for sure in a few minutes."

In response, I nod resolutely. It doesn't really clear my uncertainty, but knowing that I've got Coda keeping my back makes me feel more certain about leading us into this encounter. After a few minutes, right on time, Barbariccia shouts down from the drake's nest that a ship's been sighted at three o'clock. With this, we can finally get a look at it. And it certainly is worth a look.

Maybe it's because I've only ever seen ordinary ships, but seeing a fancy, swirly, overly detailed ship of the same size and luxury as a yacht feels oddly unreal. The hull—which is made of a pearlescent, pink metal—is so well-polished that it gleams in the sunlight, swirls and creases done along the sides and tops guiding any stray bits of tar back down into the sea. I can't see the actual cabin or anything, but something tells me the wood is no less expensive than the metal it insulates.

"That sail . . ." Coda's one eye widens in awe. "Is that *dragonskin*?"

Following his gaze, I observe the sail, which is a fairly large piece of RED hide, though it's currently furled atop the sails. What truly astounds me is that despite the sails being furled, the boat is practically skidding across the surface of the tar sea faster than a speeding rocket. Coda's baffled mutterings about steam and paddles alongside the prominent exhaust vents on top of the boat tell me that this is not a matter of magic but of science. Steam power. Here? Now?

Actually, now that I think about it, why isn't the *Frisky Lady* powered by steam? Considering that we're surrounded by four-hundred-degree tar, it would be beyond easy to create steam here, which would make steam-powered engines an obvious asset.

Either way, the fact remains that the steam-powered luxury yacht is shooting toward us at what I'm pretty sure is around a hundred fifty kilometers per hour. We, in comparison, are standing still, our sails likewise furled, angled on our side to completely block the path of their advance. The simple fact on display here is that when you're going *that fast*, it's not very easy to make sharp turns to avoid, for example, a pirate ship bobbing nefariously in the way.

Instead, they'll have to stop, which is exactly what they do. Or, rather, *try to do*.

The steam abruptly stops being vented, the sails are unfurled, and the yacht goes from a hundred fifty to fifty kilometers per hour in less than five minutes. However, they are still coming at us with a frightening speed, so Coda orders Dragon to show them what we're all about. He loads a cannon, aims, and fires. The ball of iron shoots true, flying straight for the mast and sail, only to harmlessly skip off the leather sail like a marble slipping off a silk napkin. It's honestly a surreal sight, with the cannonball crashing into the sea just behind it. Despite leaving us a bit baffled, though, it doesn't stop us.

Once our target is close enough to aim the harpoons, we fire, the force of two of the three harpoons striking its hull being enough to halt its terrifying speed the final bit. It groans to a stop right next to us, which means that it's time for the most fun part.

"Kitty, Nazzo, Dragon, Cocco, you help me take the deck; Cal, Scar, Cir, Cante, you find and capture the captain; Cane, Farello, Al, Bar, you protect the ship. Alright, let's head out, everyone!" Coda shouts, his orders meeting with an enthusiastic roar. As per his instructions, the majority of us rush across the harpoon chains onto the yacht's deck, my clawed hand quickly finding a snug and warm place in the chest of a nearby sailor.

No, not a sailor. A *guard*. A proper one, too, with a full-on uniform and a shiny, polished halberd at his side. That's strange. What's a royal guard doing all the way out here?

"Come at me, man! Let's have a—whoa, whoa, hey, wait a minute, halberds are totally cheating—" Still grumbling to myself, I quickly toss myself across the deck, kicking the feet out from under a guard harassing Nazzo before crushing his neck and windpipe in a single stomp. Nazzo, still on the ground, takes a few shaky breaths. The body under my foot is *also* a royal guard. Weird. Nazzo swallows and looks up at me, relief and excitement tugging at his face in equal measure. "Th—thanks, Kitty; that was a close one!"

"No problem," I mumble, leaning down and pulling him to his feet. Once he's standing again, I take care of the guard who just stabbed me through the stomach. He's more surprised to see me alive than he is to see his heart in my hand, but soon enough, he's too dead to show any other reactions.

"Kitty, six o'clock, three of them!" Coda barks across the deck. My body moves faster than I have time to think, claws ripping out throats, slipping between fabric to get at the skin beneath, using my teeth when necessary. Within less than a minute, three more bodies lie at my feet. Not lingering on them, I quickly move to Coda's side, dispatching a guard he was having trouble with. "What in the Gods are royal guards doing here?" he mumbles, a sentiment I second. Shaking his head, he quickly turns to me. "Status report on remaining people?"

I take a few quick breaths through my nose. "Seven in the captain's quarters, four in the general area, and . . ." I do a double take. "Eleven in the hull?" I frown. The heck are they doing down there?

He nods at me, eyes focused as he makes his decision, speaking loud and clear enough for everyone on deck to hear. "Alright, take Nazzo and clear out the hull. The rest of us will handle the people in the general area and try to find the captain. Oh, and . . ." He shows me a little smile. "Try to leave a few hostages alive, alright?"

I salute him, only partially sarcastic. "Aye-aye, Cap'n."

Nazzo, who is still a bit shaky in the knees, blinks at us. "Wait, what?" His hands fly up defensively. "Wait, I, um . . ." He tugs at the collar of his leather coat. "Can't Kitty handle himself? I'm sure I'll just be in the way, so . . ."

"Are you defying my orders?"

It's always interesting to watch the color drain from a goblin's face. This time is no different, though the beading sweat is a nice added touch. "N—no, Captain."

The severe look on Coda's face drains away as fast as the blood in Nazzo's face had. "Good!" he chirps. "In that case, I suggest you get going before Kitty gets any ideas."

Nazzo's eyes slide over to me. "What is it?" I ask him. The look of suspicion doesn't leave his face, which isn't unwarranted in the slightest, since I had been quietly contemplating if I could still handle eleven guards with him slung over my shoulder like a potato sack.

Coda claps his hands, again drawing the attention of all gathered members. "Alright, let's get to it, everyone! No time to waste!"

And since we did, indeed, have no time to waste, I did the fastest thing possible and grabbed Nazzo by the scruff of his collar, swung him into the air and onto my shoulder, and ran for the nearest flight of stairs leading down into the hull.

Say what you will, but for a goblin so small, he's surprisingly loud when it comes to complaining.

With an unwilling but subdued Nazzo on top of my shoulder, I head down into the hull. I would've been more wary of a possible ambush if I hadn't been able to smell exactly what was going on down there. Going by the scents of metal and weapons, I'm dealing with seven guards, two civilians, one mage, and . . . a human. Yeah, a *human*.

And you'd think this would explain the whole *familiar scent* deal, but it actually doesn't. The familiar scent is up in the captain's cabin, where I would have liked to go if I hadn't been given clear and obvious orders. Instead, I'm heading down here to do away with a few loose ends.

The guards are waiting in an ambush, so before I head down, I set down Nazzo and tell him to wait in the staircase while I handle it.

His brows scrunch up. "Wasn't I supposed to come along?"

Humming, I shrug. "Well, yeah, but I think I'd prefer to know that you were safe than have you in the way. Just scream if someone comes at you, okay?"

Hesitant but trusting, he nods. "Um, okay."

"Great. I'll be right back!"

Coda probably sent him with me to act as a lookout and to ensure I left a few of them alive enough to be used as hostages, but with a human down here, I don't think I want him put in harm's way. Humans can be very frightening fighters, after all—I, if anyone, should know. If Coda knew what I know about humans, I'm sure he'd agree with my decision.

After only a bit of moving down, I emerge into the hull, which isn't quite as freezing as they usually are. No, unlike the artificially cooled hull of the *Frisky Lady*, this one is almost room temperature. It feels weird. Also unlike the hull I'm used to, this one isn't used to store food and grain but rather appears to be mainly taken up by a row of cells on each side, making for a total of six, though only one is occupied. Since the hull is rather small, it's a bit crowded, with three guards protecting the wizard, two more at the front, and a pair of turnkeys huddling behind the wizard. A fun ensemble, all things considered.

Either way, as soon as I enter it, a pair of halberds stab into my stomach and chest. To pay the guards back, I reach out and rip out their carotid arteries. Blood sprays, and I'm once again covered in RED. Two down, five left. Not counting the—

<Stop.>

Wizard. I turn to him.

<Stop broken.>

Ah, that's a pretty good facial expression. His robes are really nice, though, so I'd like to loot him afterward. Once I beat this floor, they'll be sure to sell for—

I shake my head.

Once I bring them back to Stainshore, I'll be sure to get a few dozen yills for it, which I can then trade for various goods and services. Yeah, that's it.

Anyhow, my strategy is simple and the same I've used for over two years now. I go for the wizard.

Dropping on all fours, I dash across the floor, scurrying between legs and hastily stabbing halberds before emerging at the wizard. He tries to shoot some kind of spell at me, but I'm not really interested in sticking around here for too long. If the strongest fighter on this ship happens to be protecting the captain, I'll need to finish up here quickly so I can go assist Coda.

So I leap up and grab the wizard's throat, smashing him onto the deck as soon as I have him. He gasps and his eyes go wide and beady, so I knock his skull against the hard wood a few more times. The wood is of very good quality, so with only a bit of effort, his brains soon go *splat* all across the floor. I was able to avoid getting most of his clothes bloody, so they should still sell fine.

"A—*AAAAAAHHH!*" one of the guards screams, willingly throwing himself at me, halberd raised and eyes wide. It was almost too easy to reach out and let him impale himself on my raised arm. That leaves me with only a few guards left.

Since I've taken a bit of damage, I do away with one of them by biting clean through their neck, my improved tooth skill easily shearing through skin, sinew, and bone like it's nothing. Crunch crunch crunch, swallow, and the wounds I took heal for the most part. For the sake of on-the-go snacking, I bite off one of the arms, carrying it in one hand as I dispatch the final three soldiers, taking a bite of the arm whenever I let them get a hit in. In the end, it's just me and the turnkeys. Hrm. Should I let them live? Is it worth the effort? I kind of just want to do away with them to spare myself a mild headache, but then Coda might scold me again . . .

Turning toward the stairs I came down, I shout, "Hey, Nazzo! Coast's clear!"

While Nazzo warily descends the stairs, I tie up the two turnkeys with a spool of intestine I found in one of the guards, only pausing to swipe one of their key bundles. Once Nazzo arrives in the doorway, I lead them to him where he stands frozen stiff. I hand the end of the goblin-gut rope to him. "Here," I say, nudging the mostly emptied small intestine to him. "Hold this while I finish up some business."

Eyes still wide, he takes the rope. This was probably by instinct, since he jerks back a little when the rope makes a squishing sound in his gloved fist. He should be able to handle them, though, so I turn back toward the cells.

Let's see, sniff sniff sniff . . . Ah, here we go. I stop outside the farthermost cell.

In there, I find a middle-aged dark-skinned man looking up at me, hands and feet chained together, clad in clothes so tattered you can easily see his thin, bony frame. Did they never feed this guy? Or maybe they don't know what humans eat?

Before I have time to figure out the answers to these pressing questions, he suddenly stands up, legs shaking like overcooked spaghetti as he takes one, two steps toward me. His face is awash with relief. "Oh, oh, my God, I can't believe that I'd be rescued by another real person . . ." Heavy tears streak down his scarred and sunken-in face. "Tell me, did Sail send you? Please, we have to get out of here before—"

And now he's close enough to see my face. Sure, I'm drenched in blood, but it's still clear that he recognizes my features, not that I have any idea who he is.

"No fucking way," he breathes. He stumbles a step back. "How—how are you alive? You—you *murderer!* How are you alive?! You should be dead! Why the hell are you—"

"Why are you in there?" I ask.

His face twists in confusion. "What are you . . . ?" A tiny shake of the head. "You don't even know who I am? Why are you . . . ?" With my silence as incentive, he straightens his back. "I'm Grief. Lieutenant of the Africa Server. As for why I'm here . . ." His face twists into a snarl. "I can only imagine how much you relate to my position. Except, unlike me, you weren't *falsely* accused. Not to mention that your crime was actually killing a king, rather than attempting to."

"You tried to kill a king?"

"No!" he says. "I didn't! But oh, no. Of course they wouldn't believe the *human.* Never mind that I didn't even know that little greenskin was supposed to be the king of Acheron. I just happened to be nearby, and that was proof enough to arrest me, stick me on a high-speed ship across the tar sea to be put on trial at the royal court, and treat me like dirt. What a fucking joke. And the server leadership didn't even *try* to protect me—*me!* A *lieutenant!* What a sick—"

"What level are you?"

"Pardon?"

"What level are you?"

His lips shape themselves into a frown of confusion more than suspicion. "I'm level ninety-seven. How so?"

Ah, that's good. I'm level one hundred two.

I unlock the cell, step inside, and place my hand against his bare arm.

<[Touch of Reversed Concussion Resistance (Lv.8)]>
<[Touch of Reversed Organ Failure Resistance (Lv.8)]>
<[Touch of Reversed Stroke Resistance (Lv.8)]>
<[Touch of Reversed Internal Damage Resistance (Lv.8)]>
<[Touch of Reversed Bleeding Resistance (Lv.8)]>
<You have learned:
Touch of Reversed Resistance Lv.9>

Ooh, nice! That one's been a long time coming.

"Wh—what the hell did you—?!" I look up from my status message to watch him falter, stumble, and collapse back onto the bench he was sitting on. He's still alive after that? Impressive. So this is the strength of a level-ninety-seven challenger?

Blood trickles down his ears, and his eyes, and then his nose and mouth. He touches a hand to the trail of blood running down his nose, then pulls it back to gawk open-mouthed at his bloodied fingers. "What? What . . . ?" His face twitches in weird, inhuman ways, like a corpse being shocked with electrical pulses. Twitch, twitch. The left side of his face falls and his right eye widens, bigger and bigger, while the left slumps into a half-lidded nap. "What did you—"

He tries to stand up, fists balled to attack me, but instead he falls face-first, collapsing to the floor in a mess of immobile limbs. "I don't . . . What happened? What did you do to me? What is happening?" Squatting down, I watch him from up close as he tries to push himself to his feet with trembling arms, a trail of bloody saliva connecting his lower lip to the dirty floor. His legs shake and shiver and his breathing suddenly hitches. "I can't . . . why can't I feel my . . ." And then he falls again, a raggedy puppet dropped. Limp like a corpse, but still alive. "I can't . . . Why . . . Where . . . ?"

It's almost starting to be a bit pathetic, so after a bit more of watching him writhe on the floor in painless horror, I stab my hand through his chest, only hearing him mutter a final little "Mommy . . ." before he's properly gone.

<Human (Lv.97) Defeated.>
<The Administrators do not endorse the killing of fellow challengers.>
<Repeated killing of fellow challengers will result in penalization.>

Oh? Interesting. Anyhow . . .

I look down at the body below me. It'd be kind of a shame to leave him like this . . .

Just for the sake of it, I slice off one of his arms. It tastes the same as goblin, which doesn't surprise me. The lack of nutrition did, unfortunately, leave the flesh rather lean, which isn't very tasty.

Out in the hull, I find Nazzo, anxiously tapping his foot while still holding the rope to the turnkeys. His eyes light up at seeing me. "Oh, Kitty! Will you take these agai—"

Striding past him, I head up the stairs. "Come on, Nazzo," I say to him. "We don't want the others to wait for us too long, right?"

Vann

He grumbles something at me about this being terribly unfair before making the two hostages follow us up back onto deck. Going by smell, I can tell that everyone is gathered all nice and tidy in the common area. Perfect.

Without any hesitation, I head there, Nazzo following behind me, only marginally less unhappy than his captives.

The common area is surprisingly quiet, even before I open the door and head inside. Since the room serves as both a relaxation and dining area, it's fairly open, with plenty of space to sit, stand, or huddle on the floor. One corner of the room has been converted into a corpse-disposal area, containing five guards and one former sailor. The five remaining members of the ship's crew are all gathered in another corner, kept in place by the threat of violence and various other forms of hooliganism.

The seven pirates in the room turn to us almost as one. Jumpy, as usual. All but one.

Coda lights up upon noticing my arrival. "Kitty, there you are! You're just in time." Nazzo enters behind me and Coda turns to look at him, a shadow of disappointment flashing across his face. "It's a shame you couldn't keep your claws off at least one or two of them. Having more hostages would—"

Before Coda can finish scolding me, the two turnkeys enter meekly, still tied up with goblingut.

I cross my arms and smirk. "You were saying, Coda?"

A look of shock is quickly replaced by pride and he smiles at me. "Nothing of importance. Good work, Kitty! I didn't have a single doubt about your aptitude."

We look at each other for a few seconds before bursting out laughing.

It takes a little while for us to return to our wits, at which point the atmosphere in the room is positively frigid. Coda wipes at his eyes and takes a deep breath. "Right, right, sorry. Where was I? Oh, yes! We have no idea what these people are saying, so I can't tell who to blackmail for their release. Can you ask them where they're from, where they're going, all that stuff?"

"Sure thing, Cap'n," I say, casually walking across the floor to where the five hostages are sitting. There's the captain, dressed in appropriately fancy gear for the occasion, and then four sailors who look fairly experienced, except one, who looks—

My nose twitches. I stare at the young sailor.

Vann?

He stares back at me, with all the ferocious resistance of a wronged puppy. He's partially hidden behind the broad back of one of the other sailors, but it's his smell I recognize. Yeah. That's him, alright. What the heck is he—

Coda clears his throat and I realize that this isn't really the time to be needlessly intimidating. Hunching down, I turn back to the captain, trying not to look at Vann's scowling face. While still trying to make it clear that I'm totally not noticing him, I'm able to extract some information from the captain despite my sweating and stumbling over words, the contents of which I then relay to my own captain.

In the end, Coda nods thoughtfully, his face set in a look of worrying seriousness. "So this vessel not only belongs to a high judge but is actively transporting a suspected regicide for judgment?" The way he says it, like all of the words are the names of princes and demigods, makes me feel beyond cautious, so I just nod at him. He hums. "A high judge . . ."

I glance between the two captains. "Is a high judge really that—"

"Can you ask him where the high judge is right now?" Coda says with what almost sounds like mild panic. I've never heard him like that. I almost want to ask him if he's okay, but there's clearly no time for that.

Gulping, I turn to the other captain and repeat Coda's question. He frowns at us. "Didn't you see him? He was down in the hold with the prisoner."

He was? But the hull only had the guards and the turnkeys, and—

My clothes suddenly feel very hot and stuffy. "Uh, just to make things clear . . ." I tug at my collar before leaning in, asking in close to a whisper, "This high judge . . . he didn't happen to be dressed like a wizard, did he?"

"Tynus the Sage of Three is known as one of Acheron's greatest wizards, yes."

Ah.

A meter or so away, just over my shoulder, Coda asks, "What's he saying?"

"Um . . ." I turn to him, trying not to look half as pathetic as I feel. Doesn't help much, though, and my ears are still left RED. "There's a fairly good chance that I might have killed the high judge."

Coda doesn't even flinch. The captain of the ship, on the other hand, flies into a ferocious rage, eyes flashing. "*You murderous beast—!*" Only barely restrained by his employees, he thrashes, throwing curses at myself and every ally I've ever made, and also my mother. Kind of impressive, but I'm too busy being buried beneath a mountain of shame to really listen to it.

I lower my face to the floor. "I—I'm sorry, he attacked, and I . . ."

"No, there's no need to apologize," Coda says evenly. "Even if he'd been alive, it wouldn't have changed anything."

"What do you mean?"

He looks at me, eyes shining with something close to envy. A wry smile tugs at his lips. "You're more innocent than you look, friend." Before I have time to understand what he's saying, he turns to the rest of the gathered members. "We're sinking it."

"We're—" The words fall from my mouth heedlessly. "What are you saying? Why would we—we can't possibly keep the hostages on the *Frisk*, we don't even have a hold! What are you—"

"We can't let them live." His voice is calm. Rational. "If the kingdom of Acheron finds out that we killed one of their high judges, it won't end with just one army, or one fleet. They'd go after us until we were dead. Each and every one of us." There isn't a single fault in his logic. And still, I find myself foolishly refusing.

"Well, sure, but . . ." My gaze falls on Vann.

"Or are you saying you'd rather we put our lives on the line for mere money?"

"No!" I say. "I just . . ." My hands ball into fists. "They shouldn't need to die because of us. Because *I* went out of my way to get us wrapped up in this." My chest tightens. "Wouldn't that be too cruel?"

"Maybe," Coda admits. "However, we can't afford to prioritize their lives above our own." His eyes sharpen. "Or do you have some other reason to argue with your captain?"

My jaws snap shut. I can't argue. Not against that. Still, my eyes fall back on Vann. As I stand, feet fixed firmly in place, Coda begins to order the rest of the crew to leave. A few of them complain about how this was all a waste of time, but Coda placates them with the promise of greenberry pudding for dessert, which they accept with only minor grumbling. As they're leaving, Coda explains what'll happen next, and I listen, a hollow feeling carving a place for itself in my chest.

"We'll leave the hostages here with you, and you'll handle it. Take care of them, and when you're done, come out and we'll sink the ship properly. Is that alright with you, Kitty?"

Yeah, of course. Of course it's okay. What else could it be? This is more merciful than simply barricading the doors and letting them die from the tar and smoke and fire. Not to mention that I get more experience. Of course this is the best option. I nod at him. This is right. He smiles at me, and then he leaves, closing the doors. And for close to a minute, I'm standing in the room, and the hostages are watching me. There are seven of them, and one of me. As I'm futilely waiting for the horrible WHITE numbness to leave my chest, they all reach the shared, incorrect conclusion that maybe, just maybe, if they all went at me at once, they could defeat me.

So they attack me. The coordination is almost impressive. But it's just not possible.

<Goblin (Lv.11) Defeated.>
<Goblin (Lv.10) Defeated.>
<Goblin (Lv.9) Defeated.>
<Goblin (Lv.12) Defeated.>

The captain falls dead at my feet. The room is a bloodbath because I fought with reluctance. All the while I was hoping that once I killed this next one, I'd finally find the duty and loyalty needed to kill Vann—that I'd be filled with some kind of fulfillment, and I wouldn't feel so unsure anymore. But it didn't come. All but him are dead, and I feel nothing but hollow.

The hollowness isn't enough to make me kill him. He's on the floor, atop the fancy, blood-soaked rug, clutching at his arm. I scratched it by accident. Not deep enough to actually have him bleed out like that, but . . . But if I don't help him soon, it might get infected, or he might bleed too much, or . . .

I shake my head. What the hell am I thinking? Going against Coda's orders, all for the sake of some random sailor I came to know in passing almost a year ago? I must be insane.

I look down at him. His murky, dark eyes stare up at me in a mixture of terror and animalistic determination. I grit my teeth.

Damn it.

My hands, previously balled into fists, fall open-palmed and I hiss a sigh between clenched teeth.

Kneeling down, I quickly grab his shoulders and force him to face me. His eyes shine with BLACK hatred even though a light fog of blood loss. "Hey," I say. "Vann. Listen to me. Can you hear me?" His eyes widen slightly at the mention of his name. Good enough. "You have to listen to me. I might be able to get you out of here alive, but you'll need to follow my lead."

His voice, although thin and weak, is perfectly clear. "D—damn you . . . demon . . . !" He drags a raspy breath down his dry throat. "I would rather, haah, haah, die than . . . f—fall to your . . . temptations . . . !"

I take a nice, calming breath. "Yeah, sure, but for now, I just need you to . . ." While I'm still holding him, he passes out. Excuse me? "Hey, wake up, damn it!" I whisper-shout, shaking him by the shoulders. Damn it, damn it, damn it . . . !

There's a knock on the door. "Kitty?" Nazzo calls from outside. "Uh, is everything alright in there? Are you . . . *done?*"

"Just a minute!" I call out. "I have to, um . . . bite through a bit of cartilage!"

In the meantime, I try to get Vann awake by gently slapping him, but when that doesn't work, I get a bit more violent, which *also* doesn't work. Shoot.

"Kitty?" Coda shouts from the other side of the door. "Is everything going well?"

Okay, shoot, damn it, I'll just—

"I'm coming in," Coda says, the doors opening just in time for me to heave Vann onto my shoulder. Coda's eyes move over the small bloodbath for a moment, whistling at the sight. "Excellent work as always. I trust you got your fill of—" His eyes fall on me, or rather, at the goblin hanging limp from my shoulder. "What's that all about?"

"Oh, it's, uh . . ." I smack Vann on the back. "A snack. For the road. Which is standard human behavior and not to be questio—" Atop my shoulder, Vann groans. Ah. Shoot.

"He seems awfully alive for a snack," Coda comments.

"I like them fresh," I say suavely. Now that I think about it, it isn't even a lie, which makes it easier to tell and make him believe. "Do you have an issue with it, Captain?" And, then, to really lay it on thick, I add, "If you want to, I can leave it here . . ."

"Ah, no, of course not—it's no issue. Just . . ." He gives a slightly tense smile. "Nezzo and Farello don't really like seeing that kind of stuff, so take it somewhere private, alright?"

"Will do, Cap'n."

And that I do.

I carry Vann over to our ship, avoiding the uncertain looks from the younger members of the crew. I'm sure I could explain it away by saying that humans have a biological craving for goblin meat or something, but I don't want to taint their impressionable brains too much, so I simply tell them I've got a rumbly in my tumbly that no greenberry pudding is able to cure.

With my permission granted, I carry Vann down to the hold belowdecks. It's cold as usual, a pair of dragonheart-powered engines keeping both the hold and ship as a whole cold. Scar once told me that earlier ship models didn't have the holdcoolers, causing most early deaths on the tar sea to be because of heatstroke. The holdcoolers are then—being the only magically powered engines on the ship—the most expensive parts. However, with the hold downright chilly, it's the perfect place for storing foodstuffs. And, also . . .

I look at Vann, still slung over my shoulder. But will he really be alright down here . . . ? We don't exactly have any other place to keep him. This is the only storage area we have, and the only singular room we have is the captain's quarters.

Grumbling to myself, I prop Vann up against a wall as far away from the holdcoolers as possible. Then, after considering the situation for a moment, I pull a few hides from my inventory, draping the fluffy things over Vann to keep him warm. Oh, and I also tie a piece of my shirt around his arm to stanch the bleeding.

There. Good. I wish I could write a note for him to see once he wakes up, but I'll be back soon, so it should be alright.

After hesitating for a few more seconds, I quietly leave the hold, returning to the main deck in time to watch Dragon gleefully fire cannonballs at the slowly sinking yacht. Nazzo watches me approach, inching away a little once I'm close enough to the railing. He looks me up and down, eyes scanning for evidence of feasting. "Are you . . . *done?*"

I freeze up a little. "Not . . . quite. I'm saving it for later."

"Ah, I—I see . . ."

Nazzo turns back to look at the burning ship, his ears folded back and trembling slightly. Even though the burning ship is a truly magnificent sight, I find myself looking at Nazzo instead. His behavior is curious. After a few seconds, I reach out to touch him, watching with interest as he recoils. My eyes fall to look at my hand; at my claws, still RED. Scarlet blooms across corpse-pale skin. I look back up at his face to find him quickly turning back to the ship.

Ah. He fears me, doesn't he?

Not that I can fault him. Anyone would be afraid of me. Most people are, as a matter of fact. But seeing it here, in him . . .

Reaching out, I put my hand on his shoulder. He jerks away, practically jumping at the touch, but I keep my hand on his shoulder, keeping him in place. Like a rabbit caught in a trap, he turns around, only to freeze when he sees my face. I smile at him. "Hey," I say. "It's alright. I'm on *your* side, remember?" Hand still on his shoulder, I squeeze it a little.

He turns away shamefully to look back at the burning ship. "Well, yeah, of course, but it's still . . . You know . . ." His face twists in uncertainty. "He looked a lot like my brother. And—and then with the human . . . It felt more *vivid.*" He shakes his head, frowning at himself. "I don't know."

I see how it is. I pat him on the back. "I get it." I smile softly. "But you do know that I'd never do something like that to you guys, right?"

His eyes widen, as if the mere suggestion was blasphemy. "Of course! That would be—" He makes the kind of face you do when trying to eat a whole lemon in one bite. "Completely unthinkable."

"Yeah!" I chime in. "I mean, with how little meat's on *your* bones?" I grab and pinch his cheek. "I'd starve to death!" As he rebelliously shakes off my arms,

I chuckle and double down. "Not to mention that you *stink*. When was the last time you took a bath?"

"I wiped myself yesterday!" Nazzo shoots back once he's freed himself from my grip. "I'm basically clean!" Despite his tone, the smile on his face tells me that my hijinks have gone through.

While he's still on guard, I lean in closer, sniffing at him even as he tries to fight me off. "Ah, now that you say it, you *do* smell quite clean. Mmm . . ."

"H—hey, hands off!"

Before I have time to go all in on the bit and playfully nibble at his arm, Scar strolls by and slaps me on the back. "Didn't you promise Coda to stop eating the younger crew members? What is this, the third one?"

Smirking back at him, I mournfully reply, "Well, yeah, but it's only a single bite! He won't miss it, I'm sure." Then, after a moment's pause, I add, "Also, it's the *fourth* one. Can't forget Reggie."

"Of course, of course. Good kid. Shame he had to go and disobey Coda, but I'm sure his departure will serve as a reminder to all rookie members that Coda is not someone to be trifled with."

Nazzo, who until now had been in on the bit, turns pale. "W—wait, what?"

While nodding at Scar, I pretend to pick at my teeth. "At least he tasted good."

We keep the joke running for almost a full five minutes before deciding to let Nazzo in on it. At that point, both Cocco and Dragon had joined in, so when the jig was finally up, Nazzo was a fair bit miffed about being strung along for so long. However, we all had a good laugh, and Nazzo forgot all about his silly fears. Around that time, I also noticed that Vann had woken up and was wandering around the hold, which meant I didn't have much time to hang around. I bid farewell to the people on deck and headed down to the hold.

Although it felt wrong at the moment, I'm now a bit happy that I bolted the door to the hold so he couldn't wander out and mess up my cover story. Since I can smell that he's close to—but not leaning against—the door, I take a deep breath before unbolting it, and then another before opening it, the cold air of the hold rushing out to prickle against my skin.

And there he stands, covered in several pelts all draped around his shoulders, bent over at a ninety-degree angle, head lowered to face the floor. *Bowing.* What the heck is he—

"Thank you for rescuing me, sir, from those dastardly pirates and their horrific tallthing. Being a mere sailor in training, I would expect no more than being kept in your cozy hold, however, with the cold being so terrible, I ask that you allow me up on deck to warm myself. Even if not, sir, I thank you deeply for—" And here, he finally takes the time to raise his head and look at who he's talking to. His eyes meet mine. The change that comes over him takes less than three seconds. No longer is he trembling merely because of the cold. The grateful smile falls off his face. His wide eyes fill with BLACK hatred. Like BLACK, transparent ice, his eyes are so clear that I can read his heart easily. Will he fight? Will he flee? Will he freeze?

I don't want to take the chance on the first two, so while the ball is still rolling in the roulette wheel inside his head, I gently close the door behind me. Darkness falls between us. My eyes adjust instantly, but it takes a moment for him, his eyes widening, pupils trembling and focused on me to ensure I won't move anymore.

Merely by looking at him, at the guarded way he stands there, I can tell he won't believe a word I'll say. I can't fault him.

Even knowing it won't be any real help, I sit down on the steps leading to the door going up. As I sit like this, my head is a little lower than his. He's looking down at me, and I'm looking up at him. Before he has time to act, I take initiative.

"If you kill me, you won't leave this place alive."

Even in the darkness, I can clearly see his brows scrunch up in confusion. "What are—"

"You are on board the *Frisky Lady*, the ship of the Evil Claw Pirates. And right now, you are only alive because of me. You can kill me, injure me, throw whatever insults you want, but it will only shorten your life span." I sit, relaxed, as I say this. There is nothing emotional in my inflection, no hint of fear or reluctance. Nothing but calm certainty. "Unless you follow my lead, you will die, Vann. Maybe not down here, maybe not at my claws, but you will certainly die."

"How do you know my name?" Within less than a minute of conversation he has already asked the dreaded question.

Hesitantly, I let the semitruth spill from my lips. "A while, maybe a year back, we met while I was undercover. I doubt you'd recognize my name or face. However, you were kind to me at a dark time, and I appreciate you for it. That's why—"

"Is that why you've spared me?" he says in disbelief. "Because I was *kind* to you? What favor could I possibly have done for you to spare my life? You—a *human*?"

"It isn't important," I say, trying to wave off the fact that all he did was give me some tripseeds and treat me like I was an actual person. "It meant a lot, and that's all that matters."

He approaches me, fearless. "No. No, I recognize your voice. The words you say aren't the same, and you look completely different, but . . ." My eyes are on the floor, on the cold planks of wood beneath my feet. "You're Fennrick, aren't you?" Hot shame burns at my ears and cheeks. "You are!" The disgust in his voice is too much. Like he's appalled by me. By what I've become. And it makes me feel so *small*. "Is that seriously why you're doing this? I heard you speaking before, when you took me on your shoulder. Don't underestimate the hearing of us goblins. Your excuse for doing this is ridiculous." His voice drops to a growl. "*What makes you think I want to live?*"

I fly to my feet. My hands hover, half-raised at the level of his neck. The breath I draw in trembles.

What was I about to do just now? He stands below me, defiant—*strong*. I think I was going to grab him by the shoulders. Shake sense into him. I *hope* that's what I was about to do. My hands are shaking. But when I look into his eyes, although they were so fearful only a minute ago, now they're certain. He isn't putting on a show of defiance. He's honest.

I see that, and I see myself in his eyes, and my heart calms down.

I take a deep breath. Then I meet his gaze, as steadily as he meets mine. "If you want to die," I say, gently, "then I will make it painless."

For a moment, he simply looks at me, no expression save for mild surprise gracing his young face. "You've changed," he mumbles after a while. I neglect to ask him if it's for the better or worse. In my silence, he turns away from me. "So," he says, "what's your plan, tallthing?"

It takes a second or so to reel from the realization that I won't actually have to kill him, at which point I hastily blurt out, "I need you to agree to join the Evil Claw Pirates."

"To join the—" Turning back to me, he stares me right in the face, waiting for me to drop the act. After a few seconds of staring, he chuckles bitterly. "You're actually serious. And what then, genius?"

Strange question, but . . . "And then, you remain a pirate."

"And you, me, and all your barbaric pirate *friends* go adventuring, pillaging boats, killing women and children left and right, stealing life and limb from innocent civilians until we're eventually killed in turn; or better yet, die on this sea from which the gods have turned Their eyes?"

"Yes."

He laughs bitterly and begins pacing back and forth across the hold, leather soles clacking against the hard wood. "This is sick. You're sick. No—no, I'm being too generous. You're a *human*. You're all sick in the head. Ungoblic monsters, the lot of you." He turns back to me, pausing only to give me a glare. "Are you really *that* naive? To think that I would join you? That I would somehow be able to spit over my shoulder and not think about how you killed my captain, my *friends*?" A sudden scowl usurps his lips. "And you spare *me*. They were all a hundred times better than me. Did you think about that? That maybe Sir Tynus was anxious to try to get that disgusting human acquitted? That my senior, Sir Franze, who died bravely at *your hands*, was as good a father as anyone to me? And my captain—oh, my poor captain! What do you think he was to use the money from this mission for? Did you justify your actions by falsely believing that he would spend it all on snailspit and liquor? That he didn't have a wife and two children at home, bravely awaiting his return? *Dreading* the day when he would not?" He spits on the floor in front of me. "No. No, I can see it in your face. You didn't think *anything*. Because if you took the time to think of them as *people*, then you would no longer have been able to slaughter them. And that's why you spared me. Because unlike with them, you couldn't delude yourself into seeing me as a hunk of flesh to be carved for the amusement of your barbaric overlord."

I watch him carefully, my fingers folded tenderly atop my lap. I let my eyes fall to look at my claws, and then rise again to meet his burning gaze. "Yeah," I say, simply. "You're right."

Still standing in the same place, he takes a few shallow breaths, filling his chest with energy before speaking again. "You agree, then?" An air of doubt hangs in his words, almost demanding I show my true colors, maybe by disagreeing or making it clear I'm only doing this to get him on my side. But there are no true colors. What I'm saying—what I'm telling him—is the truth.

I nod. "Yeah. It's as you said." I speak softly. Gently. I'm talking to myself as much as I am to him, but it feels right. I just hadn't let myself hear it before. "If I'd known the people on your boat for even a single day, I would have spared their lives. And if I'd known them for a week, a month . . . I would have trusted them not to tell anyone about what happened. In a different world, we could all have shared a meal, and there wouldn't have been anything foul between us."

"But that isn't how it turned out," Vann snarls. "You killed them, and now they're dead, and you expect me to move on."

My eyes fall to the floor again. I don't know what I can say to that. After a little while, a few quiet words fall from my lips. "If you don't, they'll kill you."

"Or you will," Vann says bitterly, almost sarcastically. As though I wanted this. An uncomfortable silence falls between us. Striding across the room, he plants himself atop a barrel I'm pretty sure we're using to salt fish. There, he huddles a bit, pulling the furs covering him closer around him. He scowls at me from across the hold. "So that's your ultimatum. Either I join you, or I die."

"Yes."

He looks away from me. I can't read his body language at all. "I need some time to think about it."

"Okay."

He turns to look at me again, and we share a silence staring at each other before he breaks it with a simple "*Alone.*"

"Oh," I say. "Y—yeah. Of course." Standing up, I move for the door. Placing my hand on it, I chance a quick look back at him where he sits covered in pelts. "Do you need another—?"

"No," he says sharply. "I'm fine."

I don't think he is, but it isn't my place to tell him. I nod at his reply. "I'll be back in half an hour to—"

"An hour," Vann says. "A full hour."

"Yeah, okay. An hour." Mentally noting down the time—ten to twelve—I pull open the door and leave the hold, only pausing to say, "I'll knock on the door when I come back." Once I receive his answer, I close the door and bolt it behind me. That was . . . a bit draining, I suppose. It wasn't horrible, though. Really, it could have gone a lot worse. Hell, if he'd actually asked me to kill him, I would probably have had to eat him to keep up the cover story, which wouldn't have been very—

"There was really no need to make up that ridiculous cover story," Coda says where he sits on the stairs leading up. I freeze in place. Shamefully, a tiny part of my brain hastily tells me that it would take less than a minute to kill and dispose of him. I push it down alongside the urge to run away and adopt a new identity.

I muster a smile, though it's clearly as false as they come. "Oh, hey, Coda! How long have you been—"

"Long enough," he says, casually interrupting me. His head is leaning on his metal claw, but at the facial expression I make, he removes it, sitting up straight. "Why did you think that you would need to lie about this?"

In the span of about five seconds, I go through all seven stages of grief, from denial to anger, to finally settle on acceptance. Coda isn't someone I can lie to. If anything, lying to him just makes things worse. "You said we *had* to kill them all, so I assumed that . . . But I didn't want to have to kill someone I knew . . ." His facial expression says everything for him. "And I didn't want anyone *else* to kill him, so . . ."

"So you concocted this plan, hoping that if he chose to join us, then we'd spare him."

No point in denying it. "Yes."

Coda takes a deep, careful breath. "I couldn't hear exactly what he said down there, but would I be incorrect in assuming that he has yet to show any real intention of becoming a pirate?" I nod. "And if I said that it seems like he hates us, would you agree?" I nod again. He takes another breath. "And you still want to try to recruit him?"

"Yes."

He pulls his lips into a thin line. "I see. Alright. Alright . . ." Using his metal hand, he scratches at the back of his bald head. For almost a full minute, he sits there, thinking. I let him think. I'm in no hurry anywhere. Still, if only because it feels like I'm about to get scolded, I feel fidgety. Once the minute is up, he nods to himself and looks back at me, his eye shining clearly. "I'll give you a month."

"A month?"

Coda nods again, affirming it. "If you haven't been able to convince him to join us within the span of the coming month, then we have to do away with him." I feel like saying something in defense of Vann, but Coda stops me, holding up one hand. "It will be painless and quick and—most importantly, *you* won't have to do it." He smiles wearily. "More crucial, though . . . I'm sorry. I acted hastily in putting you in charge of doing away with the hostages. Next time, I'll be sure to heed your opinion beforehand." I'm not sure how to respond, so within my silence, he continues. "However, for now, we have to deal with this situation. You act best with clearly defined parameters, so . . ." He scratches his chin for a moment. "He has to agree to join us of his own volition. If we dock and he bolts as soon as his feet touch shore, we will capture and do away with him, and you'll have to sleep in the hold for a week.

"During this month, until he either chooses to join us or leave this mortal coil, he may not leave this ship. He is your *prisoner*. If you want to treat him like your friend, then make it quick and painless." His eyes hold neither cruelty nor dishonesty. He's being fully serious. "My only advice for you is to remember that whether or not he joins us is one thing; whether or not the rest of us will accept him is another."

"Yes, of course," I reply numbly. He's right. Still . . . "Do you really think he'll be able to stay in the hold all that time? Won't he get frostbite and die?"

Coda tilts his head at me. "Of course he will."

I stare at him. He stares at me. "What are you—"

"Clearly," he enunciates, "he will need to stay somewhere private." Continuing his musings, he says, "Someplace where you can lock the door. A room with a suitable bed. Preferably with a window, so our dear prisoner can see the sun and avoid going mad." He taps his chin exaggeratedly, like a schoolteacher baiting their brainless students for an obvious answer. "Someplace like . . . ?"

"Like . . . ?"

He waves his metal claw. "Like . . . *my* . . . ?"

"Like . . . your . . ." I stop myself. I swallow dryly. Is he really . . . ? "But we can't possibly keep a prisoner in *your* room! Where would you sleep?"

Coda shrugs. "We have extra hammocks."

"But for him to stay in *your room* . . ."

He watches me. I watch him. After a few seconds, his eyes narrow. "I'm not going to offer it." He stands up, suddenly shadowing me. "If you want it, you'll have to ask for it." In the darkness, his one eye shines like a moonlit topaz. "However, you have to remember that this is far more to ask for than the life of a mere prisoner."

I stare silently at the silver lining around his silhouette. A dry swallow claws its way down my throat.

Lowering my head, I say, with all the gravity I can muster, "Please let me keep my prisoner in your room."

A hand falls on my shoulder and I look up to find his face once more in the light, wrinkles creasing by the width of his smile. "Granted."

That day, I felt more need to celebrate than I had upon joining the Evil Claw Pirates.

At the agreed time, I returned down to Vann and told him the good news. He told me that he had decided not to join, and that a month, even if spent in the greatest luxury among the best possible company, would not be able to change his mind. I didn't pay any attention to his words. A month wasn't a very long time, but I felt confident that it would be enough. I myself had been convinced in only a week or so.

So, without waiting, I brought him to the captain's cabin, explained the new rules of conduct, and asked him kindly not to mess up Coda's room too much. I don't know if he heard me, though, as he spent most of the time I was there staring at Coda's wanted-poster collection. Or maybe it was at *my* wanted poster; it was hard to tell. I felt like bragging about how good the art was since Simel was such a good artist, but then I realized he probably didn't care all that much, so I restrained myself.

Since it was almost lunchtime, I quickly brought him his meal. I wanted to eat with him, but he refused my company, so I left him to his business. This, in turn, gave me the horrific pleasure of explaining the situation to my crewmates. I had naively hoped that Coda would do so for me, however, since this was *my* situation, he left it to me to explain why he'd be sleeping with us in the common room all of a sudden.

It would be a lie to say they were happy to hear about how I'm keeping one of the sailors as a pet, but I also can't say that I didn't notice Nazzo breathing a sigh of relief at the declaration that he hadn't become my lunch. At that, both Farello and Cir patted him on the back. So maybe Vann living isn't all that bad.

The day passed quietly, and then the evening too, and my tenth month with the Evil Claw Pirates came and went almost eventlessly.

What Does That Make Me?

Three weeks came and went with no real development.

I tried my best, okay? It just . . . It didn't go quite as well as I'd hoped, is all. Vann wasn't too cooperative, and my crewmates were likewise unwilling to really be part of my efforts, so . . .

But in the end, it wasn't as though they *wanted* it to go badly. For one, Vann didn't even speak their language, so it was obvious that there were going to be some difficulties in communication. Not to mention that plenty of the members disliked him from the get-go for essentially stealing Coda's room. I, of course, tried to deflect their blame onto myself, but it was an impossible situation.

Barbariccia took the whole situation to heart and ran with it. Even after close to ten months, he still refused to consider me a full member, and now he was using this whole thing with Vann to try to convince everyone else that I was a traitor. He did so with little success, but a number of the members did share the opinion that my endeavor was a futile one. And after three weeks, I'm having difficulty in finding reasons to disagree.

Vann is not making much of an effort. I understand why, it's perfectly reasonable, but it still upsets me that he isn't fighting harder for his life.

I recommended that he try to learn Yinnic, but he refused. Something about how he didn't want to spend his last month alive trying to learn a new language. He used the same excuse to dodge around a third of everything Coda cooked. Absolute insanity. Even weirder, he was completely fine with eating what I cooked for him, even though I'm objectively a worse cook than Coda is. When I asked him about it, he said that he liked the novelty of eating otherworldly food.

I tried to make him join in on game night, and on storytelling night, and theater night, but he loathed the hassle of translation too much to enjoy it.

So in short, he would spend his days in Coda's room, only emerging when forced to. And what would he do in there? Well . . .

A large portion of the time he spent there was used for writing letters. Yeah, it was weird. I used my own pocket money to buy paper and ink and a quill for him, and then a bit more to get wax and a stamp for the seal alongside the actual letters. It wasn't especially expensive, but it was still perplexing. As soon as I asked him about it, he explained himself openly.

"When I'm dead, I want you to give these letters to the people they entail."

Yeah. No matter what I said or how often, he simply would not accept the fact that he would live more than a few weeks more. So at the end of every week, he'd hand me a pile of letters and ask me to get them to the right person. Some of them were intended for people like family members—mainly his father and older sister—but the majority of them were for people I didn't know, with titles that seemed a bit too lofty for Vann to know personally. Three of them were intended for various kings, one of them being Simel. I wanted to refuse it, but he forced it on me, chiding me about "refusing a dying goblin's wish."

So now my inventory contains a few dozen letters that I have no idea how to actually deliver.

Aside from that, if only to entertain himself, he kept me around. He asked me to talk to him, to tell him stories, to keep him entertained, and to make his last few weeks slightly less boring.

The only light in the darkness of his dreadful existence was Nazzo.

Although Vann refused to learn Yinnic, Nazzo was more than willing to learn Aetongue, which was fairly similar to Eentongue, which he already knew. So Nazzo slowly learned, and after a week or so, they could kind of communicate.

However, it wasn't enough. Three weeks in, and he still refused to join us.

With not much else in terms of options, I went with what some might consider a bit of a hasty decision. But it was a last-ditch effort, so I took the chance.

I had actually asked for permission one week in, but it was only after three weeks that it went through.

"Are you still sure about this, Kitty?" Coda asks.

My eyes lie square on the small caravan cruising along the horizon. "I am," I say, hands squeezing the railing. "If this doesn't work, then . . ."

"Then you still have another week, right?" Nazzo comments, popping his head into my vision. "A week is a long time. Anything can happen."

"Yeah," I reply without much conviction. Maybe Vann's pessimistic outlook has started to infect me, but with every day that passes, I'm less and less certain that he'll turn around in the end. Sure, there's a chance that he might proclaim his new alliance at the very last minute, but I doubt that kind of halfhearted commitment would last. It certainly wouldn't be able to withstand the kind of scrutiny Coda would place on it.

Clapping his hands, Coda grabs the attention of the gathered members. "Alright, to your stations, friends!" He turns his eye to me. "And you . . . bring our rookie-in-training." As I'm leaving, I hear him mutter under his breath, "Maybe with this, the kid will be lucky enough to die honorably instead of having to be put down like a drake . . ."

Numbly, I recognize that I don't disagree with him.

I move down to the captain's room, a path I could now walk blind. Before I enter, I knock in a certain rhythm, waiting for Vann to tell me that I'm allowed in. Sometimes this takes a second, sometimes I've stood waiting for tens of minutes. Never more than an hour, though it certainly felt like it at times. After less than a minute, I hear a call on the other side: "Come in." I enter.

He looks up from where he sits at the desk, appearing so much like Coda it briefly scares me. There's a letter at the desk, one he's still writing. If he didn't put it away when I entered, it must not be too important. Still . . . "How much do you have left of that letter?"

He glances down at it, then back up at me. "Only a few sentences, and the signoff. How come?"

"Finish it, and then we have to go," I say stoically.

The quill falls out of his hand, rolling to a stop atop the letter. He stares at me without picking it up. "Is it time?"

"It is."

"I see. In that case . . ." He fumbles for the quill a little, eventually grabbing it with trembling fingers. "This won't take more than a minute. Will you leave me for a moment? I'll call for you when I've finished."

"Of course," I say, leaving the room and closing the door behind me. After what I counted to be two minutes and five seconds, he calls for me and I enter. He's standing in front of the door, with a small pile of letters in hand. I glance through them only briefly before putting them in my inventory, noting absently that the most recent one, upon which the wax seal has yet to fully dry, has a few wet spots on it. I don't ask him about it. Instead, I simply say, "Are you ready?"

"I am."

Nodding solemnly, I lead him up to the deck. The thunder of cannons is already exploding across the sky, plumes of smoke billowing from their wide-open iron mouths. Our victim doesn't have any openings for cannons, leaving them defenseless against such an attack. Once we're close enough, we shoot the harpoons. I'm not surprised when Coda calls for Vann to join us in taking the deck.

When I take his arm to lead him across the double chains acting as our ramp, I find him trembling. I squeeze his arm a little. "It's okay," I whisper to him. "I'll be right beside you, so just try to . . . *enjoy it.*" As I'm saying the words, I can feel the absurdity in it, but it's the truth. From my personal experiences, if he doesn't enjoy it the first time, he won't enjoy it the second, third, or fiftieth times, either. And if he can't ever enjoy this—*the most crucial part of our job*—then . . .

I shake my head, pushing down the thoughts with a heavy swallow. He'll enjoy it. He *has* to. At the very least, he needs to be able to stand it.

We board the small vessel, I reap the neck of a nearby sailor, and Vann freezes in place. Scar and Cir run past us, darting for where I previously told Coda I could smell the captain. I move to look at Vann, maybe to tell him something calming or encouraging, but a sword lodges itself in my chest before I have time to. Briefly annoyed, I sink my teeth into the neck of the sword's owner, my jaws clacking together so easily I might as well have bitten through whipped cream. After chewing for a second while pulling the sword out, I swallow and almost instantly regenerate the damage done. I turn to Vann. "Hey, Vann, are you—"

His terrified, trembling eyes turn to me. Or, rather, a spot that coincides with where I'm standing. Ah. Yeah, no, he is *not* okay. I move closer to him, but he recoils away from me with a gasp. All things considered, he seems to be having a bit of an episode. Why would he . . . ?

I turn to look at the deck. It doesn't look like that of his own ship in the least, but with these bodies covering it, and with *me* standing right in the middle of it . . .

I look back at him. He's having a flashback. Because of *me*.

My jaws tighten and I feel the urge to squeeze my eyes shut. But that wouldn't help. It'd only make things worse. Maybe if I touch him on the shoulder, or tell him something nice, then . . . I shake my head. Excuses. Justifications. What he *needs* right now isn't *me*, it's . . .

On the other side of the deck, I notice Nazzo, trying and half failing to once again fend off a sailor. Always thrown into the fray, never suited for it. With one eye over my back to make sure Vann isn't murdered where he stands clutching the railing, I stride across the deck, effortlessly killing Nazzo's enemy before putting a hand on his shoulder. "Nazzo, could you help Vann?"

The grateful smile on his face swiftly twists into a confused frown. "Help . . . Vann? Why? How?"

I pinch the bridge of my nose. "He needs someone to stand next to him and not be threatening. I'm sure I don't need to explain why that can't be me."

"But why does he . . . ?"

"Nazzo, you're his friend, right?" With that half-veiled accusation, Nazzo has no choice but to nod in reply, indignation shining in his eyes. "Good. If you stand next to him for a few minutes, maybe he'll tell you why he needs it."

Not waiting to hear his excuses and reasons for not being able to do what I've asked of him, I grab both his shoulders, spin him around to face where Vann stands, and then send him away with a push on the back. I watch his path for a few seconds to make sure he gets to Vann alright, and that he doesn't do something dumb. Thankfully, he's able to do his duty of standing still quite well, leaving me to my own without hindrance. A sailor comes charging at me, and I'm just about to disembowel him when I remember how I'm still in Vann's line of sight. So instead of gorily discharging him, I simply grab his neck and crush it in one hand.

I dispatch the rest of the sailors on deck in a similar fashion, the pillaging being successful in all areas but one. In the end, we take the captain and a few key people hostage, the harpoons doing their job by ensuring that they can't escape us without sinking.

That's all a bit overshadowed, though, by the fact that Vann was still in a state once we got back, and even when we got him all calm and secure in his room, he wouldn't come out, or even talk to us. He wouldn't even open for Nazzo.

It was up to me.

It's dark now. The sun fell almost an hour ago, and I'm still waiting. It's been seven and a half hours since the pillaging, and it's been seven hours since I knocked on Vann's door. Since then, I've been standing here. Waiting. Not patiently, but at the very least without training my resistances. I can't imagine the effect it would have if he called me in and I was covered in blood.

So I'm standing here. My exhaustion protection went up a level an hour ago, which was nice. I also sent Moleman a message about what happened with Vann while we were pillaging, though I've yet to receive a response. He's so busy nowadays that it's almost worrying. The last time he messaged me, he told me that he was trying to get a falsely accused human acquitted, an effort I encouraged.

While I was waiting, Coda brought me supper, which I ate standing.

Another hour passes. The time is now eight in the evening. I've heard him in there, walking around. At one point I could hear him writing a letter before tearing it up and throwing it out the window. A waste of paper, but I'm in no place to scold him. He kept writing during the coming hours, as well.

Another hour passes. And another, and another.

Midnight comes and passes, marked by Nazzo coming to visit me again, bringing a few pieces of crackbread. I eat it gratefully, sharing a few with him. We talk in low tones, and then he leaves. I wait more.

At two thirty in the morning, after over twelve hours of waiting, I finally hear a response.

"Come in."

I enter. The room is lit by a lone oil lamp on the desk, which is also covered by a pile of torn-up paper and spilled ink. A few of the papers have fallen to the floor. Coda's collection of wanted posters has been torn down from the wall and is missing—I presume they've been tossed out the window. This includes my own poster. I can't find it in me to feel indignant about it.

I instantly locate Vann on the bed, though it takes a moment for my eyes to realize that he's beneath the covers and not atop them. Closing the door behind me, I move toward the bed, taking a seat at the foot of it. "Hey," I say to the bundle of covers and hides. "Are you in there, Vann?"

"Monster . . ." I hear him mumble from inside the covers. "You're a monster . . ."

I turn to look out the window. With the stars dangling down in the sky, and their reflections bouncing up from the quiet tar sea, it looks as though the entire world, as above, so below, is covered in nothing but stars and inky sky. I take a little breath and look back at the pile of covers. "You aren't going to join us, are you?"

Now, finally, his face peeks out from within the covers. REDdened eyes set in dark circles: wide and big yet infinitely wrathful.

I smile slightly at his beyond obvious answer, but it falls off just as quickly. "Then what *do* you want?" I ask, genuinely. "You don't want to die. I know you don't. Someone who wants to die wouldn't be writing letters for people to read once they're dead." I weave my fingers atop my lap, feeling how cold my skin is: no warmer than my claws. I clench them. "How do you expect to live when you refuse the only option you have?"

From within the covers comes only a tiny murmur in response, "—ve me . . ."

"I'm sorry?"

He sits up, removing the covers from his upper body. His mane is completely tangled, his cheeks sunken with exhaustion, and his brow furrowed by grief, but his eyes are clear, almost glittering as he speaks again, saying with absolute certainty, "Save me."

I can feel my face scrunch up in confusion. "What are you . . . ?"

"Save me," he says, again. As though repeating it is supposed to make every-thing clear.

"I don't . . ." I pause to shake my head. "I *am* trying to save you! It's just that you won't accept my help. There's only one way for you to survive this week, and that is to—"

"No," he says. "You can save me."

"I *can't.*"

"You can."

A frustrated frown forces itself onto my face. "Oh, yeah, okay, *sure,*" I sneer, "I *could* save you. All I have to do is kill my friends, leave one alive so I don't clear the floor, and then *single-handedly* steer the *Frisk* to port, *all the while dragging a hostage ship with us.* Yeah. That's realistic. And what should we do at port, huh? Keep the final one as our pet? Or maybe you'll want to go your own way, and leave me to mine? Of course. Because, after all, I've only known these people for close to a year. Killing them will be easy peasy, right? Hand goes in—heart comes out. Easy. Simple—"

I bite my own tongue. My jaw snaps shut and I quickly swallow the bit-off part, regenerating it in a matter of seconds. During that time, though, Vann starts talking again.

"No, not like that. Not that extreme." He makes a face. "I don't want to live at the cost of someone else." He sits up straighter, closer. "There must be some other solution. A world in which I live, and you don't have to kill anyone to make that happen. That's what you want, isn't it, Fennrick? For me to *live?*"

I turn away from him. The answer forces its way up my throat like a fat toad. "Yeah," I croak. "I want you to live."

Carefully he removes the covers and takes a seat on the side of the bed, next to me. "I want to live. Everything else, about me joining your pirate friends . . . It's as irrelevant as it is impossible. I've been trying to tell you this for almost a month now." I can't bear to look him in the eyes. My gaze lies square on my hands, clenched tightly across my lap. "You gave me the choice to either become a murderer or die. I gave you my answer to that cruel dilemma. You didn't like my answer. What is the solution?"

BLACK hot shame burns my head all the way to my ears. "There's none," I mumble, even though I know I'm wrong.

His hands reach out and touch my clenched hands. "There is," he says, tenderly. "There is a solution." I can hear the smile in his voice when he says, "Isn't that wonderful?"

My hands relax. I blink down at them. But that . . . But . . . Out of pure confoundation, I look at him, finally. "Is there really . . . ?" But I'm struck frozen when I see his smile, and the tears welling out of his eyes, streaking down the creases made by his smile, down his chin. Making the front of his shirt damp.

"There is," he says with joyous finality.

Something dark and heavy lifts off my chest and I can finally breathe again after three weeks of drowning. "There is a way?" The words don't even feel real, but then my head catches up to my heart and the words are quickly followed by real, tangible logic. "Well, yes, I guess, with the hostages, then . . . ." I continue talking aloud to myself, hand stroking my chin. "If we took you up in the middle of the night, and then boarded the hostage ship, and hid you somewhere, maybe with the help of the hostages . . . Then, when we trade in the hostage ship, you'll be safely out of our grasp and maybe even with a group that might treat you well . . ."

Vann stares at me, eyes wide and foggy with yet unshed tears. "So there is a way?"

I hesitate to answer, but since it isn't technically impossible . . . "Yeah." I nod sharply. "There's a way."

"There's a way . . ." he mumbles back at me, and then his eyes flutter closed, and he collapses back onto the bed, already asleep when the back of his head touches the pillow. Just like that.

I watch him for a second. Then, softly enough to not wake him, I mutter, "But I might not be able to . . ." The words elude me. I shake my head, stand up, and put the covers on him again. "I'll be back in the morning," I say, mostly to myself. "So don't go anywhere, alright?"

I leave him, making sure to close the door behind me. A deep sigh tumbles its way up my throat. "What the heck should I . . ."

Nazzo stares at me. I stare at Nazzo. My brows wrinkle up. What in the—

Before I even have time to recognize that he's there, he folds into a bow, eyes facing the floor. "Please let me help!"

My eyes widen. "H—hey! How did you—" His massive ears waggle. Damn it. My eyes dart back and forth through the hallway and I take a hissing breath. Some people are still awake. Damn it, damn it, damn it . . . "Be quiet, Nazzo! Someone could hear you!" He quickly falls silent. Good. However, he's still facing the floor. Not good. I clench and unclench my hands. "How much did you hear?"

"Everything," Nazzo says. "Exactly everything." While I'm still trying to find the words to tell him off, he quickly adds, "That is why I ask that you *please* let me help."

I almost want to ask why I should trust him, but I know that it's the wrong question. Rather, I ask, "What makes you think I'll actually go through with it?"

After almost a full minute of bowing, he looks up at me, the shining face of sheer confusion. "Why wouldn't you?"

His question strikes true. Why wouldn't I do it? It's basically foolproof. Vann would survive, I can't imagine him trying to report what happened to the authorities, and even when Coda notices that he's gone missing, they can't punish me in any meaningful way. If I let Nazzo help, we could even construct a false narrative to make it seem as though he was still in his room even after the hostage situation is done and over with. So why am I hesitating? Has Coda's position as my captain taken such a hold of my heart that I can't even imagine disobeying? I don't know.

Logically, everything points to this being the best choice. A compromise.

There is no reason not to do this.

I let myself sigh. "I don't know. Sorry, it was a . . ." I shake my head. Then I look him up and down. "Are you sure you want to help? If we get caught, Coda might punish you too."

He smiles simply at me. "Yeah, but that's only if we get caught."

His confidence is almost blinding. Worst of all, the more I think about it, the more I find myself agreeing. And after a moment of thought, I finally say, "Alright. Fine, you can help. But if I find out that you ratted us out . . ." I inch closer to him, letting my size speak for me. "I won't let you off with just a single bite. You got that?"

The smile on his simple face doesn't even twitch. "Got it!" And not even a hint of fear in the air.

With Nazzo's assistance procured, I head to bed. The next day, in the morning, I speak to Vann again, presenting the plan with more detail, including dates and specific times. The hostages would be turned over in two days, so we decided that on the evening of their being turned over, the plan would be put in place. We decided not to enlighten the hostages about the plan—unless they discovered us, that is. Once the hostages were turned over, Vann would pretend to be a stowaway who somehow sat out the entire ordeal.

It was simple enough, and I had little reason to assume anything would go wrong.

Funnily enough, on that day, it rained. Rain on the tar sea was rare, and when it happened, the first hour or so would be horrible; the entire sea filled with the hissing of water being turned to steam, the steam itself being so hot it was impossible to be outside. After that first hour, though, the upper layer of tar cooled down enough to not instantly vaporize the falling water. A few hours in, the rain was still falling with a smattering vengeance, thunder crashing across the heavens, the tar sea covered in a thick mist that made it next to impossible to see anything beyond our own boat and the hostage boat.

When the sun fell and darkness came to reign, the rain had become little more than a drizzle, and everything was ready.

We agreed to do it at half past one in the morning. I had wanted to do it later, but Nazzo and Vann ganged up on me, arguing that since they were the ones affected by sleep deprivation, they were the only ones who should have a say in the matter. Foolishly enough, I let them.

So at a quarter past one, I slip out of my hammock and tap Nazzo on the shoulder where he lies in his own. Then I wait for him to climb out of his hammock before I grab him and carry him out of the room, my superior stealth skills keeping us both well-hidden as I sneak across the hallway and down to the captain's room. There, I almost knock on the door by sheer instinct before pulling myself together and simply open the door.

Vann stands at the foot of his bed, fully dressed but without the shoes. The shoes are too loud, so I had told both him and Nazzo to omit them. Vann was a bit more reluctant to go barefoot, but Nazzo was able to convince him. Apparently, he still chose to wear socks, even though the wet deck is sure to get them damp. Once he notices us in the doorway, he nods at us resolutely. We nod back, and I let Nazzo down. A quick hand movement is enough to send him away, and he slips back out the door, going ahead of us up the stairs and onto the deck in order to distract Barbariccia, who should be in the drake's nest right about now. I can't really tell anything that's happening abovedeck since the rain has dulled the scents on display, and I don't desire Barbariccia enough for the great values sniffer to pick up on him.

With Nazzo going ahead, I turn to Vann. He meets my gaze with determination and readiness, though I can smell the anxiety lingering around him. Reaching out, I pat him on the shoulder and mouth, *It's okay*. I'm not sure if it helped, but regardless, I pick him up and carry him in the same way I did Nazzo. I'd like to try if FPB works while holding someone, but Vann refused it earlier, so I'll have to try it out later.

We head out and into the hallway, up the stairs, and then wait a moment to see if Nazzo will return to tell us not to go out on deck. Then, when he doesn't appear, we head out onto the deck. It's still raining, though nowhere near as harshly as earlier today. The deck is slippery, and I remember how Coda warned us earlier today to be careful and only be up and about when necessary. Since I didn't have any business on deck, this is actually the first I've been up all day. When it rains, the surface of the tar sea thickens to the point where it's difficult to move, so today has mostly been a rest day for all of us.

I can't see anybody on deck, so after a moment of hesitation, I let Vann down, motioning for him to remain quiet. Then I lead him across the deck to the hostage ship.

I freeze midstep.

Wh—where did the hostage ship go? There's just *nothing there*! The harpoons have even been returned to their cannons. What the heck is—

"Kitty!"

I spin around, almost slipping, ready to either hiss for someone to keep quiet or force them to be silent before realizing that the look on Nazzo's approaching face is anything but positive. I look up and down the deck. There's no one to hear us. "Nazzo?" I whisper-shout. "What's wrong?"

Nazzo pants for a second or two, rain pouring down his face and mixing with what I think I can smell to be sweat. "H—he wasn't there, Kitty!"

"What do you mean?"

"Bar wasn't up in the drake's nest—it was totally empty!"

"There was no one in the drake's nest?" I ask incredulously. "Why—" I'm just about to ask him a question he can't possibly answer when my nose picks up the answer. My heart drops in my chest.

"On an evening like this, there's no need to have someone tending the drake's nest," Coda says as he steps out of the shadows across the deck. The rest of the Evil Claw Pirates soon follow suit. Barbariccia, Scar, Dragon, Cocco, Cal, Al, Cir, Farello, Cante, Cane . . . Most of them look disappointed. Some confused. Others angry. Coda is part of the first group, though with an added touch of what I think might be *grief*. Or maybe it's betrayal? "After sailing with us for ten months, I thought you would have picked up on something that simple, Kitty."

I can feel my claws clicking together, and I take a step forward, positioning myself between my two allies and the pirates. "Ten months is less time than you'd expect," I say, mostly just to fill out time while my heart stops beating so damn fast. I almost smile. "How'd you figure it out?"

His smile turns melancholic. "I eavesdropped."

"Again?"

"Again."

I grin, teeth clenched tightly. "Did I tell you that humans consider it *very rude* to eavesdrop?"

"In that case, it's the same as for us goblins," Coda says. "However, being a pirate, such customs aren't the kind I respect too often." He drops the smile. "Would you call me a hypocrite if I said that I never expected you to do this? To betray us over a *sailor?*" His eye twitches. "If anyone else had overheard your conversation, and they had told me, I would have had them walk the plank for even *suggesting* that you'd turn your back on us."

"I—I haven't . . ."

"It will be painless," Coda says, interrupting my incohesive mutterings. "As I promised. And you will be punished as we agreed to—having to sleep in the hold for a week." A crackle of thunder booms in the sky, and I remember having heard similar thunder all day. Thunder as loud as the boom of cannons. "Because that *is* what we agreed to. You remember that, don't you, Kitty?"

The rain is eating into my clothes. Behind me, I notice Vann, trembling not because of the freezing rain but rather out of fear. I grit my teeth.

"Why?" I shout above the smatter of rain. "Why should he have to die?"

"Him dying is the norm," Coda calmly answers. "Him living was the exception. But it couldn't last forever."

"Yeah!" Barbariccia yells savagely. "He's a filthy friend of a traitor! And you, as the traitor, should—"

Coda puts his hand on Barbariccia's chest. "Calm down, Bar," he says softly. Not for me to hear. "We agreed to not punish him too badly, remember?"

"*You* agreed to be coddling with the human!" Barbariccia spits. "The same creature that would eat children—*children!* And now, showing him preferential treatment? Bah! We should kill him and—"

"Then kill me!" I howl. The rain falls silent and the deck likewise. "Kill me, and let Vann live! I've committed enough sins to be smitten by lightning a hundredfold and deserve every shock *and more!* But Vann?" I wipe the rainwater from my face. "He's innocent. He hasn't done a single thing to deserve your ire, and you want to give him the death penalty?" I can feel my teeth grind together, the grating noise effectively replacing the rain. "If you'd known him as long as you've known me, you would spare him."

I pant where I stand, the exertion of shouting making my legs tremble in their wet-cloth bindings. But across the deck, Coda stands calmly, stoically.

"No," Coda says. "We wouldn't."

My heart stops beating in my chest. The cold of the rain chews its way into my very bones. "You . . ." I swallow a mouthful of rainwater. My voice is broken when I speak again, shards scraping together. "Why not?"

His eyes are as calm as the WHITE fog clinging to the BLACK sea around us. "Because you need to learn a lesson."

I stare at him. The world doesn't feel real anymore. Nothing makes sense. "What?"

"We made an agreement, one heavily favorable to your wants. For the rewards of his life, you signed off on two risks, one being your punishment, the other being his life: forfeit." His voice is soft, smooth. Like aqua regalia. Although it had only ever made me feel calm and relaxed, it now grants me the overpowering impression that, all this time, I've been in the presence of a devil as silver-tongued as any. His eyes shine in the darkness, all too similar to the sea of tar itself. "You agreed to it, you broke it, and now you will face the consequences." His eyes narrow. "Do you now refuse it?"

My breath is ragged. Cold air in, cold air out.

I'm a hypocrite. I gambled and lost and now I'm too childish to pay my due.

I bite my lip, warm blood mingling with rainwater. If only it had been my own life on the line, it would have been fine. "No," I mutter, the lead-heavy weight of a thousand sins piled atop one another slowly crumbling off, one piece at a time. "No, I can't refuse your orders, Coda." I clench my hands into fists. "But I can't let him pay for my stupid mistakes. So please—"

"Are you disobeying the direct orders of your captain?"

I shake my head, my wet hair splashing water. "No, I'm just—"

"Stop arguing with Coda!" Cir shouts. "You know better than that, Kitty!"

"Yeah, come on!" Cal says. "He saved your life, can't you be grateful for that?"

"Nazzo, you won't be punished, so just tell Kitty not to do anything stupid!" Farello chimes in. "Because, let me tell you, arguing against Coda is *beyond* stupid!"

Coda holds up a hand, silencing the group. "You won't have to do it yourself. Just step off this deck, go down to the hold, and when your week is up, he'll be gone. Simple as that." He shows an expression of remorse. "I can't make this any kinder for you, Kitty."

"This ungrateful human keeps rejecting his own captain's wants!" Barbariccia shouts. "He's a traitor, the damn thing! Let's treat him as traitors ought to be treated!"

Again, Coda stops him with a quick shake of the head, turning to me again. "Please, Kitty. Do as I ask."

I'm trembling. How long have I been trembling? I don't know what to do anymore. I'm frozen in place. My feet won't even move. The weight of the world is on my shoulders and it's crippling. Is this the weight of a single life? This soul-crushing weight?

I'm paralyzed. I can't do anything anymore. Everyone's looking at me, waiting for me to make a decision, to choose between what's right and what's right. I can't . . .

Vann pokes me. I turn to him. He smiles at me, a big, broad smile that holds enough joy for an entire lifetime. "It's okay," he says, eyes filled with tears and rain. "You can go. They'll make it painless. I won't feel a thing, so—"

I put my hand on his head. My smile mirrors him, if only in part. "Don't worry. I'll figure it out. You won't have to—"

"Conspirators!" Barbariccia cries. "That little drakeborn is trying to turn him against us even more!" Coda tries to calm him down, but he's barely even consolable. Scar and Dragon both have to hold him back, almost slipping on the wet deck in the meantime.

I clear my throat. Adapting a more calming tone, I start to speak, approaching them as I do, "Listen, we can talk about this. Let's all take a deep breath, and—" And as soon as I come close, they move back. I freeze. Coda stands tall, firm—but the rest . . . They look at me *like that*. I try to move closer. They restrain themselves, but only barely. "Why are you . . . ?"

"Just stay calm, okay, Kitty?" Coda says, smiling again, holding up his hands placatingly. "All I ask is that you leave the deck, go down into the hold, and—"

"Could you stop me?" The words come out as an inquisitive whisper, but I'm close enough for them to hear it. "Could you actually get to him?" I ask. Or maybe I'm musing aloud to myself. Why does he want me to leave? What are they afraid of? It isn't me. They know me. I've eaten with them, fought with them, played with them. No, that isn't what they fear. They don't fear my smile— they fear my teeth. "Could you get *through me*?"

Coda backs away, just one step, but it feels like a mile. "Please, Kitty, this isn't the time—"

I take a step forward, and all of a sudden Barbariccia flies out at me, his sword drawn and ready, and then, I've got my hand in his chest. No, not *in* his chest. *Through* his chest. My hand is RED. By pure instinct, I'm holding his heart. The thick organ beats against my fingers, once, twice . . . I count twelve times until it stops.

<Goblin (Lv.22) Defeated.>
<1/12 Evil Claw Pirates Defeated.>

Ah. He's . . . dead?

I lower my arm and he slides off into a pile on the floor. There he is. He's just . . . *lying* there. Motionless. He doesn't smell alive anymore. He smells dead, and he looks dead, and he *is* dead. I'm still holding his heart. It feels like a sick joke, like he'll jump up at any moment and shout, *Hey, that's mine! Give it back!* But he doesn't, because he's dead. The rain rinses my hand of blood but the heart is still there. A question pokes at my brain and I take a bite of it, to find that even though I knew him, it still tastes the same as every other heart I've eaten. It's all the same.

I feel . . . nothing.

A fist flies at me. Scar. His eyes are flashing, angry. "*YOU—!*" he screams, but I don't know what he was about to call me, because my claws go through his neck, and he can't speak anymore. I hold his intact spine in my right hand. His eyes go dim. That's weird. I thought Scar disliked Barbariccia? He was always joking that he was going to aim a cannon at the drake's nest some time, just to check if Barbariccia would notice.

I remove Scar's heart and taste it, but even though I knew him, and even though I liked him, it still tastes the same.

<Goblin (Lv.23) Defeated.>
<2/12 Evil Claw Pirates Defeated.>

And I feel nothing.

Dragon and Cocco don't bother to say anything as they go at me, their years of experience allowing them to fight in sync. But it isn't enough. They slice me, one of them getting my left eye, but it changes nothing. When fighting pairs, I usually focus on the strongest, so I reach out and grab Dragon by the shoulders, just like I did two months back when I hugged him for the first time, and I sever his spine in a single bite.

<Goblin (Lv.20) Defeated.>
<3/12 Evil Claw Pirates Defeated.>

Cocco uses the moment to slash me across the back, but it doesn't matter. I grab his arm, lift him into the air, and slam him back onto the deck. Then I crush his throat and neck in a single stomp.

<Goblin (Lv.21) Defeated.>
<4/12 Evil Claw Pirates Defeated.>

I didn't know him as well as I would have wanted to. He never did tell me why he left his wife and children behind. But it doesn't matter anymore. He's dead, so whatever led him to this place is irrelevant.

"Kitty, why would you—" I slash my claws across Al's abdomen before I even realize he's the one I'm killing. He falls to the ground in a mess of organs and membranes, rainwater pooling between no-longer-folded intestines.

"Al—" Cal falls to the ground, to his knees, bundling Al into his arms. "Oh, oh, gods, Al, why would you—"

Experimentally, I take hold of his head, and he only has time to look up at me in wide-eyed horror and betrayal before he's gone, his skull crushed between my fingers, brain matter splattering the deck and my shirt.

<Goblin (Lv.14) Defeated.>
<5/12 Evil Claw Pirates Defeated.>

All that's left of his head is his face, still confused, still so utterly betrayed. But the feelings of an empty face don't matter. All that he was, every pun, bad joke, and ridiculous taunt, is what is now splattered across my hand and the floor. That's all. It doesn't exist anymore. My memories are all there is of him.

At my feet, Al writhes, his trembling hand moving toward what used to be Cal. I step on his hand, crushing his wrist. "*AAAAAAAAHHHHH—!*" he screams, but as I'm hearing it, I realize that it doesn't matter. Once he's dead, none of the pain he ever felt—be it now or before or in a second—will matter. He'll be dead, and his pain, too. So I do the most merciful thing and place my foot on his chest, pressing my clawed sole onto his sternum, feeling it crack beneath my toes alongside his ribs, a bit more pressure allowing me to finally crush his heart fully. And like that, he's gone, and his pain with him.

<Goblin (Lv.19) Defeated.>
<6/12 Evil Claw Pirates Defeated.>

I remove my foot. I didn't actually break the skin of his chest, but now there's a deep dent, into which the falling rain is pooling. If we'd been out in the forest, it might have made for a nice bird bath, or a tiny watering hole for frogs to gather in. The thought makes me smile.

"Now!" someone shouts, and a pair of swords are stabbed into my back, into my lungs. Since that might not be too good, I turn around and swipe the feet out from under Cir. The fall makes him gasp, but the bloodied deck makes his gasp almost turn into a scream. The sound would be a bit irritating, though, so I waste no time hunching down, picking him up by the throat, and then grabbing his shoulder, tearing off his entire head with little issue. I take a few bites of the exposed neck, healing the damage they did to my lungs.

<Goblin (Lv.20) Defeated.>
<7/12 Evil Claw Pirates Defeated.>

"A—ah . . ." Farello drops his sword. His wide eyes tremble in horror. "*CIRI-ATTO!*" His broken scream grates my ears, but when I try to grab him, he runs for it, in the direction of where Vann and Nazzo stand. But the floor is slippery with more than just rainwater, and he soon slips. I stalk up behind him. Now that I'm approaching Vann and Nazzo, I notice that Vann is actually standing in front of Nazzo, as opposed to before, when it was the other way around. Curious.

Picking Farello off the floor by the leg, I stab my hand through the opening beneath his rib cage, easily getting a hold of his heart, which I then pull out and bite into. Same taste as everyone else. Same nothingness as he falls.

<Goblin (Lv.12) Defeated.>
<8/12 Evil Claw Pirates Defeated.>

I turn back to where the others had been just before. There are so few of them left now. I sniff a little.

There.

"Please, Cante, we have to—"

"I'm not going without—"

"But we can't—"

Cante and Cane. Hunched, trying to do . . . something. I pace up behind them and stab them both through the back, removing both hearts in a single, simple little movement. There. That was easy. Too easy. If I remember correctly from the way Cane told it on theater nights, he used to do fencing as a kid. And now he's an adult. But he couldn't even . . .

I shake my head.

It doesn't matter anymore. They're dead. They don't exist anymore, so I don't have to think about them.

<Goblin (Lv.22) Defeated.>
<Goblin (Lv.21) Defeated.>
<10/12 Evil Claw Pirates Defeated.>

On the floor between them lies Coda. I squat down next to him. Is he dead? But I haven't done anything yet. I sniff him a little.

No, he isn't dead. Then why is he on the floor? It doesn't make any sense.

I pick him up by the head, letting his feet dangle before trying to put him down in a standing pose. But his knees buckle out under him. That's weird. I slap his cheek a little. "Hey," I say. "Coda? Are you in there, Captain?"

It takes a second, but he suddenly draws in a quick shallow breath, his eyes fluttering open and looking around in confusion before finally falling on me, on my face, mere inches away from his. He smiles warmly. "Oh, it's just you, Kitty." He chuckles. "You wouldn't believe it, I had the *strangest*—"

I put him down. He stumbles a little on shaking knees before his feet finally give away, making him fall to the floor, to the blood and the bodies. He hisses in pain. "Ouch, what is—" And then he sees it. The bodies. What used to be Cante and Cane, and Cir and Farello, and Scar and Dragon and Cal and Al and Barbariccia and Cocco, but isn't them anymore. His mouth, now open, trembles.

I look at him, and I say, "Coda—" and I'm just about to say something else when I realize that *Ah. It doesn't matter.* Because Coda isn't really Coda anymore. I've decided that he's going to die, so he isn't really Coda anymore. I'm looking at him, of course, but it's much closer to looking at a moving doll of flesh. He's already dead. So what's the point?

"K—Kitty, what have you . . . You've . . ." He turns to me, eyes glistening, and all he has to say after all that is, "Why?"

Why?

Because . . .

I frown. Why . . . ?

I stab my hand through his chest. His heart beats between my fingers, alive. He's alive. But he's dead. That's weird. He coughs, his chest spasming around my hand. I look at his face. The way it twitches and twists into expressions of pain and horror and betrayal and countless other emotions that won't matter in as little as a single minute. Ten months I've known him. Ten months . . . that was as long as I was ever to know him. It was a good ten months. I enjoyed them. He was kind to me.

I smile at him. "Thank you," I say. "For everything."

I pull the heart from his chest and let Coda's body fall to the deck again. I count the final beats. Sixteen beats. That's all, and then he's gone.

<Goblin (Lv.25) Defeated.>
<11/12 Evil Claw Pirates Defeated.>

I stand up. It's hard to believe everything felt so big and world-encompassing only a few minutes ago. And now, what seemed to be my entire world is just a collection of meat and organs and bones being washed by the rain. I look down at my RED and bloodied hand, at the claws that did this. The weight of a life is light. Like cotton, or a single marshmallow. It's nothing.

My heart feels light.

I turn to Vann. To Nazzo. I only have one left. I might as well.

I move toward them. Vann tries to hide the smaller, younger goblin behind him. "It's okay," I say as I approach him. "I won't hurt you." There's no point in hurting him. Now I stand above them, a flash of lightning splattering them with my shadow. A rumble fills the air with heavy mumbles.

Their eyes are so big, like little prey animals. Squatting down, I reach behind Vann and grab Nazzo. He trembles in my hands. But he isn't saying anything. I lean in toward his neck. One clean bite should do it.

A little hand grabs hold of my torn and bloodied sleeve. I look down at Vann. The way his eyes plead. I understand. I let my gaze soften as I look at him, assuring him that this won't hurt one bit.

"A—ah—" Nazzo mumbles, and then I bite. Blood splatters—across me, across Vann, across the deck. I swallow the mouthful of tender flesh before tossing the still-alive goblin to the side. I look down at Vann.

<Goblin (Lv.8) Defeated.>
<12/12 Evil Claw Pirates Defeated.>

<The floor clearing has been temporarily postponed.>

<The God of Cruelty watches you with anticipation.>

I don't pay the messages any heed. Instead, I turn back to Vann and show him my blood-soaked hand, or rather, my claws. He stares at me instead of them, so I move them closer to his face. "Look," I say. "Look at it." His wide, staring eyes turn to the claws. "See?" I say. "You were wrong."

"I was . . . wrong?" Vann croaks, more in confusion than defeat.

"Yeah," I say, still showing my claws. I almost chuckle. "*I'm not shaking.* Not even the slightest tremble. So . . ." I smile at him. "You were wrong, Vann. I could have done it. They could have been as close as friends, and I—" A tiny, bitter laugh escapes my lips. "And I would still have been able to do it." Blood. Blood below me, on the deck. Blood on my hands. Blood in my hair. Blood on and in me and around me and *everywhere*. I step closer to him, squeezing him up to the railing. "What does that make me, Vann? Why did I kill them? And why—" I take a haggard breath. "Why won't I kill you?" I can feel the smile fall off my face. I look down at him. "*What does that make me?*"

"A monster," Vann says, with as much dawning realization as I feel hearing it.

I pause for a moment. "Yeah. That's it, isn't it?" I smile again. "*A monster.*"

I turn away from him, toward the bodies. Toward what I've done. Toward the emptiness, the numbness, the hollow weightlessness that it granted me.

Toward the future.

<THE GOD OF CRUELTY IS PLEASED WITH YOUR DECISION TO SPARE VANN, SON OF PETTERE.>

<You have cleared the twenty-second floor.>
<Congratulations!>
<As a special reward, the God of Cruelty wishes to grant you some of His power instead of the normal floor clear reward. Do you accept?>
<Yes/No>

Nothing about being the first to clear the floor, nothing about full clear reward . . . Just a lame little congratulation.

I press the Yes button. There was no other choice.

<You have obtained:>
<[To Make A Martyr Lv.MAX] The God of Cruelty, who watches over those that show cruelty above mercy, has granted some of His powers to His plaything.>

Is it supposed to say that thing there at the end?

I don't really have time to consider it too deeply before the rain and the wind and the blood and the reeling sea disappear, once more dragging me back to that horrid lobby.

FLOOR 23

THE HORRID SEWERS

XIX

Here We Go Again

Ah, the lobby, the wonderful lobby. Eternally imperfect. Well, nothing to do other than—

My eyes get stuck on a pillar. No, not on a pillar. On the thing that's plastered *on* the pillar. As I stare at it in a mixture of horror and awe, a status box appears to explain everything.

<Gift from the God of Comedy>

It's a poster. A poster, with a kitten on it. A kitten hanging from a tree. And above said kitten hanging from a tree, written in rainbow-colored Comic Sans, it says *Hang in there!* Signed, *God of Comedy.*

I don't even . . .

Where I stand, I stare at it for almost a full minute before walking up to the poster and tearing it off the pillar.

Only to find another, exact replica below it. When I rip the replica off, I find another one. And then another. And then another. And then another. And then . . .

And then I give up, spinning on my heels, only to find the poster on literally every single pillar. *All of them.* I feel my eyelid twitch. Alright. Okay. I see how it is. But can it handle the unbridled force of my arteries?

I try to paint the lobby. Focus on *try.* The damn posters are hydrophobic. Nothing sticks! *Horrific!*

However, my effort to somehow cover up the posters *does* give me time to check out a few other things, such as—for example—my new, slightly suspicious skill.

<[To Make A Martyr(Lv.MAX)]
The God of Cruelty, who watches over those that show cruelty above mercy,
has granted some of His powers to His potential plaything.>
<The user gains the ability to fully heal any wound using the fresh heart of
a goblin, human, or dragon. Cannot be used to heal user.>
<[SOVEREIGN SKILL]>

Excuse me? What is . . . ?

Any wound? On anyone? To what degree? Can it heal death? How fresh does the heart have to be? Does the recipient have to want it, or can it be done unwillingly? Why are dragons included? Why can't I use it on myself? How do I actually use it? What is—

<THE GOD OF CRUELTY CHUCKLES.>
<[ONLY ONE WAY TO FIND OUT.]>

I'm starting to kind of like the way this guy thinks.

Still, that doesn't explain why the *God of Cruelty* would give me a skill that *heals people*. Isn't healing good? Especially if it's any wound, then it's *really* good! How could a good skill like this be cruel? I don't get it.

Anyway, I can't test it out here and now, so while I'm waiting for the next floor to open, I decide to send Moleman a message to explain my situation.

<PrissyKittyPrincess[F23]: Hey moleman. just beat f22. u doing good?
gg>

And off it goes. Now, I just have to wait for the next floor to open. I guess I might as well use this time trying to get rid of these horrible posters.

<Top—Status—Community>
<02:45:21 Day 855>
<The twenty-ninth attempt will begin in 25:21:14:39>
<The twenty-third floor will open in 0:00:10>

Here we go.
I hope this floor will have lots of people I can test my new skill on.

<Floor 23 has opened. Do you want to enter?>
<Yes/No>

I press Yes. There is nothing else to press.

The world sways, briefly reminding me of the calming rocking of the *Frisky Lady*, only for the sensation to end as soon as it began with my feet plunging into ankle-deep gunk. What the heck is—

<Tutorial stage, Hell Difficulty Twenty-third Floor: The Horrid Sewers>
<[Clear Condition] Reach the depths of the sewers.>

Of course it's a sewer. I should have realized that by the smell, the lack of light, and the gunk I'm standing in. Eugh. The description of the place is certainly flattering enough . . .

I take a few cursory sniffs. *Oof.* Yeah, that's horrid alright. The smell is actually making it difficult to use GVS, but I can use it well enough to tell which way I'm supposed to be heading, so there's no confusion there.

Drawing myself up, I set out into the horrid sewers.

Elsewhere

<PrissyKittyPrincess[F23]: Hey moleman. just beat f22. u doing good? gg>

The message hung still before Emil's eyes, the simple words presenting themselves with little ambiguity. The same as it had when he received it almost a month earlier.

He had beaten the twenty-second floor. Emil could remember his own experiences with that floor; he and his comrades appearing in the middle of the sea in a small iron caravan, forced to fend off horrible sea beasts and live off what little food they could catch from within the oily depths. At least they could buy food when they eventually reached the edge of the sea.

As far as he could remember, Kitty hadn't even been given so much as a dinghy on which to survive the turbulent black sea. The fact that he was alive was a miracle. The fact that he had beaten the floor was an omen.

Didn't he say that he'd befriended a band of pirates? Emil thought, shifting where he sat awaiting the royal audience. The seat he occupied was worryingly comfortable. If he'd been given the choice ahead of time, he would rather have sat on the floor. The embroidered design on the seat was hand-sewn, put together with the finest threads of lightsilk by the most prestigious seamstresses in the kingdom of Acheron. It was nothing for a simple man such as Emil to sit on. However, an envoy of the Server Alliance had to be presentable. This included sitting well, wearing the proper official clothes, and not staring into space trying to think of the best way to ask a buddy if they killed their entire friend group.

He didn't want to be accusatory. Accusing Kitty out of nowhere could get him on the defensive. But sometimes accusing him was good. Sometimes it let him confront himself and realize that maybe he had been doing things that were a bit bad for the people and world around him.

Balance. That was it. He had to have *balance* in it. The golden middle road was the correct one even if the extremes could look platinum-paved.

Ensuring that no citizen was watching him, Emil pulled up the writing service.

<SuperMoleman[F67]: Hey Kitty! I'm sorry to ask this, but what happened with your pirate friends? Did something happen? You can tell me . . .>

Delete. Again.

<SuperMoleman[F67]: Hi Kitty! I'm so happy to hear from you! I was starting to get worried about what was happening with Vann, since you hadn't written in a while, but if you beat the floor then it must have gone . . .>

Delete, delete, delete. Emil sighed in frustration. Was he just overthinking things? Maybe he was going about all of this in the completely wrong light? Kitty *had* recently started being kinder. Less . . . *murderous.* Like that thing with the Goddess of Innocence. Didn't he choose to spare a child? Emil allowed himself the relief of smiling at the thought. Yes, Kitty *had* been getting better. Especially in the tutorial tournament. A man who would willingly spare his enemies, even knowing they wouldn't die from his attacks, couldn't possibly do something as cruel as killing people he had known for close to a year. Because if he *had* been able to do that, then . . .

Emil shook his head. No. *No.* Those kinds of thoughts weren't fitting of a friend.

And still, despite all of that, he couldn't find the words. The last message Kitty had sent was almost two months ago, where he explained how he'd bumped into an old acquaintance while pillaging a ship. Whatever happened to him? Did he join Kitty's pirate band, or did something happen? Then again, if he *did* join, then that would mean that Kitty would have had to kill him to beat the floor as well. But if he *didn't* join, then would that mean he survived? Or did he kill him, too, just for the sake of it?

He felt his hands clench, the white silk gloves he wore keeping his nails from digging into his palms. This wasn't helping. Assuming that Kitty would do something that terrible wasn't making things better for anyone, especially not Emil himself.

There was, after all, a chance that Kitty had chosen to test those strategies Emil had presented him when he first explained his fresh plight. Changing the name of the Evil Claw Pirates to something else, trying to get the pirates to disband altogether, leaving them behind to pretend he had already gotten to the Purgatory section early—there were a number of ways that might possibly have worked to circumvent the cruel clear requirement. Kitty, at the time, had rejected these suggestions. And Emil had been proud of him for it. How could he not have been? The clear requirement was an obvious attempt from the gods to restrain Kitty to the twenty-second floor, and for once, Kitty went along with it. He chose to settle down. It had made Emil so happy that he almost wanted to head to the black sea to congratulate him in person.

But now . . . *With this* . . .

Taking a deep breath, Emil resolved himself. He had to ask him. He had to know.

Before he threw himself into it, though, Emil cast another look around him. The waiting lobby was a big, ornate hall fit for at least three dozen waiting members. Currently, though, it contained only him. Him, and the dozen guards there to ensure he didn't do anything befitting the *hoeksak* moniker. Four guards stood at the entrance to the room; four guarded the massive, well-carved doors that led to the throne room; and the final four were at his side. Emil was fairly certain that if he so much as pointed a little finger at one of them, he'd be stabbed full of holes before a single word could leave his lips.

In terms of audiences, this was the most difficult one Emil had ever procured. So far, he had met with seven kings, queens, and emperors; fifteen princes and princesses; and over a hundred judges of higher or lesser rank. Most of these meetings took place either at the dining table or in their private offices. Never like this. Meeting the envoy of another kingdom in the throne room was unheard of, only justified by Simel the Survivor's infamous disdain of humans.

This disdain was also the reason why Emil was alone. Barred from bringing his party members alongside any object of magical power, he was more vulnerable now than he had been on the first floor.

The only reason he had been able to procure an audience at all, however, was thanks to that same disdain. Three times had he sought an audience, and three times had he been rejected. Only when he told the wronged regent that he personally knew Kitty was he able to find any success. And even then, he could only gain permission with the promise that he knew where Kitty was. For this reason, the fact that Kitty had left the twenty-second floor was almost a good thing.

It didn't elude Emil that he was, in large part, using his concern for Kitty to ignore the much more difficult worry of his own position.

Agreeing to let himself use Kitty to procrastinate on the audience, he took to writing his message again.

<SuperMoleman[F67]: Hey Kitty! Congratulations on beating the floor! How did it go? Did you use the strategies I mentioned to clear it, or did something else happen? You can tell me whatever happened, even if you

think I might not like it. We're both almost adults, after all. And how did it go with Vann? Did he choose to join you in the end? I look forward to hearing from you, and good luck with the twenty-third floor!>

Emil let his fingers leave the keyboard. As always, he spent a minute or so reading it through, ensuring it was written properly, without any misspellings or similar. It looked well enough, so—

"SuperMoleman of the Server Alliance, His Majesty Simel the Survivor, Blessed of Three is now ready for your audience," one of the guards next to the throne room's doors stated loudly, making Emil twitch at the sudden noise. "Please enter."

Emil's eyes darted back to the message. As he stood up, he quickly sent it away, hoping Kitty wouldn't be too busy with the twenty-third floor to answer it within the coming month or so. The guards at his side followed him as he moved toward the throne room. Since he knew that it was customary to mainly ignore those of lower rank, he fought down the urge to smile and say *Thank you* to the guards opening the door. Instead, to distract himself, he kept his mind focused on the way Plus had taught him to walk properly. His back had to be as straight as a ramrod, something the trendy male corset helped a lot with; his steps had to be the exact right length—not too long, not too short—to let him walk with gravitas, while still keeping in mind to not walk too fast lest the guards at his side were outpaced by his superior stature.

Unfortunately, the straightness of his back and neck meant that he had nowhere to look save for straight ahead—right into the throne room.

The red-and-black carpet—woven with a motif of flames and phoenixes— although soft, was not soft enough to make the tight shoes Emil wore any less uncomfortable. The main source of light for the long, tall room was a row of windows on the left. The windows were quick to draw Emil's attention, as the lower parts were made up of stained glass in the shape and color of flames, making it seem as though the city was on fire. However, as interesting as that was, to not face the room's ruler was beyond rude, forcing Emil to turn his gaze to the main focus of the room.

A pair of dark, perpetually fearful eyes met him. The sight froze Emil in place for a moment, from which he emerged with the intuitive understanding that the king before him wanted him to bow.

It was humiliating to make an envoy bow before them, and yet this was exactly what this king silently demanded. Any other envoy would have stormed out, showing the same rudeness in turn. An envoy was the face and voice of the person they represented. To ask an envoy to bow was to ask the illustrious person they represented to bow. This was the kind of demand that could cause and had caused wars in the past.

Emil knew this. However, he also knew that few nations in this world had any respect for the authority of the Server Alliance—least of all the Acheron kingdom.

Removing the headscarf he was using to hide his hair and lack of mane, Emil went down on one knee. He let his gaze fall to face the floor. "Your Highness Simel the Survivor, Blessed of Three—"

"Put it back on," a strained voice said from across the room. The half-veiled panic in the words, the downright urgency of the statement, briefly convinced Emil that he must have heard him wrong, or that he had said something similar but completely different, as was common with foreign languages. He raised his head briefly, readying himself to ask for clarification, only to be met with eyes of fire and another demanding shriek: "Put it back on, hoeksak!"

Only barely avoiding fumbling the thing, Emil quickly returned the headscarf to his head, pushing his curly locks beneath the band and adjusting it to cover his head properly. With that done, he returned his eyes to the king.

Simel the Survivor sank back into his throne. It was a beautiful throne, but the fabrics draped behind it drew Emil's attention for a reason far more disturbing. They were dark brown in a way only dried blood could be, creased in stiff ways that suggested it had at one point been completely drenched. And now that he was actually looking for it, he found the floor likewise stained. In some places only lightly splattered, tiny dots of dark brown; elsewhere, puddles bloomed across the tiles, partially disturbed by handprints and the swiping of movement.

Something wet and slick crawled up Emil's back and he felt himself shiver.

To keep the thoughts away, the memory of what he knew Kitty to have done here, he turned to look at Simel the Survivor. But it didn't help much. The goblin was pale and thin even by goblin standards, his cheeks sunken and his eyes set in deep, dark holes that made it look as though he was constantly staring at everything in wide-eyed, twitchy horror. The regal clothes he wore, including the crown, did nothing to hide how much he looked like a child.

"Have you finished surveying the pilak of your ilk?" the king said. Although his face hid any emotion under a veneer of sheer-constant terror, his voice was nowhere near as subtle, his vindictive loathing seeping into every spoken word. Although Emil had no idea what a *pilak* was, he could assume by the context that it was the devastation left in the room. No, rather, the devastation Simel the Survivor had chosen to immortalize.

Realizing the rudeness of his touristlike perusing, Emil quickly lowered his head again. "Thousand pardons. As I say, I thank you, Your Majesty, for allowing me this audience, and for my humble friends to—"

"Silence, hoeksak," the king hissed, one hand hovering over his ear, as though he was about to hold it shut. Not acknowledging the impoliteness of his words in the least, the king turned away from Emil, forcing his loathsome and bitter gaze to fall on the guards in the room. "Leave us."

After only a moment's hesitation, the guards relented, the close to a dozen well-armed soldiers leaving the room in a well-organized line. Leaving Emil alone with the cruel king.

More confused than anything else, Emil asked, "Why would—" only for his inquiry to go unheard as the king abruptly rose from his throne, wandering over to the window to stare out at the city, his hand resting on the windowsill.

"Do you know why I want you on your knees?"

Unsure whether he should angle himself to face where the king was now standing, Emil eventually chose to only turn his face toward him. "As the group I represent have yet to find much respect in Purgatory, you decided to show your authority by—"

"Because I don't like when your kind looks down on me." Now his eyes turned to Emil once more, burning in the red light of the sunlit stained-glass windows. "Your species has caused me more ret'rah than any blade or prayer. Can you repay me that debt?" His face set in an expression of terrified determination, the king turned away from the window, his form cast in darkness, save for a single sliver of fiery red light framing him, making it seem as though he was on fire. Outside, the city remained in a state of rebuilding, as it had for the past two years. "Can you undo this nation's ret'rah?"

"We . . ." Emil shut his eyes. He took a deep breath before opening them again. "I cannot. Nobody can."

The king stared at him for five agonizingly long seconds before giving a small, almost imperceptible nod. "Yes—yes, that is right. You cannot. Not even our gods can save us. In the time I was his prisoner, I prayed more than I ever have. I still do. Do you see this little book?" Within his hand, pulled from a small, perfectly shaped satchel on his belt, was a tiny notebook, as well-worn as it was plain. "In here, I have written all of the names he has erased. Nine thousand, seven hundred forty-two. For the ones I knew, I wrote down how it happened. When. Why." A broken smile accompanied the ruthlessly bitter chuckle he mustered. "Why . . . as though that was ever part of it."

Nine thousand, seven hundred forty-two. The number circled inside Emil's head, a shark introduced to a koi pond. His throat felt parched. Swallowing didn't help, but it gave him the strength to try to speak. "Surely, Your Majesty, that number must—"

"Every night, I pray this book. It takes a month to clear through it. Do you see? I live for this. I live because they didn't. The gods let me live so that I may pray for their souls, that they may rest, and that the people left in his wake may find peace." His eyes burn with empty darkness. "So that they may be avenged.

That justice may be wrought. Do you understand, hoeksak? Do you understand the burden that is this crown?"

No, Emil thought. *I don't.*

The silence in the room was deafening, but it was enough to rouse Emil to use one of few trump cards Kitty had left the Server Alliance. "We have called for his execution as of a year back, and he is currently an outlaw. His actions do not represent the Server Alliance, nor the wishes of all hoeksak, and—"

"Is he dead?" The king's simple question cut the well-trained, well-used line short, leaving Emil slack-jawed, the echo of the question weighing heavy on his mind. "Is he dead, hoeksak?"

"We can't . . ." Emil bit his lip. "No. He isn't dead." The mere thought that Kitty could be killed was, at this point, almost laughable. He'd survive, no matter what. Emil could only envy holding that kind of conviction. "But if we ever catch him, then . . ."

The king strode up to him. Although Emil was kneeling and the king was standing, the height difference wasn't very significant. Still, the king was looking down at him, and that was all the king wanted. "If you catch him, you will let him go."

Emil blinked at him. "You—Your Majesty, what are you . . . ?"

"He will die here." His resolute words were as steadfast and heavy as iron chains. "I know he will. He will return to this place, because this is where he was born. He is the phoenix that burns, but all phoenixes must return to their home eventually. And when he does, he will meet our justice. Not yours. You are a creature of fraudulent mercy." A scowl crawled across his face, narrowing his eyes into disdainful slits. "You would spare even a four-winged dragon if it told you it was sorry."

"We . . . We simply strive for a world of forgiveness. Where we come from, death for death is an ancient philosophy that we are moving away from."

"So your world is without war?"

Emil bit his tongue. "I believe that we may have come off on the wrong foot, Your Majesty." Gathering his spirits again, Emil smoothly spoke the lines he'd been taught. "As an envoy of the Server Alliance, I have come to ask that you open your nation and city to our influence. As the Acheron capital contains the only known instance of a church of the Goddess of Fire, we ask that you grant permission for challengers to enter into Her service to complete the quests She grants them." He paused to take a breath. "Furthermore, we also offer services in construction, communications, dragon-slaying, healing, bodyguarding . . ."

The king held up one hand. "You ask that I should allow a swarm of hoeksak into this scarred city?"

"Yes," Emil answered confidently. "It may not be to your pleasure to hear, but even if you refuse, it is likely that those seeking the quest of fire may still attempt to sneak inside the city. And, as you may know . . ." It took a moment for Emil to gather the courage needed to twist the knife in fully. "An untethered hoeksak is a dangerous hoeksak."

Simel the Survivor's face twisted into a grimace of indignant horror. "You dare threaten me?"

Emil quickly shook his head. "I am merely speaking the truth. As a hoeksak, and as someone who has met the one you fear, I know the damage our sort can cause."

The king's expression softened considerably. Then he turned around and went over to look out the window again. For almost a full minute, he simply watched the hustle and bustle out there: the men and women moving up and down the streets, the patrolling guards, the salesmen and their wares . . . "Stand."

Doubting his ears, Emil needed a moment to actually follow the demand, rising to his feet. Now, he was looking down at the king.

Simel the Survivor briefly glanced behind him, at where Emil stood, awkward and confused. "And remove that yitteh."

Silently, Emil took the headscarf from his head once more, pressing it to his chest.

The king's lips twitched down into a frown before returning to neutrality. He turned away from him to look at the throne—or, rather, at the little flakes of red on and around it. "You look nothing like him," Simel noted. "You are both hoeksak, but you are dignified." His eyes moved back to look at Emil, a newfound, newborn clarity glistening deep inside them. "Tell me. Have you ever killed one of our kind?"

"No" came Emil's quick and honest reply. "Never have I killed either goblin or hoeksak."

A small smile formed on Simel's pallid face. "Good. I only wish I could say the same." He turned back to look at the window, the light turning his ears reddish, his crown glistening in the midday sun. And for a moment, he didn't look like a king, or an adult, or even a goblin. He looked like a child, wistfully gazing out the window, hoping for snow, or for the rain to end. "You shall have it."

"Have what?"

Simel turned his head and smiled at Emil, no longer a child, but once again an adult; a king. "Permission to exist in this city—in this nation. I grant it. I will give you the housing you'll need, and your kind may enter and exit with the same scrutiny as any goblin." He became thoughtful for a second. "What is your kind called?"

The question caught Emil off-guard, to the point where he forgot to thank the king. "We are called humans," he answered, hoping that this was the word Simel sought.

"Humans," Simel repeated in a whisper. A slight frown marred his face. "Doesn't have the same ring as *goblins*." After a small silence that Emil spent fighting the urge to disagree, Simel nodded to himself, turning his eyes back to Emil, as though surprised to find him still there. "Was there anything else to discuss, human?"

Emil almost bowed again by pure instinct, recovering himself by wiping at his forehead. "Yes—it was in regard to Grief . . . to the human suspected of attempting to assassinate you. We have good reason to believe that he was falsely accused, and if you'll allow me, I would like to argue in his favor, or at least against using capital punishment against him."

"Ah, that one . . ." Simel mumbled, his voice trailing off. "I'm afraid that he's dead."

"He's . . . ?" Something sharp and hollow stabbed through Emil's chest, impaling his heart on dread and the inescapable premonition that something was very, very wrong. "Wh—what happened? Was he . . . ?" A shake of the head. "I completely understand if you chose to execute him; however, even a posthumous acquittal would—"

"He was killed en route," Simel said, enunciating the *en route* part. "Not by any order of mine."

Emil paused. Curiosity clawed at his insides. And yet, deeper down, suffocated by the need to know, a tiny voice tried to pipe up, telling him that some things aren't worth the pain of knowing. He shut it down. "How did it happen?"

The king's lips twitched. "We are lucky to have a firsthand account. A young sailor survived the encounter." Something familiar, downright nostalgic warmed his smile. However, his eyes showed a different emotion. Mourning. For himself, or for someone he saw himself in? Emil couldn't tell. "Not only an encounter with pirates, but likewise an encounter with yet another hoek . . . a human."

Warning bells rang inside Emil's head and he took a step toward Simel, trying his best to keep his face from appearing as panicked as he felt when he asked, in a trembling voice, "What was the name of the sailor boy?"

"Vann," Simel answered unhesitatingly. "Son of . . . I can't recall."

"But he . . ." He clenched and unclenched his hands. Even when he balled them together as hard as he could, he still found himself trembling. "He couldn't have . . ."

"Since the situation related to him, I had the sailor tell me his story personally. It was lucky he was rescued so soon after it ended, lest he might have been forced to use the bodies of his fellow-victims as provinte."

It was wrong. It felt wrong. He shouldn't have been hearing it. It wasn't right. "Y—Your Majesty, this is . . ."

"The sailor was very descriptive. He had a way with words. Though he didn't see everything in regard to your peer, his captor was more than willing to share details." Simel scoffed. "And to think that I had been under the impression that humans might show each other more mercy than they did goblins."

Everything Emil wore felt stuffy and hot. Too much. The corset, tighter than ever. He could barely even breathe. Kitty wouldn't. He'd been getting better. Hadn't he? So why would he . . . No, this wasn't . . . He couldn't be certain. Simel hated Kitty. For good reason, perhaps, but hatred twisted everything. Surely, there had to be some explanation, something that tied all of this together and showed that Kitty was, at the very least, doing what he thought was right.

"As for the events that led to the young sailor boy, alone on an iron ship filled with mutilated, half-eaten corpses . . ."

Emil buckled over and emptied the contents of his stomach.

The king jerked back, almost as though he thought the puddle of vomit staining his carpet was going to start eating through the floor next. "What are you . . . ?"

"I'm sorry, I'm sorry, I . . ." Trying to talk made the nausea worse, and another mouthful of stomach acid and bile soon shot up his throat. He tried to swallow down whatever was left. His teeth hurt. His throat hurt. The world was misty. His trembling hands frantically groped through his pockets for his handkerchief, only for a light purple one to be handed to him by the king himself. Hesitating only for a moment, Emil mumbled his thanks before taking it and wiping his face and eyes. Gulping down whatever remained in his mouth, he readjusted himself to speaking Aetongue properly. "I'm sorry, let me just . . ."

"I'll handle it," Simel casually replied, pointing at the stained carpet with a non-ringed finger before mumbling the prayer to clean. After only a few seconds, the carpet was clean once more, the king standing next to him with an expression of worry and enlightenment. "You humans . . . to think that you would have your types, as well."

Emil smiled sheepishly. "We're alike in that way," he muttered, using the clean spell on the handkerchief before returning it to Simel. The king gave it a slightly suspicious look before accepting it with a nod. Emil took a few deep breaths. "I thank you for the permission you have granted the Server Alliance, and for the information you have given me."

"I will have it in writing for you by the end of the day," Simel casually noted. "One of my servants will bring it to your abode."

"Thank you," Emil said. But if he were to be honest, he was more thankful for not having to hear any more about what the young sailor had experienced. Maybe, if he was lucky, the young sailor had simply aggrandized the situation in order to . . . because . . . something. There was sure to be some reason. There *had* to be a reason.

If there wasn't, then . . .

What did that make him?

Rats!

Aaaaaaaaaaand . . . *there* we go!

The rats look at me disapprovingly, which is really rich, coming from *them*.

What? Don't you like the taste of your master's flesh? Well, I'm sorry, but we've been here for almost a month, and I need to wait for a few more hours before I beat this floor. So if you want to *not die*, then you'll just have to keep nibbling at this wizard guy. I wonder who chained him down here, anyway? I almost feel like pitying him, but at the same time, I'm too tired of rat meat to not dislike him at least a little. Couldn't he have summoned something else, too? Like, I don't know, a flabby pig, or even a cow? Mmm, I can't imagine how good those would taste right now . . .

"Haah, haah, haah . . ." The wizard in question draws in a few raspy breaths. His tired eye peers out from beneath a furry WHITE eyebrow. "K—kill me . . ."

"More magic," I tell him. "*More rats.*" But he isn't making more magic *or* more rats, and the rats he's summoned so far aren't nearly enough for me to finish my full-body ratsuit with accompanying cloak, boots and top hat, so my words fall on deaf ears. Annoyed, I grab his no-longer-chained hand and waggle it around a bit. Or, I guess, what *used* to be his hand. Now, it's basically just a stump. When I first fought him, he wore rings, but then they all exploded, and without the rings, his fingers exploded. In the end, he got so desperate that both of his hands exploded. And that would be all nice and dandy, but now he isn't even *trying* to summon more rats! Very disappointing.

The few rats still scurrying around aren't too impressed by my top hat, which is likewise upsetting. Now I have a top hat and boots and cloak, but the actual ratsuit—the tour de force of this outfit—is tragically missing. Really, at this point, I'd do basically anything for more rats, including but not limited to: torture, homicide, wrongful imprisonment, arson—

<You have received a message.>

Oh? I haven't been receiving many of those as of late, so with any luck, this might just be the one message I've been waiting for! Absently stroking the rat currently gnawing off my hamstrings, I open up the message.

<SuperMoleman[F67]: Hey Kitty! Congratulations on beating the floor! How did it go? Did you use the strategies I mentioned to clear it, or did something else happen? You can tell me whatever happened, even if you think I might not like it. We're both almost adults, after all. And how did it go with Vann? Did he choose to join you in the end? I look forward to hearing from you, and good luck with the twenty-third floor!>

I pause my rat-stroking. Ah. Hum.

Well . . . that's a good question, actually. How *did* it go with Vann? Last I saw him, he was on the boat, with all the . . . Yeah. It isn't really important, so I don't see any use in talking about it. Now, how to express that to Moleman . . .

Bringing the plump rat in my hand to my face, I absently bite off its head, chewing and swallowing the crunchy thing before bringing my fingers to the keyboard.

<PrissyKittyPrincess [F23]: Nah. dunno. btw how r u doing? gg>

And . . . send! There we go. I'm really curious to hear what he's been up to since the last time we spoke. Honestly, not meeting him every other month at the Server Symposium is making me a bit antsy. Hm. Then again, now that I'm no longer on floor twenty-two, can't I go to the Server Symposium again? Yeah, sure, they want to execute me and whatever, but if we ignore that, I'm sure we can have a nice meetup!

Ahh, I'm already looking forward to it . . . Oh! And now, since my inventory works properly, I'll be able to bring him the things *I* find! So it won't just be him treating me to various foreign delicacies, but rather a mutual sharing of yummy foods.

I look down at the half-eaten rat in my hand. Hm. I take another bite, tiny bones crunching and little organs popping. I think I read somewhere that the French enjoy eating frogs and birds whole, organs and heads and all. Maybe this is a delicacy somewhere? It isn't too bad, honestly. Good fat-to-muscle ratio, and the bones are sure to strengthen my teeth, as well as my internal bleeding resistance.

If only I had more rats . . .

I look down at my captive wizard again. He doesn't look very responsive. Let's see, the time is . . .

<Top—Status—Community>
<14:33:59 Day 880>
<The twenty-ninth attempt will begin in 9:26:01>

Well, would you look at that? It's beat-the-floor o'clock!

I stab the wizard's chest and pull out his heart. Huh. Now that I'm looking at it, this heart looks a bit darker than it does for most people. Might just be the lighting, of course. It *is* quite glum down here.

If only to liven up the mood a little, I take a bite of the heart. It tastes the same as all other hearts I've eaten, so there's nothing to mention.

<Sewer Wizard [BOSS] (Lv.135) Defeated.>
<[Level Up]
<You have reached Level 123.>
<Agility has increased by 2.
Strength has increased by 3.
Stamina has increased by 2.
Don't-Worry-About-It! has increased by 1.
Bacteria Protection has increased by 1.>
<You have cleared the twenty-third floor.>
<Congratulations!>
<For your efforts, you have received the following skill:
[INSERT SOME RANDOM SKILL HERE]>

I stare at the message in front of me. Uh-huh. Great skill, guys. I'll be sure to use it well.

To make my deadpan expression twice as powerful, I grab a nearby rat and hold it up next to my face. See? Double the judgment. Twice the emotional damage.

<THE GOD OF HARVEST SIGHS AND REQUESTS A VOLUNTEER TO OVERSEE THE GIV-
ING OF SKILLS AND ITEMS TO HELL CHALLENGER LO FENNRICK.>
<THE GOD OF COMEDY EXCITEDLY VOLUNTEERS HIMSELF.>
<[OOPS,]>
<*HIMSELF>
<THE GOD OF HARVEST SCANS THE AREA FOR ANY SUITABLE VOLUNTEERS TO
HANDLE THIS GRAVE TASK.>
<THE GOD OF HARVEST NOTES A STRIKING LACK OF SUITABLE VOLUNTEERS.>
<THE GOD OF COMEDY WOULD VERY MUCH LIKE TO BE OF ASSISTANCE, PRETTY
PLEASE?>
<THE GOD OF HARVEST PRETENDS NOT TO SEE ANYTHING.>

I don't even . . . Okay, listen, man . . . God of Harvest? I don't know if you're listening in on this, but just . . . get it over with. I didn't expect anything anyway. Let the man have his fun.

<THE GOD OF HARVEST THANKS HELL CHALLENGER LO FENNRICK FOR HIS AGREE-
ABLE AND SENSIBLE NATURE.>
<THE GOD OF HARVEST HESITANTLY PETITIONS THE GOD OF COMEDY TO OVERSEE
THE GIVING OF SENSIBLE SKILLS AND ITEMS TO HELL CHALLENGER LO FENNRICK.>
<THE GOD OF COMEDY SWEARS FULL ALLEGIANCE TO THE TUTORIAL TEAM AND
SOLEMNLY DECLARES HIS WILLINGNESS TO FULFILL THIS DUTY TO THE GREATEST OF
HIS ABILITIES, WITH THE GREATEST CARE, AND ALSO THE GREATEST RESPECT, AND
THE GREATEST [INSERT BUZZWORD HERE].>
<[OOPSIE,]>
<*HIS>
<THE GOD OF HARVEST ACCEPTS THE GOD OF COMEDY FOR THE ROLE OF LIMITED
OVERSEER WITH THE GREATEST RELUCTANCE.>
<THE GOD OF HARVEST WISHES LUCK TO THE GOD OF COMEDY.>
<THE GOD OF COMEDY DOES A MOCK SALUTE.>
<THE GOD OF HARVEST INSTANTLY REGRETS HIS DECISION.>
<THE GOD OF COMEDY ASSERTS THAT HE THOUGHT FOR SURE THE GOD OF HAR-
VEST HAD LEFT ALREADY.>

You know what? I'm starting to relate to the God of Harvest. I know I've clowned on this dude over the years, but now that I'm faced with an even bigger clown, I can't help but wonder what kind of working conditions he's under.

<THE GOD OF COMEDY WAITS A MOMENT BEFORE NOTING THAT THE COAST IS
CLEAR.>
<[HEHE.]>

That's not a good sign. Should I be worried? I'm worried. I'm still in the floor with all my lovely rats, alone with *this guy*. And, sure, *hopefully* the God of Pain is also watching, but I doubt that He's the kind of guy who would stop any ongoing shenanigans.

<[HEY.]>

I squirm a little where I sit.

Hey?

<[HOW BADLY DO YOU WANT MORE RATS?]>

Um . . . I pull a few of the rats closer to me. *Fairly badly, I suppose. If you want someone in particular killed, I can handle that, or . . .*

<[NOT NECESSARY. ALL I'M SAYING IS . . . IF YOU WANT MORE RATS, I CAN GET YOU RATS. HOWEVER, I NEED YOU TO NOT RAT ON ME IN TURN. HARVEST WANTS ME TO PICK A RANDOM TRASH-TIER SKILL FROM THE BIN, BUT THAT'S BORING. LIKE WHAT USE COULD A GUY LIKE YOU HAVE FOR [AMATEUR JUGGLING (Lv.1)]?]>

Well—

<[DON'T ANSWER THAT ONE. THE ANSWER IS: NONE. BECAUSE IT'S BORING! DULL! IDIOTIC! NO, WHAT YOU NEED IS GOOD SKILLS. THE FUN TYPE. AND I'LL GIVE IT TO YOU. BUT ONLY IF YOU DON'T TELL HARVEST!]>

Okay, listen, man . . . How the heck would I even tell Harvest? I'm literally just a human! I have no way of even contacting your sort! What, do you expect me to pull out my little totally existent cell phone, dial the number for emergency divine services, and then expect someone of importance to answer? It just won't happen.

In short, just hand over the rats and no one gets—

There's an echo of laughter. From . . . somewhere. It isn't young or old, female or male . . . Mere laughter. Barely even human. This is how I'd describe the laughter of a rat, I think—if only rats *could* laugh.

<[YOU WILL HAVE IT! YES, MY FRIEND, YOU WILL HAVE IT. HAVE YOUR RATS! AND, IN THE MEANTIME, I WILL BE WATCHING YOU. DON'T LET ME DOWN, BUDDY.]>

I don't exactly know how or why, but I can tell that he's gone. And in his wake, I find . . .

<For your efforts, you have received the following skill: Summon Rat Lv.1>

Wait. Seriously? No way. Did he actually . . . ? I can't believe it. I *have* to test this out right this very—

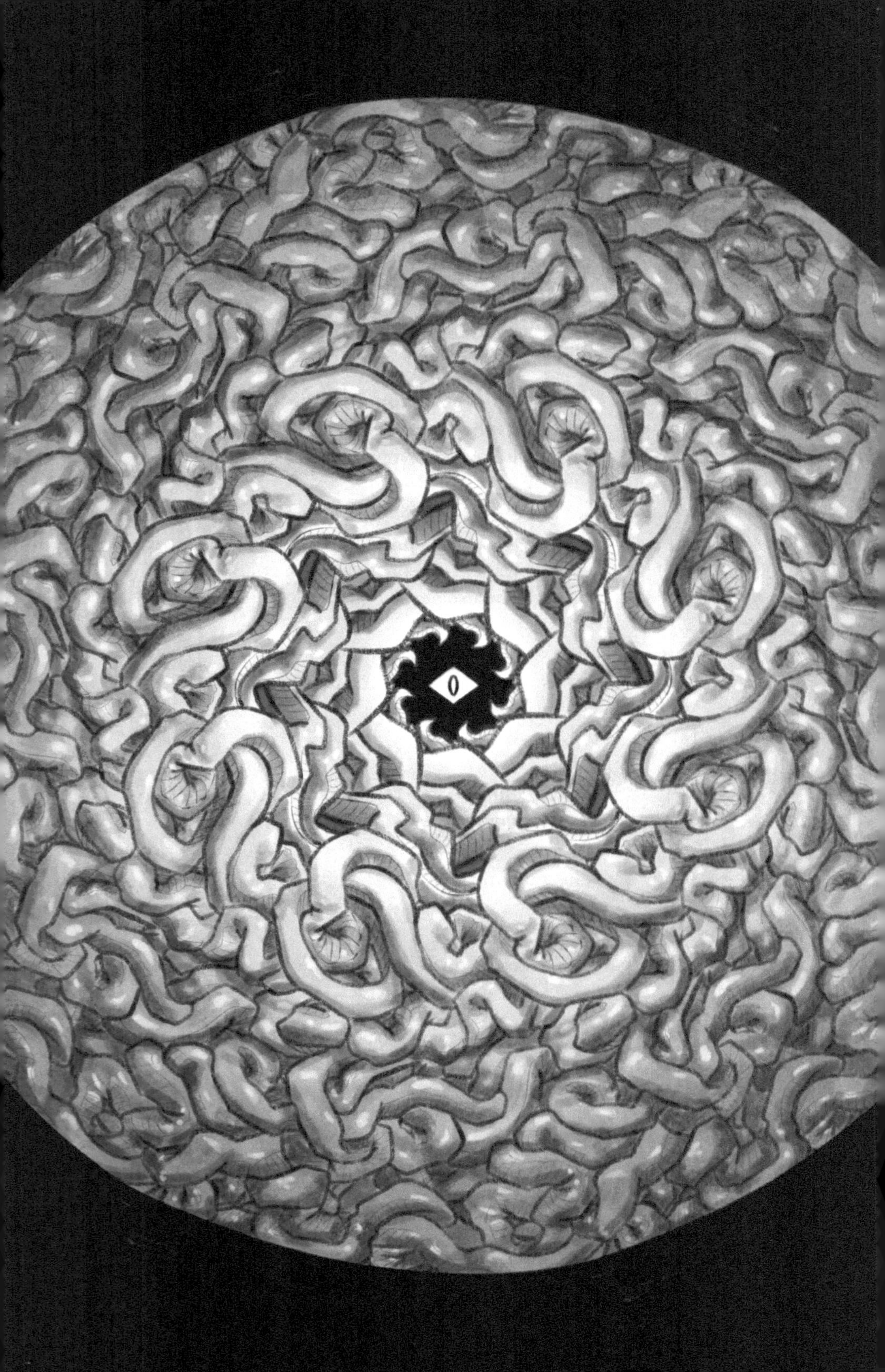

FLOOR 24

THE SNAKE PIT

A Pit with Snakes in It

—second! Oh, hey, I'm back here.

Mrm. WHITE. *And* the poster.

Before I rush right into playing with my newest toy, I take some time to give the lobby a new coat of paint, briefly angsting over the poster, finding my only solace in the fact that, at the very least, I can enjoy the catharsis of ripping it off and eating it. Not that it tastes any good, of course. But that's to be expected.

No, now that my duties to sanity have ended, I can reward myself by indulging in this new skill I've lawfully received. *Summon rat.*

Should I just go for it? Do I even need to check the skill description? It's just *summon rat.* I can't imagine that it would be anything other than, you know . . . *summoning a rat.*

Yeah! Easy peasy, right?

I point a finger to the floor. [Summon Rat]!

Nothing's happening. Did I do something wro—

My hand is gone. Severed at the wrist. I could barely even feel the way it crunched up, bones cracking and folding and skin being compressed into a tight nothingness before it was gone. And in its place, as though replacing my very hand, is a rat. The second it arrives into existence, it plummets down, hitting the still-wet floor with a meaty *plap!*

I stare at it, dumbfounded. The rat, in turn, watches me with an equal amount of dumb, animal confusion.

<Rat (Lv.0)>

It's a rat. It doesn't even have a level.

As our eyes interlock in mutual bewilderment, the [Summon Rat (Lv. 1)] skill description helpfully takes its place in my vision.

<[Summon Rat (Lv. 1)] Summon a rat (Lv. 0) at 500 grams using an equivalent volume of your own flesh, bone, fat, blood, waste, cartilage, or organs. Current Rat Limit: 1/1>

I see. So, hypothetically, I could turn my brain into a rat? Half a kilo per rat. Since a human head weighs around five kilos, I could use my head to summon ten rats. Except I can't do so for two reasons: one, my Rat Limit, or RL, is only one. Two, if I made my entire head into rats, I would die, which is counterproductive to my goals.

This skill is . . . I don't know. Is it good? Is it bad? It's . . . *rats.*

Then again, if I can increase the skill and summon a bunch of rats, maybe I can make them attack someone and choke them with rats? That would be pretty cool.

I look down at the plump rat sitting squat at my feet. *Hey, you.* The rat blinks up at me. *Yeah, you. Go run in circles for me—can you do that?*

It stares up at me.

Maybe it needs verbal commands?

"Hey, Rat Number One. I order you to run in a circle and bite your own tail."

It stares up at me.

I shoot a quick look at the skill description.

Nowhere does it say that I can actually *control* the rats.

This skill literally only lets me summon rats. Nothing else.

I glance at the clock.

<Top—Status—Community>
<15:20:03 Day 880>
<The twenty-ninth attempt will begin in 8:39:57>
<The twenty-fourth floor will open in 23:02:21>

I've got twenty-three hours.

I look down at the rat.

Might as well grind a bit, right?

The fastest way to grind rats, I found, was to hold my hand in my other hand, use the flesh in my hand to summon a rat, and then grab the rat with my other hand to instantly eat it whole, sometimes alive. I experimented with using my various organs to summon the rat in the hopes that it might instantly go into my stomach, but this was fruitless and only left me with a live rat in an abdomen that instantly healed any wound caused by said live rat. Not a very pleasant experience. If only I could somehow use this on other people, it would become an excellent strategy. Unfortunately, with the way the skill is progressing, there's no hint that it might ever evolve to let me do that. Might be too powerful for even the God of Comedy to sponsor, I suppose.

Eventually, it did level up.

\<You have learned: Summon Rat Lv.2\>

Deep down I had hoped that this would maybe let me summon bigger or smaller rats, or that the rats would have a level so that killing them would let me get stronger, but no. It just increased the Rat Limit to three. So now I could summon three rats at once. Wow! How magically useless!

To make use of this new and increased RL, I began doing my grinding seated, turning my feet into rats and then grabbing them with both hands at once to eat them. This was also quite effective.

By the time the floor opened, I had gotten the summon rat skill to level four, which allowed me to summon a whopping seven rats at once. Amazing! I kind of wish I could somehow find out the total number of rats ever summoned, because I'm starting to think it might be in the hundreds—maybe thousands.

Either way—floor!

\<Floor 24 has opened. Do you want to enter?\>
\<Yes/No\>

You know what I pressed. I know what I pressed. There was no other option. With a press of the Yes, I allow myself to be summoned into the floor.

\<Tutorial stage, Hell Difficulty Twenty-fourth Floor: The Snake Pit\>
\<[Clear Condition] Survive in the snake pit. Time left: 29:59:57\>

It's a pit of snakes.

I'm in a pit, filled with snakes.

I can't climb out of it. It's very deep, being a pit and all.

There are many snakes in it.

I am reminded of being swallowed alive and turning into a meatball.

This upsets me, and during my first day in the snake pit, I act in a fairly bestial manner. However, as I quickly came to learn, the snake pit is not a place where killing as many snakes as possible is the best strategy. No, the amount of snakes would always be the same. If a snake were killed, another snake would replace it. Considering this, in a more beautiful world where things were nice and I had never been born, the best tactic would be to permanently cripple all snakes by, for example, displacing their vertebrae slightly—however, this was not possible. This world was not so good.

There were too many snakes to cripple.

I was stuck in the snake pit, my only relief being the eventual realization that the snakes couldn't really kill me. They could poison me, inject me with acid, paralyze me, turn my flesh into necrotic goop, and—yes, they could *eat me*, but not kill me. I could probably have allowed them to kill me, maybe by willingly bashing my own brains in, but my distractions kept such a fate at bay.

Firstly, there was my rat skill. It leveled up pretty quickly since I could simply let the rats be eaten by snakes, all the while using the snakes to regenerate the lost flesh.

Was this . . . productive? Was it making me stronger? Would it let me survive the next floor? I don't know. What I *do* know is that it kept me from acknowledging the fact that my fingers would sometimes meld together into fleshy mittens, or that I was starting to see scales no matter where I looked.

The level-up messages were nice.

<You have learned: Summon Rat Lv.5>
<You have learned: Summon Rat Lv.6>
<You have learned: Summon Rat Lv.7>
<You have learned: Summon Rat Lv.8>
<You have learned: Summon Rat Lv.9>
<You have learned: Summon Rat Lv.10>
<You have learned: Summon Rat Horde Lv.1>

Somewhere deep inside, I had hoped that maybe with this skill evolution, it might become useful. Maybe I'd be able to summon rats of different elements or sizes, or I could tame them to my will, or I could use flesh other than mine to summon them.

Not so. All it did was increase the rat limit again. Now, the rat limit was at fifty. I could summon fifty rats at once. Wasn't that wonderful? It made me . . . *so happy.*

After a week or so, the number of snakes in the snake pit began to increase. I'm not sure of the exact rate, but I think it was one snake per hour. The pit was too deep for me to ever hope to escape, but having more snakes meant I had more snakes to eat, which meant I could summon . . . more . . . rats.

Soon the snake pit was filled with bloated snakes and panicked rats. The rats were actually beginning to get bothersome, since their little claws and their gnawing teeth were more effective at getting through the epidermal layer of my abdomen than the snakes were. Maybe it was instinct that led them to believe that the abdomen I used to keep my organs in would somehow be safer than outside? The rats that didn't fit inside my stomach made do with scurrying up as high as they could, perching themselves on my head, shoulders, and arms to get away from the hungry snakes pursuing them.

<You have learned: Summon Rat Horde Lv.2>
<You have learned: Summon Rat Horde Lv.3>
<You have learned: Summon Rat Horde Lv.4>

The level-ups made it worth it.

Two weeks into my stay in the snake pit, I finally found a reason to be happy the snakes hadn't been able to kill me yet.

<SuperMoleman[F67]: Hi again Kitty! Just saw you beat floor twenty-three, congratulations! You're really blasting through these, huh? Keep up the good work! I'm doing pretty well. I've been getting to know a former humanphobe . . . sapiophobe? Human-hater. He's pretty nice, not as expensive with his tastes as most rulers I've met. We're both followers of the God of Knowledge, so he's taught me a bit. It's nice. Recently, he gave me a task to help out a city undergoing a plague or something. Since my party is composed of humans, we won't be susceptible to the disease—or so he says. I'm unsure, but we'll see. If I'm lucky, I might get to help more people! But that's just what I've been up to. Your message has confused me a little . . .**

**So Vann didn't join you? That's sad to hear. But what happened with everything else? How did it actually go beating the floor? I've been hearing some nasty rumors about what happened to the Evil Claw Pirates, and I just wanted to hear your side of the story before making any assumptions. So, again, how did it go? Of course, if you'd rather take this in person, I'm sure we can figure something out. This sounds like a very sensitive subject, all things considered. I hope to hear from you soon, and good luck with the twenty-fourth floor!>

As I read, I grab a nearby snake and slowly move it toward my wide-open mouth, mentally charging it with various crimes against humanity before sentencing it to death by decapitation. *Your neck will be severed, your head removed, et cetera et cetera, and* here comes the airplane*!*

Chomp. Nomch. Mmm. Crunchy, with a tangy taste that leaves my tongue numb and my throat itchy. A Longboi number four, I see. The size and coloration should've given it away. Nevertheless, the venomous nature of these make them very attractive for—

<You have learned: Paralysis Protection Lv.10>
<You have learned: Paralysis Immunity Lv.1>

Hey, nice! That's been a long time coming! Alongside poison and bleeding, that's my third one now!

I look down at the twitching snake corpse still in my hands. *I have so much to thank you for. Guilty as charged, however . . .*

I gingerly kiss the severed neck. Then I slurp down the rest of the body. He was a good one.

I need to tell Moleman about this!

<PrissyKittyPrincess [F24]: HECKK YEEH JST GOT 1 MORE IMUNITY PARALYZE THIS TIME FRIGGIN EPIK>

Not thinking any more of it, I send it off in a rush, eager to share this wonderful development with my closest friend.

Giddy with excitement, I continue my mindless rat-grinding, waiting for his response.

And, after a few minutes—our quickest exchange in many months—his answer drops in.

<SuperMoleman[F67]: Wow, congratulations! That's your third immunity, right? However, and I'm sorry for asking again, but would you mind telling me how beating the twenty-second floor went? Again, I know it can be a sensitive subject, but it's important, okay? Take the time you need.>

Oh, yeah, I didn't actually respond to his message. That was a bit silly on my end, I suppose. Right, let's see here, what can I say . . . ?

<PrissyKittyPrincess [F24]: Idk it wasnt rlly important. had 2 beat da floor so i did.>

I send it away. A response soon dings in.

<SuperMoleman[F67]: So, just to ensure that we're on the same page . . . You killed them? Your captain and crewmates . . . You killed them all?>
<PrissyKittyPrincess [F24]: yeah>
<SuperMoleman[F67]: . . . Why?>

I pause, staring at the message—at the tiny, minuscule little word.

<PrissyKittyPrincess [F24]: wym>

It takes a minute or so for me to get his response.

<SuperMoleman[F67]: Sorry, that might not have come across the right way. I mean . . . Why would you kill them? Did they mistreat you? It's okay, you can tell me even if it feels shameful. I just want to understand your reasoning.>

Why . . . ?

<PrissyKittyPrincess [F24]: idk>
<SuperMoleman[F67]: . . . You don't know why you did it?>
<PrissyKittyPrincess [F24]: yeah>

It takes almost half an hour before I get another response out of him.

<SuperMoleman[F67]: Sorry, I have to go, our carriage just arrived. I'll message you again when I have time. Good luck with the twenty-fourth floor!>
<PrissyKittyPrincess [F24]: gl with da city>

I close down the messages. For some reason, I feel hollow inside. In a very not-nice way.

For the first time in over half a month, I'm happy to be surrounded by so many living creatures.

With my efforts, by the time my month in the snake pit is up, my Summon Rat Horde skill has reached the max level and evolved into its final form: Infinite Rats Lv.MAX, which had a rat limit of, well . . . infinity. Nothing else about the skill changed.

Despite maxing it out, I felt emptier than before.

<You have cleared the twenty-fourth floor.>
<Congratulations!>
<For your efforts, you have received the following skill: Peel Lv.1>

Luckily for me, I soon got a shiny new toy to play with.

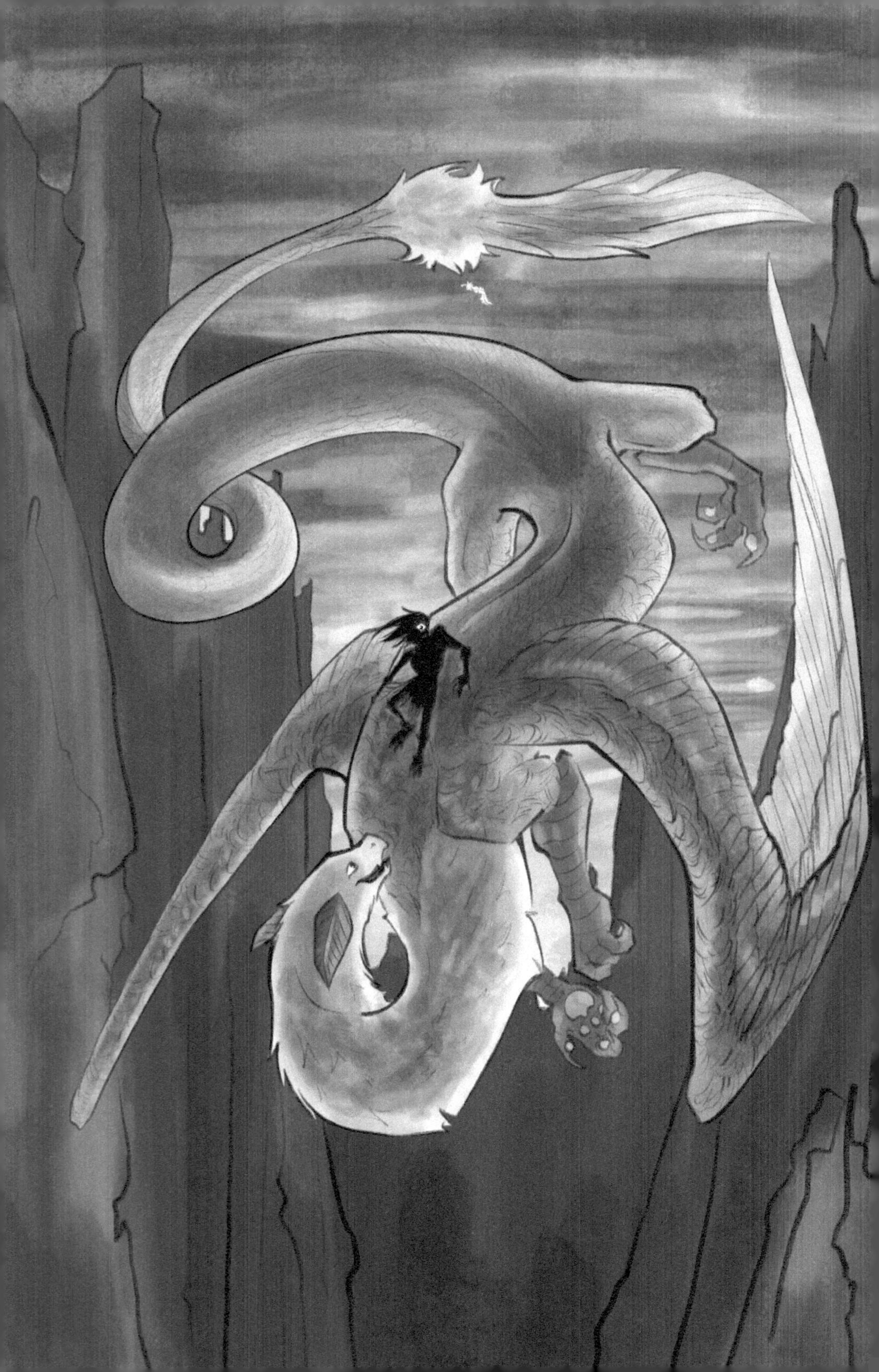

FLOOR 25

THE MOUNTAIN SERPENT

XXIII

That Gentle Knight

When I return to the lobby, I find my eyes hallucinating scales, and I can feel the phantoms of non-existent snakes wrapped around every part of my body. Luckily for me, I have long since figured out how to handle this. Simply put, if you remove the limb or area experiencing phantom sensations, the feeling will typically be gone once said part regenerates. Easy!

So I tear off all my limbs, rip out my eyeballs, and get to try my hand at using my latest trinket of a skill.

<[Peel Lv.1] Peel off your skin! Current Peel Area: 10 cm²>

I can peel off my skin! It's honestly criminal that this skill comes at absolutely no cost. Yes, for the low, low price of exactly nothing, I can peel off a square decimeter of my own skin. How useful! I'd probably be more upset if it hadn't been for the fact that the skin peels in slices, like a banana.

That aside, I'm starting to seriously consider the theory that the God of Comedy is a sadist. I can't see any other explanation for these skills.

However, that obviously doesn't mean that I won't grind it as much as I can. It *is* a brand-new skill, after all.

So during my one-day stay in the lobby, I train the peeling skill.

<You have learned: Peel Lv.2>
<You have learned: Peel Lv.3>

<. . .>
<You have learned: Peel Lv.10>
<You have learned: Shed Lv.MAX>

Shed, as the name suggests, allows me to shed my entire skin. All of it. In one piece. The weird thing is that it peels off the same as before, much like a banana, but then once it's on the floor in a heap, it magically re-forms itself into a complete and unbroken skin. For the sheer sake of it, I experimented by cutting a slit across the back of my own skin and then wearing it.

It felt . . . weird. On the one hand, it fit *perfectly*. The second I stepped inside it, I felt all snug and calm, like a cat in a cat-shaped vase. But on the other hand . . . It's a *little* weird to wear two sets of your own skin.

<Top—Status—Community>

<20:24:03 Day 910>

<The thirtieth attempt will begin in 3:35:57>

<The twenty-fifth floor will open in 4:10:13>

Nevertheless, I have a few more hours, so . . . I might as well, right?

<Top—Status—Community>

<00:34:11 Day 911>

<The thirty-first attempt will begin in 29:23:25:49>

<The twenty-fifth floor will open in 00:00:05>

With five seconds remaining until the floor opening, I can proudly report that I am able to wear seven sets of my own skin in total. Any more than that and the joints start ripping. Of course, while wearing seven sets of skin, I'm not exactly able to move very well. In hindsight, this might not be the best way to enter a floor.

<Floor 25 has opened. Do you want to enter?>

<Yes/No>

It would appear that I no longer have any choice in the matter. Oopsies!

I poke the Yes button without hesitation.

The world swirls around me, and as stiff as a man in a mascot suit, I stumble once, twice, before falling face-first onto the floor. Ouch. Did I mention that I have tunnel vision in this thing? With some creative bending of the limbs, I'm able to heave myself onto my feet again, wobbling like a penguin going down a Slip 'N Slide standing. Yeah, this might not be too good.

Or, at least, that would've been the case if I actually happened to be in any kind of mortal danger. The semibarren tundra wasteland around me presents lit-tle to no danger, especially since I'm ridiculously well-insulated. It's cold, rocky, and not threatening. The sky is an annoyingly vibrant blue, the sort it can only really be in midwinter. Considering that it's supposed to be early summer right now, that means that I am far from the central continent—far from the only place I've really known so far.

The only thing in my sight that could be even slightly threatening would be if I had to somehow climb that jagged mountain range in the distance. But I can't see why I would have to—

<Tutorial stage, Hell Difficulty Twenty-fifth Floor: The Mountain Serpent>
<[Clear Condition] Reach the summit of Mt. Apathy.>

Ah. Yeah, okay, I see how it is. Should've guessed. Is the God of Comedy running this show now? Ha ha, very funny.

However, I have a better question. What do you mean, *mountain serpent*? Am I supposed to fight a snake on the summit? I don't know if you watched me for the entirety of the month I spent in a literal *pit full of snakes*, but if I have to fight *another snake*, I'm pulling my veto card. I'm not playing anymore.

As usual, no response meets me. Figures. Now that I think about it, most of them have been fairly silent recently. Might be because their disdain no longer does anything, but it still feels strangely lonely to not hear their opinions.

I know they're watching, though. Those grubby divines can't keep their eyes off their favorite channel even if they wanted to.

And if the viewer polls demand that I must scale a summit and fight a snake, then it shall be done. It's not like I have any choice, after all.

Pulling my skins closer, I head out.

My nose guides me down the right path to the right mountain, but it's still one heck of a trek. For one, it's frigid. But it isn't very snowy. The chill is in the air, and there isn't a single sign that it's going to snow anytime soon. It's just cold. Very, very cold. My extra skin, not being warmed by my blood and veins and whatnot, actually freezes around me. Eventually, it did trap me, at which point I helpfully discovered that the peel skill also peels any skins I'm wearing on top of my own skin. So by using the peel skill seven times, I'm freed of the stiff, constricting epidermis I was wearing. For a moment, I almost considered wearing a warmer hide on top of it all, but then I realized my folly. Wear warm clothes? And miss out on an excellent cold protection grinding opportunity? No way!

So, sticking the bear hide I was holding back into my now-reliable inventory, I continue my journey. It's worth noting that since the great values sniffer skill only told me the location of what I wanted, I didn't actually know the best route up the mountain. If the rocks had been covered by moss or something I might have been able to ascertain the general outlay of the region, but as it was, all I knew was the direction and distance, and that was it. So I had no other choice but to head straight for it.

Routes? Walked paths? *Roads?*

No such things here. I scaled it, barehanded and barefooted, ignoring the biting of the cold and the stiffness of my body. Lost fingers, toes, limbs, and teeth grew back as long as I survived.

<You have learned: Scale Lv.4>
<You have learned: Scale Lv.5>
<You have learned: Scale Lv.6>
<You have learned: Cold Protection Lv.10>
<You have learned: Cold Immunity Lv.1>

With my previous immunities, the effect wasn't very obvious. Poison immunity meant I didn't die, bleeding immunity meant I didn't die, and paralysis immunity meant I didn't die. But cold immunity? Suddenly, the temperature in my body dropped by at least five degrees. Or maybe it adjusted to better fit the environment? I have no idea. All I can say is that I don't feel colder. I just feel more . . . *numb*, I guess. The sensation of cold is lesser. It feels very strange.

As I exhale between clenched, frozen-shut teeth, I find with some degree of trepidation that my breath is no longer milky-white. That's a bit worrying. Now that I'm thinking about it, the needle-like sensation piercing my limbs and joints might be shards of ice forming in my flesh. Which is also not optimal.

Still, I trudge on. Despite the fresh hell I'm now experiencing, it doesn't feel like I'm close to death. It hurts enough to make me wish that wasn't the case, but I can tell that I'm not going to die from this. Hooray.

As I'm contemplating the meaning of life, death, and the universe, my foot snaps off from under me. Not much of a loss since I'd already lost the toes somewhere, but unlike the left arm I displaced a few days back and still haven't fully recovered, I kind of need my foot to live. So even though it's a bother on several levels, I hunch down and rip the foot from where it froze stuck to the icy ground. And now for the annoying part.

My teeth, and subsequently my jaws, froze together the other day, leaving me unable to open my mouth. Or, at least, unable to do so without effort. An effort I now require.

Sticking my foot between my legs, I use my one good arm to smash my clawed hand into my mouth, snapping off and cracking enough teeth to make a hole. I don't want to remove all my teeth in case I get ambushed, so with this hole open, I spend upwards of an hour sitting squat on the side of a fairly steep cliff, ripping off pieces of my own foot and sliding them into the hole in my face. Without teeth and unable to move my jaw, I have no choice but to swallow the pieces whole, which becomes a lot more difficult when my tongue starts getting frozen, too. I try to thaw it by massaging it, but that just makes the icy needles formed inside shuffle around even more.

Maybe I should be happy that bleeding immunity makes me bleed less? If my mouth had been full of blood right now, I would have had to act as a bloody Slurpee machine. Instead, I just have to swallow marble-like teeth and frozen flesh. Very fun.

Normally, I would have eaten the bones too, but I can't be bothered. This will have to be good enough.

I continue my trudge.

After almost two weeks of trekking, as I began to scale the correct mountain properly, I noticed that the environment wasn't becoming colder. It was getting *warmer*.

My eyes, which had been frozen in a permanent half blink for several days, suddenly became warm enough to open again fully. I can see! Well, I could still understand the world around me even without sight, but finding the area in front of me to be not only snowless but actually *green* was a stunning sight. Grass. There's grass!

Breath caught in my throat, I run, something I didn't know my legs were capable of doing anymore. Falling to my knees in front of a patch of green, I clutch at the little blades of grass, feeling something soft and harmless for the first time in half a month. It's almost unreal. Painful, cold tears trickle from my thawed eyes. Ah, it's wonderful. It's . . .

I sniff.

It's close.

My knees creak as I push myself to my feet again. I stagger into a stiff, deadman's walk. Yes, now that I can actually look at the area around me, it isn't barren anymore. The grass surrounds a flattened, walked path. However, the road is weirdly broad, as though it was mainly walked by elephants, or maybe quadrupedal whales. But it started in the middle of nowhere, so I can't see why that would be the case.

Well, it seems to lead exactly to the top, so there's no reason not to follow it.

Walking on a real road after so long feels strangely rejuvenating. No steep cliff faces to climb, no crevices to lose fingers and toes in, no jutting rocks to stumble on—and, best of all, no freezing cold to make me consider the pros and cons of cordless bungee-jumping. It's kind of nice, honestly, and makes me forget that I'm heading into what I can only assume to be some sort of lair. What shall I find at the top? A snake? A sea serpent? Something else? Who knows. Either way, the summit approaches, and I feel about as ready as I can be.

As I pass a bend in the road, I begin to hear voices. Two of them. With a quick sniff, I can tell that the owners are also the only people there. They smell weird, though. Sure, they clearly smell like goblins, but then they also smell like fresh, warm rice. Feathery. Kind of like drakes do. Not to mention that the area close to them is positively warm, like a hot day in August.

Sitting down behind a rock, I let myself replicate Coda and listen in.

"I hope they send someone strong," a young, adolescent voice chirps. "That would be so scaly."

"I hope they send no one," an older, mature voice replies, sighing. "Or perhaps a flapping fiend. Would that satiate you, Goss?"

"No way! Didn't I tell you? I'm a type seven, so the only way this'll work is if they send a human, and preferably a super-strong one so they'll sob like little goblings when I rip it apart and wear its hide as a glove!" The younger one, Goss, squawks a laugh. "Oh, I can't *wait*! Do you think it'll be here soon?"

"Going by the sun, I'd say we've been here close to three hours now. If they wanted to send someone to 'save' me, they would have done so by now. Not that I'd see the point in such an exercise, save for them losing another champion."

As I'm devoting myself to the art of eavesdropping, a status window helpfully assists me in explaining my position.

<Tutorial stage, Hell Difficulty Twenty-fifth Floor: Boss Stage>
<[Clear Condition] Defeat the despicable dragon and rescue the pious priest.>

A dragon and a priest? Now that's an odd combo. A dragon . . . like I saw in the tapestries at the empire? Then again, it *could* just be an overgrown drake rather than an actual monstrous beast of fire and fury capable of burning the world to ash with a single burst of its hellflame breath. I suppress the urge to cough into my hand.

Well, I suppose I've heard enough. Before heading out, I briefly make a check for limbs and appendages. Hands, check; fingers, check; legs, check; feet, check . . . Yeah, good enough. I stand up, cross the final part, and emerge onto an unusually flat platform that's apparently supposed to be the summit. It's covered in healthy flora, with grass and flowers and even fruitful bushes covering it. I'd call the view unsuited for the title *Apathy Summit* if I hadn't been more focused on what's actually up here.

"I—it's here! Scales and feathers, it's really—" The one that's apparently Goss puffs himself up, wings spreading in a display of size and power. "Greetings, human champion of the pathetic gods!"

It's a dragon. It's actually and literally a dragon.

I grab my own hand to prevent myself from trembling too hard.

Goss, the dragon one of the two, is about the size of a double-decker bus. And that isn't even *counting* the tail. Is that feathers? He's all covered in feathers? No, not completely. The face, a pale yellow like cartoon lightning bolts, is uncovered and scaly. And the horns. A bit stubby, but he has horns. His eyes are bright yellow. His body is almost fluffy in parts, kind of like the down of a baby bird, and especially his tail, which, right there at the end, has long fluffy parts that look awesome. And the wings? Sure, they have a little tiny-chicken fluff to them, but otherwise?

I clench my jaw. Damn, that's cool. He's way too cool.

The dragon stares at me. I stare at the dragon. I'm trembling. If I look closely, his cheeks are a little deeper in color than the rest of his body, kind of like he's blushing. His wings are trembling almost as badly as my hands are. "Human!" He points at me using his trembling wing. "You have come to rescue this idolater, have you not?" His magnanimous wing moves to point at a robed goblin sitting casually in a small wooden cage off to the side. As I'm looking at him, the goblin in question waves using one of his wings. Carried by the atmosphere, I wave back at him.

Hang on, wings?

Yeah, now that I'm looking at it, the supposed priest in there has a pair of large, parrot-RED wings on his back, covered with patterns of BLACK, yellow, green, and blue. Very tropical, and very out of place on an otherwise modestly dressed priest.

The dragon stares at me. I stare back at him.

Oh, he's expecting a response, isn't he?

I go to tug at my collar but find that, as always, I'm wearing nothing. Exactly nothing. Not even a—

I look down at my nethers and then back up at the dragon. He's also in the nude, technically speaking.

"E—excuse me," I mutter, turning around and pulling out the first-best hide from my inventory, which happens to be goblin. I can feel the priest's gaze on my back. D—damn it . . . !

Sticking it back in, I pull out my rat coat, tying it around my midsection almost as a kilt. Good enough. I turn back to the dragon and the priest, coughing into my hand, clearing my throat to speak properly. "Uh, I . . ." I cough again. "Yeah! I'm here to rescue that priest, and to . . ." I bite my tongue. "To, to . . ." I swallow. Man, I must look *so pathetic* right now. This is not how I'd imagine my first time fighting a dragon to go. Now that I'm thinking about it, I never expected myself to *fight* a dragon either, per se. More to ride it across the skies. Man, that would be so awesome . . .

"To . . . ?" the dragon asks gently, more confused than anything.

I point a big finger at him, hoping that clenching my hand might suppress the trembling. "To slay you, you despicable dragon, you!"

The dragon's eyes go wide with unadulterated glee, his wings flapping with excitement as he grins childishly and turns from me to the priest, then back to me again. "You—you're really—" The dragon swallows, stepping back and forth like an excited dog, the tip of his tail wagging. "Champion of the gods! Tell me your name, so that I may announce your death to the gods, your perishing giving me the final push needed to loosen my remaining ties to the ground and emerge into the skies as a fully fledged four-winged dragon!"

"I am . . ." My real name? My username? My jaw clenches. "Lo Fennrick. But you can call me *Kitty*." I try to make a show of bravado. "And what name should *I* announce to the heavens when I slay you, oh great dragon?"

The dragon's chest puffs out with pride and excitement, feathers ruffling and unruffling. "Goss!" he announces. "It's Goss Fletchling, but you may call me Goss!"

"Goss," I say, if only to sound it out. Damn. That's a cool name.

Across the summit, I can hear Goss mutter breathily, "Lo Fennrick . . . What a name . . ." Which I hope isn't in the *what a dumb name* sense, because if it is, my heart might just break. He looks at me again, face split in a toothy grin. "Very well, human Kitty! We shall battle. My claw shall face your . . . What weapon do you use, anyway?"

I see a chance and I take it. Holding up my hand, I use the summon rat skill, instantly transforming it into a plump rat, grabbing it before it can fall. I hold it up like it's a grenade of some sort. "I use the rat."

"The rat?"

He isn't laughing. I cough a little. "The . . . rat. Yes."

He stares at me. I stare at him. I'm just about to throw the rat into my maw to eat the feelings away when he gives a full-body shudder, uttering with the greatest awe, "What an ability, what power . . . !" Before his eyes can fully transform into glimmering stars, he catches himself, coughing into his wings. "I—I mean, no matter how amazing your powers of rat are, my powers as a *dragon* will be more than a match. I'll turn that rat of yours into roast meat with a single breath!"

"Oh yeah?" I say, grinning back at him. "Not if I can do it first!"

"What are you—"

<[Touch of Reversed Heat Protection (Lv.1)]>

A single poke and the rat erupts into flames, turning halfway to ash before I come back to my senses enough to stick it in my mouth, extinguishing the flames and regaining enough flesh to recover my hand again, if only partially.

Using the three fingers I was able to re-create, I do a pose, including jazz hands. Ta-da!

He hasn't moved a single inch from the spot where he's standing, nor has his expression shifted by a single muscle.

Twirling around, I do the pose again, including jazz hands. Ta-da!

His jaw falls open. "Are . . . Are you . . . ?" I pause my jazz-handing. He takes a trembling breath. "A *half dragon* . . . ?" I stand before him, midpose, unable to find the proper way to respond to that. Frankly, I want to say yes, but that would be like a mouse declaring itself half cat just because its ears are a bit pointy. Before I have to express that fact in gentle words, the dragon continues, saying, "But that shouldn't be possible, you can't get *half-corrupted*, that makes no sense, so maybe . . ." Its heavy brows sink down across its eyes. "Do humans not become dragons, physically?"

"Um," I say sheepishly, "I don't think humans can turn into dragons at all."

His wings fall a little. "Oh, um . . ." He tilts his head cautiously. "I'm sorry for your loss?"

"All the better," the priest suddenly chimes in. "Becoming a dragon is nothing but cruelty. And not only for the ones around you."

I take personal offense. "No it isn't! It's—"

"It's *awesome*!" Goss says, finishing my sentence. We turn to each other, our jaws slacked open. I shoot him a thumbs-up. He gives me a thumbs-up in turn. Since he's obviously the expert on this, he continues, saying, "Being a dragon is totally scaly. You can fly, shoot fire, become immune to almost all kinds of dumb magic . . . *And* you don't have any stupid parents to get you down anymore!"

The look the priest gives him is one of deep, bottomless pity.

Before he has time to say anything else to get the mood down, I add my own piece, saying, "*And* you get to live for thousands of years to become an ultra-mega-strong super-dragon, totally unkillable by mortals and gods alike."

The dragon and priest both stare at me like I just declared that the world was a ball of fire.

"Wherever did you hear that?" the priest asks.

"Yeah, um," Goss says, "that's only . . . Like, yeah, I guess if you go and become a mumbler, you could live for a while longer, but that's not really . . ." He hums hesitantly. "Sure, four-winged dragons can live to be over a hundred years old, but most get defeated before that, so it still isn't exactly *thousands* of years . . ."

I blink at them. "Wait. You're telling me that you aren't super-long-lived?" I can feel myself squint in suspicion. "How old are you, anyway?"

Goss, forgetting all about the previous topic, puffs up again, grinning proudly as he says, "Three!"

I sway a little where I stand. "Three . . . *hundred* . . . ?"

"No, I'm three."

I cross my arms. "There's no way in hell that you're three years old."

The dragon flaps his wings indignantly. "Am so!" After a second's pause, he soon adds, "Well, if you count my years as a skinny goblin, then I'm thirteen. But I've been a dragon for three years!"

I turn to look at the priest in the hopes of perspective. He looks solemn where he sits in the cage. Once his eyes meet mine, he gives a defeated shrug.

I turn back to the dragon. He's younger than me by almost seven years. He's . . . just a *kid.*

"Well?" Goss asks across the peak. "Aren't we gonna fight?"

Goss doesn't seem to understand why I care. In all honesty . . . Why *do* I care? The clear condition is simple. He's all aboard and doesn't seem to mind killing or dying. The priest doesn't care either way. Yeah, sure, he's just a kid, but he's still a dragon.

I crack my knuckles. "Yeah, yeah. Fight. Let's do it."

The dragon nods. "Yup. We're gonna do it."

"Yeah. Exactly. *Fight.*"

The air thickens with tension. He stares at me. I stare at him.

Neither of us makes the first move.

Five seconds pass, and then ten, and then fifteen, and then . . .

The priest sighs loudly. "If neither of you wants to fight, then—"

"I want to fight!" Goss chirps.

"Y—yeah, that's right!" I say. "We're totally going to fight. I just . . . I need to gather myself a little, okay? Dragons are supposed to be super-strong, so I need to be ready." Even if said dragon is literally a *tween.*

"Exactly!" Goss says, pacing where he stands. "I've heard that humans are super-strong, unkillable beasts who would just as soon eat a baby as defeat a dragon!" I can tell by the awestruck tone in his voice that he admires the qualities mentioned, but I still kind of want to correct him and explain that not *all* humans eat babies. "In other words," Goss continues, "I have to prepare myself. Um, *mentally.* This is my first real fight, after all!"

Because he's only thirteen. What the heck is he even doing, being involved in all of this? He shouldn't be here, being called a dastardly dragon, kidnapping priests . . . Sure, he's happy about this, but doesn't he know I'm going to kill him? Or maybe he's too arrogant to realize it. He *did* mention something about how killing me would let him become a four-winged dragon, whatever that is.

I cross my arms. "So, um, Goss . . ." He turns to me, a quirk at his lips making it obvious that he's trying to suppress a smile.

"Yes, K—Kitty?"

I pause a moment before speaking. "Are you ready?"

He flaps his wings happily. "Yeah, of course I am! I'm totally—" The look in my eye makes him freeze in place. He folds his wings across his back, his tail no longer wagging for the first time since our meeting.

I take a step closer to him, keeping my face neutral and my words measured. "Are you ready, Goss?" And below that, an earnest question: *Is this really what you want?*

He draws himself up slightly, his eyes gaining a hint of determination as sharp as any blade. "Y—yeah. I'm ready."

I let my shoulders fall a little. "Alright, then." My eyes slide back to the status message hovering above his head.

<Dragon (Lv.173) [BOSS]>

That's a ridiculous level. Just to compare, I glance at my own stats.

<Top—Status—Community>
<PrissyKittyPrincess
Human Level 133
Agility: 371 (+47)
Strength: 288 (+47)
Stamina: 404 (+47)
Magic Power: N/A>

I am completely outmatched. As always. I can only imagine what Goss must have done to gain such a high level in such a short amount of time. Nevertheless . . . It doesn't matter anymore. Soon he'll be dead, I'll be a few levels stronger, and I'll be one floor higher. That's how it's going to go.

Turning away from my stats, I look back at Goss. The look on his face tells me everything, but a quick sniff affirms it. He's scared. More than that, though, he's excited. I can smell it. He wants this. So it's okay.

I loosen up a little, take a step to the right and then one to the left, and while Goss is still confused, I fall into a dash. The world blurs around me and within a flash, I find myself next to him, my sharp claws shooting out to gouge into his side, only to find them harmlessly bouncing off hard scales. No, not scales. Now that I'm close enough to look at them, the scales in question are actually the folded-down feathers previously puffed up in pride. Harder than steel.

I leap back, finding the dragon blinking at me, eyes wide. "Whoa, that was so fast!" His shock is soon replaced by a cocksure grin. "But is it faster than . . . *this*?!"

The air cracks and something the approximate weight of a semi-truck smashes into my side, my chest buffered only barely by my left arm, though I can still tell that a few of my ribs have been not only broken but indeed pulverized, my arm following a similar fate. My body, as limp as a rag doll, flies several meters through the air, the airborne status giving me plenty of time to recover my thoughts enough to somersault, spin into a ball, and hit the ground in a gracious and ready cat-stance. Wary of further attacks, I look up at the dragon between stray strands of my hair, only to find him alternating between looking at me, looking at his outstretched tail, and looking at the priest.

"Whoa!" he exclaims, the feathers on his tail unfurling back into their fluffy form. "That was *awesome*! Totally hornific! Did you see that, Kitty—"

The second his eyes fall on me, he realizes his folly. Kind as I am, I give him a few seconds to regain his composure, his tail's feathers folding back into a sleek and heavy club. Once these seconds are over, I leap into a roll, the confused glances he shoots to the left and right informing me that, at the very least, FPB works on him.

It's been a while since I fought such an annoyingly massive opponent. Hopefully, the general strategies should still work. Rolling at my fastest speed, I go straight at him, swerving only to dodge the erratically whipping tail and also a random strike from his massive paw that looked as though it had weirdly soft paw pads, to then eventually get behind him. For a moment, I don't do anything as I bide my time, waiting for him to stop moving so much. While waiting, I accidentally make eye contact with the priest. He's looking straight at me. I blink at him. He waves at me. I wave back at him, accidentally breaking the FPB.

Goss snorts huffily. "Why are you—"

Before he has time to turn around and ask why I'm sitting right underneath his ass, I leap at his ankle, attaching myself to it by the jaws. Thanks to my endeavors on floor twenty-two with chewing on metal, I was able to get my dragon fang skill to level two. A skill I now make good use of by successfully chewing through the feathers and getting at the tough flesh underneath. Unfortunately, even with that, I'm not quite able to get through, so I'm left chewing and gnawing while the dragon begins jumping around, going "*Ow, ow, ow!*" and kicking his leg in an attempt to get me off.

I am, unfortunately, as tenacious as a tick, so I just keep biting.

"You bloodsucking . . . !" His wings unfurl and begin to beat powerfully, air being displaced and leaves going flying as he heaves his heavy body into the air, legs dangling beneath him. And as for my own part . . .

Holy shit. Holy shit. I'm flying. I'm literally in the air!

With every wingstroke, he brings us higher, the summit we were on becoming smaller and smaller until the priest is little more than a dot. The world around us is massive. From up here, I can see *everything*. Is this what it's like to ride in a plane? It's exhilarating! But also kind of scary. But still—

"If you don't let go," Goss shouts above the roaring of the wind, "I'm going to drop you, and you're gonna crack like a wooden doll!"

What the heck is he . . . ? Grabbing hold of his leg, I stop biting to chastise him for his dumb logic. "Okay, first of all, what are you even going to do if *not* drop me? We're literally like a thousand feet in the air, so if I stop biting you, you're obviously going to—"

He kicks his leg slightly. My fingers slip on his scales and I go plummeting.

Daaaaaaamn youuuuuu Gooooooooooooooooooooooss—!

The ground approaches rapidly, and an old instinct in the back of my head starts counting the seconds. I get closer and closer. I passed ten seconds a few moments back, so I feel fairly certain that this is it. Frankly, by all the metrics, this is probably the dumbest way to die. When I come back as a ghost, I'm going to haunt the shit out of this guy. Though, on the other hand, considering that I've yet to be haunted by anyone, the chances are low that the afterlife is of the ghost type. Anyway, pretty good run, all and all. I'll see you all in He—

A pair of massive clawed hands grab me mere meters from the ground, decreasing my plummet from dozens of meters per second to only a few as Goss cackles loudly and sets me down on the ground. "Haha, I got you, Kitty! Now, let's get back to—"

I take a few steps away from him, hunch over, and barf up my liquefied intestines. Acting more on instinct than anything else, I quickly begin to scarf down my mangled left arm, swallowing the bone bits and mushy tissue like it's the first thing I've eaten in weeks, which wouldn't be entirely incorrect. As I'm wolfing down my own flesh, I focus the regeneration onto my stomach, ignoring the reeling sense of disreality coming over me.

Alright. Alright. That wasn't too good, but there was enough flesh in my arm to regenerate it partially, so I don't have to eat all of it. I turn back to Goss.

He seems oddly worried. "Are you, um . . . ?"

I fly at him. My claws are ineffective but my teeth work. Still, his folded feathers are thick enough to use as footholds, so I rush up the side of his arm and onto his back, where I stand between his half-folded wings. The back is usually the weak point of large creatures, so I should have some time to—

His long neck twists around until he faces me, his head being larger than I am. We stare at each other for a long moment, trying to understand each other's thought processes. Am I going to attack him? Is he going to attack me?

I take the safe before the unsafe and throw myself at his head like a leaping facehugger, trying to get hold of his tongue so I can gouge it out, but his lips are sealed tight. Oh, well. Might as well go for his eyeballs then—

He cranes his neck back, squeezes his eyes shut, and slams his face into the ground.

Ah . . . Arghhh . . .

With both of my arms broken, I can't hold on to him anymore, and I think my spine broke, so that's no good either. He leans back out, sighing. I draw in a ragged breath that fills my lungs with warm liquid, the resulting cough making my chest rattle. But that's alright. I eat the last parts of my arm, shifting my back as I do in order to place the spine back in its proper place. Broken bones aren't too bad to handle since they don't need much tissue to heal. With my bones back in place, I leap to my feet again, good as new.

I crack my neck. He stares down at me. With my various battle meditations active, my arm is quickly healing. I wipe the blood from my face.

He frowns at me. "You're, um . . . kind of hard to kill. You know that, right?"

Quickly deducing that he isn't the type to attack while talking, I answer, saying, "Yeah, I know." And after a moment's pause, I continue. "And you," I say, "are really hard to hurt."

"Well, I *am* a dragon, after all." He grins proudly. "And a type seven, at that!"

"I don't know what that means."

"Do you hate the gods?"

His words give me pause. How is that related to anything? Well . . . I hum into my hand. "*Most* of them," I say. "A few are alright."

"Well, I hate all of them," Goss says with the pride of someone who probably doesn't know who he's actually denouncing. "God of Goblins, Goddess of Dragons, God of Knowledge . . . They all suck, and I'm living proof! See, I hated the gods so much that they made me into a dragon, which means that—"

"If you'd attend my sermons," the priest abruptly says, "you'd know that that isn't how it works."

"Is so!" Goss barks. He turns to me, his ruffled feathers falling back into place. "Anyway, it isn't important. We were fighting. And I'm about to show you my secret trump card that will totally incinerate you and destroy you forever, leaving not even a body to be buried! Mwa-ha-ha—"

"Don't you dare burn my garden!" the priest says in a rare display of actual anger. Standing up in his cage, he affixes the dragon with his strict gaze. "If you burn this place, I'll ensure you don't get so much as a hare in provisions for a *month*!"

Goss's jaw slacks open. "I—I was just . . . You can't seriously . . . ? But I—" One look from the priest shuts him up properly. His wings slouch across his back and he looks down at the ground, muttering, "Okay, Father Moonlight . . ."

The priest takes a seat once again, huffing. "You've already made a mess of it enough with all this blood and claw marks . . ."

"S—sorry . . ."

I'm listening to the back-and-forth, but more than that, I'm looking down at my hand. At my fingers. My claws might not be able to get through, but I have more weapons than that. Specifically . . .

<[Touch of Reversed Protection (Lv.2)]
**Any [Protection] skill can be used in the reverse to cause the effect that it protects from, to the strength of the skill. The protection level that may be reversed depends on the skill level. The touch may only be used once per protection level.
Current power: Level 2.>**

I clench my hand into a fist and turn to look at Goss again. "Are you done, Goss?"

"H—huh?" Goss says, turning to me. "Oh—yeah! Of course, yeah. I just . . . I'll show you the flame breath later. I suppose . . ."

I run at him, ignoring the prickling feeling in my chest as I slide under a massive claw swipe, leap over a whip of the tail, and finally take a spot beneath his exposed belly. I put my hand to it, tapping my fingers in a certain rhythm.

<[Touch of Reversed Stroke Protection (Lv.1)]>
<[Touch of Reversed Cold Protection (Lv.2)]>
<[Touch of Reversed Hallucination Protection (Lv.1)]>
<[Touch of Reversed Heat Resistance (Lv.10)]>
<[Touch of Reversed Dehydration Protection (Lv.2)]>

That should just about do it. It was a shame that I couldn't kill him in a less painful way, but—

A massive hand suddenly grabs me, dragging me out from under his stomach and up to his face. "Aha, gotcha!" He grins like a cat with its mouse caught. "Thought you could scurry out of my reach, eh? Well, not so! I may look like a big lunk, but beneath that, I'm all muscle! It's just that my down hasn't all gone away yet, which is totally normal for dragons my age, I'll have you know. Well, one thing that *is* fully developed is my breath, and if I just shoot it right up and you above me, then I probably won't burn any of Father Moonlight's garden. So it should be okay. R—right?"

I follow Goss's tentative gaze to the priest. He gives a look of unbridled suspicion before shrugging. Goss turns back to me, grinning. "Right! Prepare yourself for your last moments, human Kitty!" He holds me up by the back of my rat kilt—my rilt, if you will—his mouth opening dramatically. Down below, I can see a piercing light forming in the back of his throat, his chest swelling and feathers rustling as fire gathers in his bosom, before . . .

His mouth snaps shut. He looks me up and down. "Um . . ." he says, glancing away shyly. An orange blush warms his cheeks. "You wouldn't mind, like, um . . . giving me your seal, right?"

"My . . . *seal?*"

"Y—yeah!" Goss says. "You know, like when you seal a letter? Or do you not have . . . ?" His eyes look me up and down, clearly realizing as he does that I don't really carry much of anything. "Oh, yeah, um, no, forget I said anything, it was totally dumb, I just . . ."

"No, no," I say, understanding what it is he's asking for. "We humans don't really use *seals*, but we do have *signatures*. Would that work?"

"Signature?" he asks, skeptically.

"Yeah! All I need is some ink and a quill, and . . ." And I don't have either of those. Going by the look on Goss's face, the chance that he owns one is in the negative. Right. My brow furrows. I look down at my claws. "Or, I mean, my claws and blood should work just fine, I think? It'll turn brownish and gross-looking after a while, but it should still work, no?"

"Yeah!" Goss replies excitedly. "Yeah, that'd be scaly!" His face suddenly falls a little. "But don't you need something to sign?"

"Well, yeah, but . . ." Frowning, I remember something I grabbed a while back that mysteriously wasn't purged by the floor being closed. "I got just the thing."

I summon my wanted poster from inside my inventory. While Goss is still oohing and aahing, I force him to set me down before using the palm of his hand as a desk to sign on. Simply put, I use my own blood as ink and my sharp claws as quill, which allows me to successfully jot down the worst-looking signature I've ever done—or seen, for that matter. Putting the dot at the end damn near spreads enough blood to hide everything else, but Goss is absolutely ecstatic about it, jumping about and overall causing a ruckus enough to shake the earth. After a minute or so, he finally calms down enough to apply logic. Hunching down, he hands the rolled-up wanted poster to the priest. "Um, can you please hold this for me while I beat this human?"

The priest doesn't answer, but he also doesn't refuse the poster. With his loot safely secured, Goss returns to me. As he reaches out to grab hold of my rat kilt, I put my hand on his finger.

"Hm?" Goss says. "What's up?"

TRP didn't work, nor did TRR. My claws can't get through. My teeth don't sink deep enough. There's only one thing left to try.

Close to three years ago, I gained a tolerance without levels that has never improved. A tolerance whose effect has been uncertain, to say the least.

<[Death Tolerance] Grants tolerance toward death.>

I don't know what this does. I don't *think* it makes me unkillable. It certainly doesn't feel like I've been immortal all this time. Then again, I haven't died. Not for realsies, at least. But I don't know. Maybe this is the only thing keeping me alive and I've never known.

If I used touch of reverse tolerance with this, then . . .

"Well, Kitty?" Goss asks. I look up at him—at his excited, starry eyes. "Are you ready? My breath is awesome, it can turn absolutely anything to ash!"

I swallow a dry bit of saliva. My hand slides off his finger. "Yeah," I say. "I'm ready." A thought hits me and I hold up a hand before he can grab me properly. "Just—I have one last thing I want to do before I go. Is that okay?"

Goss tilts his head quizzingly. "Yeah, of course it is!"

"Thanks," I mumble, and turn to my messages. With only minor searching, I pull up the right recipient, writing in my brief but honest message.

<PrissyKittyPrincess [F25]: Hey Moleman, ill b going now, thank u 4 everything, im sorry i couldnt b as good a friend as u were 2 me bye, good luck with everythign, gg>

I send it away. Then I turn to Goss. "Now I'm ready."

He grins, grabs me, and lifts me again. Holding me above his open maw, I watch calmly as the back of his throat fills with light and flames. At least it'll be painless, I suppose.

After only a few seconds of powering up, there's a massive rumble in his chest, thunder paradoxically coming before lightning, his forked tongue squirming in glee as flames fill his throat and his mouth and then everything else as a concentrated beam of pure flaming WHITE shoots out of his mouth, bathing me in a blinding cascade of light and fire and burning, flames everywhere, and then . . .

The fires end. I look down at Goss. He looks up at me.

"Why aren't you dead?"

Human for Dinner

So, to summarize, he tried his breath on me a total of six times before we both realized that it wasn't going to work. My heat protection evolved into heat immunity, my fire protection rose to level 9, and my divinity protection reached level 8. As a matter of fact, in the time it took for us to collectively figure out that he couldn't kill me that way, I healed my arm and thus returned to being nigh unkillable.

Following that, we tried a few other strategies. He dropped me from up high, he tried crushing my spine, and he actually succeeded in breaking my neck, but in doing so I bit my tongue off, which healed my neck and allowed me to once again escape death.

And at this point, you might be wondering why I'd let a juvenile tween dragon try his hand at killing me for the better part of an hour. Had I been a coward, I might have pointed to how my protections rose nicely, even gaining one more immunity, but that wasn't it. See, while he tried using my face as a punching bag, I got a message from Moleman. And then another one. And another, and another, and another, and . . . yeah.

In short, if I threw in the towel, that meant I had to face Moleman.

I'm basically in the situation where I left a suicide note on the kitchen table, went to take a bath with my toaster, and only then realized that my house had breakers, making the self-toastification impossible. Like, what do you even do at that point, assuming the person had already come home and was banging at the door? Do you open it and smile sheepishly, all *Oh, sorry, I goofed up! Whoopsie!* and face the incredible awkwardness of such a situation?

Or do you avoid that awkwardness at any cost, because there's no way in hell I'm telling someone to their face that I was too dumb to check if we had ground fault breakers ahead of time and that's why I failed?

So, yeah. That's the situation. He's trying to kill me, and I'm trying to get killed because I can't kill him. Funnily enough, we haven't tried beheading yet. When I asked him about it, though, he wouldn't give me any straight answer.

I guess, in the end, we're more alike than I originally thought.

"So, what are we up to now?" Goss asks, holding my liver between two of his claws.

"That would be . . ." I look down at the tally marks written in the earth. I add another one. "Number fifty-six."

Goss frowns at the liver before handing it back to me. I eat it in a record-breaking four bites. Even as I make a small pose at the success, his frown persists. "Don't you think it's about time?"

"Time for what?" I ask him. Struck by inspiration, I pull my spleen from my abdomen. "Time for *dessert*?"

He shakes his head, frown twitching at the sight. "No, I mean . . . It's been almost an hour. I don't think there's any way left to kill you, Kitty. We tried everything!" For some reason, I can't muster the strength to say the obvious. Goss sits down in front of me, lowering his face enough to put his eyes at my level. "Shouldn't we try something else?"

"Like what?"

He shrugs his wings. "I mean, what do *you* need to win? You said you couldn't just leave, but what can you do, then?"

"Well, the clear condition says that I need to *defeat the despicable dragon*, and that I have to save your priest guy."

"Despicable dragon?" Goss parrots, a smile dawning on his face. "They called me that? *Despicable?*" After a moment of grinning to himself, Goss shakes his head, regaining his serious expression. "It doesn't say, like, *two-winged dragon Goss Fletchling*? Just *dragon*?"

"Yeah, but I don't see any other priest-kidnapping dragons around, so I can't imagine that it would be anyone but you."

"Sure, sure, but . . ." His brows fall into a contemplative furrow. "Hang on a moment." He turns around briefly, unhooking the simple clasp holding the priest's cage shut. Father Moonlight steps out after a second and Goss turns back to me, saying, "Well? Did it change?"

<[Clear Condition] Defeat the despicable dragon.>

I look up from the status message. "Yeah, now it just says that you need to die."

"Me, or some nondescript dragon of uncertain wing amount?"

"Nondescript one."

"Well, in that case," Goss says, trotting back up to me, eyes glinting, "I think I might know how to solve it." He clears his throat before speaking again. "You see, we have a killing rite coming up in a month or so, and—"

<A CHANGE HAS BEEN MADE.>

<[Clear Condition] Defeat Goss Fletchling, the two-winged dragon formerly known as Gohm Trahl.>

"Ah, no, wait," I say, cutting Goss short. "It changed. Now it wants me to kill you, specifically."

Goss—or maybe Gohm—freezes midstep. His eyes inch over to face me. "Seriously? Like, me-me?"

"Yeah, you-you." I squint at the text. "Gohm . . . *Trahl?* The hell kind of name is—"

Goss flashes across the space between us, delicately putting the tip of a claw to my lips. "Don't—" He bites his own tongue. "Don't say that name. That's my old, skinnie name." After a few moments of staring at a range closer than one yard, he removes his claw from my lips. His wings fold up behind his back. "Still, that would mean that it really means *me* specifically, huh . . ."

"Yeah. Goss Fletchling, the two-winged dragon," I read straight from the clear condition. "I just need to beat you, and—"

"Two-winged dragon?" Goss repeats, his voice bearing a striking hint of epiphany. "So not just me as an individual, but me as a dragon? A *two-winged* one?"

I cross my arms and try to radiate only half as much suspicion as I feel. "Yeah?"

"So . . ." He grins at me. A real toothy one, like only a dragon can do. "*Not a four-winged one.*"

I don't know what that is. I purse my lips at him. "I don't know what that is."

"You don't know what a—" Exasperated, he turns to Father Moonlight, who had taken his sweet time walking up to join us. "Father, he doesn't even know what a four-winged dragon is!"

Father Moonlight shrugs. "He's a human; I've heard they know nothing."

Ah, *finally* a sensible stereotype! As I'm nodding and smiling at some true words for once, the priest continues. "How he knows Twotongue is beyond me, though." Suddenly his brows furrow as he looks at my hair and then my neck. "You *are* a he, right?"

"I am!" I say with absolutely no defensiveness. "I am a man. A manly human man who just happens to speak and understand all languages. Don't ask me why or how, it's a long and weird story." I pause a moment to let them ask about my cool and dramatic backstory. Neither of them says a thing. "Let's just say that the gods and I have a few hatchets left unburied."

Goss frowns. "I don't know what that means, but . . ." He takes a deep breath, sitting down. Following suit, I sit down as well, the priest carefully folding his massive wings to let him sit on his feathers before joining us in our little circle. "I'm a dragon, right? A two-winged one. See, because I have, you know, *two wings*. But!" He raises a finger for dramatic effect. "If I were to offend the gods and thereby fulfill the criteria inherent to a type seven such as myself, I'll ascend and become a four-winged dragon, forfeiting my arms to a life of eternal freedom and—"

"That's dogspit and you know it," Father Moonlight scoffs. "Types? Criteria?" He shakes his head. "Reach rock bottom and you'll find a pair of wings waiting for you. Can't be in pain if pain's all you feel."

"You were a type *five*," Goss says dismissively, rolling his eyes. "You wouldn't get it."

"Type seven, type five . . . There's only one type, and that's—"

"Suicidalist, yeah, I know. Well, if you're the only type, how come the only member of the suicidalist party is old Ymir? On that note, what's going to come of the party once he gets his turn in the killing rite next month? Are you going to step in to keep it from dissolving?"

"The fewer parties, the better. This whole political ordeal is ridiculous and should be—"

"Okay, hang on," I say, butting in. "What the heck are you even talking about anymore? Can we please stay on track?"

Goss sits up a little straighter, his ruffled feathers falling back into place. "Oh, y—yeah, of course. Er-hrm . . ." He coughs into his hand. "What I'm trying to say is that if I become a four-winged dragon, then, you know . . . ?" He looks at me expectantly, waving his hand a little. I feel a tension irritatingly similar to a headache pass across my skull.

"Then you'll no longer be Goss the two-winged dragon," I finish. And I'll no longer have to defeat him.

Goss tries and fails to snap a finger. "Exactly! That way, I get my wish, you get to *beat the floor* or whatever you called it, and—"

"And Purgatory is plagued by another heartless disaster." Father Moonlight's words are like a balloon popping at a Vietnam vets' get-together.

Ignoring him fully, I turn back to Goss. "And how do you turn into a four-winged dragon?"

"I don't know!" he freely admits, like a lunatic. Plucking the signed wanted poster from Father Moonlight's hands, he unfurls it, comparing the portrait to my face. "But I have a feeling that you could help."

"Help how?"

He smiles at me. "I think you'll be able to tell me that better yourself." His smile shifts into a feline grin. "How about we continue this conversation at Loathe Summit?"

* * *

"They *should* be okay with it. I mean, it's just one teensy human, right? Those grumps in the aliusist party bring skinnies for dinner basically every *week*, so a single little tallthing shouldn't be seen as any weirder, even if he's coming willingly. At least, I think so . . ."

I look over at Father Moonlight, trying to understand whether he can also hear Goss. Considering that we're currently a few thousand feet in the air, each of us held in one of Goss's massive hands, it's impressive that I can hear the dragon's words at all. Father Moonlight meets my inquisitive gaze with a light shrug, which probably means that either it'll be okay or I won't have to answer Moleman's message. A win-win, in other words. While I'm trying not to fawn too much over the speed and altitude and *holy shit I'm kind-of-almost riding a dragon*, Father Moonlight shouts out over the roar of the wind, "Don't forget that we have feast in an hour!"

Goss blinks. "Feast? O—oh, yeah! I almost forgot . . ." Suddenly struck by a thought, he turns to look at me, a new, predatory glint in his eye. "Father, do you think a human would count for the—"

"Is he smaller than a dog?"

Goss pulls his lips tight, turning back to look at the air ahead of him. "No, he isn't," he grumbles. "But I've been so busy! How am I supposed to find a share if I'm in the middle of ascending from the rungs of the merely two-winged?"

Father Moonlight makes the understandable decision to not grace Goss with an answer.

"I mean, isn't self-fulfillment more important than grub? And, sure, I'm still a whelp, but I barely get hungry anymore, so—*whoa*!" Swerving in midair, Goss quickly takes a right around a cliffside, bringing us into the shadow of an immense mountain. "Whew, that was a close one! I keep forgetting where the entrance to this place is . . ."

Despite his casual words and general aloofness, Goss has proved himself to be an adept flier, so even though I feel about as safe as a parent going test-driving with their kid for the first time, I don't *think* I'll die here. Probably.

As I'm trying to make sense of where I'm going and what's happening, Goss zips in and through various tunnels and openings, eventually lunging into a hole that almost looks as though a laser melted a hole straight through the rock. Once we start flying through tight tunnels and cavern systems, Goss begins to keep his mouth open in a strange way, producing a whistling sound between two of his teeth. This practice appeared completely senseless until I began to hear a similar, lower-pitched whistle, the sound making Goss abruptly land, squeezing his body to the floor of the cavern, letting another, larger dragon pass by overhead. With the speed that thing was going, they would've no doubt collided had Goss kept going.

Getting back in the air, Goss flew us the last bit, at which point a number of other tunnels began to merge with ours into one big one, which finally ended at the entrance of a large, dome-shaped cavern. The cavern, in turn, connected to various other tunnels, but I wasn't looking at that.

No, the real centerpiece of this room isn't the size of it—easily rivaling a stadium—nor is it the various vibrantly colored dragons lounging around it. Rather, I'm drawn to the beauty of its design. Someone, I don't know who, must have spent months upon months in here, carving intricate patterns out of stone, chiseling out statues and horns and various intricate details to create a splendor that easily rivals the Sun Emperor's palace. The roof, which has been rigorously shaped into a perfectly smooth ordeal—only broken by a small opening at the very top letting in a stream of light—is fully painted, depicting what I think might be the genesis of dragons. There are two central characters: an intricately detailed dragon and a small female goblin held in the dragon's hand. The area around these two is split, the haloes protruding from their heads basking goblins and dragons in light. Funnily enough, the goblins are on the side of the dragon, and the dragons are on the side of the goblin woman.

The art continues down the sides, becoming so detailed and descriptive that I can barely make out what it's supposed to be. Every dragon painted is unique and detailed, whereas the few goblins present outside the centerpiece are either drawn with little detail or presented as straight-up ugly. From what I can see, the overall piece is split into a number of smaller ones, often depicting battle, or romance, or winged goblins, or . . . flower petals, I think?

While I'm trying to crane my neck to look at the art, Goss puts me and Father Moonlight down, which makes me stumble a little before catching my footing. Father Moonlight follows my gaze to the ceiling. "The pride of dragons—a testament to their foolishness." He smiles bitterly. "I can only hope that should dragons ever go extinct, this will be our legacy, rather than the spiteful atrocities scattered across the world."

Goss looks like he wants to disagree, but I'm quicker. "I hope you get remembered for how awesome you look," I mention offhandedly, which luckily gets Goss happy enough to not pick a fight with a priest.

Father Moonlight chuckles lightly, turning to me. "It's been a while since I could converse with someone at my own level. You'll join Goss for the feast, won't you?"

"I still don't know what that is," I say, "but okay." Feast means food, food means I eat, and eating means yummy. Also, it doesn't hurt to get to talk to more dragons. Dragons are good. I really like dragons.

Nodding, Father Moonlight turns toward the room, his eyes following the stream of light shining in through the hole at the very top as it hits a specific place on the wall. Now that I'm looking at it, someone has painted a pair of bows running across the floor of the room, numbers from one to twenty-four painted along it. The stream of light hits a spot in between sixteen and seventeen. "Looks like we have about an hour and a half until the feast. As I've told you before, unless you bring your share before seventeen, I won't be able to skin it in time, which means—"

"I won't get to eat, I know, I know," Goss huffs. He looks more annoyed than he did finding me functionally immortal. "I'll find something, okay?" Without waiting for a response from Father Moonlight, Goss grabs me beneath my armpits, lifting me up again. "And now, I have to go show Kitty my—erm, *look* for grub. Goodbye, Father." He's just about to turn and fly away when a look from Father Moonlight stops him in his tracks. Goss gulps. "Oh, and uh . . ." A stubborn blush forces its way onto his cheeks. "Th—thank you for helping me catch a human. And also for, um, letting me use your garden. Highly appreciated. Or—or something."

Father Moonlight's stern face melts into a genuine smile. "You're welcome, Goss."

"R—right!" Goss stutters, turning his back on the priest. "I'll be going now. Bye!"

"I'll see you at mass, Goss!"

"You won't, but okay!" Goss shouts back as he beats his wings, getting back into the air. I only have time to wonder about why he left so quickly until I spot the small, gentle smile on his lips.

I look up at him. "Are you *sure* you're a type seven?"

Goss jerks in surprise, accidentally clutching his hand enough to break all of my ribs at once. "What do you mean? I—I have no idea what you're talking about!"

"I'm just saying that," I choke out, feeding myself my own fingers to heal the broken ribs, "if you're supposed to hate the divine, then I understand kidnapping priests or whatnot. That's sure to get the gods upset. But you don't even *know* the gods, and Father Moonlight . . ." I take a small break to swallow down the bones and tendons. "I've only known him for like an hour or two, but he seems nice. More than that, *you* don't seem to dislike him in the least. If you're supposed to hate the divine, I'd imagine you were also supposed to hate the lackeys of the—"

A high-pitched whistling approaches us in the tunnel, lasting for a little more than two seconds before we smash into it, Goss going tumbling atop another dragon, only barely larger than him. "Oh, hey, Goss!" the dragon beneath him, colored a light green with blue spots, chirps. "Did it work with Father Moonlight? Did you get to fight a human?" It smirks. "Are those arms I see? Shame to hear that the ascension attempt failed. Better luck next ti—" The dragon's eyes fall on me. I smile and wave at it.

Before I have time to shout *Howdy, neighbor!* at the top of my lungs, Goss covers me with his hand, sealing away both me and my pranks. "S—sorry, no time to talk, I have to go find something for the feast, bye!" And in a flash, the world becomes weightless and he speeds off again, the other dragon's shouts echoing down the tunnel, telling him to bring the skinnie to the feast. But even after we're away from the dragon, he still won't unseal me. It's hard to exactly tell his emotional state since the feathers hide the telltale smells of fear, but I can tell that he's far from calm.

It takes close to seven minutes—I counted them—before he finally lets me see where I am and what's going on.

"This is my room!" Goss says as he lets me down to see the magic. And . . . uh . . . Honestly, going straight from the splendor of the hall we were in just now to *this* feels a bit jarring. So, for one, it's only barely big enough to fit him. There's a groove in the middle of the room that's shaped like a curled-up cat, filled with animal hides. I'll assume that's his bed, but he doesn't spend any time on it. "There's my wall, and here's my hoard! So far I only have a few pieces of armor that I got off a rose knight down the side of the mountain. I kind of wish he'd been alive so I could've gotten something to brag about, but it's okay. All hoards have to start somewhere, right?"

I approach his little hoard. Can this even be called a hoard? Then again, he's only gone at it for a few years, so it makes sense. While I'm looking through the sad excuse of a dragon's hoard, Goss lumbers up to one of the walls, puts his face close to it, and shoots fire at it until it starts melting. Then he simply grabs the molten piece of wall, fashions it into a hook, and sticks the signed wanted poster onto it. Once it's properly affixed, he takes half a step back—as far as he can step without his body bumping into something—and hums at the sight. I nod at the barren wall. Yup, now there's a sight for *Better Homes and Gardens.*

When he turns to me, I make sure to assert my approval by doing a thumbs-up. His face splits into a smile. "Hehe!" he laughs, turning away from the wall to begin picking through his hoard himself, mumbling about whether bones count for the tribute. As for me, I'm left with a very strange feeling.

Is this what it feels like to have a younger sibling? With my older sister, I was kind of like this. Always seeking her approval, not always getting it, but once I got it . . . Hoo, boy!

I let my eyes rest on Goss for a few moments. "What are you looking for, anyway?" I ask.

"Huh?" Goss pulls his face from the hoard, emerging with a helmet stuck on his nose. "Oh! Yeah, right, you don't . . ." Making a slightly annoyed face, he plucks the helmet off, flicking it back into the hoard. "It's really just a thing for us whelps, but . . . Every day, we have a little feast. Everyone brings something they've caught, as long as it's smaller than a dog, and then Father Moonlight prepares it and we all share whatever we caught. I usually keep a few rabbits around just in case I forget to go out to find some, but I must have eaten them yesterday for a midnight snack . . ."

"Happens to the best of us," I say, nodding as I recall my various midnight snacks across the past three years. All those goblings . . . Ah, now I'm drooling again. Wiping the drool off my chin, I'm struck with a thought. Frowning, I look up at him. "A rabbit is enough to feed you for a day?"

He pauses briefly. "Oh, um, we don't actually *need* to eat, it's more of a comfort thing. Once we mature into full dragons—which I'll do in less than two years, for the record—we swear off needless goblin pleasures like eating and sleeping. Some dragons also choose to do a sort of fast, like never speaking or never using their arms, but I think that's weird and dumb, so I'm not doing that." He glances left and right, even poking his head into the tunnel leading out of the room for a moment before turning back to me. "Between you and me, though . . ." He grins. "I might not even stop eating."

"How controversial," I say knowingly, even though I actually don't know what's so wrong with eating. My fake confidence gets through to him, though, and he snickers uncontrollably, like some kind of villain sidekick. However, my mind is elsewhere. "So, what you're saying is that if you have something to bring to the feast—hopefully something smaller than a dog—then you get to eat?" He nods. I purse my lips. "Do you think there's any chance that if I also brought something, they'd let me join in?"

"Well . . ." Humming, he taps his chin, eyes sliding from me to the wanted poster hung on the wall and then back to me, where his face erupts into a grin. "Sure! You're basically a dragon in all but form, so I don't see why not!"

I fight the urge to sob violently at his compliment. This . . . might be the greatest compliment I've ever gotten. Turning away from him I wipe at my face, snorting down the last bit of gratitude before returning my eyes to him. "Okay, that's good, because I think I might know what to bring to the feast . . ."

"These are the fattest rats I've ever seen, but I'm not sure if—"

"But they're smaller than a dog, aren't they?"

Father Moonlight's face crumples up slightly. "Of course, but that require-ment is mainly an *upper* limit, not . . ."

"Aw, come on, Father!" Goss mewls, pushing his face closer to the two of us. "Don't you know those cost him an arm and a leg?"

I move to high-five Goss for completing the joke we agreed to do earlier; however, since I'm no longer holding onto Goss's wing, I plummet to the ground face-first, unable to catch myself with my single arm. Before I have time to groan about my predicament, Father Moonlight grabs my shoulders and pulls me to my one foot. "Are you alright, son?"

Something tightens in my chest. "Y—yeah, I'm okay."

The worried look on his face reminds me of someone I'd rather not think about right now. "Look, Kitty, these rats are sure to be a delight for the whelps, and I will gladly accept them, but only on the condition that you don't do this again."

"What? No more rats?" I ask incredulously, wobbling on my one leg, my one hand clutching onto Father Moonlight's arms with a little more desperation than I'd like it to. "Rats are the bread and butter of any child—errm, *whelp's* diet. If you're worried about the possibility of disease, I can assure you that I produce only the finest-quality rats, organic and certified non-plagued, so there's really—"

"Didn't it hurt?"

My jaw clamps shut. I can feel the sweat beading on my face. "I, erm, hehe . . ." I want to wipe at my forehead, but I only have one hand, and that hand is currently clasping a certain man's robe. "Only a *little*, so . . ."

He pats my arm. "I will accept them, but please, don't hurt yourself like this again."

Even though I know that this would be a good time to celebrate, I can't bring myself to. "Okay," I mumble. "I won't."

Still holding on to me, he turns to look at the close to forty rats I used a literal arm and leg to summon, all piled on top of a repurposed cloak, their necks severed. His frown deepens. "However, the feast will be in only a quarter of an hour, so I doubt I'll be able to skin them in time . . ."

I'm not sure why they want the rats skinned, but . . . "If that's a problem, I would gladly help out."

He blinks at me in what seems to be genuine surprise. "You would?"

I almost want to shoot back a simple *Why wouldn't I?* but in the end, I'm able to stifle it by merely nodding instead.

He smiles and squeezes my arm. "I will gladly accept your help, then. Goss, will you help the others in preparing the dining room?"

"Okay, Father!" Goss says chipperly, clearly excited to get to partake in a feast wherein his contribution amounts to almost twenty rats. A respectable number, if you ask me. Before he leaves, though, he gives me a little look. "You'll be okay, right, Kitty?"

"If someone dies while we're skinning rats, I doubt it'll be me," I say with a confident smile.

Convinced, Goss smiles and bounds off down the hallway we arrived through. I turn to Father Moonlight. Without needing to say anything, he takes my side, placing my one arm over his shoulder to help me walk. However, with me on his shoulder, he has a brief moment of internal conflict as he glances between the pile of rats, me, and the small, goblin-sized hallway ahead of us. I smile at him. "If you help me over to that pile, I'll show you some human magic."

Not questioning it, he brings me over, and with only a few movements, I will the entire bundle of rats into my inventory, where they belong. Father Moonlight whistles at the sight. "Impressive magic, indeed."

I puff my chest out to gloat, only to realize that bragging about something that every single human challenger can do is kind of dumb. I deflate a little. Trying to keep my spirits up, I quickly add, "Not as impressive as my rat-skinning skills, I can promise you that."

"I trust you," Father Moonlight says. I pause in my tracks, shooting him an uncertain look.

He didn't even hesitate. Something deep inside me wants to cackle and call him foolish for trusting someone like me, to assert that even with only one arm and leg, I can still make it quick. Another part, even deeper, wants to sigh and pity him for falling for my ruse.

But I don't do any of that. Because, above all of that, there's a softer, gentler realization; one that brings a smile to my face. "Thank you," I mutter at him, understanding that I'm in the presence of a truly kind person.

Although it takes a while, he's eventually able to bring me to what is more of a workshop than a kitchen, complete with tanning racks and instruments that assist in skinning and cutting. If anyone else had led me in here—save for Moleman—I would have assumed I was about to get skinned. Instead, I look around the place with curiosity, absently wondering if he might let me use any of the tools.

He leads me to the center of the room, furnished with a large workbench made of . . . obsidian, I think. Either way, he motions for me to join him at his side, which I do. He nods at the workbench. Understanding his signs, I summon the rat horde. The sight of it makes him sigh, which is understandable. While I'm still thinking about the most effective ways to skin rats, Father Moonlight wanders over to a small closet, from whence he pulls a pair of leather aprons and a pair of matching obsidian knives. "Here you are," he mutters warmly as he stands on his tippy-toes to thread the loop of the leather apron over my head. "We're a bit tight on time, but that's no reason to ignore safety."

He almost hands me a pair of leather gloves alongside the knife, but by then, I've finally been able to pull myself out of my mild reverie to refuse, saying, "Ah, uh, no thank you, I've got my own," and presenting my hand. He takes the hint well, but I can see the slight disappointment in his eyes.

We position ourselves on opposite sides of the workbench and grab a rat each. I start skinning it without really having to pay attention, my wandering mind eventually falling on Father Moonlight. I watch him feebly try to skin the tail. It might not be my place to tell an actual adult like him, but . . . I hold up the tail. "Here," I say, grabbing his attention, "you don't have to skin the tail, it's got too little meat on it. Just cut here, and here, and the tail comes off easily. And then with the smaller legs, there's this trick I found . . ." As I talk, I feel a RED heat come to my ears. He isn't saying anything and I'm blabbering about skinning *rats* of all things. This guy has a whole-ass tannery! The *last* thing he needs is some human runt to strut in and try to tell him how to do his job. I must sound like such an arrogant prick right now—

"Like this?" he asks, his knife deftly severing the tendon I mentioned.

I blink at him. "Y—yeah," I say. "Like that."

We keep skinning rats. Sometimes, I tell him a little trick, and he thanks me, and implements it without fighting it in the least. After a few times, I started waiting for the other shoe to drop. At some point he'd have to hit back, right? Tell me that I was horrible at this and that it was unhygienic to use my bare hands and whatnot. But he never did. Eventually, I got desperate enough to try to strike up a conversation. "So, um . . . What are you using these skins for, anyway? The dragons don't wear it, and . . ." I look down at the finely crafted apron he put on me. "And why do you have two of these? Is there some other goblin living here or something?"

"No, there's only me," Father Moonlight says casually as he slits the skin across a plump rat's back. "Goblins are brought here occasionally, but they aren't exactly guests. And among formers, there's only myself."

"Former?" I ask, pulling the skin off a rat in a single piece, tossing the rat into the rat pile and the skin into the skin pile.

His wings rustle slightly and he looks up at me in innocent amusement. "A former dragon, that is."

"You used to be a dragon?" Bullshit.

"Long ago, at least," Father Moonlight says. "But I got better. After the last dragon priest retired, I took his place. Since then, we've had two new formers, though both are still on their maiden journeys as of over ten years back. Whether they choose to return here and join me as dragon priests is up to them. In the meantime, I can only hope that one of the current dragons that live here might get better, too."

I can't tell if he's happy or sad. All I can do is look down at my apron again, overcome with the feeling that this is like a mother sitting day in and day out, sewing baby clothes for a child that may never arrive, the little caps and tiny socks building up in one big pile of unsaid tragedy. "I'm sorry to hear that," I mumble.

"Thank you," he says softly. He carefully places his latest rat in the pile, putting the skin in the skin pile with equal care. "As for the leather, tanning and such . . . It's mostly a way for me to keep things running. Once a month or so, I bring down the pelts and whatever I've sewn to a nearby town and sell them to a merchant whose family has been doing business with our parish for generations. I save the money for things needing repairs, as well as funds for any new formers."

"Don't you get lonely?" I ask, beginning on a new rat. "I mean . . . Everyone else here is a dragon. Assuming they are anything like I've heard, your presence here is nothing short of a miracle."

He chuckles warmly. "There's nowhere I'd rather be. She . . . The Goddess of Dragons saved my life. To be able to repay Her by helping Her unfortunate children is the greatest joy I could ever imagine." If he hadn't said it with such reverence, I'd almost want to jeer at him. But there isn't any hidden bitterness to his words. He isn't pretending or willfully deluding himself into thinking that everything's okay. He's like Moleman, in that way. This is what he truly feels, and I can't find any reason to laugh at him. In fact, such a strong belief makes him nothing less than admirable.

Nodding, I toss my latest rat into the pile, moving to grab another one only to find the rat pile emptied. What in the—

"Done already?" Father Moonlight remarks happily, turning to me with a big smile. "You must be the fastest rat-skinner I've ever seen!"

"Thank you," I say, at first out of habit, but then with actual weight. "*Thank you.*"

"So," he says, looking at the pile of skinned rats. "Are you ready for a glorious feast?"

I can feel myself drool.

Oh boy, am I.

What's Your Type?

I help Father Moonlight bring out the skinned creatures for the feast. Alongside my and Goss's pile of forty rats, there's also a small boar, a dog, an unskinned gobling, two drakes, a green rabbit, and a pair of worms. All and all, there are eight pieces of meat and forty rats, with the rats making up a solid fifth of the total mass presented. It is certainly a pride-inducing sight.

Since there's actually a table for these to go onto—a large and round but squat one fit for ten house-sized dragons to sit side-by-side around—Goss and I place everything where it should go. We might have gotten a little overexcited, though, spending a few minutes too many arranging everything into a fancy pattern. However, by the time the other whelps arrive, it's proven to be more than worth it.

Of the seventy-eight denizens of Loathe Summit, four of them are whelps. I know this because Goss was very helpful in explaining it to me. Whelps are smaller than normal dragons, still haven't lost the down, and have yet to fully come into their own colors and patterns. After five years, they have a coming-of-age rite where they decide which type they are and whether they want to remain at Loathe Summit. Most remain, some leave. Not that they can't leave earlier than that, of course; it's just seen as leaving the nest too early.

The other whelps in question number only three, of which two are older than Goss and one is younger. They arrive by this same order, with the two older ones arriving together and the youngest slipping inside almost five minutes after we were originally supposed to start.

And now everyone's sitting around the table, most people staring at me, and me staring at Father Moonlight, who has joined us for some reason.

"Oh, Goddess of Beasts," Father Moonlight begins, making me twitch in surprise. But before I can loudly ask what's going on, I notice that all of the whelps—with greater or lesser reluctance—have laid their wings atop the table. Even though I don't know what I'm doing, I replicate them using my one arm instead of wings. "We thank You for these creatures whose lives have been laid down for the sake of ourselves."

There's a pause, and I wonder if this is the part where we say *Amen*, but then the dragon sitting on his right—the oldest one, introduced by Goss as Kempt, starts talking, his blue wings rustling, "Oh, God of Goblins, we thank You for this gobling, granted for our nourishment and benefit. Bring her into Your arms and let her heart be laid to rest."

The word quickly moves to the one on his right, who is the second-oldest dragon and the same one Goss bumped into earlier, introduced by him as Frey. Talking with routine calm, she continues the prayer, saying, "Oh, Goddess of Dragons, watch over us, that these lives laid to rest may serve to strengthen us and make us stronger, so that we may one day become super big and strong."

The dragon on her right is the youngest one, barely half of Goss's size, and doesn't realize at first that it's her turn. It takes Goss to elbow her in the side for her to start speaking, at which point she goes, "Oh, um, I, uh . . ." She gulps. I think Goss called her Fink earlier, which feels suitable, for some reason. "G— God of, um . . . God of Fighting, please—"

"That's not a real god," Frey hisses at her with a sneer. "Do you mean the God of Duels, or the God of War, or the God of Combat, or the God of Hunting?"

Fink, who's a pure, annoying WHITE, turns pink around the cheeks. "Um, I—I never really . . ."

"It's okay," Father Moonlight says from across the table. "You don't have to. I can teach you more about the gods later, okay?"

Seemingly holding back tears, Fink nods, unable to so much as speak.

Father Moonlight turns to Goss. "Would you continue, Goss?"

"Oh, yeah!" Goss says. "Oh, God of . . ." He pauses, turning to me. "Is there a God of Humans or something?"

"Uh, well . . ." I recall a somewhat disheartening memory. "The god of our world is the *god of love*, if that's who you're looking for." Ugh, it still feels kind of gross even just saying it.

"God of Love . . ." Goss says, his voice bearing a worrying amount of reverence. "Right, okay! Oh, God of Love, I thank you for letting there be humans. Very scaly. And I also thank you for letting me meet one. Extremely awesome."

He stops talking. Now nobody's talking. I blink at him. The word has moved to me. A—ah. I gulp. "W—well, I, um . . ." Think, brain, think! There has to be *something* I can say! "Oh God of . . . of . . ." I bite my lip. You know what? To heck with it all. I might as well, right? If it's expected of me, then there's no reason not to. "Oh, God of Pain, thank You for getting me this far. And the God of Cowardice, even though you're a coward. And Want too, even though you're crazy. And also Cruelty. You're weird, but you gave me a skill, so . . . thanks." I close my mouth. Now I will talk no more. My piece is said. If you want to pry my lips open, you'll have to get through my teeth too.

Better bask in it, you divine douches, because I am *not* saying it again!

Father Moonlight's simple smile pulls the wind out of my sails. "So say we all in praise of the God of Multitudes, aye."

"Aye," the gathered dragons reply in unison, even Fink, which means that I have no other choice.

"A—aye," I say.

There's about a zero-point-two-second pause before Frey bodily throws herself across the table, jaws snapping at the small boar, only for Goss to leap atop the table, hissing and snarling like a wronged macaw while Fink silently tries to slide one of the rats closer using only her tail, the arrangement Goss and I worked so hard on being thrown into the air as the table turns into a gladiatorial arena.

"*STOP IT!*" Kempt shouts, his wings bared and his nostrils flaring. The gathered dragons all comically freeze in place, the boar half-torn between Goss and Frey. Everyone looks at him. He huffs angrily. "Can't you even wait for Father to leave before acting like beasts?"

The younger whelps look away in shame, but Father Moonlight doesn't seem to mind as he takes a step away from the table. "No, it's nothing to worry about. I'll leave you to it. I hope to see a few of you at mass," he says. Then he smiles, bows slightly, and walks away. As I watch his back moving into a hallway, I can't help but wonder why he doesn't fly. Maybe it's a matter of taste.

Even after Father Moonlight's silhouette has faded down the hallway, the whelps don't move. Kempt gives them a glare before finally sighing. "Alright. Get to it, alrea—"

Not waiting to hear him finish that word, the whelps return to their chaos, the boar stuck in a tug-o'-war between Goss and Frey quickly torn in half, their jaws snapping at the severed pieces of meat flying, their hands grabbing for whatever meat remains as they bat their wings at each other threateningly. In the surprisingly captivating cockfight, I'm able to use the moment to sneak away two rats and the gobling. Fink is only barely able to get hold of a single rat, while Kempt, unhindered, grabs one of the drakes. The rest of the meat is split between the furiously fighting Goss and Frey, who growl and fight like animals over not only the dog and drake, but also the rats, and even the two little worms.

I watch them in a kind of reverie, unsure whether they remind me more of a pair of dogs fighting or two siblings. Either way, I was able to get some grub, so I'm happy. I dig into my gobling, wondering why it hasn't been skinned like the rest. Then again, despite saying that he was once a dragon, Father Moonlight doesn't strike me as the type to enjoy looking at dead children, so it might once again be his personal preference.

After a minute or so, Goss and Frey finally stop fighting like a pair of alley cats, settling down on either side of the table, popping rats like Skittles and glaring daggers at each other. Meanwhile, the drake Kempt took has mysteriously ended up with Fink, who's eating it with grateful care.

As I look at the whelps, Frey meets my gaze. She gives me a cautious look. "So you're a human, huh?"

Goss almost leaps onto the table again. "Yeah, he is! And his name is *Kitty*!"

"I was asking *him*," Frey says, rolling her eyes. "Show-off . . ." Eyes back on me, she looks between me, the knee in my hand, and the gobling from which I got the knee. "Is it any good?"

I consider her words for a second, letting myself chew fully before I swallow. "Haven't you ever had gobling?"

"O—of course I have!" she says, but her puffed-up, defensive feathers tell a different story. "I was just . . . I mean, that one was frozen when I found it, so I didn't know if it'd thaw in time, and . . ."

"And even if it did," Kempt says, "you didn't know if anyone would have the guts to *eat it*." Considering that he's a dragon, I'm surprised to find so much venom in his words.

"It's smaller than a dog, isn't it?" Frey shoots back. "Besides, Goss would've eaten it. He'd eat *anything*."

Despite what sounds like an insult, Goss straightens out pridefully.

Kempt, on the other hand, isn't about to let her go for that. "Smaller than a dog, yes, but it's still a *goblin*."

"Yeah, so?" she says. "It climbed the mountain itself. Even if the country we made that pact with some thousands of years back still existed, it would still be fine."

"It's a *child*!"

"Yeah, and a *goblin*!"

Using my nails as saws, I pull off the gobling's head and start chewing on the neck. The neck is kind of weird. Depending on the goblin's lifestyle, it's either the toughest or most tender part. In this case . . . "Mmm." It's good. While Frey and Kempt are snapping at each other about the ethics of child-eating, I turn to Goss. "So," I say through a mouthful of meat, "you're awfully quick to thank the gods, considering that you're supposed to be a—"

"Fine!" Goss abruptly barks, splattering a bit of sinew from the drake he was eating. "Okay, sure, so I'm *not* a type seven." Across the table, Frey and Kempt have quieted down. "What do you suppose I am, then? A type two? Type eight? You don't even know what the types are! My coming-of-age rite is in less than two years and you expect me to retract my type *now*? It took me over a year to come to terms with being a type seven, and now you think I can just toss that aside, all because—"

"I think you're a type four," Frey says from across the table. Goss turns to her, his face set in a snarl. She raises her brow at him. "What? It's not *my* fault you've got your hate painted across your chest."

"I do *not* hate other people! Not enough to be a type four, at least. I mean, come on! When I talked to Lutz, he told me that he seriously killed every single person in his city, *methodically*. One by one. He sealed the gates with fluid stone, and then he just . . . I am *nowhere* near that. All I did was—"

"Burn down your home village, yeah, we know," Frey says. "Which is totally not exactly what Rew did."

"Rew did it because he was jealous, not because—"

"I think you're a type five." The table turns to Kempt as one. Calm and collected, he slides his icy blue eyes from Fink, to Frey, to Goss. "Like me."

Goss bristles. His claws scrape against the table as he pulls them into a fist. "You think I'm a suicidalist? Like you and your buddy *Ymir?*"

"Yes. That's exactly what I think."

"No. *No.* I did *not* kill my family and friends and everyone else because I hated *myself.* How does that make any sense? Nobody does something drastic enough to become a dragon because they despise *themselves.* Everyone knows that!" Goss exclaims with a lot of certainly for being a tween. His face twists into a sneer. "Everyone except for you and that dying skinnie, Ymir."

Kempt's wings flare out, his eyes widening in sheer anger. "How dare you—"

"Hey," I say. Even though I didn't speak loudly, my tone is enough to get them to quiet down. I wait for them to turn to me before I speak. "What's so important about types?"

The anger buzzing like a hive full of wasps in the air dissipates.

Goss almost looks despairing. "What's so important about . . . ? Types are *everything!* Your type determines why you became a dragon, and what keeps you as a dragon, and what can get you to ascend." His brow furrows deeply. "Since kidnapping Father Moonlight didn't let me ascend, I'll assume I'm not a type seven, but . . ." He looks down at the table, eyes cast in a bit of shadow. "If I don't know what type I am, how am I supposed to know how to ascend . . . ?"

"Well, uh . . ." I tap my chin thoughtfully. "What's the difference between types? Do all type sevens have flame breaths and type twos ice breaths, or is it the colors, or . . . ?"

"Not quite," Kempt says across the table. "There's no physical way to tell, and the actual events that caused you to become a dragon don't have anything to do with it, either. It's a personal feeling." He hesitates slightly before continuing. "However, I tend to agree with Father's perspective, in that there aren't nine types, but rather only a single—"

"That's dumb," Frey says as she chews on at least fifteen rats at once. "The parties have been using this system for like fifty years. Why would they design all of the parties after the types if it wasn't correct?"

Kempt pauses for a moment. "I'm not sure. However, Father has been here for seventy years, so—"

"So that means he knows everything? Hah!" She pulls up her lips, giving a nice view of her sharp teeth. "If he hadn't had the sacrament of absolution, he would've been served at the feast by now. That's the only reason anyone bothers letting him hang around, at least. Faith? Devotion? *Friendship?* Ridiculous! Heck, even if he hadn't been here, we could still do the killing rite just fine. Throw some dragon in there, stick that feathery whatchamacallit on them, and have *them* pummel the would-be mumbler to death!" Leaning in closer to Kempt, she gives him a front-row seat of the toothiest leer I've ever seen. "Maybe then we could even have goblins over for dinner, *every single day.*"

He seems completely unimpressed. "No, I think we'd better not serve goblins for dinner every day. I'd hate to see you starve."

Frey's eyes widen. "Why you . . . !"

Turning away from the bickering whelps, I give my attention to Goss. He doesn't even seem slightly amused by the circumstances, which is worrying. "Hey, you alright?" I ask him, putting a hand to his foreleg. I look at the untouched pile of meat in front of him. "You've hardly touched your rats."

He jerks back in surprise, head swiveling to face me. "H—huh? Oh! Sorry, Kitty, I was just . . . Heh, um, all this talk about types got me a bit confused, that's all." He tries to smile but fails, the edges of his lips dipping into an uncertain frown. He falls into silence, but I can tell that he has things to say, so I keep quiet. After a couple of choked seconds, my efforts are paid off. "Thinking about when I turned into a dragon feels weird. I don't remember hating much of anyone. When it happened, it just felt *right,* and I've never really questioned it. It still doesn't feel wrong. In all honesty, it doesn't feel like much of anything." His eyes fall to the little pile of meat in front of him. "But I must have hated *someone.* Why else would I . . . ?"

I pat him on the arm again. "You'll get there," I say as though I know anything. A small epiphany strikes me. "No, as a matter of fact . . . *We'll* get there."

He blinks at me. "Huh? What do you mean?"

I fight back the urge to cackle maniacally. "It's quite simple, Goss. You said it yourself, right? We just need to figure out who you hate, and then we can use that to turn you into a four-winged dragon, and then . . . !"

"And then . . ." Goss says quietly, "you'll go away."

I ignore it. "So how do we best figure out who you hate . . . ?" Well, frankly, to know which type he is, we'll kind of need to actually know which types there are. "Goss, about those parties you mentioned . . . Could you explain them a bit more?"

"Oh, uh . . ." Turning back to look at his pile of meat, he begins absently tracing lines using his claw. "Well, there are nine parties for all the nine types. You join the one that shares your type, so if I was a type seven, I'd join the religist party once I came of age. Right now, the biggest party is the socialist party, with . . . Fifteen or sixteen members, I think? I can't remember who the leader is, but since they're the biggest party, they have the most sway at the monthly conference."

"The—the *socialist* party?" I ask, trying not to let the shock show on my face. "You have a socialist party?"

"Yeah," Goss answers, completely missing my incredulousness. "There's the socialist party, the deist party, the progressivist party, the naturalist party . . . one for every type, as I said. Oh, and the smallest party is the suicidalist party. It only has a single member, so Ymir is party leader by default. Ah, but Kempt will be joining in two months or so, so by that point . . ." His words trail off as his brow folds over his eyes. "No, wait, Ymir turns thirty-seven next month, which means that he'll have his killing rite, so . . ." His brows squish together. "I guess that means that by the time Kempt joins the party, he'll be alone. Weird. Strange to think that we'll have a month or two without any type fives." His thoughtful expression abruptly shifts into a jarring grin. "Good riddance!"

Across the table, while still keeping Frey in a choke hold, Kempt quickly shouts, "Hey, I heard that!"

Ignoring him, I keep my mind running. Not just about the fact that there are socialist dragons, but rather because this makes our path forward fairly clear. "Alright. Got it. In that case, I think I know how to best figure out which type you are." I smirk up at his confused, reptilian face. "We're going to go interview a few politicians."

If they're even a fraction as corrupt as the real-life versions, this might be a bit mentally draining. But it'll be worth it.

No, wait, sorry, *Earth* versions. Not sure where that came from . . .

Either way, during the few minutes it takes for Goss to finish eating his rats and such, I'm able to convince him to join me in questioning the political parties about why they are the type they are, why their type is the best, how they became dragons, et cetera, et cetera. He's skeptical, of course, but since I'm the one asking, he goes along with it.

"So, first up . . . type one?"

"No, it'll probably be easier to do it in order of size," I say from where he's clutching me tight in his hand. "I doubt they'd all be collected in one place, right?"

"Not quite, but kind of? I haven't been to all of them, but they have their party locales."

"Locales where they party?"

"Locales where party members gather," Goss clarifies. "I haven't been to all of them. Since I'm a whelp, they should let me in alright, but I'm a bit worried about *you* . . ."

"I'll be fine," I assure him. "I'm too charming and witty to kill off."

He chuckles. "Maybe so. But if they make any quick movements . . . I'll try to protect you."

"I can say the same for you," I comment. Then, after a moment's consideration, "But thanks."

"No worries. Let's see, the socialist party should be down here and to the right . . ."

We swoop down a few more completely dark tunnels, Goss flying as per the guidance of his whistling. Echolocation? Possibly. Since I don't have anything of value to add, I allow myself to lean back and enjoy the ride a little. I've only been to an amusement park once, but it was pretty similar to this. The only difference would be that this is a smoother ride. Not to mention that considering the difference between the way I am now and the way I was when I was ten or something, this is probably safer. Hm. Now that I think about it, couldn't I technically survive a roller coaster crash by now? Remind me to test that hypothesis when the opportunity arises.

As I'm thinking about theme park accidents and my own mortality, Goss takes an abrupt right, goes up through a hole, climbs a stark tunnel wall, and eventually finds a big, fancy door. I can only barely see it in the darkness, but . . . Yeah. It's a door. Like, an actual wooden door, big enough for several dragons to enter at once. While I'm still reeling from the existence of the stupidly ornate door, Goss walks up to it, bumping his short horns against the wood. After a few seconds, a slot opens. A massive, flaming eye peers down at us. "Who's there?"

"Um, it's Goss," Goss says. "One of the whelps?"

The eye shifts from Goss down to me. "What is that creature in your hand?"

Goss lights up with pride. "Oh! This is actually my new friend, Kitty. He's a human!" In the same vein as a child presenting their parents with a cool lizard, Goss holds me up to the slot, putting me mere yards away from the eye. Going by the eye's size alone, the owner must be over twice as big as Goss.

To alleviate the tension a little, I give the eye a casual wave. It remains, staring at me, unblinking. Ah. This is awkward. I wonder if TRT would work if I applied it directly to the eyeball?

There's a sound of locks and chains being undone, and while I'm still reeling a little, the door slides open. In its place stands a dragon, easily the size of an entire gymnasium, with horns large as trees, said horns being partially covered by lacy pink dresses. My sense of reality completely leaves me. The dragon as a whole is a vibrant shade of orange, with striking patterns in yellow and pink. The arms and legs, the lower parts which are usually not covered in feathers, are also covered up by torn and repurposed ball gowns. If I hadn't been carried by Goss, I would probably have collapsed with the sheer disillusion taking hold of me.

The dragon in question nods for us to enter, which Goss does, his head only barely reaching up to the level of the other dragon's folded wings. Compared to Goss's hand, I'm like an action toy, but if this dragon were to carry me, I'd be more in the size category of a tin soldier.

As we enter, the dragon closes and locks the door behind us, allowing my jaw to drop once more. The place we now find ourselves in is not only absolutely massive, but likewise stupidly fancy. The floor is covered in a ridiculous mishmash of different carpets, some woven as finely as any tapestry, others more simple, but all of them spread out with the casual indifference of the wealthy. There have to be at least several hundred of them, if not thousands. The walls are similarly diverse, made up by an unfathomable array of paintings, the majority of them set in frames that could probably buy a normal person their entire pension. And that isn't even to mention the various pieces of decorations, ranging from vases and armors and weapons to entire regalia outfits, artifacts, and masterpieces worth more than entire castles lining the walls and ceiling in a casually grotesque show of indifferent wealth.

My eyes finally fall on the main sources of illumination, namely a pair of crystal candelabras hanging from the ceiling, the finely polished and tempered glass effortlessly refracting the light of the dragonhearts contained within to create stunning spectacles of light across the room.

What the hell is this place? More importantly, why are supposed socialists hoarding wealth?

"Hello, Hart!" Goss says chipperly as he bounds up to one of the five or so dragons in here. The dragon in question is currently discussing something with another, equally massive dragon. They don't seem to mind his approach too much, though. As a matter of fact, the dragon Goss addressed seems almost delighted to see him, his aged face wrinkling up as he turns his massive, green body to face us. I'm unhappy to notice that he, too, has covered his arms and legs in dresses.

Hart gives us a smile that strikes me as more predatory than pleasant, his great head lowering until he's level with Goss. "Why, if it isn't the little religist-to-be!" He taps a claw to his chin, his tunnel-sized neck moving back and forth. "Mind telling me what a type seven is doing in here?" With only those little words, the air around us seems to take on a chill. His eyes turn to me, narrowing slightly as he takes in what I am. "And a *human*, too." He leans in closer, until I can feel his breath against my face. As hot as fire. His eyes roll to Goss. "Religists aren't welcome here, Goss. Or are you trying to make a statement?"

I can sense it. I don't know if I've ever really felt it this clearly before, but the look in his eye . . . This man—no, this *dragon* is ready to kill. Even more than that, he's willing. I can practically taste his eagerness in the air.

Goss, however, doesn't seem to notice it in the least. "Oh, yeah, sorry, I changed my mind. I realized earlier today that I'm actually not a religist." Smiling innocently, Goss looks up at Hart, eyes almost sparkling. "So it's okay that I'm here, right?"

Hart's wings shift where they lie folded across his back and he leans back, his face melting into an expression of slight amusement. "Well, why didn't you just say so?" He grins, pacing a little before lying down properly. "About time, if you ask me. Religists . . . They are too narrow-minded. What use is there in blaming priests and churches when the real fault lies in this cold and unwelcoming society?" With a small pat on the floor, Hart invites Goss to lie down as well, which Goss does, letting me down as he does.

Man, these carpets are even more comfy than they looked. "Yes," Hart says, continuing his monologue, "if only those shallow goblins had been more accepting of our kind, we would not have had to live secluded in mountains such as these, cooped up like caged beasts! What injustice, to deem us cruel merely because of how we chose to react to the cruelty of society." He pauses briefly to look down at Goss, maybe to make sure he's still listening. "Tell me, Goss. You came from a poor family, did you not?"

"Um," Goss says, the question clearly taking him a bit aback. "Well, kind of, I guess? Dad was a farmer, Mom kept the family . . . But it's not like we were *poor* or anything. We could eat. Not as well as I do now, sure, but it wasn't like *that*, you know?"

"Ah, the son of a poor farmer," Hart says, shaking his head as though that's the same as being the child of a worm. "It's no wonder, really. I myself was the third son of an impoverished worker family. Can you imagine it? Owning no more than three full outfits, barely enough food for everyone . . . Yes, indeed, anyone would do the same thing in our positions."

Sitting cross-legged on the floor, I pull out the seam of a nearby carpet. "They didn't, though."

"Exactly. Economical strain is the cause for—" Hart almost bites his own tongue off. His head slowly turns to sneer down at me. Then he looks at Goss. "Excuse me, did your pet try to say something?" He catches his own mistake. "Oh, sorry, I meant to say *snack*."

Goss, with wide-eyed naivety, shakes his head. "He's my friend! Also, I think he said something like *They didn't, though*. Is that true?"

Hart clicks his forked tongue. "I suppose so. Not *everyone* under economical hardship becomes our kind. However, how many of us come from working backgrounds? How many have been put down by the heartless society that failed to rear its weakest members?"

"No idea," Goss says.

"No idea," I parrot.

The fact that we both said it gives Hart some pause. "Yes, exactly. We cannot know. However, I'm sure that you can find no fault in my argument." I can, but I'm not going to mention it because he seems like the easily annoyed sort. "Now, to return to the tyranny of class society . . ."

By the time Hart finishes his speech, I'm completely certain that he's off his rocker. He doesn't have a shadow of a doubt in the theory that society as a whole is to blame for dragons existing. However, at the same time, he also seems weirdly proud of being a dragon. I don't get it. Can't he just accept that dragons are awesome and should be revered as the ultimate life form? Weird. He even recounts how he transformed into a dragon, and . . . I'm sorry, but it was totally his own fault. He covered it in a bunch of flowery words, but in the end, it can be summarized as a family squabble going out of control. He felt unseen in his family, purposeless and too sheltered not to fear going out into society, so when they finally got enough of him to throw him out into the streets, he lashed out. Burned down the family home, killed his childhood sweetheart . . .

I can see why he'd blame the whole not-having-money thing, but in the end . . . Wasn't it his own choice?

Once Hart finished his monologue, I grabbed Goss, pulled him to the side, and told him my thoughts.

"Yeah, I think so too," Goss agrees. "But, I mean . . . Doesn't he kind of have a point? A thief steals because he lacks. If society had been kinder to the poor, he wouldn't have lacked."

I roll my eyes at him, my voice taking on the tone of a preschool teacher. "Yeah, sure, but what about when the nobility steal from those poorer than them? Not to mention people who kill for no reason, or people drunkenly fighting in bars."

"Maybe so," Goss admits. "At the very least, I don't think I'm much of a socialist. All this economic stuff, and *society* . . . I wasn't thinking about that in the slightest."

"Good." Nodding, I try to withhold my own enthusiasm as I ask, "So who's next?"

With that done, we head to the ali . . . alui . . . *aliusists*! That is, the guys who blame their becoming dragons on their family, friends, and acquaintances.

They felt pretty promising when Goss described them, but once we showed up to visit, those hopes were dashed. For one, they were all crammed inside this tiny cavern, piled on top of another like sunbathing snakes. And that's another thing—*all* of them were there! All fourteen dragons, each one big enough to eat an elephant like an apple, were present to form the pile, arms and wings and tails and necks intertwined. When we tried to converse, they all talked above each other, chattering about how much they hated the people they blamed for turning them into dragons. And, sure, some of it was absolutely deserved, but for the most part, it came across as more of a blaming game.

"And my mother? That witch of a goblin ran me ragged, she just . . ."

"My brother would hit me, and my dad would hit me, and honestly, they got what they deserved, so I don't see why . . ."

"Purgatory is better off without those kinds of people—if you'd only *heard* what they called me behind my back . . ."

It was difficult to make out any one of them. At the very least, though, I could hear Goss as he said, "Sure, they pushed me pretty far, but it's not like I did it because of them alone. My mother could be kind of harsh, but I don't think I hated her enough to become like *this*."

I agreed, and off we went to the next party; namely, the universalists.

"If only that detestable General Warsson hadn't invaded at that moment, then Lithia would have remained pristine, and this would never have happened!"

"Blame us all you want, but *you* began this war!"

"Oh, blame the oppressed! How goblic of you, Gut!"

A lot of shouting, and even more arguing, half of which I was too distracted by the numerous flags, military statues, and royal portraits to pay attention to.

They tried to convince Goss that he did it because of the famine that struck the Tenn Dukedom, which in turn was a result of the ongoing conflicts with the nearby kingdom of Ret-inn, which was tumultuous because of the arduous state of the princess and prince, the latter of which had been provided by the Empire. By this point, though, I felt it pertinent to mention that this wasn't possible, since the princess and prince would only be mysteriously killed a year after Goss's transformation.

In the end, Goss and I both dismissed his being a type six on account of the fact that he didn't even know he was living in a dukedom.

The next ones, the progressivists, could hardly be seen over the piles of books covering their small shared space. Only one of them was willing to step away from his frantic research to explain why the unstoppable march of time was to blame for their becoming dragons. He was very adamant that the reason Goss became a dragon was out of despair of his aging parents, alongside his own becoming older. Unfortunately, since Goss was ten at the time and neither of his parents was older than thirty, we dismissed these guys as well.

"So who's left?" I ask him as we leave, watching with curiosity as he begins counting on his fingers, eventually using the ones he's holding me in.

"We've gone through five of the nine types, so that leaves us with . . ." I can see the formulas circling behind his eyes. Nine minus five equals . . . ? "Um . . ." The question of whether dragons can or can't sweat is answered as beads of sweat roll down his forehead.

"Four?" I say, to which he turns orange around the cheeks.

"Heh, um, yeah. My brother didn't finish teaching me plus and minus before he, before I, you know . . ." His smile fades slightly. "But, thanks."

"You're welcome," I say, already deciding that I need to teach this kid how to do his math.

We head to the next ones, called the metaists. Unlike the religists, who hate the gods that actually exist, these guys have made up a new god specifically for the purpose of hating them. That is, a singular god, who reigns over not only Purgatory, but also the world humans came from, and every other world, place, and person, too. According to them, this singular god has created everything there is, has been, and will be for the sole sake of its own cruel entertainment. Dragons, then, are merely another piece of tragic comedy, their plight of karmic indifference and their wants of no matter.

Goss and I both agreed that these people were lunatics.

The solitarists, who we met with next, shared our opinion. In fact, according to them, both the metaists and religists were completely off their rockers. There were no gods and no god, no purpose or meaning, and no reason behind why they became dragons. Even if they had transformed following a failed murder attempt, even if it followed betrayal, despair, and agony, it didn't matter. They had a lot of credible sources for this, their small room filled with more academic literature than the progressivists had.

Listening to them, I thought their opinions mirrored Goss's thoughts a little, only to find him making a face of reluctance, almost disgust. When I asked him about it, he was quick to clarify, saying, "Sure, I don't know exactly why it happened, but I do know that there was a reason. It just wasn't any of the reasons everyone else has mentioned so far."

We moved on. The second-to-last ones, the naturalists, were a bit difficult to find. Apparently, they actually lived on top of the mountain rather than inside it, roaming about and sustaining themselves on the land. Goss doubted that we could find them, but with my nose, such doubts were trivial. We left the caverns and headed out, using my nose as guide until we found one.

Despite hulking over the trees, the dragon we found was not especially visible. Without my skill, it would've been difficult to tell his striped green feathers apart from the foliage he surrounded himself with. Nevertheless, we found him, though he wasn't especially happy about it. Even explaining that I could find anything I sought didn't placate him. It almost seemed like he would attack us for a moment, until Goss explained that he was curious about what made him a naturalist. At that, he softened a bit.

As he told it, anyone who was a dragon would always have become a dragon. They were simply predisposed to it from birth. Trying to find meaning in it was like trying to figure out why the sun shone. It simply did. He didn't understand why I took issue with his analogy, but it didn't anger him too much to continue his tale.

Essentially, to him, there was something inherently different about dragons. Not everyone could become one, but everyone with the predisposition would eventually become a dragon.

The annoying thing about his argument wasn't that he was right, but rather that he couldn't be disproven. At the same time, he couldn't be proven, either. Everyone who's become a dragon was always going to become a dragon. It's circular reasoning and doesn't actually prove anything. Though, of course, when I tried to explain that, he got annoyed and lumbered off. I was kind of scared Goss would be upset with me, but he was actually okay about it, since he agreed with me.

"If I was always going to be a dragon," he said, "I would have come out of the womb with feathers on."

I couldn't disagree with that one.

With type one done and over with, we head back to the mountain. It's gotten fairly dark now. "That was the eighth one, right? Including the religists we didn't visit, that is."

"Yeah," Goss answers. "And with that, there's only one type left." He falls silent for a moment.

"That type being . . . ?"

"Huh?" Goss says absently. "O—oh! Um . . . that is, type *five*. Suicidalists."

Suicidalist? Haven't I heard that dumb-ass name somewhere before? . . . "You mean, as in Kempt, and . . ."

"And Ymir, exactly," Goss finishes for me. "That's the problem. There's only Ymir, and I don't know where he is, so . . ." He pauses for a moment, focusing on his flying as he swoops through a bend in the tunnel. "But it's not like we *need* to meet him or anything. Clearly, there's no need to go on. Everyone else knows who they hate and why they turned, and I don't. So there's something wrong with me. It doesn't mean I'm a *suicidalist*." The chuckle he shoots out is desperate at best. "But you can still hang around, right? There's no reason to—"

"If you follow the tunnel going right a few paces down," I say, "you'll start heading toward him."

"Wh—what?"

"Didn't I tell you?" I say, looking up at him from between his fingers. "I can find anything I'm looking for. *Anything*."

His eyes dart down at me, then back up at the tunnel spiraling ahead of us. "Yeah, sure, but . . ." The tunnel loops, closer and closer. "Do we really have to—" The fork in the road approaches swiftly. "I don't . . ." He falls silent. I can smell it. Closer, closer. His eyes squeeze shut. A glint of light shows the fork in the road only seconds away, and I barely have time to wonder if we're going to bash our brains out on the midpoint before Goss abruptly rolls to the right, bringing us down the proper road.

"Good," I say, loud enough for him to hear. "This is no time to be a coward, Goss!"

In the darkness, I can't tell if he's smiling or frowning. But I can hear his words as he chokes out, "I will try, Kitty."

I ask nothing more of him.

Dragons

The tunnels get smoother and smoother, inexplicably becoming broader as we keep going. But we don't talk. The only sound is the flapping of his wings and the whistle of his echolocation. Usually I can tell if a silence is nice or awkward, but right now, I really have no idea. Goss seems nervous, but I can't tell any more than that.

Still, we're getting there. Oddly enough, though, the closer we get, the stranger it smells.

At first, it was just some little scent, tickling my nostrils. But now it's starting to become almost overpowering, though not in an entirely unpleasant way. It kind of reminds me of the smell of a fireplace, but without the smoky overtones, leaving only the deeper, purer fragrance. Is something burning? Is that it?

To determine whether I should be worried, I turn to look up at Goss, brushing away a bit of wind-caught hair to see him better. Even in the darkness, the tentative look on his face is clear. Tentative, but not worried. So it's probably okay. One funny thing I've noticed in being flown around by this guy is that dragons have remarkably flexible necks. Right now, even though his neck is normally about the length of a bus, it's been pulled in to decrease the effect of the wind on him. It makes him look absolutely ridiculous, but laughing at him would be kind of mean, so I abstain.

The smell becomes more and more omnipresent, and by the time we can see the light at the end of the tunnel, I'm starting to wonder if someone set a monastery on fire. But no. As we emerge into the light, it becomes all too clear what we've been heading toward.

In the middle of a lovingly formed dome-shaped cavern, hanging from the ceiling like a big carved stalactite, is a church. I have no idea how it got there, and I have no idea how it works physically speaking. Did someone literally carve the ceiling into a circular church? Why? My questions are only intensified by the way the church looks. The sides are all filled with frankly beautiful stained-glass windows, each one depicting a dragon or a winged goblin in some state of grace.

I think the most important thing to mention at this point is that unlike what you would expect from a church presumably designed to be attended by dragons, it isn't big. It's the size of a normal church—no more, no less. The question of how a dragon who wanted to attend would even join is answered by the position of the single dragon in attendance. He's sitting beneath the church, his head stuck into one of the many windows. I can't see him inside, but going by the casual way he's sitting, I can only assume that this is the regular state of things.

As we approach, Goss comments lightly, saying, "I think that's Ymir."

Since I can't smell any other dragons around, that should be the case. Still . . . He's far from a pretty sight. All other dragons so far have been fairly pompous, or at least nice to look at, with their colorful feathers and saturated hues. This guy, though? Fleshy. Almost all of his feathers have either fallen off or been plucked out, leaving the majority of his form exposed. If I hadn't known he was an awesome dragon, I would have assumed someone grabbed a skinned chicken and elongated it. Not even his wings have more than a few solitary feathers on them. Can he even fly like that?

Once we're close enough to maybe call out to him, we both simultaneously realize our mistake. Above us, in the church, as clear as day, is the sound of singing. It's . . . beautiful, honestly. I can only smell two presences in there, but it sounds as though four people are singing.

"Double-throat singing?" Goss mutters, low enough to not disturb what is quite obviously the evening mass. The mass Father Moonlight asked us to attend. The mass that, clearly, nobody attended, save for some featherless old bonebag.

We turn to each other. Goss makes an expression of physical pain. I shake my head.

It's not like I'm part of this dynamic, and he didn't even invite me personally, but . . . *Still* . . .

Goss turns away from the church, his heavy footsteps padding against the cavern floor.

I squint up at him. "Where are you going?"

He meets my gaze, more confused than outraged. "What do you mean?" he says in a hushed tone. "I'm going away so we don't disturb them. We can return later."

I cross my arms. "So that's it? You're just going to leave? Like a little *chicken*?"

"What's a *chicken*?"

"Someone who's very cowardly," I quickly explain. "Ergo, someone like you."

"I—I'm not *cowardly*!" Goss shoots back, quickly glancing over at the church to check if they're still singing, which they are. In a whisper-shout, he says,

"Listen, I don't know how you humans do things, but here, if mass is in session . . . You can't just *join in* out of nowhere. Walking away is the respectful thing to do, so that's what I'm doing."

"Respectful," I concur, "and exactly what a chicken would do."

"I'm not—"

"Bwok bwok bwok!" I tease, replicating the beating of a chicken's wings.

"What is that? What are you even doing?"

"This is you," I explain helpfully. "Bwok bwok—that's the cry of a chicken, and then the wings . . ."

"I don't—" He heaves a big sigh, loud enough that they should definitely have heard us. "Okay, okay. You know what? Sure. Let's join in the middle of mass. Why not? I'm sure Father will be delighted to see us and not at all ask us to leave because, hey, we *literally just barged in.*" He huffs in frustration and turns around with a big dramatic flourish, but the second his eyes fall on the church, he freezes in place.

"Well?" I say. "Are you going to join mass, or . . . ?" I flap my fake wings at him.

Gritting his teeth, Goss strides forward, taking a seat opposite Ymir. He brings me up to his face, scowling darkly. "If he asks anything," he says, "I'm blaming you."

"Cool with me," I say casually. I wonder if blaming me would be enough to create a new party? Ah, I can see it now—type ten: *Fernrists.* I chuckle to myself like a madman. While I continue my insane mental imagining of what I could do to create a dragon, Goss deposits me atop his head, right between his horns, which is . . . This is *such a nice place to sit!* Why haven't I been sitting here all this time?

I get my answer as Goss raises us both into the air, the movement almost making me tumble right off his head. I'm able to regain my footing, but from now on, I will be clutching onto his horn, thankyouverymuch.

And soon, one of the many large stained-glass windows stands before us, easily bigger than Goss's head. I frown at it. How do we . . . ?

I notice a shadow moving behind the window, and with the tiniest click, the window opens outward, making Goss and me jerk back a little. Father Moonlight quietly affixes the window in place. Both Goss and I stare at him in mute horror. Straightening out, he looks at us and gives us the biggest smile I've seen in months. Then, saying nothing, he walks away from the window. Goss isn't moving, so I bonk him on the head, which gets him out of it. He carefully slides both of us inside the church, his chin easily finding rest on a well-carved wooden stand. It's a little too big for his head, but Goss seems to find it comfortable enough.

Looking around the church itself, I watch with curiosity as Father Moonlight returns to stand in the middle of the church, atop a small, well-engraved stage—or, I suppose, an altar? I never did learn all the church terminology. Either way, the stage is as round as the room as a whole, and Father Moonlight stands in the middle of it, wearing different robes from before, now dressed all in RED, matching his wings. Not a bad color.

Across the room, a wrinkled and aged dragon smiles at us. His face is covered with scars, and I'm pretty sure one of his horns has been chipped, making him look strangely war-torn despite having the complexion of raw chicken.

When I look down at Goss's face to see if he's politely smiling back, I instead find his eyes wide and staring and his lips drawn into a tight line. I bonk him on the head again, but it doesn't help. Ah, if only I could control him like a certain chef rat . . .

Apparently, I have to do everything myself, so I look up at Ymir and give him the biggest smile I can muster. I have no idea if he saw me or not, but I'm not bold enough to wave.

This place feels . . . weirdly *real*. I don't know how else to put it.

The smell I felt before is here, in all its glory, but it isn't as strong as I expected it to be. It's here, relaxed and calm. A light spirit of smoke, gently moving around the pews, some of them large enough to hold the heads of dragons, others small enough for singular people to be seated. There's space enough for a total of twelve dragons, and maybe thirty normal people. Right now, though, there's only me, Goss, and Ymir.

Under the light of a dragonheart lamp, Father Moonlight abruptly begins speaking. Or maybe continues. "Such a pair of lovers had never been seen before. Her parents, fearing her draconian suitor, refused to allow her back into their home. And he, being so pitiful as to fall for a goblin, was chased from the top of Loathe Summit." I have no idea what he's talking about, and where I sit on top of Goss's forehead, I can feel every twitch of his face as his brows furrow in confusion. "Their love was such that it could have saved any heart, purged any dragon, and made any goblin fall. With none but each other, their plight was finally recognized by the Gods, who numbered only seven at the time. They took the two of them into Their fold, granted them the titles of God of Goblins and Goddess of Dragons, forever to watch over Their eternal offspring. Even now, They see our every pain, share our mishaps, and forgive us our trespasses. When we fall, They fall with us; when we fly, They fly with us." He smiles out at us. "So tells Borrh the Witness, Apostle of Dragons. Aye."

"Aye," Ymir says.

"A—aye," Goss and I say in equal hesitation.

Apparently, there wasn't much left of the mass. After the reading, we sang two hymns—neither of which I could really join in on—listened to Father Moonlight talk, and kissed a small box containing a single WHITE feather that he brought around. Apparently, it's the feather left by the God of Goblins as he was chased out. I have no idea if that's actually true or not, but everyone else was doing it, so I followed along.

<The God of Goblins is pleased.>
<The Goddess of Dragons is pleased.>

I'm going to ignore that.

"The mass is finished; go in peace."

Nobody leaves. Goss and I are here to see Ymir, and Ymir is smiling lightly, waiting for Father Moonlight to finish up with putting the things for the mass inside the altar. Weird place to put it. This includes the big weird robe he was wearing, so once he's finished, he looks the same as always. He looks around at us, clearly unsure who to talk to before finally turning to Goss and me. Another smile lights his face. "I'm so glad you decided to join us!"

Sitting atop Goss, I can feel him start to tremble lightly. Right. Sliding off Goss's head, I join Father Moonlight in standing on my own two feet. "Yeah, haha," I say, "funny coincidence, really. We actually came here to see Ymi—"

"It was nice!" Goss blurts out. "We—we just got, the drafts were really bad, and, um, I didn't know the way, so, uh . . ."

I frown at him. Turning back to Father Moonlight, I lean in close, whispering right into his ear, "He's lying, but he feels bad about not showing up. Be nice, okay?" I pause for a moment. "Please?"

Father Moonlight chuckles, stepping away from me. "Oh, Ymir told me all about it. Something about an abrupt downwind?" Goss, despite how confined he is, begins nodding fervently. Still smiling, Father Moonlight walks over to him, patting him on the nose. "Never you fret, Goss." Some cruel glint appears in his eye, like a disguised devil. "We shouldn't have any such issues for tomorrow's high mass."

Goss gulps, the movement of his throat making his whole head bob up and down. "Y—yeah, of course."

Hand still on Goss's nose, Father Moonlight turns to me. "Now, what was that about meeting with Ymir?"

Since Goss is still incapacitated by Father Moonlight's casual show of affection, I speak in his place. "Yeah, so, it's about his type . . ."

It doesn't take long to retell our day's adventures, and by the end of it, Ymir has decided to join in on it as well.

"So after all that, now, you suspect you may be one of mine. A *suicidalist.*"

Goss lifts his head off the seat. "I—I'm not! I was just—"

"We're *considering it,*" I clarify. "In all honesty, so far . . . Well, I'm not sure if it's my place to say it, but nobody seems to have any clue why they turned into dragons."

Father Moonlight shares an almost imperceptible smile with me. "A most astute observation."

"If I didn't know better," I continue, "I'd assume that all this about types was a load of hogwash."

The priest's smile widens.

Ymir, for his own part, appears far less amused. "And you expect my testimony to prove your suspicions?"

"I don't expect anything. All I want is to hear your thoughts and experiences, and if what you say resonates with Goss, then we have our answer. If not . . . who knows? I'm not here to figure life out for you. Your business is yours, and my business is mine. Blaming random people and things for your own actions is dumb, but if you guys want to do that, who am I to stop you?"

The old dragon's wrinkly face twists into a light smile. "I can see why Father spoke so warmly of you."

He did what now?

I turn to look at Father Moonlight. In the time I was monologuing, he took a seat next to Goss. He smiles at me sheepishly. Can he do nothing but smile? Still, I can't find it in myself to be annoyed at him.

"So," I say, "spill the beans."

His heavy brow wrinkles down. "Spill the . . . ?"

"Tell me your story. Why should Goss be a type five, why are *you* a type five . . ." I wave my hand in the air. "Everything like that."

"Ah, I see." Ymir shifts his head. "The simple answer is that, had they not been too farsighted to see their reflection in the mirror, all dragons would be suicidalist. It is the only true choice." His voice is heavy but unlabored. "Yes, I could blame society. Or even my poor parents, my comrades, perhaps even the opposing army . . . Perhaps it is the fault of my king and their king, who started such a meaningless war. Or it is the fault of the goblin who invented spears and arrows." He speaks evenly, voice apathetic to the horrors he must doubtless have experienced. "I wasn't the worst off. Dennetter, my comrade, lost his leg. I returned to a pair of parents who may not have loved me as much as my brothers, but at least they were *there*. I may not have had all that a prince might, I had my share of losses, but in the end, I could have been happy."

Somewhere in the back of my skull, I can feel something itching, like a cluster of termites, gnawing at the inside of my head, reminding me of everything that's happened, everything I did, every voice that uttered the same question. I swallow down the memories, turning to him with barely hidden desperation. "Then why did you . . . ?"

"*Because I wanted to.*" His words slice through the air like a knife through my chest.

I stagger where I stand. Clutching at my chest, I find nothing but scarred skin and a brand emblazoned deep enough to reach my heart. Blinking doesn't remove the film of RED falling over my eyes. "Because you . . . *wanted to . . . ?*"

"Yes," he says, the serpentine word slithering through the air to bite at my already opened wound. "That is why. I killed my mother, and my father, and my siblings, and I burned the town to cinders, and I tore my priest to pieces, and when my former comrades took arms against me, I laughed in their faces." His lips twitch in disgust. "I was a pathetic creature back then."

"But—but you . . ." I say. Something cold burns in my chest. My heart is on fire. I can feel my hands, clenching and unclenching. My head buzzes. "How— how *could* you? Weren't they your *friends*?! Your family? And you killed them, all for—for your *selfish* wants? That's it? That's your grand explanation? Your majestic, all-encompassing justification for why you did what you did?" I pace up to him, hands trembling, jaw clenched. "And now it's all okay, because you blame yourself? Do you seriously think that that's enough to be forgiven?"

I'm close to him now. His massive head, his infernal breath. His eyes, cold and all-encompassing as they stare down at me, what little surprise he had suddenly melting away into apathy. I stand, my chest rising and falling quickly, watching with wide eyes as his head slowly slides out of the seat, disappearing out of the window and into the darkness of the cave outside.

I blink at where he was mere moments earlier. *Th—that's right! Run away, you pathetic little—*

A massive clawed hand reaches inside, the thumb and forefinger pinching around my chest, pushing my breath out of my as my ribs makes a sound similar to hard candy being crushed between teeth.

"K—Kitty!" Goss shouts in vain as the hand pulls me outside.

Gh . . . ghhhh . . . !

<You have learned: Fracture Protection Lv.8>

Haah, haah, haah, alright, okay, I deserved that one, I get it, so . . .

He dangles me in front of his massive face, both rows of man-sized teeth bared. His eyes burn, endless darkness burrowed inside them, deeper than any tunnel. Face twisted in something that might be rage, might be grief, he takes a deep, shaking breath. *"Do you believe that I've forgiven myself?"*

Ragged breaths are about all I can take now. My heart pounds against the cracked remains of my sternum, mere inches from his massive finger. The world is starting to look blotty. I look up at him.

His shallow, quick breaths hit me. His featherless wings are flared in a show of threat. Eyes wide, heart pounding quickly . . .

Ah, that's it. I get it now.

I smile at him. "You're just like me."

He blinks at me. The fury fades from his face, his wings slowly fold themselves, and his lips fall to hide his fangs. "Yes," he says, softly. "Yes, I am."

"Kitty!" Goss shouts from across the cave, finally having gotten his head out of the church. "Kitty, I'll save you! Are you—" He notices the look on Ymir's face. "Oh. *Oh.*" He retreats a little. "S—sorry, I didn't know that . . ."

"Hold out your hand."

"Huh?" Goss says, looking back up at Ymir. Nevertheless, he follows his demand, holding out his right hand, and then watching with some surprise as Ymir drops me from a hundred or so feet in the air and into it, both of my legs breaking on impact. Ow. I look up. The sight of Goss's jaw falling a little brings a smile to my bloodied lips. Apparently, this only made Goss more worried, as his wings beat in terror. "Kitty! By the—Ymir, why would you . . . ?"

"No, no, it's okay," I say, pulling myself to my feet, biting off my fingers to heal my legs as I do. "I'm fine."

"But . . . !"

Before he can protest anything else, a voice from up above makes itself known. "Hey, mind if I join in?" Father Moonlight asks, leaning out of one of the church's windows.

Ymir looks up at him. "Of course—pardon me, Father." He holds up a hand, letting Father Moonlight step onto it before lowering him down, very softly, without breaking a single one of his ribs. Ah, the perks of the clergy. Maybe those Frenchmen in the late eighteenth century had a point after all . . . Turning to me again, Ymir squints slightly. "As I was saying, I was a *pathetic* creature back then."

Goss perks up a little. "But you got better?"

Reading the facial expressions of dragons isn't exactly easy, doubly so when the emotions being conveyed would be too nuanced for even a normal human face to show properly. I *think* he's frowning in some kind of misery, maybe even regret, but . . . Deep in his eyes, there's also what I think might be relief. "No," he says after a long pause. "I have not."

The words make Goss's expression fall. "B—but hasn't it been almost forty years since then? Surely, you *must* have—"

"I haven't!" Ymir snaps. His clawed hand grasps at the barren rock below. "I *haven't.*" In his other hand, I see how Father Moonlight gently places his hand on the far larger dragon's thumb. Ymir turns to him briefly, his jaw working as he keeps his eye away from us. When he turns back to look at us, there is resolution in his eyes. "I haven't, because I *can't.*" He lets his wing flare out, barren, featherless, and grotesque. He scowls at it. "No matter what, I will always be a dragon. Ever since that day. I am not forgiven, because I can *never* be forgiven."

Father Moonlight looks up at him, his face transparent in its worry. "Ymir . . ."

The dragon almost winces away from the tiny priest in his hand. His tail beats behind him, thumping into rock. "I am sorry. I have told you this before, Father." His eyes burn sadly as he looks at us. There is no hope in his face. If anything, all that can be seen in his eyes is the absolute certainty of a sinner. "Even if I become a former, I will still have my wings. I will still carry this unforgivable burden on my shoulders. They are dead at my hands. As there is nothing I can do to bring them back, there is nothing that can forgive me." He looks down at me, his face set in a snarl. "*Especially not myself.*"

I feel something tighten in my chest.

Unforgivable. The mere word hurts. It stings like nettles, burns like a mother's gaze. But at the same time . . . It feels *good*. Comforting. The embrace of an iron maiden. Being unforgivable . . . It means you don't have to try anymore. Like Ymir. He's a dragon. But even more than that, he's a monster. He always was, and he always will be. That's right. Even a former is defined by what they once were. *There is no forgiveness.*

I almost chuckle. How wonderfu—

Something hits me and my head snaps to face Goss. His lower lip is trembling. I grab onto one of his fingers. "Hey, Goss, listen, this isn't—"

Before I can say anything else, he closes his hand around me, pressing me close to his chest as he runs away, wings desperately flapping, bringing us away and away and away, out into the tunnel and around a bend, until they can't see us or hear us.

The second he releases me, I grab hold of his fingers. "Goss, that wasn't—" I swallow thickly, trying to get rid of my twisted and knotted-up feelings. "He was wrong. You hear me? *That isn't true.* He's only saying that because he doesn't know—"

Goss smiles at me. Tears are streaking down his face, glinting in the darkness.

"I get it now," he says. Taking a deep, heaving breath, he wipes at his face with his wing. When it pulls away, his REDdened eyes turn upward, at the darkness of the tunnel. "I'm a type five. I just didn't want to accept it before. But—but I know better now."

"Goss, you don't—"

"I do!" he says. He takes a few shallow breaths. "I do. I did it because . . . *Because I'm me.* It wasn't about Mom, or my brother, or even the village. It was because of me. There's no one else to blame." He leans back, hiding his face with his wings. "There's only *me.*"

And worst of all, I can't find it in me to disagree with him.

"Goss, where are we going? Please, I really think we should talk about—"

"I told you—I have to show you something." He flaps his wings harder, the tunnel around us becoming a blur of dark rocks and indiscernible shapes flashing by. My ribs healed a few minutes back, but I still feel like my chest is cracked and shattered. High above, Goss pants with exertion, flying faster and stronger, probably trying to drown out his thoughts at any cost. Being the softie I am, I don't stop him.

He flies and he flies and within mere minutes, the glittering end of the tunnel winks ahead of us and we burst out into the cool, comforting night air outside. The night sky yawns open above our heads, teeth of glistening stars dangling above our heads as the multiple moons gaze down, watching us as we streak up, up, and above.

Goss's grip on me tightens as he brings us into the sky, wings beating powerfully to take the world below us farther away, until the trees become like flayed toothpicks and the cliffsides mere pebbles in our eyes. The air grows colder around us, puffs of pale, smoky air huffily escaping Goss's open mouth, barely able to dissipate before the flapping of his wings causes them to spiral into tiny tornadoes of smoke.

The clouds grow nearer and the mountains go farther away, the world I knew before being left behind, replaced with a jewelry box of stars and moons.

<You have learned: Oxygen Deficiency Protection Lv.6>

"Haah, haah, haah, haah," Goss gasps as he fights to bring us higher and higher. The air around us is starting to grow cold enough to form ice on my eyelashes. He shoots a glance below us. "Just a little more, just a little bit more," he bites out, redoubling his efforts.

I have never been this high up. I'm starting to suspect that I may never be this high up again. In a way, I'm not sure if I find it exhilarating or terrifying. Maybe a bit of both, I suppose.

After a while longer, when his breath no longer runs WHITE, Goss turns to look down. He smiles.

Letting his wings fan out fully, the feathers on his tail doing the same, Goss begins to soar rather than merely fly. We aren't quite above the clouds, but we're close enough to where the world below us appears pitifully small. Holding me close to his chest, he uses his other hand to point at the world below us. "See that?" he says above the roaring of the wind. "That's Loathe Summit. And over there is Apathy Peaks, and then, if you go over there, you arrive at Misery Mountain. Then, right there, you can see Mount Contempt, and even the Silent Cliffs."

I look down at the mountains and peaks, and how small the dragons inside must be from so up high. "It's pretty."

"Yeah," Goss says. "But what I like most of all is how, when you're as high up as this—and *only* when you're as high up as this, and you look at it from just the right angle . . ." With a few shifts of his wings, he brings us around slightly. Below us, the full mountain range is visible, from beginning to end. And, honestly, now that I'm looking at it, it kind of looks like . . . Goss grins. "It looks like a resting mumbler!"

Like a sleeping dragon. Yes, with the two peaks there, and the way some of the cliffs go up and down, it looks a lot like a dragon taking a nap. But in that case . . . "Why isn't it called the sleeping dragon?"

"Huh? Oh! I asked the same thing when I first got here," Goss says, gently beating his wings every few seconds to keep us aflight. "Father Moonlight explained that it came from an old wolf's tale about a mumbler." As he speaks, Goss's voice becomes like that of a storyteller, almost in the same way Father Moonlight told the tale of the God of Goblins and the Goddess of Dragons. "Back when goblins came from dragons, there was a very mean and cranky dragon. He was a cruel dragon who loved nothing better than to break up lovers. So he would steal away maidens, and when their lovers came to rescue them, he would give them a choice. Either they let him eat their lover, or they let him eat them. Whoever lived would be released—at least, that's what he said.

"But, cruel as he was, whatever the person picked, he would do the opposite. So if you wanted to die for your lover, he would instead kill your lover, and let you go free. See, that was his biggest cruelty—the horrible mercy he always gave."

Hm, mercy as cruelty . . . Now where have I heard that one . . . ?

While I mutter about my own things, Goss continues. "And he kept doing that, until one day, when he kidnapped a poor farmer girl, and no one arrived to save her. Not knowing what else to do, he let the farmer girl live. But every day she would cry, begging him to go to her village and see if they were alright, and every day he would refuse her wishes, until she stopped pleading. She became completely silent.

"But by that point, the cruel dragon had grown to enjoy the sound of her voice. Until then, nobody had talked to him, or listened to him. So even though she didn't ask for it anymore, one night he set out to her village. When he got there, he found that it had been burned to ashes by another dragon. Blinded by rage, he fought the other dragon, only barely emerging the victor. When he returned to his cave, he found that the farmer girl had escaped. In despair, the dragon set out, wandering the world aimlessly, muttering to himself words of apology, hoping to eventually find her again and beg for forgiveness."

He falls silent. I glance up at him. "Um, is that . . . where it ends?"

"Depends on the version," Goss says. "The way Father told it, the poor farmer girl actually went away to go to the village on her own, getting there and only barely missing the dragon. Hoping to thank him, she would then set out on her own mission. However, by the time she found him, he had already become the first mumbler. Pitying his mindlessness, she gave him a kiss, putting him to rest and letting his body become the Resting Mumbler mountain range."

Honestly, I'm not sure if that's a happy ending or not. "Isn't there an ending where they end up together? Or at least where they meet, and she can forgive him properly?"

Goss pauses a moment, humming to himself. "I guess there might be, but since it's supposed to lead up to the presence of a mountain range, it would need at least a bittersweet ending."

"Yeah, probably." As we circle around the mountain range, my eyes fall on the empty hollows at the head of the mountain range, their blank voids staring up at me, simultaneously tearless and mourning. "Hey, Goss?" He blinks down at me. I tilt my head at him. "What even is a mumbler? You said this guy was the *first*, so that suggests there are more dragons that wander aimlessly and become mountains."

"You don't know—well, I knew that, but . . ." He shakes his head. "Um, okay . . . You know Ymir?"

"Yeah?"

"Unless we kill him within like five years, he's going to become a mumbler."

"What?"

"Usually, the killing rite happens when a dragon is thirty-seven and a half years old, because the youngest-ever mumbler was thirty-eight. If we don't do that, then they become mumblers. It takes a few months once it starts, but once it's done, they turn into these mindless wandering things that do nothing but mumble incomprehensible gibberish and, well . . . *walk*." I perk an eyebrow at him. "Which sounds unproblematic when you hear it first, but, like . . . They're still *dragons*."

"Ah."

"Yeah. So if you don't kill them before they become mumblers, they'll start to walk through basically anything. Walls, trees, buildings, forests, *people* . . . They aren't as bad as four-winged dragons in terms of destruction, but to the goblins, they're still kill-on-sight."

"So you're telling me," I say measuredly, "that when a dragon hits their middle age . . . they get *dragon dementia*?"

"Maybe? I'm not sure what that is, but I guess?"

I stroke my chin. Killing rite. Ymir. Killing Ymir. Type five: suicidalist. Type five, hatred of the self. Killing rite. Kill Ymir. Kill . . . Ymir . . .

I feel a lightbulb flash in my head. "Goss," I say.

"Hm?"

"I think I might know how to turn you into a four-winged dragon."

Goss lights up into a surprised smile. "Really? Wow, that's awesome! What did you have in mind?"

"You're a suicidalist—apparently. So you hate yourself."

"I'm not sure if I—"

"*So*, you hate yourself. In order to become a four-winged dragon, if I've understood it correctly, you need to confront the thing you hate and kind of defeat it or something."

"That's a bit simple, and we really don't know exactly why—"

"*So*, you need to defeat the thing you hate. You hate yourself. I can't condone you killing yourself, because if that doesn't count as me defeating the floor, then I'm stuck here forever. Hence, you need to defeat yourself without defeating *yourself*." Dramatic pause. Goss doesn't say anything. I continue. "So, what's the next best thing after you?"

"You?"

"Not me." I grin. "*Another type five.*"

Finally, it hits him. His jaw drops open and he briefly stops flying, causing us to plummet a second or so before he's able to catch himself. "You can't seriously mean—"

"I can."

"But the killing rite is usually handled by Father Moonlight, I can't possibly—"

"You can."

"There's *no way* that the parties would be willing to let a *whelp* commit the killing rite—"

"There is."

Goss pauses. He turns to me slowly. "Is there really?"

I cross my arms in an attempt to exude an inch of the confidence I'm lacking. "They're *politicians*, Goss." It doesn't take any effort to let the grin split my face further as I affix him with my gaze. "Haven't you ever heard of *lobbying*?"

As it turned out—he had not. Getting him up to speed was easy, though, and by the end of it, he understood quite well that I was very serious. It did take a couple of minutes, though, so while I explained lobbying practices and my personal disdain for them, Goss brought us back into Loathe Summit, and then all the way back to his room, where we are currently sitting on his bed.

"But even if it *were* possible . . ."

"It is," I interject by pure little-sibling-ness.

"Okay, sure, it *is* possible. But you'd still need all nine parties to agree, *including* Ymir himself! If he disagrees, we're dead in the air," Goss laments. "And even more . . . What if we get it through and it fails? I mean, what if I do it, and kill Ymir, and *don't* become a four-winged dragon?"

"In that case," I say, "we'll find something else."

He frowns, looking away. "Something else . . ." The way he says it almost feels bitter, even though it should be at least slightly triumphant. I watch him where I sit, absently stroking the fuzzy hide beneath me. The quality is surprisingly good. While I'm waiting, I keep one eye on Goss as he vexes himself over whether to kill some old dragon. I would love to kill the skinbag myself, but that wouldn't get us anywhere, so I keep myself from offering it. Goss frowns, burrowing his head into his wings. "And what would Father say . . . ?"

"I'm sure he'll be cool with it," I say, even though I'm not sure in the least. "He doesn't seem like the type to enjoy killing anyway." Which makes me wonder why he would be the one in charge of the *killing* rite in the first place.

"Sure, but . . ." Goss continues grumbling to himself for almost a full minute.

I sigh. I didn't want to pull this card, but he leaves me no choice. "Look, if you don't want to, it's fine. We can find something else, so—"

"N—no, it's not that!" he says, popping his head out from between his wings. "I just . . ." He clenches his teeth. "I *could* do it. I think. It's not like I'm a . . . What did you call it? Shiekenn?"

"Chicken?"

"Yeah! I—I'm not one of those! So . . ." He looks away. "I'll do it. If you really want me to."

I slap my knees and stand up, making him twitch. "Great, happy to hear it! In that case, how about we get right to it?"

"Get right to . . . ?"

"The lobbying, that is," I say.

"What, *now*? It's the middle of the night!"

I frown at him. "Well, sure, but . . ."

"Even though proper dragons don't need to sleep, whelps like me . . . We still need a little bit. Especially since we've been doing so much today. It's been a long day—for me, at least."

I let my foot slide back and forth over the soft hides. Turning away from him, I put my hands on my hips. "It's not like I have to sleep personally, but if you need it, then . . ." I return my gaze to him with a smile. "I'd be an awful guest if I didn't permit my host his rest."

Goss brightens up into a full-faced grin, fanning his wings out. "Really? Yippie!" Before I have time to comment on his word choice, he steps over to the torch we had burning on the wall, blowing it out and returning to the hide-filled cavity that is his bed just as fast. There, he plops down next to me, only barely avoiding crushing me to death beneath his girth. Without giving me time to complain, he grabs me where I stand and pulls me close, hugging me to his chest like I'm a very small plush toy or something. "Good night, Kitty!"

"G—good night," I grunt out, hoping that my near lack of breathing might clue him in to the fact that he's holding me a bit too tight. He doesn't catch it. With a bit of struggling, I'm able to pull my arms free. "Sleep tight, Goss."

He doesn't respond. Did he . . . ?

Soft snoring reaches my ears.

Yeah, he fell asleep. Just like that. What was that—seven seconds? At most. I'm honestly impressed, not that I can find any real use for such an ability. Not in a dragon, that is. Sighing, I try to replicate his reptilian feat, cozying myself down into his hands as best as I can. It's far from a comfortable place to sleep, but it's better than other places I've slept in. It should be doable with a bit of effort.

I close my eyes.

Sleep. Yes, now I will sleep. Rest. When did I last sleep? It isn't important, I suppose. Sleep is good. I used to love to sleep. Even more than being awake, though marginally less than beating other people at things they were proud of.

I *have* changed, haven't I? In more ways than one. Fundamental ways. Ways I didn't even know I *could* change.

Moleman was—

The name forcing itself into my skull instantly pulls me awake and my eyes flash open. Sitting up, I start frantically looking around as though I'm expecting him to be around, standing next to me, smiling at my dumb hijinks. But there's no one there. All is dark, and all is quiet, save for Goss's light snoring. I try to take a few deep breaths, only to find them unwilling to go down, big and struggling like toads. I swallow them forcefully.

N—now that I think about it, I've been receiving messages all day, haven't I? I kind of tuned them out since I was hoping I'd get killed sometime during the course of the day, but now it's night, and I still haven't told him I'm alive and that everything is alright.

I still haven't . . .

I pull up my menu, navigating to Moleman's profile without checking my messages. Then I choose the little button to send him a personal message, and . . .

I stare at the empty message box.

My fingers itch. I gulp again, but the lump in my throat isn't going away.

What do I tell him? *Hey man, sorry I said I was going to die and then disappeared for hours on end, it was a prank, haha* wouldn't go over well. Maybe *Hey Moleman, buddy ol' pal, remember that message I sent today where I said I was about to go die? Yeah, haha, I totally failed! Apparently I'm kind of unkillable, so I'll have to find some other way to escape responsibility for my actions. You're still cool with me, though, right?* Because that's exactly what Moleman wants to hear. Ugh. How about, while I'm at it, I just send *Hey Moleman, I don't value our friendship or your feelings enough to spare literally two minutes to tell you I'm okay. Anyway, if you were to try to lobby dragons into letting your new dragon friend kill other dragons, how would you do it, hypothetically speaking?*

Bringing my hand to my face, I take a bite, shearing through skin and flesh and bone and sinew. The pain lets me briefly ignore everything else. I chew slowly before swallowing, almost upset to see the area I bit out regrow within seconds. My eyes roll to look at the status box in front of me.

I close down the empty message.

Even if I don't tell him, he'll still know I'm alive. And that's the important part, isn't it? I'm alive, he's okay, and when I end this floor, either by making Goss digivolve into his no-armed form or by straight-up dying, I can explain it then. Right now, I need to focus. If Moleman was here, he'd understand. He always does.

I try to relax a little more. In the morning, we'll go around to try to lobby the different political groups. Let's see, with the socialists, I should probably tell them that the clergy are an oppressive class and that Goss, as a member of the working class, is far more suited for ending the life of one of his kind. And for the naturalists, I'll say that the young killing the old is simply how the cycle of life goes, and for the universalists, I might look into . . . if Ymir comes from some enemy nation or whatever . . . and the metaists, I can probably say . . . well, something, probably . . . I'm sure . . . It'll all work out . . . in the end . . .

My eyelids flutter closed, Goss's breathing becomes like a cradle around me, and I feel myself relax, well and fully.

XXVII

Ugh, Politics

Morning came quickly, though by the time I was awake, Goss was already up and about, calling me a sleepyhead, a snoozer-loser, a nightcap-haver . . . Every slur in the book. I would've been more upset if he hadn't been right. Yes, indeed—for once, I was as snug as a bug in a rug.

Being an effective worker to a T, I wanted us to start lobbying straightaway. Unfortunately, Goss—my ride and guide—wanted us to go hunting first. With yesterday's failure in terms of food brought to the feast, Goss was desperate for us to have something better to offer.

And so, at four in the morning—yes, that's *before* the sun goes up—we went out hunting. Naive as I am, I expected us to hunt in the nearby area, but not so. Goss took us to the neighboring country, then circled around until he found a forest lush enough to hunt in. As he explained it, to keep themselves from completely wrecking the local ecosystems, they limit themselves in terms of their prey size and amount. So no bigger than a dog, and they have to grab it from a new region every day, resetting weekly. Apparently, this gives them a fair bit of variety. Neat.

So we hunt for a bit. With my help, Goss is able to capture a number of small-to-medium-sized animals. Since he has no sense of how to keep meat tender, I had to teach him to slit their throats and suck out the blood to let them hang a little. How does Father Moonlight survive with these beasts around him? Ah, then again, he doesn't have to eat any of it himself. It's not like the whelps themselves are gourmets or anything, but I prefer my meat either fresh or old enough to no longer be in a state of rigor mortis.

With little effort and only a bit of bloodshed, we're able to leave the forest with a few hares, two winged drakes, and a single dog-sized tarantula. Mmm, tarantula . . . Goss was hesitant, but I promised to teach him how to cook it so it becomes yummilicious, which convinced him.

Before we fly home, I get Goss to take us on a little detour, flying high above the nearby surroundings. I know he sees it as casual, being a dragon and all, but I can't get over the novelty of it. It looks way too cool. Even if I hadn't adored dragons, this sight alone is enough to make me bitter about humans not being able to transform into dragons.

Then again, considering all the dragons I've met so far, maybe being a dragon isn't all it's hyped up to be.

I glance up at Goss. Well, aside from this guy, that is. The more I think about it, the more amazing it is that he's still got all that childishness. Not in the way where he's immature or anything, though. It's more that he lets himself be a kid.

Something cold and hard forms in my chest.

By the time noon rolls around, we've returned once again to Loathe Summit. For Father Moonlight's sake, we drop off our loot straight away. As soon as we do, though, I have a thought. "Hey, Father?" I ask, sidling up closer to him where we walk in the tunnel to his workshop.

"What is it, son?"

I pause a second to regain my strength. "Well, uh . . . So far, it looks as though I'll be staying here for a while. A few weeks or so, maybe." My statement makes Goss, who's walking a little behind us, noticeably light up. I pretend not to see it. "I was just wondering if, since I'm here anyway . . ." The words are elusive, but I'm able to grab them by the throat. "Maybe you could teach me how to tan leather? A—and sew with it, and such?"

"You want to learn tanning?" he asks, eyes widening incrementally.

"Why?" Goss shoots down from just above us. I try to telepathically tell him to keep quiet with a look, but it doesn't really work, and he just ends up even more confused. Nevertheless, he isn't speaking, so I overcome my hesitation and continue talking.

"Yeah," I say. "So far, I've been skinning things and keeping the hides, but it's not like I've actually been able to tan them properly, so after a few weeks or months, they kind of . . . *break down*." For his own sake, I avoid going into detail about what kind of activities I partake in to cause such wear and tear.

He blinks at me. I feel myself sweat. D—did I say something wrong . . . ? "Do you really want to learn tanning? From *me*?"

Oh, lord, here it is. I turn away from him. "It's not like I know anyone else who's as good at it as you, but if you've got your hands full, then it's not like I can force you to—"

Before I have time to finish making my excuse, he's crossed the distance between us and slung his arms around me, his head pressed against my chest. I freeze in place. Wh—what is—

Taking a step back, he removes himself from me, wiping at his eyes. "Thank you—yes, of course, I would be delighted to teach you all that I know." Smiling warmly—way too warmly—he touches a hand to the leopard hide I'm wearing. "I had noticed the tattered things you wear, so hearing that you'd like to learn how to dress better . . ." He chuckles—no, *snickers* to himself. "I will gladly be of service to you, my son."

"Th—thank you," I croak, the words only barely overcoming a sob to force their way out. "It . . . it means a lot."

"Not as much as it does to me," he sighs.

We bring the meat for the feast to his workshop, and then Goss and I get guilted into joining Father Moonlight for high mass. Okay, that's a bit harsh, we could definitely have refused at any point and he'd have been completely fine with it, but the thought of him saying mass for a single attendee overpowered any such wants. Also, since Ymir was set to die in like a month, it would do Goss good to talk more with him. That way, we could extract more information, Goss could get closer to ascension, and I would be privy to more odd stories.

We attend the high mass. It was, dare I say . . . *pleasant.*

Unlike yesterday, there were three more dragons in attendance, a number that included Kempt, allowing the parish to reach a full six members, myself counted. The difference between three and six members doesn't seem like much, but it made a massive difference in the hymns sung, alongside the overall reverie.

Dragons, as I have come to learn, actually have two throats, one being for fire-breathing and the other for normal speaking affairs. The funny thing, then, becomes how they use both of these throats to sing, creating music I'd describe as strange, but far from bad. It was . . . interesting.

We remained, and afterward, Goss took the time to talk to Ymir. It wasn't really my place to listen in on their private conversation, so I dislodged to go learn tanning from Father Moonlight.

By the time evening and the feast arrived, I had learned the basics of tanning, been taught how to properly cobble simple loafers, and forgotten all about lobbying. Shoot.

The feast would have been nicer if Kempt hadn't sat smirking at Goss and me the entire time. Gloating little tick. I wanted to tell him off, but Goss wouldn't let me, insisting that if we blew up at him, he'd be the winner. I was loath to find him correct.

To update on the tarantula situation, Goss liked it. Everyone else thought he was a freak for not only eating but also *liking it*, but we didn't care. Tarantula is good. Can recommend.

After the feast, we finally got around to lobbying. With so much time leading up to it, I had given plenty of thought to what arguments could be used to sway each party. However . . .

"You're okay with it? Just like that? But I didn't even explain the economic reasoning behind—"

"It's fine," Hart says, waving his hand casually as he continues carefully assessing a golden plate of some sort. "I really don't care."

Goss glances between me and Hart. "Don't . . . care?" His countenance takes on all the properties of a wronged puppy. "But isn't he your fellow party leader? You must have known him for over ten years by now!"

"Yes, I have known Ymir for . . . close to fifteen years now, I believe," Hart agrees. His massive eye turns to look at us with what can best be described as boredom. "Why do you ask?"

Goss paces where he stands. "B—but if you've known him for that long, then . . ."

I hold up a hand, silencing him. Then I take a step forward, hoping that even though he's now turned back to the little plate in his claws, he might still listen to me. "What we're trying to say, party leader, is that considering how this is usually a very ritualistic practice that's been going on for hundreds of years, we had expected a bit more resistance from you leaders." I pause, checking to see if he's listening at all. "So if it isn't too much of a bother . . . Could you elaborate a little?"

He turns to us in equal parts confusion and frustration. "Are you deaf? I don't care how that saggy old skinwing dies as long as he croaks before he starts mumbling." Sneering, he puts the plate in his hand, absently rolling it around with his thumb. "If you *really* want to hear my thoughts," he says, giving Goss a meaningful look, "I wouldn't care even if you decided to let that little pet of yours do him the honor."

Not sure whether to thank him or question his morals, we instead decide to keep our silence and leave.

Within a few minutes, we reach the religists, gear up to do our well-researched pitch, only to be met with the same reaction.

They don't care.

Not how he dies, not who does it, or even *why*. Their attitude alone told me that they wouldn't have cared even if I personally decided to tear him apart and use his blood as two-in-one shampoo and conditioner. They just . . . didn't care.

None of them did.

Not even Ymir.

"You'd be fine with it?" Goss asks, his voice hoarse. "With me k—killing you?"

The aged dragon simply shrugs where he sits, absently basking in the sundial's sunray. "Why would I not be?"

"It's your *death rite*," Goss enunciates. But both he and I know that the ritual nature of his death doesn't make any difference. "And—and Father Moonlight is your *friend*, so I don't see why . . ."

"It doesn't matter," he says simply, in the same bored, indifferent way as everyone else. "To die is to die. Whether it comes at your claws or his kiss is unimportant. At the end, I will return to dust, and my sins die with me." His aged, deep-set eyes slowly move from Goss to me. "However . . ."

That small word gives Goss hope, as he looks back up at the larger dragon, eyes twinkling tentatively.

"I would rather not be killed by someone who is unwilling."

"Unwilling?" I parrot. "What's that supposed to mean? Goss is *beyond* willing to do this. I mean, look at him! He's practically trembling with excitement!" As a matter of fact, now that I'm dramatically pointing at him, I notice that Goss is actually trembling for real. I hide my flusterness with a weak chuckle. "Heh, um . . . Yeah. He wants—no, *needs* to ascend, and he's willing to fulfill the ulti-mate type-five thing to do so. You understand, don't you?"

Turning to look at Goss, Ymir lets his nose crumple up into an expression of distaste. "I see how it is." Without waiting for me to explain the facts and how everything really is, Ymir stands up, turning his massive back to us. Before leav-ing fully, he turns to look over his shoulders and folded wings, brow furrowed over his eye. "I do not care if it is you, or that priest, or even your human friend who should kill me. Neither, I suspect, do my fellow party leaders. However, if you decide to take Father Moonlight's role, I expect that you should be able to follow through as well. Otherwise, your sins will only weigh heavier."

And with those words, he walks away, crawling into a tunnel and out of sight.

I nudge Goss's arm with my elbow. "I'd say that went pretty well! I was afraid he wouldn't be up for it, so it's great to hear that he's cool with it. Right, Goss?"

As I turn to look at Goss to examine the reason for his silence, I instead find an answer to a question I didn't even know I had.

Apparently, even dragons can turn pale with dread.

The day ends, and the next one arrives, as they always do. The monthly confer-ence was a little under two weeks away, meaning that we had plenty of time to just hang around, not doing much of anything. However, that changed following a single, small discussion.

"So, assuming they're okay with it . . ."

"Which they are," I respond confidently. The rats I was trying to juggle to impress Goss struggle and fall out of my hands. "Damn it—just . . ."

"Right, okay, and . . . And if I do the killing rite, become a four-winged dragon . . . What then?"

I pause my frantic attempt to gather the rats again, turning to him slowly. "What do you mean, *what then?*"

"I mean," he continues, "I'll be a four-winged dragon, right? I'm not sure if I told you this before, but normal dragons don't really *like* four-winged dragons. They're of the same opinions as goblins in that matter—same as when it comes to mumblers and such. Four-winged dragons have a tendency to ravage ecosystems and cause general havoc, so they're kill-on-sight even for normal dragons." He quiets down for a moment, giving me an odd look as I stuff my face hole with two rats at once. "Since the killing rite will be attended by most of the dragons in Loathe Summit, it means I'll be surrounded by a bunch of dragons, all wanting to kill me."

"Really, now . . ." I say, slurping down a rat tail like it's a big fat spaghetti noodle. "Well—that's only if they *can* kill you, right?"

"What do you . . . ?"

"I'm just saying," I say, strolling up close to him. "Thanks to my skills, I'm basically unkillable. That's why you had to let me live. If you were similarly unkillable, they wouldn't be able to stop you from leaving." Now that I'm close enough, I lean myself onto his folded arms. "So, in short, you need some training from a real master of unkillableness."

"Training . . ." Goss breaks out into a small smile. "I *like* the sound of that!" His expression falters. "Though there was one more thing I was thinking about . . ."

I use a rat tooth to pick at my teeth. "Hm? What's that?"

"Well, it's just . . ." Brows furrowed, he hunches down closer to me, eyes darkening slightly. "What if we go through all this trouble, I turn into a four-winged dragon, and then you don't beat the floor? What then?"

"In that case . . ." I hum to myself. "Assuming you become as monstrous as four-winged dragons have been described . . ." I turn to him with a grin. "I guess I'll have to kill you, then!"

"Kill me—" His eyes flash wide, jaw falling slightly. "Would you actually . . . ?" I stare at him blankly. Of course I would. He stares down at me. Something small shifts in him, and his frown twists into an uncertain smile, like a finch trying to replicate the grin of a crocodile. "W—well, if you train me like you should, I won't let you! I'll be so strong and unkillable that you'll be laid flat before the power of my new form! A single beat of my awesome clawed wings will send you *flying*!"

"Oh, yeah?" I say back, matching the teasing nature of his words. "That's only if you actually *do* turn into a four-winged dragon. As you are, I could take you on easily!"

His grin gains much-wanted sincerity. "Oh, you're *on*!"

On I was. From that day on, during the course of the two weeks leading up to the monthly council meeting, we sparred on the daily. I call it sparring, but it was really more of a brawl, the two of us going at each other like a pair of siblings fighting over the last cookie. It was difficult to crown a winner since we weren't exactly fighting with the intent to kill, but the one who ended up on top of the other by the end was always yours truly. Sure, we were both nigh invulnerable to each other, but that didn't mean that we couldn't get tired. Or, more specifically, that *Goss* couldn't get tired. By the end of a good match, he'd always be panting in the dirt, and I'd be the proud winner, telling him to give up or else I'd never stop tickling him.

Does this make me a dragon slayer? I have no idea what the specific requirements are, but it would be a pretty funny title to have. If nothing else, I've been able to ascertain a good number of weaknesses specific to dragons.

For one, when they gear up to breathe fire, their chests swell out, and in the seconds following the breath attack, a pair of small vents open up on the sides of their chest to let out residual steam and heat. These vents are about the size of my fist. When I tried shoving my hand in there, Goss actually retreated across the room in genuine fear and pain. So, in short, I'm not doing that, but if I *were* to want to kill a dragon, that's where I'd put my claws. Of course, the sheer heat coming from them is enough to cook my entire hand and arm to braised perfection, but that's not really an issue for me.

Other weaknesses include their featherless arms and legs, their heads, and their throats. You'd probably need some kind of RPG bazooka-type thing to actually lop off a dragon's limb, but it's still more realistic than going after their actual hide.

Finally, and I couldn't prove this, but I think the bones, flesh, and organs of a dragon aren't as strong as their feathers and skin. If you took a massive hammer and pummeled them silly, you'd probably be left with a perfectly unbroken bag of jellified flesh and shattered bones. Unfortunately, I'm not strong enough to wield such a hammer, and even if I was, I have a feeling that they might be in short supply.

We sparred, sometimes with the other whelps as referees, and we spent our time in a rather casual fashion. Hunting, going to mass, flying to new, distant places, and most enjoyable of all, talking to other people. I spent more time than I'd like to admit in Father Moonlight's workshop, not always with him in it, training my tanning and leatherworking. It was . . . *fun*. Making things was weirdly enjoyable. The time-consuming nature of tanning leather was very suitable for my position, and I threw myself into it with zeal.

During the time I spent in the small workshop, Goss would take a form of apprenticeship under Ymir, learning all about what it meant to be a type five. According to Goss, Kempt would often join them, but from what I can infer, their relationship wasn't too close.

Either way, the end of the month approached with quick steps, and soon, the time for the council meeting had arrived.

"And you know what to say to them, right?" I ask Goss, adjusting the leather top hat I made for him. It's comically small atop his massive head, but we need to be presentable for this. "You're ready and willing, and . . ."

"And I am under no duress or threat," Goss finishes, completing the saying I drilled into his head. With the top hat properly affixed to his head, he cranes his neck straight up, trying to make his back equally straight where he sits waiting in the tunnel leading into the dining room. Or, I guess, the general meeting room. He shoots a look down at me. "You're sure it's now? Maybe we should check the sundial just in case . . . ?"

"I'm sure," I say, one eye on the clock.

<Top—Status—Community>
<21:38:40 Day 940>
<The thirty-first attempt will begin in 2:21:20>

"Assuming everyone else operates on the same time frame as we do, they should be here in just under seven minutes." At my words, Goss turns again to look down the tunnel, tentatively shooting out a little whistle, just in case. With no echo returning, it seems like there's no one there yet. I affix my gaze onto Goss's back. "Are you nervous?"

His head snaps back to face me. "Am I—" He forces a chuckle. "No, no, I'm not, I'm just . . ."

"What did I tell you about trying to lie to me?" I say, purposefully re-creating the tone my own mother would use.

The words make Goss slouch a little. "S—sorry . . ."

I watch him for a moment. He's such a kid. Sighing, I pat his hand. "There, there." He raises his head slightly. I smile at him. "It's okay to be nervous. Sure, I can't see why they'd shoot it down when we've already gotten the green light from them all, but there's always a chance. We're only here to look pretty, remember? Whatever happens is outside our control, so there's no use in worrying about it."

"I suppose . . ." Despite my well-measured words, Goss still looks blue. I guess I'll have to pull out my trump card.

"I'll tell you what—how about, when this is all over, we go out, catch a few tarantulas, and I prepare them how you like them?"

Finally, Goss perks up, wings flapping with barely withheld excitement. "Really? With that special sauce, too?"

"Of course!" I say. "Wouldn't be grilled 'tula if it didn't have the special sauce."

"Grilled tarantula . . ." Just the words are enough to get him to drool, and I can only relate. Food is the best. Ah, now I'm drooling myself . . .

I sniff. Down the tunnel, I can hear faint whistling. "Hey, Goss—they're coming."

"They're—" Off-guard, it takes a second or so for Goss to pull himself up, back straight, tail curled around him, and wings at half mast. Without the wings and tail, I can't really replicate the formal salute, so I opt to simply stand with my back straight and such.

Down the tunnel, the first of the nine party leaders arrives. By the smell, I'll assume it to be Hart.

Goss bows his head as Hart sets his feet to the ground, folding back his wings. He nods slightly at both of us before entering the dining hall.

As his back fades into the room, Goss lets out a breath. I catch his eye, giving him a thumbs-up and a smile. He replicates the thumbs-up, though his smile trembles a little.

The remaining leaders soon arrive, dropping in one by one, their reactions to me and Goss ranging from total apathy to a pat on the shoulder. The final one to arrive was Ymir, who walked alongside the tunnel's floor, his heavy tail dragging behind him, and—oh, so *that's* where Father Moonlight went! Riding atop Ymir's shoulder, no less. I can respect it.

They sidle up next to us, their eyes turning to us with more confusion than anything else.

Father Moonlight speaks first. "What are you sitting out here for?"

"Come, children," Ymir says, waving for us to join with his wing. "This is no honor to give people such as us."

Sharing a brief look, Goss picks me up, puts me on his head—my new preferred seat—and heads inside the dining hall alongside our mentors.

There, the monthly council meeting begins.

The large round table finally finds proper usage as a total of nine dragons sit side-by-side around it, filling out its circumference with little room to spare. If my knowledge of dragon politicians isn't failing me, it would seem that they're arranged by type, going from one to nine clockwise.

The other people in attendance—me, Goss, and Father Moonlight—are all seated to the side, outside the discussion but present enough to hear it. Since I want to be able to see things too, I'm sitting on top of Goss's head. It's comfortable.

"Looks like everyone has arrived," Hart says, drawing himself up until his head is the tiniest bit above everyone else. I think Ymir is technically taller, but since his back is slouched and his neck sagging, Hart is able to look down at him as well. "To begin with, I want to nominate myself as word-tender, and Lif of the metaist party to act as scribe. Is this accepted by all?"

"Aye," the other members say as one.

Not wanting to be left out, I go to say *Aye* as well, only to notice Father Moonlight looking at me funnily. Ah. Alright, then. I hold my tongue.

"The council has accepted myself as word-tender and Lif as scribe, so it shall be," Hart finalizes, slamming the end of his tail onto the table as Lif—a slim, brown old-shoe-type dragon—begins to carve words into the table using his claw. "Aside from the party leaders, we also have the current Priest of Dragons, Father Moonlight; Goss Fletchling the whelp; and a human named Kitty in attendance. They hold no voting power nor say in the decisions and their outcomes." The council honestly looks more bored than anything else. "The first matter on the agenda relates to the complaints of the nearby city of Volk, brought to our attention by Father Moonlight, in regard to the overhunting of nearby wildlife . . ."

The meeting begins on a note that encourages napping above all else. Still seated on Goss's head, I allow myself to zone out as they discuss the inane, unimportant affairs of the month. Before this, I was honestly a little bit curious to know what dragon politicians could have to discuss, but now that I'm here . . . Oh, God. I'll be lucky if the attempt doesn't end before they bring up our subject.

With nothing else to do, I count the seconds until they mention something that isn't to do with archives, whelp supplies, tithes, and inane squabbling. One, two, three, four, five . . .

Seven thousand, three hundred seventy-two, seven thousand, three hundred seventy-three, seven thousand, three hundred seventy—

"This brings us to our most recent topic, namely Ymir Attechilde's killing rite." I bound upright where I sit, almost falling off Goss's head in the process. Hart, unaware of my plight, continues. "As you have most likely already been made aware, we have received a petition in regard to who will execute Ymir. At Kitty the human's request, Goss Fletchling has been nominated for the role. To specify, this role will include none of the pre-killing duties, and only those pertaining to the actual killing of Ymir. This would be in the place of Father Moonlight. Are all in agreement?"

Much as they had with almost every other decision, they share a brief look before each, in turn, gives their opinion.

"Aye."

"Aye."

"Aye."

The word moves around the table, from type one to eight, repeated with equal indifference. The leader of the religist party is filing his nails. The leader of the aliusist party is preening her feathers. The leader of the metaist party, despite being the secretary, is drawing tiny scribbles in the stone before melting it with his breath and repeating the process.

The word finally moves to Ymir. His tired eyes turn to Hart, the only one who cares enough to look him in the eye. Ymir heaves a sigh. "Ay—"

"*STOP!*" someone shouts.

Huh? What is—

I turn to where the voice came from, only to find Father Moonlight standing up, his chest rising and falling and his wings partially splayed out. The gathered dragons all turn to him as well. Speaking for everyone else, Hart asks, "Is there something you would like to say, Father?"

"Th—this is . . ." In a rare show of actual turmoil, Father Moonlight looks between us, his confused, betrayed eyes falling on Goss, me, and all of the other dragons in turn, including Ymir, before finally returning to Goss and me. "What have you done?"

I can feel Goss begin to tremble beneath me. "I—I was just . . ."

I put a hand on his forehead, affixing Father Moonlight with a calm gaze. "I'm doing what I came here to do, and he's doing what'll get him where he wants to be." My voice is even, measured, and above all: certain. I'm not upset, and I really don't think he should be either. "Or are you that excited to kill Ymir yourself?"

And, lo and behold—even a former can grow pale.

Recognizing that the two of us are fully decided on this, he turns back to the other dragons. More than that, though, he turns to Ymir. "Is this really what you want?"

Ymir meets his gaze with the composure of a man already dead. "This isn't about what I want," he says simply. His heavy eyes roll to take in Goss. "It's about what he needs."

I can see Father Moonlight's wings shudder. His hands ball into fists at his side, he draws a deep trembling breath, and when he lets it out, his hands fall back into palms, and his splayed wings carefully fold themselves across his back, neat and tidy. "Very well, my old friend. I shall not take from you your choice of executioner. However, should it become too much . . ."

"You will do what you must," Ymir acknowledges, closing his eyes and waving for Hart to continue.

Hart, meanwhile, looks to Father Moonlight for confirmation to continue. After a second or so, Father Moonlight nods, though I'd be blind not to notice the hesitance in his face. Hart nods back at him. "Very well, then. In that case, we agree unanimously to temporarily grant Goss Fletchling the role of Ymir's executioner. So say we all."

He uses his tail like a gavel.

I slide down a little across Goss's face, grinning as I do. "Hey, we did it! Nice work, Go—"

Eyes wide, pupils small and trembling, he stares straight ahead and . . . And I think I can hear his teeth chattering. Uh . . .

"Hey, Goss, are you—"

<The thirty-first attempt has begun. You will now be returned to the lobby.>

Wait a minute, I wasn't finished with—

I disappear. And, just like that, I'm back in the lobby.

But I *did* succeed in getting Goss his onetime gig as a hangman! That has to count for something, right? At least, I think so. Sure, Goss didn't look too hyped about it, but that was only a temporary bit of resistance. Once he's up and at it, he'll realize that once someone's dead, there's no need to feel bad anymore. Dead is dead, after all.

Yeah. That makes sense.

And now, I have to make do in the lobby until the floor opens again. Let's see, which resistances should I train, now . . . ?

I finally decided to keep doing bleeding, just for the sake of it.

<Floor 25 has opened. Do you want to enter?>
<Yes/No>

The time passed quickly, and now that the floor is open, I press the Yes button without any hesitation.

With that, I return to the mountain range. Or, more specifically, to a random point far away from the actual place I want to go. Ah. That's problematic.

Well, I'll get there eventually, I guess.

With that in mind, I get back to trekking. I don't have to trek for too long, though, as after a few hours I start noticing massive shadows circling high above. Good. This means Goss *was* listening when I told him about how I'd probably disappear during the meeting and reappear a day later, out and about. Very nice.

From my noticing them, it only takes them a little while to notice me in turn, after which I'm swiftly rescued and brought back home. And just like that, my casual, easygoing life continues. There are only two weeks left until the killing rite, and I'm excited to continue attempting to tan leather and explore the nearby countries with Goss.

Except, after the council meeting, both Goss and Father Moonlight have been acting a bit weird. Father Moonlight I can understand—he's almost definitely upset that we didn't tell him ahead of time about all of this. I feel like the right thing to do might be to apologize, but apologies are supposed to be genuine, and I don't feel bad about doing it, so . . . yeah. But Goss? Yeah, no, I have no idea what's eating him. I can only assume that he's nervous about the whole killing rite thing, but when I asked him about it, it didn't seem to be the usual stuff. It wasn't fear that he might not turn into a four-winged dragon, and it wasn't fear that he might turn into a four-winged dragon, so I really don't know what else it could be.

Nevertheless, aside from that small bit of awkwardness, life continued as it had for the past two weeks. We sparred, we hunted—though now we could only hunt a max of five creatures each—and we fished, we lived, we laughed, we . . . We had it pretty good. Since it might come in handy, I even taught him all I'd learned about killing dragons. Weirdly enough, that got him apprehensive. Tweens . . . incomprehensible creatures, they are.

During our time, I was even able to raise my bleeding immunity to level two, which very clearly slowed the rate at which my heart beat and made me bleed less. Also, the blood I did bleed was darker than usual and strangely thick. Very odd.

Either way, after two brief weeks, the time had come.

The killing rite was at hand.

The Preparations

"Goss, where did I put my good coat?"

"The rat one or the leopard one?"

"The, uh . . . The leopard one, I think. It's not in the hoard," I say, tossing a pair of rat shoes over my head. I pull out a small nightcap made of drake tongue. What was I even thinking with this . . . ? Slightly disgusted, I put it back in the pile, already filled with my works and collected knickknacks.

Using a bit of obsidian on the wall as a mirror, Goss slicks back the feathers on the back of his head. "Are you sure it isn't in your inventory?"

"In my . . . ?" I blink at him. "Oh! Okay, wait, let me check . . ." I check my inventory, from whence I retrieve a leopard-leather coat. "Hey hey hey, I got it!" Threading it over my shoulders, I twirl around, showing off my full outfit. "What do you think? Stunning, isn't it?"

Not turning away from the mirror, he glances at me from the corner of his eye. "I never took you for the prissy sort, Kitty." He frowns lightly. "Isn't your normal outfit enough?"

"My normal outfit isn't suitable to wear for the living wake," I say, pulling at my leather shirt to tuck it into my leather pants. Doing so unfortunately got my leather belt a little loose, so I undo and retie the bow. There! Perfect. Combined with the leopard fur coat, I look absolutely ridiculous. Exactly as I want it. I can't bring myself to wear shoes, though, so my feet will have to remain bare. Smiling, I look up at Goss, letting my eyes fall to his feet with pride. "How are the sandals? Not too tight, I hope?"

Finally moving away from his reflection, he holds up his front paws, moving them cautiously, feeling how the hide bands hold the tempered leather pads in place. "They're good," he says. I smile not only at the compliment but also at the fancy patterns I carved into the soles. "It's a bit weird, is all."

I shrug. "Well, unless you're a former, if you want to step on holy ground, you've gotta cover your feet." In that sense, I'm lucky that I'm not the one who'll be Ymir's demise. I'd love to, but having to wear shoes is a bit of a deal-breaker. Another reason to become an apostle of some sort, I guess. Now that I think about it, I haven't really checked the process on that, have I?

<Want Apostleship Trials progress: 359/365>
<Cowardice Apostleship Trials progress: 22/23>

Wait, what? Seriously?! How have I not noticed this before?

I guess, with them barely ever saying or doing anything, I forgot that this was even a thing. Huh. Well, I guess it's nice that they're holding similar speeds. If I'm lucky, they might happen at the same time. I can only wonder how they'll want to do this. Going by how Father Moonlight described the apostles of yore, there's a chance that they'll try to bestow prophetic visions and divine quests upon me, something that I'm not too hyped about. Why did I do this again? Oh, yeah, the promise of power. Good ol' power.

Closing down the status screens, I do a flashy pirouette, ending it once I'm facing Goss. "So?" I ask. "Are you ready?"

His brows, which have been constantly furrowed for the past two days, somehow furrow a bit further. "Yeah," he says. "I'm ready."

With that, he scoops me up, puts me on his head, and off we go to mass.

We arrive at the church to find a total of three dragons who care enough to show up other than ourselves and Ymir. A bit sad, but Ymir doesn't seem to mind. No, that old fart's been complaining about the necessity of the living wake for close to a week, so he's probably happy that there are fewer people for Father Moonlight to express condolences to. Among these dragons is Kempt, who greets us with a solemn nod.

They put their heads in the church's windows, and the living wake begins. Despite the weightiness of the subject, Father Moonlight handles it all well, retelling Ymir's life with the comedy and wit of someone who knew him too well to tell it like the tragedy it is. Ymir, for his own part, smiles at the jokes, even chuckling at times. Father Moonlight relates his story to the tale of Uje the Romantic, the apostle of the God of Comedy. I didn't know the God of Comedy had such things, but apparently, he found Uje the Romantic too hilarious to let die, giving him his strength to keep going on. The moral of such a story, according to Father Moonlight, lay in finding strength and courage in the absurd, meeting life with a smile and a laugh even in circumstances of tragedy.

The words made Goss tremble beneath me.

"With that, my children, we are brought to the final part of our ceremony— the adornment of the absolution chasuble." I had noticed it before, but now that

Father Moonlight is actively bringing attention to it, I can't help but be in awe of the robe he's wearing. Calling it multicolored would be an insult. If a color exists, then it's on there in the form of a beautiful, shimmering feather. There must be thousands of them, covering the chasuble from the hole of the neck all the way down to the edges of the robe, both front and back. Most of the feathers are spotted or striped in different colors, others being solid, and a few shifting in a gradient from bottom to top. The vast majority are a brilliant, brightly saturated color, though a few are lighter, a select number being almost a pure WHITE. The entire vestment bobs gracefully as Father Moonlight walks across the church floor, all the way up to Ymir.

Ymir, in turn, lays his head on the side, presenting the nape of his neck. Although most of his body is naked and featherless, here, a few feathers lie bare, the lot of them in a brilliant purple sheen, shimmering from blue, to cyan, to green where the light hits them just right.

Father Moonlight draws a small circle in the air. "By the power granted unto me by the Goddess of Dragons, I relieve you of your pride, so that you may live on for eternity in Her grace."

"Aye," Ymir mutters.

Kneeling down, Father Moonlight plucks a feather from his neck. Standing up once more, he puts the feather to his lips. There, he mumbles, "By Her love, you are freed. Ymir Attechilde, you are a dragon no more." He kisses the feather gingerly. The air pulses, the room fills with warmth, and even though there are no arms around me, I feel embraced.

Ymir lifts his head, and as he does, the final feathers fall from him, turning to dust as they do. Now he is fully bare to the world.

With the feather in hand, Father Moonlight inserts it into the chasuble, securing it among all the others. Cool show. Anyway, does this mean that if Father Moonlight has anyone's feather, he can instantly make them go bald? Is this the sacrament of penance I've heard so much about? I now understand why the dragons let him stick around even though they never show up for mass. Nobody wants to go bald in their teens.

Father Moonlight turns to us. His gaze makes me jolt a little, but I soon realize that it isn't for me—it's for Goss. Goss, who, until now, had been trembling, and now goes completely stiff. Father Moonlight strides across the room. His face is the very picture of reluctance. But I can tell it isn't because of any religious piety. No, the pity shining in his eyes is enough to reject any such ideas. Within seconds, he stands before us, his eyes moving from Goss up to me. "Kitty, if you please . . . ?"

Even though I don't know why, I slide down from atop Goss's head, making sure to take a seat close enough to where I can keep my hand on his cheek. He nods thankfully at me, and I smile back.

He turns to Goss, who is doing a very effective impression of a storefront mannequin.

With only a few movements, Father Moonlight removes the chasuble from himself, holding it closely as he turns to Goss. "My son, will you please lift your head?"

Like an animatronic beckoned by magic, Goss stiffly lifts his head, eyes affixed onto the dragonheart light in the middle of the church. Father Moonlight, unbothered, approaches him closer, holding the chasuble in both hands, unbuttoning the back of it until it becomes a long robe. Then, while Goss is trying desperately not to move, he hangs it over and around his neck, tying it as best as he can without either making it fall down, tearing it, or choking Goss to death in the process. After only a minute of work, he takes a step back, the chasuble hanging like a feathery neckbrace below Goss's chin.

"By the temporary passing of the absolution chasuble, I grant onto you, Goss Fletchling, the Goddess-given right to stand on the holy ground of Loathe Summit's heart, to execute the rite of killing necessary to absolve Ymir Attechilde of his sins, and to pronounce his death to the world. As you wear this chasuble, you act in Her name, executing Her wishes, and conforming to Her desires. She sees you."

Going by the way Goss's pupils tremble, I can only imagine how nervous he must feel. Worst of all, with his head up high, I can't even touch him to let him know I'm still at his side. Still, that's a pretty extreme way of putting it. I really can't see—

<THE GODDESS OF DRAGONS SEES GOSS FLETCHLING.>

Ah. Okay, all right. I'm not telling Goss that one. Sure, maybe this will increase his chances of becoming a four-winged dragon, but . . . personally speaking, I'm used to gods and goddesses watching me around the clock like I'm popcorn television. But Goss? No way. He actually takes these divine doofuses *seriously*. If he knew they were really voyeurs, I dread to imagine how he'd start acting.

"Th—tha—thank y—you, F—Fa—" Goss pauses his stuttering to bite his tongue and hyperventilate. "F—Father."

All he gets in reply is a sad smile and a face filled to the brim with pity.

The wake finishes with a few songs, the presentation of the God of Goblins's feather, and a final hurrah to the life Ymir led.

"The mass is finished, go in peace." Of the gathered attendees, only the two dragons I didn't recognize leave. The rest of us—Goss, me, Ymir, and Kempt—all remain, our attention focused on Father Moonlight. The only one who moves is Ymir, who briefly pops his head out to properly embrace the two dragons in turn, returning his head to the window after a few seconds. "Everyone is here, then," Father Moonlight comments. "To clarify, Kitty's presence is tolerated since he stands as an outsider to our own rules and customs."

Nobody makes any show of disagreeing, which is nice. I'd rather not be left out for this part.

Father Moonlight inhales deeply, readying himself. "The ritual we are about to partake in is one of grave importance. If we do it incorrectly, Ymir may perish before the killing rite has begun. Therefore, I ask all of you to handle this with grace." We all meet his stern gaze with some measure of readiness. The sight allows him to let out a small breath, his deeply furrowed brows rising a little in relief. "Good. Then let us go together to the chamber of penance. Ymir, if you will?"

Helpful as always, Ymir removes his head from the window before reaching in and helping Father Moonlight down. Goss helps me in a similar fashion, and we leave the church in a collected group. Since Ymir can't fly and Father Moonlight has vowed not to, we walk there, our small gathering moving silently through the large, natural cave system. It's dark, none of us feeling jovial enough to try to light it with fire or humor. All I can hear is the heavy thudding of the dragons' footsteps, the rustle of their feathers, and their breathing.

It doesn't take long to arrive, but in such silence, the minutes feel like hours.

Nevertheless, we reach the place.

The chamber of penance, despite the grandiose name, appears more like the torture chamber of a medieval castle than anything of religious connotation. Neither the floor nor the walls have been tempered by dragon fire, leaving them rugged and harsh as opposed to the smooth, ornamental architecture I've seen so far. It doesn't even smell like dragon in here, or even like anyone has been in here for months, for that matter. It's cold and dry, and the only scents of note are those of rocks, water, and what I think might be smoke of some sort.

It doesn't smell like much of anything. Not even the chains hanging from the ceiling or the various tools strewn on top of stone workbenches smell like anything. It feels muted. The dim lighting doesn't help.

As we enter it, Ymir casually sets Father Moonlight down. Neither of them seems to view this dimly lit torture chamber of a place as anything less than normal. I'd almost think the same of Kempt, if it wasn't for the faint trace of fear I can smell on him. He's hiding it valiantly with that stoic expression, but it comes out in the tightness of his wings and the stiffness with which he walks.

Goss, on the other hand, makes no show of hiding how horrifying he finds the room. Gaping wide, he moves his head and neck about, trying to take in everything he sees, from the massive metal contraption in the middle of the room to the obsidian altar close by it. I pat him on the head in an attempt to keep him calm, but it isn't really working.

Ymir turns to his small comrade. "Father, do you . . . ?"

Father Moonlight shakes his head and points to the metal contraption in the middle of the room. "You know how to use it, my friend." Waving to Kempt, Father Moonlight briefly continues. "Kempt, will you please help him get into the bindings?"

"Yes, Father," Kempt says, radiating resolve that I can't smell on him. Despite his words, he hesitates for a moment before striding up next to Ymir. Together, they move the ends of several chains closer to the center of the room. In total, I count over two dozen chains, all of them made of a BLACK, dull metal that scrapes along the ground as they drag them over.

With nothing better to do, I move over to help them, only for Father Moonlight to put his hand on my chest, stopping me in my tracks. "Leave them to it. I'd like you to help me, instead."

"Ah, uh . . . Alright, Father."

Goss looks down at us anxiously, pacing where he stands. "Um, Father . . . Is there anything I can do to help?"

Father Moonlight returns his gaze, thinking it over a moment before finally saying, "Assist Kempt as best as you can, and try to put the order of the chains to mind." His tight expression of unease briefly mellows into a smile. "Who knows, one day you may be the one to assist me in this gruesome task."

Nodding dryly, unable to respond with words, Goss lumbers away to go help Kempt.

As for me, with a single gesture, Father Moonlight encourages me to follow him, which I do. In silence, he leads me over to one of the walls, where I find something I hadn't noticed before: a door. Pulling a small bundle of keys from within his robes, Father Moonlight unlocks it, opening it for us to enter. I hunch down and follow him inside the pitch-black corridor. To make sure I'm still following him, I put a hand to the wall, only to recoil back as I feel not the coarse texture of barren stone but rather the smooth, glossy surface of what I think is obsidian. This entire wall . . . No, this entire corridor is made of obsidian . . . ?

Father Moonlight's footsteps suddenly stop ahead of me and I snap out of it in time to not collide with his back. I look around us. I can't smell anything aside from us two. It's terrifying. For all I know, this darkness that surrounds us could continue for miles and miles, never stopping. Sheer emptiness.

I can feel my heart beat faster at the thought and I reach out, desperate to feel something real, something that isn't cold and smooth, my hand fumbling through the air, fingers groping for something to touch, *anything*, and eventually finding . . .

My hand touches the hem of his robe. Soft. "Is everything alright back there, Kitty?" he asks, his mere voice filling the darkness with warmth.

I take a few deep breaths, calm and easy. "Yeah," I say. "I'm okay."

"Good. Because I'm about to show you something only formers have had the pleasure to see." Within the endless darkness, I hear him draw in a breath, filling his lungs, inhaling the cold and the darkness and everything else, deeper and deeper and deeper, until I think his chest surely can't hold any more, and then . . .

He lets it out. Particles of light flow from his lips, like the breath of a dragon in the form of an aurora borealis, bright, beautiful light, shining on the world, allowing me to see that I'm not looking at his back but rather his face—his calm, aged face. And then I see it. The particles, all floating in the air like dust caught in a sunbeam, bring light to the room. The walls of obsidian show our reflections, mirrored endlessly, around and around and around, but even more than that . . .

Atop seven pedestals, within crystal cases, each leaning on a small velvet pillow, are seven branding irons.

Not asking me to release my hold on his robe, Father Moonlight moves through the particles to the first pedestal, from which he removes the first of the seven brands. He hands it to me, and I take it, even though I almost expect it to scald my skin. It doesn't. It's cold, and so is the next one he gives me, and all the rest, too. After less than a minute, he's given me all seven of them, smiling at me like a parent who's finally figured out how to best let their toddler help them bake.

I smile back at him, because I don't know what else to do.

"Come," he says. "It's time to fulfill our duty."

Not questioning him, I follow him back into the darkness of the tunnel, unable to watch as the particles fade fully. I'm still holding on to Father Moonlight's robe, and it feels a lot less scary this time.

We emerge into the comparatively lighter chamber in time to watch Kempt and Goss affix a thick metal collar around Ymir's neck, one of two, the other collar clutched around the base of his chin, keeping his head in place using four different chains. All in all, Ymir is strung like a Christmas ham ready for the oven, chains keeping his wings, arms, legs, body, neck, and tail fully immobilized. It's kind of relatable, now that I think about it. Except, unlike my brief stint in a similar cage, Ymir is completely unable to move. Not that he seems much perturbed by it, mind you.

Father Moonlight watches him with a wry expression as we approach, motioning for me to put the brands on the obsidian altar in front of the aged dragon. I put them down in what I think is the correct order, though I really don't know.

"My friend," Father Moonlight says, craning his neck to take in the full size of Ymir. "Shortly, we will begin. I know that you are ready, and have been for many years now. Nevertheless, I will say that it pains me to see you here, and I hope that the virtue you hold may rouse pity in the Goddess of Law."

Ymir can't respond. His mouth has been bound with a strip of metal as thick as I am tall, keeping him muzzled. I can't help but wonder if it's for him or us that he's tied up like this. Probably both.

Nevertheless, his eyes speak enough for Father Moonlight, who chuckles. "You are quite right—it is ironic. I will not prolong your suffering with needless trivialities. Let us begin." He holds out his open palm to me. "Kitty, would you please give me the brand of gluttony?"

The brand of . . . ? I turn to the altar, scanning for whichever one could possibly be—oh, it's the one with the teeth, isn't it? I grab the one I spotted and hand it to Father Moonlight.

"Thank you," he says, accepting it. Then, a little louder, directing his voice to Kempt and Goss, "Will you please raise his chest and lower his stomach?"

Not asking for any further directions, Kempt and Goss do as asked, chains rattling as they pull them into place, Ymir's body being moved like a puppet on a string into the position Father Moonlight designed. In the meantime, holding the brand in both hands, Father Moonlight recites a prayer to the Goddess of Law. Then he presses his lips against it and appears to feel exactly nothing as the brand instantly heats up enough for me to instinctively back off despite being several yards away.

Holding the brand tightly, Father Moonlight approaches Ymir until he's close enough to touch the skin of his underbelly. Lifting the brand, he lets it hover close to the dragon's stomach, his voice echoing through the chamber as he says, "In the name of the God of Multitudes, I forgive you," and presses it against Ymir's skin.

Ymir's eyes flare open and he begins to thrash in his chains, pulling against the groaning metal and whipping his head back and forth, his screams silenced by the muzzle and his hyperventilations only able to huff through his nose, snot and mucus webbing across his face.

Father Moonlight pulls the brand from his stomach, walks back to me, hands me the now-cold brand, and asks me for the next one. I give him the brand of greed. Ymir is pulled to the floor, thrashing and heaving, unable to even make a single sound aside from muffled grunts and snorts escaping through his nostrils as huffs. Father Moonlight says a prayer, kisses the brand, and then presses it against Ymir's right palm. Flesh sizzles and burns as a plume of steam and smoke rises from the hand, each finger tied down so that he can't even ball it into a fist of pain. Ymir's neck bobs back and forth, his eyes wide and unblinking as his jaw fights against the groaning metal muzzle.

With the brand of greed done, Father Moonlight hands it back and asks me for the brand of lust. He says the prayer, kisses the brand, and presses it against the back of Ymir's right hand. The brand doesn't go as deep this time, only barely scalding him, though it still makes him jerk in pain, chains clanking against each other as he draws in a rasping breath through his nose.

Next, the brand of wrath. Ymir's body is lowered, the two whelps struggling to bring down the massive, thrashing beast. His chest is presented, and Father Moonlight presses the brand against it. The skin around the area bursts into flame. Skin is cooked instantly, his legs kicking in their restraints like the movements of a dead animal, tears of pain streaming down his wide, unblinking eyes. His chest and stomach spasm, agonized snorts displacing little air as his windpipes fight between hyperventilating through his nose or attempting to scream through it instead.

It takes effort for Father Moonlight to pull the brand from the cauterized skin. Once it's been dislodged, he pauses a moment before grabbing the next one. Standing close to Ymir, he puts his hand on the brand. "May the God of Pain be kind to you."

After a few seconds, Ymir calms down again, though his body still twitches with every stuttering breath he takes.

At Father Moonlight's order, they bring him down on the floor fully. Taking the brand of sloth, he climbs atop Ymir's back, to the same place where I've seen him sit many times. Accompanied by a small prayer, the brand is pressed into the spot right in between Ymir's wings, Father Moonlight retaining his balance even as Ymir once again begins to thrash and fight. Climbing back down, he asks for the penultimate brand—the brand of envy. I give it to him.

Still pushed into the floor, Ymir's head and neck are pulled down as well until they're both laid flat against the cold stone. His trembling nasal breaths kick up dust, his eyes moving back and forth erratically, unable to settle on anything or anyone.

With the second-to-last brand in hand, Father Moonlight moves closer to Ymir until he reaches his neck. He says a prayer and presses the brand to his skin. The flesh sizzles and crackles, his neck twitching and his entire body jerking. The little movement his neck is capable of is enough to lift his head an inch and then slam it back into the floor, thump, thump, thump, over and over again, the chains clattering around him. "Kempt, Goss, hold him down!" Father Moonlight barks, the two whelps quickly cooperating to bodily subdue the larger dragon, struggling as they keep Ymir from hurting himself any more.

Father Moonlight steps away from Ymir. "The final brand," he asks of me. I give him the last brand—the brand of pride. As Father Moonlight steps up to Ymir's tightly restrained head, he speaks softly, saying, "Doubtless, you can no longer hear me. I know this, yet I still need to ask you to steel yourself. For all dragons, pride is our greatest sin. This will hurt more than the others. Should you die here, I will not blame you. Still, if only for the help you wish to grant Goss, I ask that you be strong. Have courage."

The brand in his hands grows hot, soon turning a bright WHITE. I touch a hand to my chest.

Climbing on top of Ymir's neck, he brings himself onto his head, until he's standing right atop his forehead, in between his wide, staring eyes. Holding the WHITE-hot brand like a sword, he plunges it into Ymir's head. The skin at his feet bursts into flames, the area next to the brand charred into coal as the tears streaming down the dragon's face are instantly turned to steam. Ymir doesn't move an inch. His eyes stare at the empty, BLACK ceiling. Blank and lifeless.

Then they close.

Goss and Kempt breathe heavily.

A rare look of hope shines through Goss's eyes. "Is—is he . . . ?"

A deep, snorelike breath drags itself through Ymir's nostrils.

The look of disappointment on Goss's face is matched in equal despair on Father Moonlight's face. "No, he is not. Though, for the moment, we will let him rest as though he was." Stepping down from atop his friend, Father Moonlight stumbles, though I'm quick enough to catch him, letting his listless form fall into my arms. He smiles up at me, eyes half-lidded. "It never gets easier," he mumbles—maybe to me, maybe to himself. "It never does."

To that, I have no response.

While Ymir slept, we undid the chains and applied a soothing cream to the brands, which would probably have been very nice to have close to a year ago. While he slept, I cobbled together some sandals for Kempt, who had apparently forgotten that he can't stand in the killing pit with his feet bare or the gods will smite him. When I called it the killing pit, Father Moonlight scolded me, and said that it was disrespectful to the deceased to call it anything but the chasm of absolution. However, *chasm of absolution* is really long to say, and *killing pit* is both more fitting and funnier.

We had to wait close to an hour for Ymir to wake back up, which he did by thrashing, fighting, howling in pain, and whipping his tail all over the place. It took everyone present to get him to calm down, and even then, he wouldn't stop shivering, every movement he made causing him to twitch in pain. It was a pathetic sight, but more than that, I pitied him.

"Yeah, these brands . . . hurt like a bugger, don't they?" I say, trying to relieve the tense mood somewhat. It doesn't work. Nobody's having any of it, and I feel silly for making the effort. Speaking of feeling silly . . .

I tear off my clothes. They were tight and constraining and did not breathe whatsoever. With them off, I'm left slick with sweat, which is even less enjoyable. Ugh. Either way, our small band sits for a few minutes, relaxing as the time ticks by. I think the reason was something in regard to keeping Ymir calm and allowing him to collect his spirits before we get to the whole killing thing. I don't really get it, though. He's going to die anyway; what's the point in postponing it?

I'd almost call it infuriating if it wasn't for the fact that Goss obviously enjoyed it. No longer trembling as badly as Ymir, he's instead sitting nice and relaxed, the tip of his tail thumping nerve-rackingly against the floor.

Sometimes, I wonder what's going through that kid's head.

XXIX

To Dust

"Everything alright, Goss?" someone asked.

The words themselves wouldn't have been enough to snap him out of his daze if it hadn't been for who said it. Turning his wide eyes left and right, it took a moment for him to remember that the person he sought wasn't at his eye level—he was much smaller. Almost the size of a wooden toy. Goss looked down at Kitty with a smile he didn't feel. "Oh, um . . . Yeah, I'm okay, Kitty."

Despite being a human, Goss had never felt any trouble reading Kitty's facial expressions. Sure, he could look as blank-faced as a drake at times, but even then, Goss felt confident that he understood what his closest and only friend meant. Right now, going by the way the little human's brows were furrowed, his thin, pale lips drawn into a tight line, Goss could tell with fairly good certainty that Kitty was suspicious. "Really?"

Memories of stern lectures explaining the virtue of honesty flashed through Goss's mind. He knew that Kitty only wanted what was best for him, but still . . . "I'm okay," he said again, withholding the little fact that *okay* didn't necessarily mean *alright*. To shift the conversation, Goss cleverly pointed at Kitty's now-exposed chest—at the brand he bore on the right side of it. A brand Goss had never asked about. "Better question, are *you* alright? I mean . . . That brand . . ."

Happily enough for Goss's communicative abilities—or, rather, lack thereof—Kitty could read him well enough to infer what he was asking about.

Touching his fingers to the brand, Kitty let them run through the grooves, imperceptibly wincing at the pain, though it was clearly more of a physical than a mental response. There was a small smile on his face, though it didn't reach his eyes. "Yeah, this is . . . I got what I had coming for me. Heh, painful as the dickens, or however you call it, but . . . yeah. If nothing else, it reminds me not to be an idiot and do stupid shit."

"Has that worked?"

Kitty looked up at him. The small shadow creeping across his face went away, the smile he wore finally reaching his eyes. "I'd say so." His smile quirked up into a grin. "Or, what? Are you trying to say that I'm doing stupid shit now?"

"N—no!" Goss said, drawing his wings in front of him as protection. "I was just—"

"Will you two quiet down?" came Kempt's harsh response. "This isn't the time for bickering like children."

The two bickering children fell silent, sharing a look between them that effectively conveyed their emotions. Kitty rolled his eyes, and Goss smiled at him—an honest one, despite everything.

"No need to fret over it," Father said, his soft voice hoarse from all the talking he'd done. Somehow, Goss knew it'd only get worse as the evening went along. The small former raised himself to his feet, straightening out to look at the few people gathered. "It's time." The mere words sent something cold and sharp through Goss's chest. Had Father turned to look at him and not Kempt, he would surely have passed out right then and there. "Kempt, will you please fly ahead of us to the chasm of absolution to ring the bell?"

Bowing deeply, Kempt spoke reverently, saying, "As you wish." Always the show-off.

Then again, if Kempt went to ring the bell, it meant Goss didn't have to go to the chasm of absolution quite yet. It meant that, for a few minutes more, he could keep being with Father and Kitty and Ymir, as though none of what was happening was actually real. If Kitty had heard his thoughts, he would no doubt have said that it was useless to prolong the inevitable, and that rejecting reality was dumb. But he couldn't help it. The world he lived in right now, and the world that would arrive in less than an hour, was a terrifying unknown.

Even though he was so much bigger, Goss scootched closer to Kitty where they both sat. And Kitty, without saying anything, leaned into him. Who could have imagined it? A small, vulnerable little human, taking comfort in a *dragon*.

And, even worse . . .

Goss allowed himself to lean against Kitty.

For the past month, Goss had lived in a wonderland. He had been happy. Happier than he'd ever been as a kid or even as a dragon. Dragons didn't trust each other. It was part of the deal. The other whelps were, in the long run, his future political rivals. Even if they joined the same party, they'd always fight for superiority. There was no such thing as friendship.

But Kitty . . . this little human . . .

He was effortless in his camaraderie.

It took days for Goss to work up the courage to suggest going to a nearby nation, or to ask if he wanted to watch the weekly shadow puppetry together in the main hall. But all his fears, all his reluctance, it was all for nothing. Because after all that, after all his worries and woes, Kitty would simply say *Yeah, sure,* and that was it. He didn't make Goss feel stupid. He didn't arbitrarily insult him. When Goss was down, he never felt like Kitty would turn him away.

He was the brother he wished he'd had.

He'd had a brother, back when he was still a skinnie, but he . . . he wasn't like this. This was different, and it was better, and the thought that in less than an hour it'd be gone, just like his last brother . . . It *terrified* him.

Becoming a four-winged dragon meant to lose oneself. Goss knew that. Before Kitty arrived, Goss had spent hours asking Father about what four-winged dragons were like. Among the dragons, Father was one of the few who had met one and survived. More importantly, he had known the person before they ascended. He knew what they were like.

To be a four-winged dragon was complete apathy. There was no god of four-winged dragons because they were inherently godless. Even mumblers were still dragons, but four-winged dragons . . . All gods rejected them. Father had even said that when you became one, your mind was made into a blank slate, and your soul reworked. You were no longer yourself. You were no longer *anybody.*

That concept had made Goss beyond excited.

But now, as he stood before the gates of such a life, he could no longer find the same attraction in severing all contacts to mortal life. Losing his arms and gaining wings in their stead meant he could no longer hold Kitty. As a four-winged dragon, he could never again attend mass, or help Father down from the church. He wouldn't be able to return to Loathe Summit, and he could never meet Kitty again.

Because either Kitty would leave, or they would fight, and be separated by death.

"Hey, Goss?"

Goss snapped out of it. He looked down to find Kitty in his hand, not at his side, and they were . . . walking? This tunnel . . . He couldn't recall ever seeing it before. How long had they been walking there? He couldn't remember, and the realization that he couldn't recall how long he'd been zoned out was even worse.

Kitty frowned up at him, his pale face filled with worry. "I've been trying to talk to you for a while, but you seemed *really* out of it . . ."

"It's okay," Goss lied. A brief glance down at his friend convinced him that even if he caught the untruth, he wasn't about to rightfully scold him for it. "I'm just, um . . . *excited* about the killing. Heh. As a proper soon-to-be-four-winged dragon *should* be, you know."

Going by the wrinkle forming between Kitty's eyes, he wasn't about to let that lie slide. "You really shouldn't—"

Heavy breathing aft reminded Goss that they weren't alone, something Ymir and his shoulder-friend were quick to point out. "Please," Ymir said, his voice heavy with exhaustion. "Continue walking. Prolong this no longer."

"Y—yeah, sorry," Goss mumbled, quickening his pace just enough to create a gap between himself and the people following him. Dissociating too hard was clearly not good for him, as he now had no idea why he was the one leading the way. If he was lucky, this was the only way, and he wouldn't have to deal with any forks in the road. If he was unlucky, then Father had spent minutes explaining exactly how and where to go, and was counting on him to get them there.

Goss felt himself start to sweat.

A tiny hand squeezing his finger almost stopped his heart in his chest. He looked down at Kitty, feeling his worries melt away because he knew that as long as he had his friend, he'd be okay. "Hey, um, Kitty . . . are we going the right way?"

"A hundred percent. I sniffed it and the tunnel only goes down one way. If you're wondering, at this rate, we'll be there in a minute or so." He smiled up at him, relaxed and easy and confident that Goss wouldn't mess it up somehow. "You're doing great."

A little quake passed through Goss's chest. In a minute, he might not be doing so great. But for now, he still had his friend. His closest friend. In a way . . . his *only* friend.

Not trying to think too much about it, Goss squeezed Kitty closer to him, feeling something tiny crack in his hand. He looked down at Kitty to find him making a disappointed expression. "Come on, man, how many times do I have to tell you?" Kitty said as he began to absently bite off his own fingers. They'd heal within a few minutes, but it still made Goss feel guilty.

"Sorry," he said. "I can't help it. You're too tiny and squishable. Maybe if you'd eat more meat, you might grow a bit bigger and become like me."

"That's a *low* blow, Goss!" Kitty said with a laugh. "I'll have you know, nowadays, I—" Suddenly, the small human fell quiet, brows furrowing once more into a contemplative expression. "Actually, now that I'm thinking about it, I can't remember the last time I ate anything that *wasn't* meat . . ."

"I can," Goss commented simply. "Five days ago, when we went to the edge of Ret-inn, you ate a bunch of suspicious mushrooms. But then when I wanted to try them, you said I'd probably die, so I didn't, even though you seemed to think they were totally scaly and yummilicious."

"Did I?" Kitty mumbled. "Oh, yeah, I did! Well, I'm not surprised a medieval guy like you doesn't know, but fungi are actually closer to animals than they are to plants, so I'd sooner count it as flesh." The words flew straight over Goss's head. For one, he didn't actually know what a fungus was. However, with the help of context clues, he could infer what it meant. Even then, though, the science refused to sink in. After a few seconds of stunned confusion, he decided to simply accept it. By that point, Kitty had already started speaking again, muttering, "Kind of amazing that you'd remember that, though . . ."

"The reason you don't must be because of the mushrooms poisoning you," Goss hypothesized. Like that, he didn't have to admit that he remembered because every day they'd shared for the past two weeks had felt numbered. Since he only had fourteen days with Kitty, he decided to put them all to memory as best as possible. Maybe if he could recall each day in detail, he could cling onto it when he became a four-winged dragon. That way, when he fought Kitty, he would know him enough to spare him. That's how the wolf tales went, at least. "Either that, or it might be because I dropped you when we were flying away, but I apologized for that, and—"

"Yeah, of course, don't worry about it," Kitty said. One thing Goss liked about Kitty was his honesty. If Kitty said not to worry about it, Goss wouldn't worry about it.

As Goss let relief wash over him, Kitty put his nose into the air, sniffing deeply. "Ah, we're here."

Goss slowed in his steps. Up ahead, a door easily large enough to fit several dragons side by side loomed, its face engraved with thousands of names. He had heard about this door. The tombstone. The mere sight of it made Goss want to shrink away, the only thing keeping his feet rooted in place being Kitty's steadfast gaze. Swallowing, Goss stepped to the side, letting Ymir and Father walk up to it. Once they were close enough, Father pointed to a spot in the middle of the right side. Without having to say anything, Ymir rose onto his trembling hind legs, his stomach spasming from the pain of the gluttony brand. Once he found his spot, he carefully carved in his own name using his claw. Despite how nervous he felt, Goss noticed with interest that Ymir wrote down not just his name, but also the name he had as a goblin. Var-jeat, son of Lemn.

With the name inscribed, he let his body fall once more, grunting as he used both his arms and wings to catch himself. Then, without any command from Father, he put his knuckle to the door and rapped on it.

The door slid open and light flooded inside the formerly dim hallway, blinding Goss where he stood. The sight made Ymir frown slightly, but he still entered, forcing Goss to quickly speed after him.

Until now, Goss had only been to the chasm of absolution twice. Once, when he was very new, to watch the last leader of the naturalist party get killed. And then, once, when he and the other whelps snuck inside to check it out. One of the other whelps had jokingly leapt down onto the actual ritual floor. He was turned to dust before he had time to gloat about it. Goss still remembered their horror, and how it had taken them weeks to gain enough courage to tell Father about it. Once they did, they held a proper wake for him, carving his name onto the tombstone gate.

And now that floor lay before him.

The ceiling of the room was open, allowing the sky and its setting sun to be seen, and to light up the chasm as a whole. Above, on a circular balcony of sorts, stood the rest of the dragons, all watching down with varying levels of haughty interest.

"They'll come for the execution, but not the wake," Kitty muttered into his hand. Goss could only agree.

The ritual floor itself was the main piece. It was large enough to appear more like an arena, big enough for all dragons of the mountain to crowd into. Not that they could. If they did, they would be turned to the same dust that made up the floor Ymir and Father now stood upon. Gulping, Goss mustered the courage to step out onto it, giving a brief prayer to the Goddess of Dragons that this wouldn't be the last thing he did.

Thankfully, his prayer was answered. With a heartfelt sigh of relief, he looked down at Kitty, glad to find the human still in his hand and decidedly not dustified. However, he was looking straight ahead in the way he only was while viewing the so-called status messages. "See anything, Kitty?"

"Uh, yeah, it says I've entered holy ground," Kitty noted absently. "Fits what you've said so far, but it's still interesting to see again."

In response, Goss could muster only a nod. His attention had affixed itself onto Ymir and Father, who now stood in the middle of the arena alongside Kempt.

"Today, we will unfortunately say farewell to Ymir, of the suicidalist party . . ."

Goss realized with horror that Father was giving a speech about Ymir's death, with Ymir's executioner standing five paces behind them, awkwardly cowering in the corner. Goose bumps spread across every inch of his skin and he ground his teeth together. What was he supposed to do? Join them? He, a *whelp*? No way. But if he kept standing there while they were really introducing him, then . . .

"Goss," Kitty said, far below, but close by. Goss looked down at the gently smiling human. "You're doing great. Just keep looking like a fearsome and ferocious dragon executioner and you'll be fine."

With those simple words, Goss felt himself relax.

"But, uh . . . Make sure that you put me on top of the bleachers before you start doing your thing, alright? I've got a feeling that if you drop me, I won't get away with a simple brain-splattering."

"Yeah, yeah, of course," Goss replied. If he hadn't been such a coward, he would have relieved himself of his one friend minutes earlier. Kitty shouldn't even have been on the ritual floor. The Goddess of Dragons was watching him. What would She think about him allowing a human on Her sacred holy ground?

There was no doubt in his head that She was gearing up to give him everything he had ever asked of Her.

"Nominated for this solemn duty is none other than Goss Fletchling. As he takes his place before our comrade Ymir, let us all join in the resting mumbler's hymn," Father announced. At the sound of his words, the dozens of gathered dragons began the hymn, their voices joining as one.

Goss felt his heart stop as Father turned to him.

Quickly ascertaining where the whelps had chosen to watch from, Goss drew back his arm, asked Kitty for forgiveness he already knew he'd receive, and threw the screaming human across the arena, the toy-sized being's screech just happening to be the exact same tone everyone was singing, making his shriek imperceptible. Before turning away, Goss made sure to watch Kitty's flight just enough to see Frey catch him in one hand—very impressive.

With that done, Goss turned toward where Ymir stood, his wings bound and his body tethered to the ground, Father at his side.

While the hymn drew into a crescendo, Goss strode across the arena, his heartbeat acting as a drum, going faster and faster as the larger dragon came closer. Soon, Goss stood right in front of him. The aged dragon's weary eyes stared blankly at him, his forehead scarred by the brand of pride, his chest rising slowly as hoarse breaths crawled out of his throat. Goss gulped.

A small hand fell on his little finger. Down below he found Father looking up at him. "It isn't too late," he said warmly. "Nobody will fault you for leaving the rest to me."

Goss drew away his hand. "I—I have to do this. I need to. I . . . *want* to."

Going only by the way Father looked at him, Goss could tell that his lie didn't quite get through. Nevertheless, out of respect for Ymir, Father stepped away. Kempt likewise followed along. Soon the two of them were far away, as was Kitty, and the whelps, and everyone else. It was just him, Ymir, and the hymn in the air. But soon, even that began to fade.

The final notes of the hymn came to a close. The last voice echoed away. Now the only sound to be heard was Ymir's labored breathing and the heavy beating of Goss's heart.

High above, a bell chimed. It was time.

Goss stood there. Alone. He couldn't remember the last time he'd felt as alone as he did then. There was only him, his victim, and his heart. He could feel it beating within his chest. Faster, faster. Tired eyes looking up at him. A hundred eyes looking down at him. A select few eyes, seeing him for the kid he really was. He could feel his breathing begin to hitch.

Ten deep breaths, he heard Kitty say, a memory away. *Count them, in and out. One in, one out. Two in, two out. When you get to ten, repeat it backward. And if that doesn't help . . . A bit of manslaughter never hurt anyone, right?*

One in, one out. Two in, two out.

Eyes watching.

Three in, three out. Four in, four out.

Mouths mumbling. Asking. Questioning.

Five in, five out . . . Six in, six out . . .

Eyes on his back, eyes on his face, eyes on his side. Everyone watching. Everyone seeing him be a pathetic little loser who had to do breathing exercises to muster the strength to kill an old skinbag.

Seven in . . . seven out . . . Eight in . . . eight out . . .

Why couldn't he just do it? Nobody else had problems with this. Father could do it easily. He'd do it in a heartbeat, and everyone would watch the pretty dust. But you can't. Because you're *pathetic*.

Nine . . . in . . . nine . . . out . . . Ten . . . in . . . ten . . . out . . .

Pathetic. Pathetic. Pathetic. Pathetic. And you think you can be a four-winged dragon. Pathetic. Absolutely pathetic. The Goddess of Dragons is watching you, and She thinks you're *pathetic*, even Kitty thinks you're—

"Just kill him!" someone shouts across the arena.

"Come on, do away with that old skinnie!"

"What are you waiting for, you pathetic whelp? Show that suicidalist what he wants to see!"

Nineinnineouteightineightoutseveninsevenoutsixinsixoutfiveinfiveoutfourin-fouroutthreeinthreeouttwointwooutoneinoneout—

Zero.

Goss struck, his right arm flying out, his splayed claws scratching across Ymir's face, drawing deep gashes in the skin, flesh opened and red, dark blood splattering, streaking down across his apathetic face because even though it must have hurt, even though it had to be painful, it still didn't hurt as much as the brand—even death wouldn't be close. Eyes blurring, mind dissolving into static, Goss took a step back, bracing himself before letting his tail whip out, aiming it for the older dragon's neck, hoping that Kitty's theory would be right, that a well-placed strike at the right spot would kill him instantly, making his suffering brief and ending this whole farce as soon as possible.

The air cracked, the club his tail had formed hit true, and all he felt was the stiff musculature of a neck in constant strain. He pulled his tail back. Ymir wasn't moving. *Maybe he's dead*, Goss thought, hopeful naivety clashing with the terrible reality of the situation. Within only seconds, Ymir drew another breath, and the spot Goss struck bloomed into a purple bruise.

He wasn't dead. Not yet. He had to kill him. He had to do more than that.

"Kill him!"

"Come on, don't waste time with mercy!"

"We're here to see the old invalid die, not your gawking!"

Looking up into the bleachers, Goss let his eyes search desperately, only stopping once they fell on Kitty. In return, Kitty met his gaze evenly, without any discernible emotion. He wasn't expectant, he wasn't unhappy, he wasn't bloodthirsty, and he wasn't disappointed. He was *nothing*.

Until Goss showed results, he would be given nothing. This was as clear as day.

Goss turned back to Ymir. With the chanting of the crowd filling his ears, he tried to kill Ymir in every way he knew how. He clawed open gashes along his body, severing arteries and leaving him a bleeding mess. He beat him, breaking bones and mincing his tawny musculature into mush. The dust-covered ground, previously a pristine white, was covered in flowering blooms of red blood.

Please die, Goss thought as he tore flesh from the old dragon's bones. *Please die*, he chanted as he pulverized bone and bit off the older dragon's limbs one by one, despite knowing that no amount of pain he inflicted would be greater than what he had already experienced. *Please die*, he prayed as he allowed himself to be covered in the viscera of his mentor, his every heartbeat reminding Goss that he was still alive, he wasn't dead, and the world was worse off because of it.

Please die. Please die. Please die. Please die. Please die.

He wouldn't die. Even as his blood covered the floor like the feathers of a slain drake, his heart still beat. Goss tore out his intestines, threw his musculature across the arena, displaced bones, and exposed his heart to the world, and yet it still beat, and he still lived, and Goss was a failure—a pathetic failure and a mistake who never should have agreed to any of this. He should be dead. He should have died long ago. But he was alive, breathing, his heart beating, and nothing Goss did could redeem him.

"AAAAAAAAAAHHHHHHHH!" Goss screamed, devolving into a petty tantrum as he beat at Ymir's open chest, at his steadily beating heart, his fists closed and useless and a disgrace to everything Kitty ever taught him. "*Die, die, die, die, die, die, die, die! Please, die—*"

"Goss, *stop!*" Father shouted, in front of him now, standing on top of Ymir's chest, his wings spread out, defending Ymir even though Ymir was unforgivable, irredeemable, the kind of monster who could only find absolution through death. How dare he? "Please, my child, I'll—"

Goss's closed fist slammed into Father's side, the small former flying across the arena to crash into one of the walls. High above, the audience raged with joy, shouting, laughing, crying for him to do what he came here to do. And as Goss looked down at the exposed heart in front of him, he finally understood what it was he needed to do. Adam, falling to the temptation of Eve, Goss leaned down, gathered the heart into his hands, and took a bite. Finally, it stopped. Finally the beating of the heart ended, the thumping finished, the roaring of the audience quieted, and like this, finally, it was time. Goss could feel it. It was time. Now he could finally—

Kempt leapt at him, tackling him from atop Ymir, both of them going flying before rolling to a stop several paces away from the body. "Goss, you have to stop! What you've done to Father is—"

Goss's face thrust out, his wide-open jaws snapping at Kempt's neck. The older dragon jumped back only barely in time to avoid the brutal attack. His wide eyes blinked at him. "What in the world are you—"

Without waiting for Kempt to initiate, Goss threw himself at him, tackling him to the ground and pushing down his limbs, his ravenous maw finding itself at the base of his fellow whelp's wing. Powerful jaws clasped around the vital limbs, needle-sharp teeth sinking into flesh, the taste of blood and flesh reinforcing the fact that *it was time. This was it. Now he could become who he was always meant to be.*

Wailing in pain, Kempt pushed Goss off, only barely doing so without losing his wing in the process. Freed, Kempt attempted to use his breath of fire, only for Goss to quickly stick his claws inside Kempt's chest vents, the sudden intrusion leaving the older dragon to gasp for air, falling to the ground in screamless pain. Goss watched as Kempt retreated, crawling in the dust, a trail of blood in his wake. Above, the other dragons clamored. This was it. This was it. This was it.

This was . . .

Silence. Emptiness. He wasn't transforming. Why wasn't he transforming? He looked down at his arms, but they were still arms, not wings. They were supposed to be wings. He was supposed to have wings. His eyes moved across the arena. Ymir was dead. Father lay in a crumpled heap on the other side of the arena. Kempt was gone. He had done everything right. But he still wasn't a four-winged dragon. So why did he . . . ?

Electrical currents shocked across Goss's skull and he turned on himself, on his own wings, his jaws snatching a hold of the base of his right wing, the pain making him feel alive, feel *real*, feel like the world was nothing save for his flesh screaming out, and not everything else, and he chewed at it, the skin giving way to flesh, the flesh giving way to bone, and the bone giving in eventually, snapping off, rent to dust, gone, and just like that, his wing fell to the ground with a heavy thud, and with that, he wasn't a four-winged dragon, he wasn't even a two-winged dragon anymore, but he was still a dragon, he'd always be a dragon, no matter what he did, and that meant that he was unforgivable, always unforgivable, only redeemable through—

Something fell onto his face. Something small, about the size of a wooden toy. Goss stared with horror into the face of Kitty. Neither of them said a word.

With a powerful shake of the head, Goss sent Kitty flying, the human's claws unable to find a grip on the dragon's smooth scales. Kitty hit the dust a pace away, where Goss fully expected his last remaining tether to mortal life to turn to dust. However, instead, he could only watch in slack-jawed shock as Kitty pulled himself to his feet—no, to the stumps where his feet used to be. He wasn't standing on holy ground barefoot. Somehow, such a trivial loophole had spared him.

Neither of them said a word. The air buzzed with tension between them.

Then Kitty leapt into the air and disappeared. For an instant, Goss felt that all-too familiar confusion come over him, though it was quickly replaced by recognition as he noticed the trail of dust left by Kitty's rolling. His tail whipped out, finding its target easily, though the attack was made empty as Kitty instead latched onto the tail, crawling up his back as Goss attempted to fight back, thrashing about and batting his tail at the smaller creature.

"Get off—" Goss grunted, bucking like a wronged drake, his attacks making contact but without any lasting damage. In the end, he could only watch as Kitty, battered and bruised, bleeding from his legs and pretty much everywhere else, crawled on top of his face once more.

For a moment, they simply watched each other, both covered in more red than anything else, breathing heavily.

Kitty placed a hand on Goss's forehead, the bruised fingers feeling soft despite the claws adorning them. "It's okay," he said. "You don't have to do this anymore. I was *wrong*. This isn't . . ." He drew a deep breath. Eyes on Goss, he allowed himself to almost smile. "Did you . . . think I was going to kill you? Because you didn't turn into a four-winged dragon?"

"I did," Goss admitted. Even now, doubts rang through his mind. Maybe Kitty was only trying to get him off-guard, playing nice so he wouldn't be able to fight back once he struck. Maybe this had been his plan all along, and all the days and hours they'd shared were for this and this alone.

"You did, huh . . ." A small smile cracked across Kitty's face, but it faltered just as quickly, a deep frown replacing it. "I'm sorry. I . . . I've changed my mind." His smile returned, though somber—almost mellow. "I'll stay, Goss. I've decided. You can be a dragon as much as you want to be, and I . . . I'll still be your friend, and I'll still be by your side."

"You . . . will?"

"Yeah. I will."

"Even though I didn't become a four-winged dragon?"

"That doesn't even factor into it," Kitty admitted with a chuckle.

"Even though . . ." Goss tried to look away, but no matter where he looked, he still saw Kitty, sitting on top of his face, smiling like a proper brother. There was nowhere to run. Strangely enough, Goss didn't even want to escape anymore. "Even though I'm . . . *me*?"

Kitty broke into a grin. "*Because* you're you."

Goss felt himself smile. It was so simple. *Ah. So that's it, then?*

"You know, all this stuff with Father kissing things and doing magic . . . it feels so much like a storybook. Did you notice that? All the kissing is super weird. I mean, kissing people into magic should be reserved for magical princesses, if you ask me. Like, could you imagine if you got kissed, and all of a sudden a bunch of magic happened? That would be ridiculous!" Kitty rambled inanely. Goss enjoyed every word of it. "I'll prove it! There's no way it'd work in real life, see, it's just . . ." Leaning down, in pure mockery of something Goss had never heard or cared about before this moment, Kitty planted a kiss atop his forehead. "See? Absolutely nothing's happeni—"

It felt as though someone was hugging him.

[MY CHILD, I HAVE MISSED YOU. WELCOME HOME.]

The world felt warm. Arms around him on every side, hugging him tightly—but not too tightly. Like a mother holding her child, in the way he had always wanted his own mother to hold him—but it was okay, because there were other people to hug in the world, who would love to hug him, and wouldn't mind being hugged by him. Holding out his arms, Goss felt Kitty in them, snuggled closely. Warm. Even though Kitty usually felt so cold, now he felt warm. And big. He didn't feel like a tiny wooden toy anymore—he was as big as a big brother should be, hunched down to hug Goss properly.

Goss opened his eyes, and Kitty was looking down at him, suddenly big, and although his eyes were big and wide with all the subtlety of a toddler pointing at a disabled person, they still held all the love Goss had come to expect from them. Goss smiled up at him. Tentatively, Kitty smiled back.

Chuckling warmly, Goss said, "You look a lot skinnier from down here."

"You—you—you're . . ."

"I got better," Goss said, finding himself to mean it completely. He felt lighter. "*You* helped me get better." Smiling wider, he pressed himself back into his brother's arms. "Thank you, Kitty. *Thank you.*"

"You're . . . welcome . . . ?" Kitty said reluctantly.

Still holding Kitty, Goss asked, "Are you going away now?"

For a second, Kitty couldn't answer. His eyes read the air. Then he choked out, "Yeah. But . . . but they're giving me a few more minutes. That's what it says."

"No exact time?"

"No, but knowing them . . ."

Goss dislodged himself, his smile feeling as casual as a dragon's natural scowl. "In that case, we have a bit more time."

Taking Kitty's hand, Goss led him across the arena. Now, unlike before, the chasuble of atonement he wore was perfectly sized, covering him in the warm feathers of all that had come before him. Below, the dust felt warm between his toes. Welcoming. Up above, the dragons watched, their eyes following the two as they strolled through the dirt, one of them tracking blood everywhere. Eventually, they arrived at where Father lay slouched against the wall. Hunching down, Goss grinned at the other former. "Father, you don't have to pretend to sleep anymore."

Without opening his eyes, Father asked, "Did you get better?"

"I did," Goss answered simply.

In response, Father peeked an eye open. Seeing Goss, he bolted upright, breaking into a massive grin. "*Goss!*" Not waiting for his fellow former to stand up, Father grabbed Goss and pulled him into his arms, hugging him so tightly he lifted him off the ground, taking the moment to twirl Goss around. "My son! Oh, I am so proud of you!"

Goss smiled sheepishly. "No, not yet. There's still something I have to do."

As one, they both turned to Ymir's body. He was a grisly sight to behold. They both knew what had to be done. Before he let him go, Father gave Goss a pat on the back. Goss returned the gesture by squeezing his hand. And then he was off. The audience was silent, wide eyes watching nervously as the one-winged former approached the brutalized corpse. To get to his heart, Goss had to step over multiple discarded organs and half-mangled limbs, his bare feet touching blood, yet remaining untarnished by it. Soon he stood upon the dragon's chest, Ymir's cold body, his heart half-eaten and motionless where it lay.

Clasping his hands, Goss muttered, "*Forgive me, as the God of Multitudes forgives you.*"

Kneeling down, he took the heart in his hands, brought it to his face, and pressed his lips against the dead organ, his kiss flooding it with light. And with that, the heart turned to white dust, and so did the rest of the body, his blood likewise. The holy ground returned to its beauty, and Ymir returned to from whence he came.

But he would always live on. Goss touched a hand to the chasuble, to Ymir's feather adorning it. And he smiled, because Ymir would never truly be gone—nor would anyone else. Not even he would ever disappear fully. The world was immeasurably kind.

With his duty to Ymir completed, Goss turned once more to his brother, who stood by Father—his lanky, awkward posture mirrored on his face. From across the distance, Goss asked, "Do you have time left?"

"Y—yeah, I think so," Kitty replied. He glanced down at something Goss couldn't see. "A little over a minute."

"That's plenty of time," Goss said, and with only a few steps, he found himself in front of Kitty again. Goss held out his arms. By pure instinct, Kitty reciprocated, pulling the smaller former into his arms. There, Goss felt at home. Hugging Kitty properly was worth everything else. "Will you come visit someday?"

"I don't know," Kitty replied honestly.

"I hope you will," Goss said. "But if you don't, it's okay."

"Is it?"

"It is. My only regret is that I couldn't do for you what you've done for me."

Kitty hesitated. "You've done plenty for me. I'm the one who . . ."

Goss smiled against his chest. "I'm glad I met you, Kitty."

"You can't know that," Kitty said. "You don't know what I might do down the line."

"It doesn't matter. Right now, I'm happy to know you. What happens later doesn't change what I feel now. And right now, I feel glad."

Kitty bit his lip. "Goodbye, Goss. I'm . . ." He took a shallow breath. "I'm happy I didn't kill you."

Goss giggled. "That's good." He sighed happily. "I'm glad I didn't kill you, either." Looking up, Goss met Kitty's gaze enough to show him the biggest smile he could muster—a smile as honest as it was pure. "Goodbye, Kitty. I'll see you around!"

And, despite everything, Kitty finally found the strength to smile back. "See you, Goss."

With that, still holding Goss in his arms, Kitty disappeared, summoned away to continue his divine service.

Goss watched his fading image, smiling.

ABOUT THE AUTHOR

Palt is a Sweden-based author of isekai, short horror stories, and some fanfiction. He is currently working toward a degree in criminology. In his spare time, Palt enjoys drawing and playing the trombone.